A Skeleton In The Closet

by

David Feeney

ISBN: 0-75964-463-2

This book is printed on acid free paper.

1stBooks – rev. 8/29/01

I would like to extend a warm thanks to the following: James Deem for helping me to better understand the mummification process; George Hademeno of the American Stroke Association for his advice on the various types of strokes; Dr. Joseph Hornak for teaching me the difference between MRIs and CAT Scans; Dr. Graham Jones for his help on the toxicology tests; Inspector Sherman Ackerson of the SFPD for explaining the rank system of San Francisco's finest; Thomas Roughneen for his advice on some of the legal matters; Jessica Bayliss, Assistant Professor Jim Fry, Corbin B. Jones Ph.D., and Randall Hayes for their advice on eye color; Dr. Mike Finnegan, Alice Lloyd, NJ-IAFN, and especially Drs. Frank and Julie Saul for telling me how to determine whether or not my mummy was pregnant. And a special thanks to my editor, Arlene S. Uslander, for the guidance and suggestions.

Prologue

She stood on the corner of Jersey and 18th Street. It was warm, though the cool breeze that blew through her hair hinted like a whisper that winter was close at hand, or at least what passed for winter in San Francisco. She brushed a few strands of her jet-black hair, professionally coifed and parted down the center, over her ear. It always fell that way on windy days.

Behind her she could hear the lively sounds of piano and saxophone that wafted out, along with the scent of cigarettes from the bar, "Great Sax." It was a one-story structure with a white stucco front and a slate roof. Two prominent windows stood on either side of a large oaken door. Inside, a live band played. The Great Sax was something of an institution in the city, having been around since the 30s. She knew the bar well, having frequented it many times in the past. But like the summer, that, too, was behind her. She had to be careful now. She had plans. She touched her stomach gently. Too much to lose, she thought.

She ran a thin, elegant finger over her ear again and caught a glimpse of herself in the windows of passing cars. Her attire was demure in style: beige skirt, jacket and a cream silk blouse, though, the skirt was a tad-too-tight and short; too short for November 1953. Short enough to make passing men look too long and their women look at them with anger. And look they did, despite her current state. They looked at her buxom build, her brown eyes, her full lips, swivel hips, long legs and gold-bronze skin. Men looked at her Italian beauty and wondered and dreamed. Women looked at her and felt lacking. She enjoyed every minute of it. She ran her tongue across dental work that had cost more than the clothes she wore. She hadn't always looked this good. The raw beauty had always been there. It was the polish that had taken time and money to acquire.

A female acquaintance, sensing her confidence, once asked her to join the *movement*, as she called it. She was, of course, referring to the feminist movement. She attended a meeting and met a few of the *sisters*, as they called themselves, but left after only a few minutes. She wasn't interested in joining anything that would have her parading around with a bunch of angry women, in what amounted to little more than begging men to give them more power. The fact that they had to ban together and organize to achieve power was to her the greatest indication of their inability to achieve it on their own.

A couple passed by. He was in his mid-thirties and his wife in her late-twenties. He smiled a boyish grin at her and she returned it, parting her lips as if she was going to say something, but didn't. The wife's face pruned and went red. She elbowed her husband. The smile came off his face and went to one of confusion.

As they passed, she could hear him say, "What? I was just being friendly."

She particularly enjoyed the fact that she had this effect despite her current state. Five months pregnant and she was barely showing. If anything, she decided, men found her more attractive pregnant and women more jealous. She didn't understand it and chalked it up to biology. She smiled. She still had it.

She was 26 and single, though she hoped that would change shortly, and pitied the women who clung to their husbands and boyfriends with child-like desperation. She never fawned or clung to any man out of desperation. But things were different now. She was different. She was in love. For the first time in her life, she could actually admit that without feeling weak. In her mind, she stood before a precipice of decision. All she had to do now was work up the courage to tell him and hope he'd leave his wife.

She thought briefly about her family back home and what they would say if they could see her now. The pregnancy wouldn't surprise them. Most would say they saw it coming years ago. It was the love part that would have knocked them over. The fact that he was married would no doubt have eased it for them.

She gritted her teeth momentarily and forced a smile. She opened her eyes extra wide and turned into the breeze so the wind would dry the tears that had sneaked up on her while she was in thought. Questions concerning her family's empathy would never be answered because she was never going back. Not even to gloat. That was certain.

She had left Brooklyn mainly because there wasn't much of a future there. That's not to say that there was not a selection of men; quite the contrary. The problem was that the men came in mainly two types, blue collar and immigrant. She didn't see herself marrying a war vet turned factory worker and settling down to one of the small apartment complexes in one of the endless ethnic neighborhoods. It was a stifling existence and with the death of her father only more suffocating. The fleeting pastimes of childhood were replaced with the responsibilities of looking after her younger siblings. Not to mention the horrors that followed. One thing not in doubt was that she had to escape.

She came to San Francisco mostly because of the weather, warm and sunny all year round, with mild winters. She had never been out West and knew nobody there, but that didn't deter her. The idea of being in a new place, unknown, appealed to her. It gave her a sense of renewal.

Upon arrival, she got an apartment in North Beach, as its dominant ethnicity was Italian. North Beach was known as "Little Italy." Like many before her, she sought safety in the familiar. She knew she wanted to be in Pacific Heights but knew enough to know that coming out of Brooklyn, she wouldn't fit in. Nor could she afford it. Reaching the status she saw herself at, would come in increments of upward mobility.

North Beach of course had its benefits. There were lots of restaurants where one could get a good meal like home. But after a time, she found it too Italian, too familiar. Too much of the Old World was present. A world she felt removed from by birth. She had worked in the city for some time and was then becoming more comfortable amongst the non-immigrants. Her job in accounting had allowed her to acquire a better wardrobe and improve her appearance. Her

Brooklyn accent had even faded somewhat. After a time, she decided that she had gotten too big for "Little Italy" So she left.

She found a better apartment in a better neighborhood. She still felt a bit out of her element but pride and determination kept her from going back.

She thought briefly about the men she had been with since her arrival, just over five years before. Mistakes, mistakes, mistakes, she concluded. Most of them were hers, but all were mistakes; all except one.

"Paper, ma'am?" a small voice asked.

She turned back and saw a little boy of almost five standing beside her, a single newspaper in his hand. He wore a pair of shorts, knee-socks, leather shoes and a collar shirt. His hair was well-combed. A very caring mother obviously had dressed him.

Behind him a few yards were three other boys, all of whom were older. They stood at the corner clad in sneakers, jeans and t-shirts. All were giggling. Eyeing them, she sized-up the situation immediately. The little fellow before her wasn't the regular salesman. He was too young to know any better.

"What's that you said?" She asked only to show the others that their friend wasn't being made a fool.

"Would you like to buy a paper?" he asked with wide and honest eyes.

"How much does it cost? She asked in mock curiosity.

"It's..." His eyes rolled about as if searching the inside of his head for the answer. "Forty-five cents," he said, holding up two fingers.

The other boys looked on with creeping jealousy.

She smiled. That was more than twice the price of a Sunday paper, never mind the daily. "Let me see if I have enough money, okay?"

He nodded.

She dug about momentarily in her purse and came up with a quarter and two dimes. She knelt down beside him and handed him the money. He gave her the paper. "Thank you," she said.

"You're welcome, ma'am," he replied.

She touched his cheek with an elegant finger and traced it up the side of his face. He hunched his shoulders and blushed while a hush fell over the others. "You are so cute," she said.

They looked at each other a few moments. He was stunned by the pretty lady. She was similar in age to his mom but her presence was unlike any mom he'd been around. She was enthralled with this little fellow, whose honesty, like her beauty, she knew would last only a few years more. She wondered what kind of man he'd be.

She leaned in close and from a distance, their faces seemed to touch.

"Whoa!" said the biggest of the boys. "She's kissing him!"

The little fellow smiled, not understanding and with money in hand, turned and ran to his friends.

She watched, and wondered whether the child she carried would be as cute as that little fellow. God, she hoped so. And in truth, there was no reason why it couldn't.

She had changed so much, she realized. It had taken time to change, she decided, or as the man in her life put it, "True change takes its own time." It was time to just go over and tell him. Tell him everything. Tell him about his child.

She had crossed the precipice.

A yellow cab with a dented rear fender and a muddied license plate slowed and came to a stop, as if reading her thoughts. The rear passenger door was right in front of her. She took a final look behind her, saw the small boy and waved. He smiled. She got into the cab thinking about the future and all the possibilities it held. It was only after she had closed the door behind her that it occurred to her that she hadn't signaled for a cab.

The cab pulled away from the curb and drove quietly into the mid-day traffic. The "On Duty" light was off.

Present Day

David Feeney

1

Nob Gardens, a large apartment building was in the midst of rebirth. "The Gardens," as it was referred to by Residents was an eight-story "U"- shaped building. It was constructed of brick and had been built in the 20s. With large glass double-doors in front that were encased in an intricately woven iron frame, the building was protected by an outer gate. A brick-wall ran along the property. Two snarling gargoyles stood atop two pillars on eternal watch on either side of the wrought-iron gate. Spacious windows lined every floor of the front, two per unit. Each unit had a fireplace.

The owners had decided that they could make more money by taking the sixty original units, renovating them and leaving in their place some thirty-five deluxe condominiums. All were to be spacious, with polished wood floors, and well-lit with natural light via the generous windows and skylights. That is, they would be once they were completed.

Each unit would cost over 100 K and would be the exclusive dwellings of the emerging IT class. Most of the new units were already sold. None had been finished, though - a fact that only encouraged "Kelly's Construction" to double their efforts and complete the job on time. At least that's what Mike Kelly thought as he moved through the dust cloud of the basement apartment.

His jeans and T-shirt were drenched in sweat, which was bad enough. The fact that the room was inundated with dust only made it worse, as it stuck to his clothes and cast him entirely in gray. Despite the fact that he hadn't started working on this unit; dust kicked up earlier had carried in from the adjoining unit.

He set down his sledgehammer and wiped his sweat stained dusty denim sleeve across his damp forehead. Mike Kelly would be happy when his part in this project was complete.

After consulting a floor plan and making sure he was in the right unit, he picked up his sledgehammer and found a spot on the wall. His job as defined by his father, Pete Kelly, was to tear down the sheet rock wall and plywood partition between this unit and the adjoining unit, thereby turning two small apartments into one large condo. He marked the spot with an X, grabbed the sledgehammer and started smashing.

The hammer tore through the sheet rock with ease, shattering it and leaving large holes. With each strike, he moved horizontal to the last one by about one foot. With fatigue creeping up on him, he spaced the holes out some, moving further with each hole.

The hammer smashed through the sheet rock and hit - brick?

The reverberation shot through Mike's hands and arms like a bolt of lightning, numbing him to his shoulder. "Fuck!" he screamed in a combination of anger and fear as he dropped the hammer.

He reached up and pulled on the cracked sheet rock. A section came loose. Sure enough there was brick on the other side, red brick to be precise. The type of brick you find on old school houses, outdoor ovens or about quaint fireplaces. "There isn't supposed to be brick here," he said to himself. Curious, he took the hammer and tapped about gently, to the left of the hole. The taps were solid, indicating that there was more brick.

His interest sparked, he took the crowbar, stuck it in a hole and broke off a section of the sheet-rock. Beneath it he found redbrick. In all the walls he'd torn down, this was the first wall that was made of red brick. "Let's see how far this thing goes." In a few minutes he had stripped a section and found that the brick wall was about the size of a doorway.

He stood back and looked at the brick. "Brick, sheet rock or board, it's gotta come down," he decided.

Seizing upon an idea, he searched about until he found a metal spike. He drove the spike into the brick at different points, breaking the mortar and loosening up some of the brick. Then he smashed the brick with the sledge. He worked like this, alternating between spike and sledge for a while. He had to be careful. He didn't want to hit a pipe. He knew they were here somewhere.

He struck, head high. The brick smashed and part of it fell back and disappeared inside the wall, leaving a small, brick-sized hole. He'd reached a hollow of some kind. *Finally*, he thought. He took a look inside the wall but could see nothing with the dust. Whatever was there, it wasn't the unit on the other side. The pipes had to be nearby. He took another few swings. Brick fell away, clearing a nice sized hole. He set down the hammer and took another look inside. He coughed. His throat was dry.

Mike reached into his tool-belt and found a flashlight. He switched it on and shook it a few times before the beam came on, cutting a path through the dust. He shone the light into the hole in the wall. He froze. It took him a moment to realize what it was. It took another moment before it registered. Then it registered. There was somebody in the wall.

"Dad!" he screamed.

2

12:16 PM

I drove my black, mid-nineties E-class Mercedes through the mid-day traffic. Declan, Con or Connor to my friends, I didn't mind the delays so much as the Mercedes was an excellent car and made driving if not pleasurable, certainly a tolerable experience. I was at a point in life and career where a sports car would have seemed silly. Besides, I had seen other men my age that went that route and always couldn't help but laugh at their mid-life predicament.

I was born and raised in San Francisco and like many of the other proud citizens; I felt a special pride in the history of the city and my part in it. It was something I got from my mother. I knew that the Ohlone Indians were the original inhabitants of the bay. The Spanish arrived in 1769 and the first colonizers established themselves in 1776.

The settlement remained small until the Gold Rush, after which people from all over the area raced in, hoping to get rich overnight. The city's population grew and prospectors of all shades set about their trade. Con-men, hustlers, and prostitutes soon provided the support and service industries. Levi Straus would go on to make a fortune selling miners what would become the uniform of the blue-collar class: - jeans. It was for this reason that I never wore them as I felt them to be the uniform of industrialized slaves.

Shipping provided the city with a large influx of Chinese immigrants who were used as laborers throughout the 1840s and '50s. Irish immigrants, many of who were fleeing the so-called famine, found their way to San Francisco and settled in the Mission District.

The first train arrived in the city in 1869, quickening coast- to-coast travel. People of all backgrounds arrived. Most formed their own neighborhoods, which were reflections of the homelands they left behind, fled or were thrown out of.

In 1906, earthquake and fire rocked the city. Over 700 people died. Following the devastation, the people set about rebuilding their city: bigger and better. Every ethnic group had its specialty; a trade or tradition that brought them some prominence. The Chinese and Italians were known for their restaurants, the Jews in finance and Precious stones. Cops, soldiers and other public servants were the domain of the Irish. It was in this way that the Irish elevated their status in America. My grandfather had been a cop in the '20s and often entertained me with stories of police work at the turn of the century. He had even pursued a serial killer in those confusing days following the quake.

San Franciscans also undertook the construction of the Golden Gate Bridge. My grandparents were one of many couples who put up their homes as collateral to ensure that the funding for the project would be secured. Several of my uncles on my mother's side had worked on the bridge. One of these uncles, Robert, died. I, of course, had never met my uncle but still referred to the Golden Gate as Uncle Bob's bridge.

Funny, I suddenly remembered that I, in fact, had been adopted. I had seldom thought of my adopted parents as anything else than Mom and Dad when they were alive. Since their deaths some eight and twelve years earlier, I hadn't thought of it at all.

I had been a pathologist for the city of San Francisco for over twenty years. In that time I had worked my way up from Pathologist's assistant as a student, to Pathologist after graduating, and finally to Chief Medical Examiner. Over the years I had been cross-trained in every aspect of the Medical Examiner offices' operations. This diversity of skills came in handy during those times when budget cuts increased the worth of employees who could take on additional tasks.

I had performed not only autopsies but had also done time as an Investigator; one of the people who visit the crime scene, gather evidence and coordinate with the police. In many ways, I enjoyed Investigations as much as Pathology, sometimes more so. I liked getting out there, talking with the police, most of whom I knew and for whom I shared a mutual respect and admiration. I liked the piecing together of information in the field.

Investigations weren't so much a departure from Pathology as a complement to it. Pathologists determined how a person died, whether it was by gunshot, knife, drowning, and electrocution, old-age or via a multitude of other causes. Investigators helped to determine the means of death, the why. Whether it was homicide, suicide, accident or natural causes. As a young Pathologist, I had often felt a sense of fragmentation in my work. A body would be brought in and I determined how it had transpired. I often wondered about the investigation that preceded my participation, and its aftermath. Despite the fact that I would be given a copy of the investigator's report and a briefing, I felt left out. I didn't like the lag-time between my questions and their answers. When the opportunity to do investigations made itself available, I took advantage of it. Investigations and Pathology, to me, were two sides of the same coin; they both concerned themselves with ending the mysteries of death. Investigations provided me with a sense of completeness that had been lacking in Pathology and I made many friends and more than a few enemies with my directness and lack of reverence for such things as ego, careerism and other such nonsense disguised as social niceties.

After a time, I grew bored with advancement within a system that would ultimately bump me up to an administrative position, which would not allow me to do what I loved most, work! Without the option of going back and not wanting to move forward, I moved laterally. All the way out of the ME's office and into academia.

I currently taught a few courses in Pathology and Medical Ethics at San Francisco City University Medical School, a job I enjoyed. I liked being in an environment conducive to learning and being around young people, as it offset the presence of death that was so much of my calling. I enjoyed teaching. The hours were good and I got to perform autopsies and teach this skill to others.

It was Inspector Cal Donaldson, my long-time friend, who suggested to me that I get a Private Investigator's license. "I'm not saying you should go hang a shingle that reads 'DR. PI,' and go peeping in windows with a camera for pissed-off wives. I'm saying that you could do independent autopsies and investigations when warranted."

"Autopsies for hire?" I remembered myself asking.

"Absolutely. It's a skill, and we live in the age of specialty."

It didn't take long before I saw the logic of Donaldson's suggestion. A PI's license would allow me to investigate unusual deaths: suicides and supposed accidents where people, family members or the insurance companies had lingering doubts as to the cause. It had been a simple task for me to obtain a PI's license. The requirements weren't as demanding as one might think, for me at least. One had to be 18 years or older, undergo a background check by the Department of Justice. One also had to have either three years, 6,000 hours of investigative experience, or a law or police science degree and two years 4,000 hours experience, or an AA in police science plus two and a half years, 5,000 hours experience. I had over 23 years and nearly 15,000 hours experience in investigations. I also had to pass a two-hour multiple-choice test that covered such areas as laws, liability and evidence handling. It was a test, aspects of which I helped to write for the city, several years earlier. I then had to submit an application, two recent photographs and two fingerprint cards, an exam fee and a Department of Justice fingerprint-processing fee. In the end, the most difficult aspects were the photographs, as I couldn't decide which one made me look professional without looking like some tough guy wannabe. After I was notified, I paid a licensing fee of $175 and was ready to go.

My background and training as an investigator made me qualified - no - overqualified for PI work. I knew the City of San Francisco well. My knowledge of the different agencies was seconded to only the mayor himself. Nobody, except Donaldson and a few other aging police rivaled my knowledge of the streets and its neighborhoods.

I had an ideal career: teaching and performing autopsies as my mainstay and doing a bit of PI work when I felt motivated. This PI work centered about performing autopsies for hire, conferring with the client as to the results and deciding with them whether further investigation was appropriate.

I kept no office hours as a PI; I worked out of the University, using the school's facilities and equipment. I used a select group of graduate students to assist me with the autopsies and test results, in return for additional credits I issued per semester. It is one of the perks of tenure.

It was a part-time practice. Insurance companies would call upon my services when an autopsy's results were unclear and clarity meant money. I was currently on retainer with three. My name was passed about from them and their lawyers and those in law enforcement. The bulk of my business came by word of mouth in these circles.

Amongst the fairer citizens of the city, I had developed a reputation as a man who was able to get the job done with the most important quality that the well-to-do and the well-connected seek -discretion.

There were several other reputations that had circled amongst this potential pool of patrons. There was one in particular that I hadn't sought to foster but flourished nonetheless. This was in part through circumstances outside my control, and partly through my own fault. That being, that I was an avenging angel for hire. That people could hire me to perform an autopsy and if I found something amiss, I would "lean" on or kill the perpetrator. My training as a doctor, they believed, allowed me to mask these "hits" as accidents.

This, of course, was not true. I had never set out to "lean" on or kill anybody on purpose and certainly not for hire. I had, however, "leaned" on several people by coincidence and killed one by necessity in the course of my investigations when the other guy came at me with a tire-iron. Charges were dropped and never brought, respectively. I had other reputations, depending on who you were and what you thought of me, but none held greater amusement or unease for me than this.

I parked my Mercedes in the Station's lot, which was two-thirds full. A shift change was in progress. Police were coming to work while others were leaving.

9

David Feeney

Some were leaving still in uniform. Some of those arriving did so in civilian clothes so that I couldn't tell if they were coming or going.

I exited the car and put on my black sports coat. I checked myself in the driver side window's reflection as my prescription glasses darkened in the daylight. For a man in his early-fifties, I looked good. That's not to say I was handsome, as I wasn't. Average height and slim, I had a gaunt-ruggedness about me, with intense green eyes that hinted danger. Something I found that attracted certain members of the opposite sex. At least that's what they told me. I didn't understand it and didn't feel the need to question it. I tugged gently at the collar of my gray cashmere mock-turtleneck shirt. My gray-flecked, black hair was cropped short. It was easier to keep that way, easier to dry, too. I adjusted my Docker slacks by moving the belt a tad to the left. Comfortable, I set off across the lot and into the aptly colored, black and white building.

3

Chief Wilson was sitting behind his desk when I entered. He was in his late forties though he looked older. I figured that he had worked long and hard to get that way. His uniform was tight and the brass buttons looked as if they might pop off at any moment. On one chair sat Dr. Michael Lukas of the Medical Examiner's office. Lukas was about my age and was similarly built. Similar to Wilson, thereby justifying my decision to get out of management. In the other chair was Inspector Cal Donaldson.

He was just past sixty, with a wife and three kids. He'd been a cop for some thirty years. He was broad shouldered, 6'2 and weighed some two hundred twenty-plus pounds. A lot of this was fat but mattered little and never stopped him from doing his job. "I can't run fast, but I can run far," was his motto. His fedora rested on the arm of his chair.

Donaldson saw me enter first and he stood. His trench coat hung off him like a cape. "Good afternoon, Declan. No trouble finding the place?" he asked professionally.

"No."

Chief Wilson and Dr. Lukas both stood. Each introduced himself, which was more of a formality than anything else, as we all knew one another. I knew Dr. Lukas from having worked with him when I was still with the ME's office. I knew Wilson well, having worked on a case with him years earlier.

"Long time no see, Dr. Connor. How you doing?" Wilson asked.

"Not bad," I smiled. "How are you?"

"Fine," he said. "Thanks for coming in on such short notice."

"No problem," I replied.

"Dr. Connor, we have a problem." Chief Wilson said. "It seems that we have a skeleton in a closet."

I contemplated this for a moment. "Have you considered confession?"

We all laughed.

"No," Donaldson said. "He means a real skeleton in a closet."

"Oh."

"Actually it's a mummified body," Dr. Lukas corrected.

"I see. Where was it found?"

"Over at Nob Hill. It was in a basement apartment. It was discovered this morning. It had been stuffed into a wall that led to the closet of the adjoining unit. The entire wall was built up around the body. It wasn't part of the original floor-plans," Donaldson explained before adding, "It was quite a sarcophagus."

"Hmmm," I said, wondering where Donaldson had picked up the new word. "I heard about that earlier. The news didn't say anything about the body being mummified, though."

"That was Inspector Donaldson's idea," Chief Wilson inserted. "He thought it best to keep that tidbit from the press until we had a chance to talk to you."

"To avoid the freak-show," Donaldson added.

I nodded. "And you want me to find out how this person died?"

"Not quite," the Chief corrected. "We're interested – actually, Inspector Donaldson suggested the idea - of bringing you on as a consultant."

"The situation is," Dr. Lukas injected, "that the body is female. We know that she was murdered and that's about all we know so far. She has no identification of any kind on her and we have no idea as to who she was or why she was killed."

"How was she killed?" I asked.

"Single gunshot wound to the left eye," Lucas answered.

"Exit?"

"No."

"Good."

"We plan to run her fingerprints," Donaldson offered.

"That'll take weeks, depending on how badly she's mummified, and besides, unless she has a criminal record, you won't get anyplace," I informed. "Any idea how long she's been dead?"

"Judging by the style of her clothes, I'd say at least thirty years," Dr. Lukas said.

I considered this. "Face intact?" I asked.

Donaldson nodded. "Yeah. Except the eye. Your best bet is to do that facial reconstruction."

Dr. Lukas shrugged. "Dr. Simpson was the man for that and he isn't as good as he used to be - arthritis," he explained. "Besides, he still does it with clay."

"I understand you got that computer thing at the university," Donaldson said.

"We do," I agreed. "We're still developing it, though it looks promising. Fact is that the clay method is still the best. Computer generation however may end up being our best shot."

"Any ideas on how you'll proceed, Doctor?" Chief Wilson asked.

"Obviously we'd do an autopsy, blood tests, fingerprints, X-rays," I listed them all. "Run CAT scans, take DNA and whatever else to see if there's anything that can help us. I could build up a picture of what she looked like and run it like a missing person's photo. We can narrow down the time she died by determining the exact make of her clothing."

Chief Wilson nodded.

I continued to pitch out ideas. "We could run the photos in local papers, hand-out flyers. I heard of a case where they developed a web-page and ran it over the Internet."

The Chief was impressed. "That's a good idea. What about television? You think they'd be interested?"

"A mummified body stuffed into a closet? I asked. "I'm sure they'll all be interested in it."

"Yes," the Chief nodded. "But would you be willing to put something together? Some sort of presentation that could be aired."

"I guess I could." I didn't like the sound of this.

"Connor has plenty of experience," Donaldson hocked. "He used to be a spokesman for the ME's office."

"Very good," the Chief said.

Actually, I hadn't been an official spokesman for the ME's office but had stood in for the regular guy on occasion.

Donaldson was enthused that his idea seemed to be bearing fruit. "Yeah. And since Connor has a PI license, he could conduct some of the investigative aspects of - - "

"No," the Chief interrupted. "That's something I want to get straight right up front. I spoke to the Mayor before you came in Dr. Connor. I'm aware of your credentials and licensing as a PI, but for this, we're interested in hiring you as a consultant and an advisor to Inspector Donaldson."

"All right," I nodded.

"I personally want to make sure right here and now that there will be a clear division of labor. I'll leave the specifics up to you two. But in the broad strokes, Inspector Donaldson will handle all aspects pertaining to the interviewing of any suspects or witnesses, the gathering of evidence and the overall direction of the case. Dr. Connor, you will handle the autopsy and the direction of the forensic aspects. You will advise Inspector Donaldson of their ramifications and follow his directions on how to proceed. Agreed?"

"Absolutely. I concur."

"Yes, sir." Donaldson added. "But you know two investigators can interview more people than one."

"I'm aware of that. However, since the mayor's office ultimately has had to sign off on the paying of Dr. Connor's fee, they have it as a precondition to his hiring that Inspector Donaldson handle all the interviewing." The Chief smiled at me. "We wouldn't want to get caught in the middle of a lawsuit."

I said nothing but merely looked over at Donaldson. Wilson was referring to the time I broke the jaw of a society man, Preston VanHeusen, after I discovered he was killing his newborn infants, making it look like crib death.

"Besides," the Chief continued, "I'm sure Connor will be more than busy with the forensic aspects of the case. The mayor's office has agreed to pay you on a week by week basis, with weekly evaluations as to whether to renew the city's contract with you."

"That sounds fair," I admitted. I looked over at Dr. Lukas. "The ME's office is all right with this?"

"Absolutely. We're two men short. Miller is on vacation and Shepherd is sick.

"Business as usual," I said with a smile. I knew both men. Shepherd had come to work for the city over ten years before and Miller about eight.

Dr. Lukas nodded. "We'll offer you any help that we can, though."

I considered this. "Thanks. We'll be able to use the University's facilities. It's fully equipped."

"How soon do you think there could be a break in this case?" the Chief, ever concerned with clearance, asked.

I thought for a moment before answering, "If it happens, it will happen within a few weeks. Our best chance here will be that the photos will jog someone's memory as to who she was and that they will provide us with an identity to work from. Television coverage could bring this case nation-wide attention. That alone could end it in a few days. However, I wouldn't hold my breath."

"Do you want the department's PR people to contact the press when you're ready or will you handle it?" the Chief asked.

I almost laughed. I had no media contacts to speak of. That was another myth that had developed about me: that I was media-connected. "The department's will be just fine," I said.

"Great. Where do you gentlemen think you'll start?"

"First, I'll organize an autopsy. Set aside a room and contact a few colleagues. We could be ready to go by tomorrow sometime."

"That soon?" The Chief was surprised.

"Sure. First we'll need to have the body brought to the school."

"We'll have it there within the hour," Dr. Lucas stated.

"I'd also like to visit the crime scene," I said, speaking more to Donaldson. "Get a mental picture of everything."

"Sure," Donaldson said. "Once Dr. Connor has narrowed down when she disappeared, I'll go and talk to whoever owned the building."

"How many owners have their been?" the Chief asked.

Donaldson dug through his coat pocket until he found a small note pad and flipped through it. "Eight since the thirties. It switched hands four times in the mid-sixties alone. I'll find out who rented the apartment once we've narrowed down the time-frame. Otherwise we'll be dealing with perhaps as much as a hundred people."

"Good. Get to it then."

The gathering broke up and Donaldson and I began for the door.

"Oh, Dr. Connor, one other thing," the Chief said.

"What's that?" I asked turning back.

"Go easy," he said simply.

"I'll go wherever the case takes me," I replied.

4

2:12 PM

Donaldson and I escorted the body to the University, where it was unceremoniously deposited in the air-conditioned morgue. News hadn't been let out that an autopsy would be done from the facilities, let alone an autopsy of a mummified corpse. The fact that the body was mummified would be mentioned on the news. Once it was, there would, no doubt, be a flurry of interest concerning the corpse. The press would not be told of the body being moved to the University or my involvement, but it would get out amongst the medical students once I selected my dieners, or assistants, no matter how many oaths of secrecy they took. That much was certain. The police press people were already fending off rumors - rumors that had no doubt been started by the workmen of Kelly's Construction who were present when the body was found.

Afterwards, we drove out to Nob Gardens, as I wanted to get a look over the crime scene. I knew it would be of little help as the event had occurred decades before and there would be little to learn. We took Donaldson's car, which gave us a chance to talk on the way over.

We arrived at the building and Donaldson parked up the street a bit. It was a one-way street lined by apartment buildings on both sides. A van and two trucks marked "Kelly's Construction" were parked out front. Life went on.

"Is that it there?" I asked, and pointed.

"Yep," Donaldson confirmed as he released his seatbelt and opened his door.

I followed suit.

A narrow driveway lay to the side of the building and wound its way around the property and out of sight in the back. We made our way past the wall that bordered the property and past two gargoyles. I was an admirer of architecture, though I didn't know much about the subject. Judging from the brickwork, I figured the building to be at least fifty years old. An assumption that was reinforced when I saw the ironwork that adorned the front entrance. We walked through the glass double-doors that were tied open and went inside. Donaldson led the way.

Echoes of workmen carried down from above. Donaldson saw a workman in an apartment, as we passed. He stopped and asked, "Hey, babe, is Pete Kelly around?"

The man looked up. "Yeah. He's around somewhere."

"Tell him Inspector Donaldson is here and that I'm in the basement apartment and when he gets a chance, to drop by."

The man nodded. "Sure."

We descended the stairs and made our way past the tape to the apartment where the body had been found, #44. There really was no need for the tape, as there would be little we could learn from the scene. Donaldson lifted the tape up, allowing me to pass under and then followed. The room was cool and had a damp smell. Donaldson noted how much smaller the apartment looked now that there was no dust flying about. He walked towards the back. "Over there," he directed.

We walked over to the wall. Our footsteps echoed in the empty dwelling. I considered the partially demolished brick wall.

"Hey, nobody's supposed to be in here!" a voice announced from behind.

Donaldson and I turned to see an annoyed man whom I assumed to be Pete Kelly enter. His expression changed when he recognized Donaldson. "Sorry, Inspector," he said. "I thought it might be the press."

"I told one of your guys that we were down here and asked him to get you," Donaldson explained.

"I didn't see him," said Kelly. "I just heard voices."

Donaldson introduced us.

"Do you have a floor plan for this room?" Donaldson asked.

"Sure. Give me a minute," Kelly announced and left. Moments later he returned with several large sheets of paper, rolled up in tubes. He found the right floor plan and brought it over.

"Thanks." Donaldson looked over the map a moment. "See here," he pointed to me. "That wall's supposed to be made of plywood."

I nodded and ran my hands on the inside of the wall. It was obvious that this was no cavity in the wall. There was no coincidence in the body's being lodged here. Someone had built up this wall to house the body.

I traced a finger along the map until I found what I was looking for. "Hot water pipes," I began. "Probably here and here." I pointed to either side of the wall. "And another one in the back. Perfect."

"Perfect how?" Donaldson asked.

"To make a mummy," I explained. "See, mummies occur very seldom in nature. It takes very specific circumstances. You either have to have a very cold climate - - "

"Or a very warm one."

"Not just warm, but dry. Dry heat like Arizona. The body has to be kept dry and bugs have to be kept from eating the body and helping it to rot. This wall here with the pipes running on either side and behind it would have been warm, sometimes hot, very dry and free of insects. You couldn't have planned it better."

"Do you think someone did plan it?"

"To make a mummy? Nah. Whoever built this put the body here as he probably figured the heat would speed up the decomposition. There'd be no point in trying to make a mummy, as it would preserve tissue and organs that could be tested later. The best thing would have been to have the body decompose completely, leaving us with only the bones."

"And limiting our abilities to do forensic testing," Donaldson concluded.

"Exactly."

"If you guys don't need me, I'll get back to work," Pete Kelly said.

"Sure, thanks," Donaldson said.

"Mr. Kelly," I started. "What's your opinion about this wall?"

Pete Kelly shrugged his shoulders. "It's not expert quality, but it's competently constructed."

I considered this. "Thanks."

The elder Kelly started for the door.

Donaldson called after him. "How's your son doing?"

Kelly shook his head. "I gave him the day off."

Donaldson smiled. Pete Kelly did likewise and exited.

Now it was my turn. "What do you think? Did the murder take place here or did he shoot her somewhere else and bring her here?"

Donaldson looked about. "I'd say that she was shot somewhere else and brought here."

"Why?"

Donaldson tilted his head in a way that told me he was sifting facts. "The walls here are too thin for someone to fire a weapon. Someone would have heard."

"True, but he could have used a pillow or something to silence the weapon," I countered.

"Yeah, but this wasn't a crime of passion," Donaldson pointed out. "It was an execution and that's premeditated. I'd say the murder took place elsewhere and the body was brought here for disposal."

"Good point. Whoever did the hiding probably didn't rent the place for very long then," I theorized.

"Probably not. He probably rented it for a month. Just long enough to do the work, make sure it was set right and then left."

I thought for a moment. "If that's the case, how did he get the body in through the front doors?"

"Who says he did?"

"What do you mean?"

"There's a back entrance," Donaldson said and indicated the way we entered. "It comes in from the yard or garden as they call it."

"I didn't know that."

"Come on," Donaldson said.

We walked back through the apartment and into the hall outside. There we turned left, walking in the opposite direction of the stairs we came down. At the end of the hall, we turned right. There, ahead of us, was a small flight of steps, six in all, which led to a door. Donaldson opened the door. The parking lot greeted us.

"Perfect," I said.

"Yeah, I saw it after I called you. A person could have parked in the back and brought a body in with little chance of being seen."

I nodded. "It's very plausible. Few apartments down here to begin with."

"Four," Donaldson specified.

"Are we sure that the door was - -?"

Donaldson nodded. "It was here. He could have parked right up here, reversed in even. Could have had her wrapped up in a blanket or carpet and carried her right down here."

I nodded. "I like the bit about renting the apartment for only a short period of time."

"Well, once you get the time she was murdered narrowed down, we can narrow our search."

"True. Let's get a bite to eat."

5

3:08 PM

Potrero Hill is an area above the Soma and Mission districts. Quiet middle-classed neighborhoods exist alongside condos of gay artisans and wealthy socialites. San Francisco General Hospital lies to its south. Parks, playgrounds, auto-body stores, antique dealers and bars all coexist within this region. There are also a few nightclubs and, Potrero Hill has the distinction of being the place where O.J. Simpson grew up.

One such bar, the "All-night Sax," had become something of a haven for lonely hearts and insomniacs. Its main feature was explained in its title: live jazz into the early hours. It was a quaint establishment. The décor was mahogany, with brass fixtures. Soft lights from above as well as from the tables and booths about the bar created an atmosphere that gave patrons feelings of privacy, protection and encouraged intimacy.

Patrons came to hear the jazz, which was among some of the best amateur performances one could enjoy free of charge. The owner had been a modestly successful saxophonist back in the forties and fifties. He bought the establishment in the sixties, in part to have a steady day job and in part because he wanted to promote new talent. He changed the name and helped launch the careers of a few locals as well as entertain a lot of people. It was the West Coast's jazz version of CBGB, only it was clean. It was warm without being stuffy. It was cool.

I had frequented the place since I was a medical student. I'd come off rounds sometimes at four in the morning and wouldn't be tired. So, looking for something to do, I drove down to hear the music. Actually, I had discovered the place years before when I was a driver for the ME's office. I recognized the building by sight, though, since I was a kid as I had had an aunt who used to live nearby and we visited often.

One night, after a late shift, I was on my way home when I saw the lights on - soft lights that bled invitingly into the surrounding darkness temporarily halting night's advance. I slowed and rolled down the window; music upbeat and pleasant, drifted out. People were entering and exiting the establishment. They seemed happy, so for want of something better to do, I went on in. I had continued to do so ever since. That was over twenty years ago. Later, when I worked the ME's office, I would often review the results of some lab test or finish a report, after coming off the graveyard shift. I had spent many a late night/early morning in the All Night Sax and had, over the years, sampled the talents of many up and coming jazz performers and could actually say that I had heard them "way back when." I got to know the owner and a few of the staff, though they changed over the years. I wasn't into the Haight scene or any of the various underground musical movements that had sprung up in the city in those days, that so many of my colleagues enjoyed. I always felt a peace and comfort about the place that I couldn't explain.

Donaldson and I sat at a booth near the back. Despite being in the non-smoking section, smoke drifted over to us. Susan, a waitress in her late 30s, divorced with no children, approached our table. She was pretty, the lack of children, obviously accounting for her good maintenance. Or at least that's what I figured. "Good afternoon, gentlemen. Good afternoon, Connor."

"Notice how she said 'gentlemen' and then mentioned Connor," Donaldson said.

I said nothing. Susan smiled. "What can I get you two?"

Donaldson ordered a Pepsi, I a club soda. Susan departed with a wink.

"Anything with you two?" Donaldson asked.

I shook my head.

"You sure? Why not? She's cute enough," Donaldson offered.

"Because I like this place."

"So?"

I explained my policy on dating women who worked in places I liked to frequent. "She's very pretty, but that's not the point. See, if I were to date her, when it ended I'd run the risk of seeing her every time I came in and that could ruin this place for me."

Donaldson laughed as he heard this. "Let me get this straight. You'd rather not have a relationship with a woman on the off chance that it might end badly and cause you to resent visiting the place where you met her?"

"Absolutely. Look, I've been in enough relationships to know that the vast majority of them end badly. Too many to risk ruining this place as it's the only one of its kind in the city."

Donaldson sighed.

"It's kind of like friends and lovers," I explained further. "Lovers come and go; friends are forever."

Susan returned with our drinks and parted.

"Hiring me was your idea, wasn't it?" I asked.

Donaldson smiled, his arms outstretched wide on either side of our booth. "Of course, babe."

"Why?"

He took a swig from his Pepsi. "I wanted to help you out. Give a boost to your business."

I could hardly believe what I was hearing. "Boost my business? I work full-time for the college and spend my days off correcting papers and you're trying to find me work? I'm flattered."

"I know that, but you know what I'm talking about. It's a case!" he said excitedly.

"I know that."

"Look," he explained. "They could have assigned me Nelson and we'd knock about, and the ME's office would run their little tests and that would be fine. But you know as well as me that murders that aren't solved within forty-eight hours have little chance of being solved. Where do you think that'll leave us after twenty or thirty years?"

"Good point. What makes you think I can solve this?"

Donaldson took another swig. "When I arrived on the scene and got the basics of this one, I knew that I would be working closely with the ME's office. I figured it would be a perfect one for you. You're something of a legend, you know, after breaking Van-Heusen's jaw."

Unimpressed with my friend's assessment of my skills, I asked, "Did you see the way Wilson warned me?"

Donaldson smiled and shrugged it off. "I wouldn't mind that too much."

"You just did what they wanted. Fact is he admires you." Donaldson drummed his fingers on the table. "You know, I always wanted to work a case with you, pal."

I nodded and smiled lightly. It was true: all of it. Several police had expressed their satisfaction after they heard about what I had done. Their only regret was that they hadn't been there to witness it, or do it themselves. It was also true that in the years since, I would confer with Donaldson on different aspects of cases that he had been involved with. It became something of a running joke between us. Donaldson would present scenarios to me when I'd drop by for barbecues or one of the kid's birthdays'. He would often begin these scenarios by saying, "Hey, Declan, what if you and me were to partner up on this case? Wouldn't that be a hoot?"

I said, "See now, Cal, if you wish for something often enough, it sometimes comes true."

Donaldson set down his drink. "That's the spirit. Let's be honest. You enjoy being out of the classroom. Hitting the streets. Huh? Am I right?"

"No doubt about that," I admitted. I had spent the better part of my career working the graveyard shift. I had no family of my own or any children. Aside from my sister, Megan, there was no other person in the world I could call family. We had a few distant relatives and second cousins, but we never kept in touch. I was a night person pretty much and when I decided to work at the University, it had occurred to me that I hadn't been in the light of day on a regular basis in years. I still hadn't gotten quite used to it. "It certainly does break the monotony. Though it looks like I won't be 'hitting the streets' too much on this one."

Donaldon shrugged. "Yeah, well that's just the Captain watching his brass. Besides, he said that everything would have to be cleared by me. So if you're not too busy, you can accompany me on some of the interviews."

I confessed, "I'd actually like to do that." Fact was the idea was becoming more intriguing as I thought about it. I hadn't been on a case of any kind in some time. It had been months since I had even been called upon to consult. I hadn't even performed an autopsy since last semester. It would feel good to apply my skills in a non-academic setting.

"You're coming around," Donaldson beamed, obviously glad that his plan was gaining acceptance.

"All right, all right," I said. "Let's get this division of labor squared away. What's the game-plan?"

Donaldson sat back, adjusting himself in the booth and thought a moment. "Well, you get started on the autopsy and narrowing down when she died and then I'll go find out whoever owned the building around the time you give me. Once we have your estimate, we can start lining up some interviews."

"Okay," I said. "Looks like I need to get started then." As is so often the case, the first break would be up to the pathologist to make.

"Yep. Once you point me to the right year, I'll be able to investigate any records of missing persons, rent records, employment and so forth. There's a wealth of information out there and most of it will be on paper, so my guys will be pretty busy."

I nodded.

"When do you think you can get started?" Donaldson asked.

"I'll do a bit tonight."

"Really?"

"Sure. Why not?"

"I thought you were just saying that for the Captain's sake; y'know, so they were thinking they weren't being taken advantage of."

"No, I meant it," I assured. "The autopsy won't get started before tomorrow at the soonest, but more likely the day after. Tonight, though, I'll do some preliminary work."

"What, no classes? Book reports?"

"No, I teach mostly in the morning."

"No *tutoring*?" Donaldson asked slyly.

"No," I said, knowing full well that Donaldson was referring to my reputation as being a man who availed myself of the numerous nubile and willing young women who tended to proliferate at the University; a reputation that had some basis in reality. I had had a few relationships and a fling or two with *former* students and graduate students. I had never had a relationship with an undergraduate, and I had never, ever approached any of them. The women had initiated all relationships.

The University had a simple and well-defined policy against student-teacher relationships; they were illegal. From a legal standpoint, however, I had been on the right side of law. I hadn't had relationships with current students. The rule didn't apply to graduate students as a few had coyly pointed out to me.

For my part, I took it in stride. I viewed it better than the other stereotype of single men who taught college and lived alone in San Francisco; one I had simultaneously endured with a pinch of salt when I was a young pathologist, which, of course, was that I was gay.

"No extra-curricular activities? Study groups?" Donaldson asked.

"Nope."

"One on one?"

"Ah-ah."

"Tete-a-la-tete?"

"No."

"Tit-a-la-tit?"

I smiled. "You really think about this, don't you?"

"Hey, I'm a fan of the man," Donaldson said expansively and then became serious. "What kind of autopsy you plan on doing?"

I thought a moment. "Possibly a limited."

"Why limited?" All joviality had left Donaldson. That was another aspect of our relationship: our ability to joke around one minute and be solemn the next. We shifted easily from the silly to the somber, from deadpan, to dead serious.

"Because we know what killed her," I explained. "There's no need to inspect every organ, so we'll take tissue samples from the major organs and see if she had any anomalies that may aid in identifying her."

"I don't get that."

I leaned forward, and explained further. "We might find that she had a disease that ran in her family, something rare. Just like the way an X-ray can show whether a bone has been broken, the presence of a disease can help us in identification."

"I see," Donaldson acknowledged.

"I'm mostly concerned with the autopsy of the head. The bullet is still lodged in there and we'll be able to determine the caliber without any trouble. If we're lucky, the bullet didn't hit any bone and we'll get good ballistics off that. I also plan to do X-rays, run tissue samples through toxicology, get blood samples, if possible, do tests on the hair as well as obtain a DNA fingerprint." These tests, I knew, would provide us with various valuable clues as to the identity of the woman, as the tissues contained a wealth of knowledge for anyone with the know-how to decipher them. I was particularly interested in what the hair samples would yield, as human hair is a repository for any drugs the victim might have been taking.

"You're going to be busy," Donaldson acknowledged and then his voice changed tone. "I don't mean any offense, but have you ever done an autopsy on a mummy? I mean, are you qualified?"

I raised a hand to allay my friend's anxiety. "Actually, I haven't." I confessed. "But I know a few people who have. I'm going to give them a call tonight and invite them down to participate."

Donaldson considered this momentarily before saying, "I hope they don't expect to get paid. I mean the mayor would have to sign off on that."

I shook my head. "No. These guys and gals will do it for the experience. It's not every day that they get to work on a naturally occurring mummy."

"I imagine not," Donaldson said. "You got a crew already picked out?"

"I've got a few potentials," I said simply. Actually, I had more than a few people. In my mind, I had already picked out the perfect team. I reviewed the team briefly. I then outlined my "dream team" to Donaldson. Dr. Cornelius Geist was a Forensic Anthropologist, who had worked on mummies in Africa, Europe and throughout the Americas. He was the only one of my fantasy team who had gotten a chance to study the now-famous "iceman." I hadn't seen him in a while. Geist was getting up there in years. Last I had heard, he'd been having some heart trouble. I was sure that only death would keep Geist away from an unusual find. He would head up the autopsy.

Next on the list was Dr. Lucian Maher, a Forensic Dentist who had taken part in various studies of the teeth of Egyptian mummies. I had only met him once at a staff meeting a year or two earlier. We knew each other mainly by reputation. His expertise could yield interesting insights into the life of the victim. Recruiting him, I imagined, would be no trouble.

Dr. Maureen Trundy was a Forensic Radiologist who would be able to interpret the CAT scans, X-rays and whatever secrets they might hold. She used

25

to work for the University but had moved over to the City's museum, where she did research. Last time I had talked to her, she said she was bored. I was sure that it wouldn't take more than a phone call to get her to leave her research behind and do some real work.

Dr. Merriam Liu was a Forensic Toxicologist. We would be depending upon her to obtain blood and tissues samples and perform tests that would determine blood type and any diseases or genetic abnormalities Maria Cialini might have had that could be of some help to us.

I would also need a couple of dieners, who would assist with the labeling of tissue samples, moving the body about and the setting up of X-rays and other tests. I would pick two graduate students for this task while I would serve as Dr. Geist's assistant.

"How long do you think it'll take you to assemble this crew?"

"Not too long, I figure. Geist will be the only difficult one, and that's only because of his health. Assuming he's okay, I'm sure he'll show. The rest are safe bets. I can drop by Maher's office as well as Dr. Liu's. Trundy I'll call later this evening."

"What about those 'diners?'" Donaldson asked.

"Dieners," I corrected.

"Right, dieners. Do you think you'll have any trouble recruiting them given the apathy of today's youth?"

"No. We'll have more applicants than positions. It'll be worse than the actual team."

"Up and coming?" Donaldson asked.

I nodded. "Good thing is that it ensures that I can pick amongst the best and the brightest.

Donaldson nodded.

I sipped my club soda. "I'll get started on the facial reconstruction this evening. I'll come up with something. Neil Thompson, the student who designed the program, is probably there right now. He's bit of a lab-rat," I confided.

"Oh?"

"Yeah." I stood. "Spends all his time wrapped up in his work. He never gets laid. Good kid, though. Kinda like you."

"Hey-hey, hey," Donaldson said in mock-protest to the mock-attack. "Why, I'll have you know that last night when I got home, I said in a loud and masculine voice, 'Hey baby, daddy's home, give me some - - -'"

"Let's go," I said and stood.

"All right," Donaldson said and added, "Hey, Kate was asking for you."

"Oh?"

"She's still hoping you might get married. Says you deserve it."

"What did you say?"

Donaldson shrugged. "Marriage is a three-ring circus: engagement ring, wedding ring, suffering."

I smiled.

"Still, if you were, you'd get a lot more pussy."

"When you're single, you get pussy." I informed. "When you're married, pussy gets you."

"Touché."

6

4:32 PM

San Francisco City University is a four-year institution devoted to medical sciences. It has a student body of nearly 15,000 full-time undergraduate and 6,000 full-time graduate students. Founded in 1910, sitting on 130 acres at the northernmost section of Twin Peaks, SFCU is only a few blocks short of Golden Gate Park. In addition to its football field, pool, tennis and basketball courts, it also has a first-rate medical center.

Donaldson dropped me off, but stayed outside to make a call to his wife on his cell. When he came in, I was in one of the morgue's autopsy rooms, which was located on the second floor of the medical building, and by that I mean it was two floors underground. I was always aware of how much more pleasant this morgue was, in so far as a morgue could be, as opposed to the city's. Actually, it always reminded me of a dentist's office. The walls were eggshell as opposed to sterile white and the tiles were of a newer variety than the city's morgue. This institution was barely twelve years old; the city's nearly eighty. The hall lights were diffused, casting it in a soft glow. Stark contrast to the harsh white fluorescent light of the city's morgue, that glared vulgarly off everything and was the cause of many a headache.

Yet, I was also aware of the overall cold-loneliness of the structure, that no eggshell or diffused light could ever mask. Not to mention the ever-present smell of disinfectants that no potpourri could ever hide. I had been in and out of morgues throughout my career. This one had been built largely on the charitable nod from one of the city's better citizens; a name that escaped me at that moment. It was used mostly for teaching and research and was immune from such problems as backlog. Being staffed by tenured physicians, there was little fear of the facilities being overused. But a morgue is a morgue is a morgue and all morgues are similar as all deal with unraveling the mysteries of death.

This one was little different from the others. A wall-mounted stainless-steel sink-station was on one side of the room. A two-hinged section cover-dissecting table sat parallel atop an autopsy table that was located in the center of the tiled room. A scale, like the kind found in a produce isle, hung from the ceiling.

A portable two-body mortuary refrigerator had been wheeled and plugged in. The unclothed mummified body lay on a tray and was, thanks to the three-piece telescoping aluminum carriage, two-thirds out of the refrigerator. Without clothing, the body appeared even thinner than it had when I first saw it. Her mouth was open and her lips frozen in a snarl, exposing her front teeth. I imagined that this had taken place after death, but couldn't be sure. Gnarled, black and pruned, it was hard to believe that this had once been alive.

"What's with the mini-fridge?" Donaldson asked. "Any beers in there?"

I ignored the joke and answered the question. "I didn't want to leave the body out. We weren't sure whether we'd do more tests after we X-rayed it, so I brought in the fridge. That way I wouldn't have to be wheeling it back and forth to storage.

"Ah. So, what were you able to get?" Donaldson asked.

I walked over to the body. Donaldson followed suit. "Quite a bit actually. We removed the clothes and wiped the body down with carbolic acid to make sure bacteria wouldn't start eating away at it, as it has been removed from its environment. Then I performed an external exam and found only one wound. This single contact-wound to the eye," I said pointing. "I confirmed that there is no exit so we'll be able to retrieve the bullet later at the autopsy. I'd say it's a .22."

"When's the autopsy?"

"Still not set. The day after tomorrow at the soonest. You going to drop by?"

Donaldson nodded. "Absolutely. What's the word on the dream team?"

"Dr.'s Maher and Liu are good for the day after tomorrow. I'm still waiting for Trundy to return my call, but I don't see any problem with her showing up. The big one is Geist. He's interested and can possibly make it. He'll call me back tonight and let me know for certain. It'll all hinge on him. I'll pick out the *diners* when Geist gives me the okay."

Donaldson was pleased. "Good. I'll mark my calendar. What else have you got?"

"I can tell you that she had no jewelry or rings. Not even a watch. Her nails were manicured. Professor Adams from anthropology dropped by and made a quick guestimation of her height being roughly 5'7 and was about no more than 120 pounds in weight."

"How did he determine that?"

I smiled. "She went by the woman's skirt and shoe size. She's the same size."

"Very scientific."

"Yeah. About the clothes, I took the names and the particulars of all her clothing and have someone looking into that now. Based on the style of clothing, an educated guess puts her as being dead since the early fifties. Her clothes were new. But we'll be able to narrow that down a bit later. From what I was able to see, her nails, hair and teeth appear to have been well kept. This woman was polished so it's a fair assumption that she bought her clothes when they first came out. She kept up with the fashion."

"Right." Donaldson had an idea. "If you figure that she was dead since the early fifties, I could go over and question the owner of the building where she was found."

"I wouldn't do that just yet," I said.

"Why? I usually question all potentials, either at night or early in the morning. I like to catch them in the off hours; that way, they're less prepared. You can come along; I meant that y'know."

"True," I agreed, "but a person usually has a harder time lying when you have particular information like a photo. It's like the whole thing is closing in on them."

"I love when they get that cornered look." Donaldson smiled in remembrance of several occasions.

"If you're worried about a potential suspect coming up with a story while we wait for these photos," I began, "I should remind you that the perp has had probably half a century to come up with one."

"Yeah," Donaldson said, and then remembering, asked, "Oh, the computer thing. How much longer do you think it'll be?"

"Soon. I took an X-ray of the head earlier. I got Thompson building up a digital image down the hall."

"Sounds hi-tech," Donaldson ventured.

"It is. This kid's good. He's developing a new program for facial reconstruction whereby you scan in the X-ray," I explained.

"Hmmm." Donaldson didn't understand, but I knew he was impressed nevertheless.

"Anyway, he's got this program where he scans in this information and then can manipulate the X-ray of the skull by introducing variables such as age, race, height and weight and so forth. The program builds up how the face would have appeared in life. When finished, it'll allow us to view the face from any angle."

"You mean like a mug shot?"

"Something like that. We'll have full front and both profiles. It's a lot of math," I explained. "I'd like to bring a copy of one along once it's printed, before you talk to anyone."

"Absolutely," Donaldson agreed. "Photos could have an effect and jog some memories. Tell me, buddy, how good is the quality?"

"As good as one can expect."

Both of us knew that computer-generated photos had an artificial look to them. They were a good aid, though, and certainly a step-up from hand-sketches.

I continued, "We tested the program by taking X-rays of some cadavers. I didn't let the student see the face of the cadaver so all he had to work with was the X-ray and the approximate weight and height. This prevented him from being influenced by memory of the cadaver's face. The results were good. Based upon the X-ray I gave him, he says he should be able to get some good images."

"Welcome to the information age," Donaldson said, impressed.

"Yeah."

Curious, Donaldson asked, "How long did the old method take?"

"Well, working with clay took hours. CT scans were a step up and took less," I said as I slid the body back into the refrigerator and locked it. "Let's go. You can see for yourself."

We exited the morgue.

"Are you ready for your TV appearance? Donaldson asked as we made our way down the hall.

"No, but I will be."

"'Unsolved' something or other," Donaldson said.

"Something like that, yes," I confirmed.

"I hear it's going to be broadcast all over," Donaldson said. "How'd you arrange that?"

"*Your* buddies in PR told the local station about the mummy aspect of it. Some producer at corporate got wind of it and offered to do a fifteen-minute segment on it once the autopsy is complete. They want to put it in the next episode."

"When will it be filmed?"

"I have no idea. They're going to get back to me on it, probably the same day as the autopsy. They'll interview me here, though." I shook my head. "When this story hits the news tonight, look out."

"I know."

"One of the producers has already put in a bid for the book rights," I pointed out.

Donaldson merely nodded, apparently well accustomed to the feeding frenzy that bizarre cases generate for the media.

I shrugged. "Anyway, it should create interest and hopefully knock something loose."

31

"Oh, it'll knock something loose," Donaldson agreed. "Like every nut and conspiracy theorist in the country." He paused a moment before continuing on a lighter note. "What are you going to wear?"

"I don't know, why?"

"Wear a trench coat, why don't you?" Donaldson urged.

"Stop with the trench coat."

"No, do. It'll make you mysterious. And when you talk into the camera, tilt your head down a bit and look up to the camera and arch your eyebrow."

I laughed. "Do you ever stop? Would you like to direct the episode?"

"I'm just trying to help," he laughed.

"How about I try to talk gravelly?" I suggested mockingly.

"Whatever works."

We walked on. I looked into the different rooms, where if nobody were present, I shut off the lights. In one room, there was a cantilever storage rack that could be used to store bodies temporarily if the staff was in a jamb for space. Donaldson wondered aloud if the facility had ever faced such a crisis and added that most likely, it was a donation. A few feet away was a cadaver lift, a device we used to lift bodies, and move them from the freezer to the autopsy table. Unlike the hand operated ones the city morgue used, this one was battery operated and was a donation.

"I've got an idea," I said.

"What's that?"

"Why don't you appear with me? *You* can wear your trench coat and look mysterious. They can interview the officer in charge and ask him his insights."

Donaldson shrugged off the idea. "I don't think so. Besides, all that attention might cause the ladies to hit on me when I'm on the street. I have to keep a low-profile."

We walked on.

"Look," I said. "Don't ask too many questions about facial reconstruction or this kid'll throw the book at you."

"All right."

7

Donaldson and I entered a well-lit room used by the staff to review findings. There, hunched over a keyboard and peering into a computer screen was Neil Thompson, third year graduate student. Tall and narrowly built with wire-rimmed glasses, he was an excellent candidate for doctoral work as well as a nervous breakdown. He had previously earned a degree in computer science and was a decent programmer. He was currently well on his way to his first patent.

Thompson looked up. "Good evening, doctor."

We made our introductions. I was anxious to see how Thompson's program had worked out. Thompson was anxious to talk about the field of facial reconstruction.

"How's it coming?" I asked.

"It's almost there. A few more minutes and we'll have it. It's working with the variables you gave me earlier."

"How'd you determine age?" Donaldson asked.

Thompson cleared his throat. "That was based on there not being a single gray hair on the mummy. That's not to say that she couldn't have been older and have died her hair. But her clothes weren't something that an older woman would have worn. Autopsy will determine the age better, though. For now, we're going with under thirty."

"So ah, Neil," Donaldson began. I shot him a look as I recognized the tone. "Dr. Connor's been telling me a bit about your work, but he doesn't make much sense. Why don't you tell me all about facial reconstruction."

I shook my head.

Thompson spoke fast, happy that he had a willing audience to hear about his area of expertise. "Well, Inspector - - "

I tuned out, as I knew the development of the technique well. Facial reconstruction was first documented in 1895 when an anatomist named "His" attempted to identify Johann Sebastian Bach. His was the first to collect information concerning the thickness of tissue about the face. He had determined that there were nine midline and six lateral points on the human face.

Soon after His came two Swiss scientists, Kollman and Buchly, who combined information gleaned from His, with their own. There was also a paleontologist named Mikhail Gerasimov. He developed what is called the "Russian method" in the 1920s. Gerasimov's method emphasized the development of the musculature about the neck and head. The Japanese, too, did experiments to determine flesh thickness about the face in the 1940s. In the 1970s, Professor Lebedinskaya furthered studies when he examined over 1,500 people of different ethnic backgrounds, such as Lithuanians, Koreans, Buryats, Kazakhs, Bashkirs, and Uzbeks.

The last twenty years had seen the development of a very accurate system of reconstruction. This system was basically a combination and refinement of several older techniques. Figures for tissue thickness were available for Japanese, Caucasians and Afro-Caribbean's. Most of the earlier techniques involved sculpting a model of the head or laying the clay over the actual skull. Today, scientists cast a mold of the skull with a derivative of seaweed called "alignite." The best method of casting a plaster mold was the two-part split where you do one half and then the other before assembling them as one piece. There had also been work done with CT scans.

I listened and nodded. The kid was accurate.

Donaldson took this all in. "What if the skull is damaged or is half obliterated?"

Thompson straightened up in his seat. "If half the face is damaged, we impose a mirror image of the good half. Even though no face in the world is perfectly symmetrical, it's close enough. Anyway, you take the mold of the skull and drill in tiny wooden dowels. These dowels are set into the plaster at a depth that reflects the thickness of the tissue in that area. Then you take Cornish pot clay and build up the muscles about the face to the depth indicated by the dowels."

Donaldson nodded. "What about the nose? How do you determine that?"

I could see that he was getting into this.

"Good question. On average, the more narrow the nasal aperture, the narrower the nose. The opposite also holds true. You can take a tangential line down from the lower third of the nasal bone until it bisects a line taken upwards from the anterior nasal spine."

Donaldson looked at me, and then Thompson. He was confused.

"The two lines will intersect at what is roughly the tip of the nose," Thompson said simply.

"Oh. Why didn't you just say so?"

Thompson continued, "Artificial eyes are also set in. This is done earlier. I should have told you that before."

Donaldson waved him on.

"OK, so the musculature of the face is built-up and then clay is applied over this, usually in layers. It used to be done in pellets, but layering is more accurate."

Donaldson considered this. "If you cover up all the musculature, then why not just smear clay on to the right depth? Why all the hassle?"

Thompson nodded as if he had anticipated this. "This technique allows the face to be built up from the skull outward so that it accurately reflects natural development. Also, if one wants to show a cross-section of the face, you have only to peel back a layer of the clay."

Donaldson seemed impressed. "This was the technique that Dr. Simpson was good at."

"Right," I confirmed.

"The difficulties of working with only a skull is determining the crease on the upper eyelid, the size of the ears, and shape of the mouth. These elements are too difficult to determine via skull alone."

"OK," Donaldson acknowledged. "How does this CT Scan you mentioned earlier work?"

Thompson continued, "CT, or Computer Tomography is a medical scanning technique where the CT-scanner is fitted to a computer-controlled milling machine. This cuts a replica of the skull in styrene. There's also a technique called 'Selective laser sintering.' Here the CT-scans are directed into a computer-guided laser that polymerizes powdered plastic into an image of the skull. The technique I use," he said with some pride, "is quicker and better as there is no clay to mess with, no molds to construct, styrene to cut and no dowels to insert into a model. The computer builds up the musculature. In this way the process is always objective. My program builds up the musculature according to race. The scientist can't be influenced by such factors as bias, fatigue, personal error or having seen a photo of the victim. The program creates a three-dimensional image."

"Sounds good, babe," Donaldson said. "How much longer?"

Thompson looked at the screen. "A few more minutes. I introduced some variations of my own."

"Oh?" I questioned.

"Nothing major," Thompson said defensively. "See the drawback of my program is the same as the others; it's difficult to determine the size of the nose, ears and mouth. But in this case, we have a good idea of what she looked like, right down to how she combed her hair as we're working with a mummified body and not just a skull. Now I've looked over the body and I believe that she was either Italian or Spanish."

"Really?" I said.

"Sure. She clearly has very full lips. Now as far as I know, there were no collagen lip implants back then, so we can assume them to be natural. We also know her hairstyle and assumed color. My opinion is that this was a very exotic looking woman. So what I did, since the program allows me to produce a color photo is that I opted to give her brown eyes, olive-colored skin, and, of course, black hair. I also factored in her hairstyle, approximate ear and nose size." He pressed a button on his ergonomic keyboard. "I'll show you the process from the beginning so you can see how far it's gotten to now."

Donaldson and I leaned in and watched as an image of the skull materialized. Pinpoints aligned themselves about the face. Then the facial muscles began to "grow." It was like watching someone decay in reverse. Slowly, the muscles became thicker. A pair of large eyes faded in. The muscles stopped "growing" and skin surfaced about the face. The picture was still in black and white. A few moments passed. Hair, black, luxurious and parted in the middle, grew out and stopped at the shoulder. A thin nose appeared, as did eyebrows. Ears too and then a mouth."

"Looking good," Donaldson said. "Coochie-coochie."

"Thanks," Thompson said proudly.

"And you created the program?"

The young grad-student nodded. "It's patented."

Color faded in. The screen came alive with the woman's face. The face took on a healthy glow as the skin went to an olive tone. The eyes went brown and the mouth smiled slightly. Despite the artificial, mannequin-like qualities of her visage, one thing that rang through was her incredible beauty.

"Here we are," Thompson said. "Finished."

Donaldson pulled up a chair as a "photo" came off the laser printer. The color qualities of the print gave her face a vitality that the computer's monitor seemed to lack. There was a greater range of hue in the skin and it had an effect on the eyes, which, while it didn't make them lifelike, definitely made them less lifeless.

Donaldson picked up a photo and took a close look at the face before him. It looked like the mummy, only filled in. The hair had a luster to it. Slender eyebrows arced neatly over the large brown eyes. The mouth had been rearranged. The death snarl had been replaced by the affable smile of two sensual lips.

"Jeepers, this is good Thompson!" I said.

Donaldson "hmmm'd" his agreement.

"Thanks. I also touched up the hair a bit."

I was impressed. "Seriously, I mean, I heard it was good but this is - she is beautiful."

"Yes," Donaldson said staring into the face. "She was."

I noticed Donaldson's strange expression. "What is it?" I asked.

"I don't know."

"You know her?" I asked jokingly.

Donaldson shook his head slowly. "I can't tell whether it was from her beauty or not but she looks familiar. I got a feeling of *deja vu*. Maybe she was an actress or a model or something?" he said finally.

"If she even looked remotely like that, she could have been," I agreed.

I, and I suspected that the others, felt a slight pang of guilt over the feelings that we were having about a woman who'd been dead for decades.

"The smile was my touch. Makes her look alive," Thompson said to break the uneasy silence.

The computer generated eyes blinked.

Donaldson gave a start. "Wow!" he said. "Tell me that was your touch, too."

Thompson nodded and looked over the screen like a cyber-Picasso admiring his work and checking the fine details.

"I can print the photos at various angles," he offered.

"Yeah," I said looking at the photo. "Do that."

"What would you like?" Thompson asked.

Donaldson replied, "Full frontal, profile left and profile right."

"No problem."

"How long do you think they'll take?" I asked.

"Couple hours," Thompson replied. "The computer has to recalculate everything and then rotate the image. It's not as simple as flipping the image over as the face isn't symmetrical and thus the image on each half has different variables."

"OK," I nodded. "I'll drop by later or tomorrow and pick them up."

"Sure," Thompson said.

We left Thompson to his own devices. As we walked across the plaza, Donaldson looked over the photo before him. "Pretty impressive work for one evening."

"All and all, we're pretty lucky to have this much," I confided.

"Why's that?"

"Due to the excellent preservation of the body."

"Oh. I hadn't considered that the body was preserved. At least not well."

"Yes, mummies do not often occur naturally. Like I said earlier, this one obviously occurred by accident. When a body dies, bacteria break down the tissue, eating away, eventually leaving only the skeleton behind. In order for these bacteria to grow, they need three things - warmth, moisture, and air. If any one of these is missing from the environment in which the remains are kept, the growth of these bacteria can be affected. If combinations of these aren't present, the bacteria may not develop at all and the body doesn't decay; it mummifies." I yawned. "The Egyptian mummies, the ones we're all familiar with, were created deliberately. Different cultures would do things like drying the body out in the hot dessert sun where there was no moisture. Others would actually smoke the body."

"What do you mean smoke? You mean like beef jerky?"

"Yes. The process is similar."

Donaldson shook his head.

"Remember the Ice Man they found in Italy a few years ago?" I asked.

"The one who had no pecker?"

"Yeah. The one who had no pecker. Glad to see you're keeping up with current events."

"Things like a poor bastard dying during the Ice Age and gets defrosted and has no pecker I tend to remember," he said flatly. "Wasn't his name Bobbit?"

I ignored the pun. "At any rate, he was preserved because of the extreme cold temperatures. Now that covers both extremes of hot and cold," I said. "Did you hear about the bog man?"

"Is he a relative of the boogey-man?"

"No," I said and took the photo.

"I thought he was."

"In Europe, they have these bogs where the ground is very marshy. In the old days, armies sometimes threw the bodies of their dead enemies into these bogs or sometimes a person just fell in. They would sink under the Pete, which would block oxygen from getting into the soil. Those mummies, the 'bog men,' were formed due to lack of oxygen. I think they found a few of them in Whales."

Donaldson nodded, impressed. "I knew you were the man for the job."

We made our way to the parking lot. Donaldson turned to me. "She must have pissed someone off."

"What makes you say that?"

Donaldson nodded as if confirming something in his mind. "A young, beautiful woman. Single contact wound to the head. Calm, deliberate, personal," he said.

I shrugged. "Maybe."

We reached Donaldson's car. "You know what kills people. I know why people kill. This was personal," he diagnosed.

This comment hung like an airborne pathogen for several moments.

I finally spoke. "I'm going to run the images Thompson develops as a flyer, like a standard missing person. Distribute copies."

Donaldson looked at his watch. "You know, now that we have the photo and the approximate year, we could go and interview the building owner."

"Fair enough. Who was it?"

Donaldson took out his notebook. "You said the body was probably there since the mid-fifties?"

I nodded.

"Well, according to what I have, that building was owned by 'Golden Gate Realty,' between 1949 and 1958."

"Fine. Who do we see there?"

"You're not going to believe this."

"Try me."

"Did you ever hear the name Michael Astor IV?"

"Sounds familiar."

"Michael Astor, the heir to the Astor fortune. Real estate mogul turned philanthropist," he recited. "Ring a bell?"

I laughed. "Actually it does."

"What's so funny?"

"If I remember correctly, it was his grant that built the University's morgue. How's that for irony?"

"What do you say we go inquire as to the body that was found in his building?"

"Sure." I placed the photo into a folder.

"But listen, let me do the talking because a guy like this doesn't brush his teeth without counsel," Donaldson advised.

"We wouldn't want to piss him off," I said officially.

"I'm not worried about that. I'm more concerned with him being offended and using his legal muscle to complicate things for us. Let me do the talking. I'll stick to the facts. You just listen to what he's got to say."

"Fine. Are you going to call him and set up an interview?"

"What the hell for?" Donaldson asked slyly. "We'll just say we were in the area and thought we'd take a chance."

"Why give anybody a warning?"

"That's right."

Donaldson unlocked the driver's door. I opened mine.

"Bye the way," Donaldson inquired, "did they ever find that guy's pecker?"

"I hate to disappoint you," I said, "but that guy's pecker was never missing. The scientists had trouble finding it due to the desiccation of the flesh.

Donaldson looked confused and hurt for a moment, but only a moment before rebounding. "I've heard of not being able to find your dick with both hands, but not being able to find someone else's?"

8

6:49 PM

The Financial District came to fruition back in the boom days of the Gold Rush of the 1840s. Then it had simply been a beach town. The influx of fortune seekers was such that the pre-Golden Gate bay area became so clogged with ships that many of the new arrivals were forced to stay. That was then.

Today the Financial District is the center of the economic life of the city. Banks, Insurance, Telecommunications and Oil companies all call this area, built on the settlements that housed the originally "49ers," home.

The drive to Montgomery Street was quiet. After winding our way from Twin Peaks, we took 17th Street to Market and rode along for a stretch. There was little traffic that hour; the post-work rush hour had largely ended and the citizens of the city were at home. I kept my window down as I enjoyed the cool evening air blowing across my hair. Before us on the left, towered the Transamerica Building, on our right could be seen the majesty that was Uncle Bob's bridge.

I knew little about Michael Astor IV as I seldom read the society pages and had refused to have anything to do with things like fundraising. Donaldson knew more, not because he read the society pages, but because his wife did.

This is what I did know; Michael Astor IV had worn many hats in his life. The seventy-four year old philanthropist was the sole heir to the Astor fortune, valued at something in excess of two billion dollars. Michael Astor the 1st, as the legend went, had come out to California during the Gold Rush and had amassed a sizable fortune during the late 1830s. Michael Astor II had continued the family's upward spiral by investing in the railroads after the Civil War. Michael Astor III had done well in shipping, with lucrative contracts throughout Asia. Michael Astor IV started with a few pieces of property and quickly demonstrated the family's knack for success by creating an empire of his own in real estate. He had been married a few times and had a couple of kids; four, if my memory was correct. Michael Astor IV had decided in the early seventies to devote half of his fortune to charitable causes and quickly established himself as the city's most munificent man, dolling out several million dollars a year to orphans, drug rehab programs, the handicapped, the afflicted and the aged.

Some said that Astor's later-in-life switch to philanthropy was due to guilt. There was a dark side to this legend that was whispered after the accolades. Michael Astor the 1st had reportedly built his gold fortune largely at the expense of others. He was said to be, by various historians and biographers, a particularly ruthless man who'd been involved in numerous "fool's gold" swindles and other unsavory practices. Michael Astor II's railroads were built on the backs of cheap Chinese labor and Michael the third had used strikebreaking Pinkertons to crush several attempts by his dockworkers to effectively organize themselves into a union. In keeping with the family tradition, Michael IV had been accused of bribing public officials to change the zoning laws back in the sixties. This reportedly enabled him to buy several choice plots of land at bargain-basement prices. Once the zoning had conveniently changed yet again, the price of the land had skyrocketed, increasing his profits disproportionately. Critics of Michael Astor IV, including a few pop-psychologists, theorized that his generosity was overcompensation, literally for the sins of his fathers. OK, maybe I knew a bit about him.

"Do you know what I've noticed recently?" Donaldson asked, effectively derailing my train of thought.

"I can't imagine," I replied, and meant it.

"How come on TV and in the movies and everything else, you always see guys getting hit in the nuts?"

"What?" I said, half-laughing.

"I'm serious. You watch TV, every other show; a guy gets it in the nuts. Movies, you got women kicking guys in the nuts, or burning them in bed on the movie of the week. You can't even watch three minutes of *America's Funniest Home Videos* without some poor hack getting a golf-ball, softball or brick in the balls. A woman cuts her husband's pecker off and women are cheering."

"All this pecker talk has really gotten your engine going, hasn't it?" I prodded.

Donaldson continued as if I'd said nothing. "All the feminists and fags, I mean 'homosexual community,' say that if you show violence towards women or 'gays,' then you increase the chances of someone else doing the same, right? Well how come it's OK to kick and bash a man in the nuts but not a woman in

41

her groin or whatever? I mean what would happen if Arnold Schwarzenegger or Stallone kicked a woman in the groin in a movie? What would happen? You know what would happen," he stated. "There'd be a line of lesbian, femi-nazis from here to Mars and back. And all of them screaming, 'Ah, violence against women!' and 'Oh, you evil man!' Now why do you think that is?"

"I don't know," I said. "But I'm sure you're going to tell me."

"It's all a part of the continuing program of the 'Pussification of the American male.'"

I laughed. "The what?"

"'The Pussification of the American Male,'" he declared. "Think about it. Who are the vast majorities of those guys that get kicked in the nuts? Huh? Middle-class white, heterosexual guys between the ages of twenty-five and fifty. You see? That's the sex, color, age and orientation that have been blamed for everything from slavery to the greenhouse effect. And ever since the sixties and the Vietnam War and all that, there has been a steady and relentless attack against the middle-class white male by feminists and gays, lesbians and other men wannabes."

"You think this a bad case of 'penis envy?'" I quipped.

"No, no, no," Donaldson said as he changed lanes. "Well maybe, you never know. What I'm saying is that there has been a coordinated effort to demasculate - -"

"Emasculate," I corrected.

"Right. Emasculate." He turned the car left on Montgomery. The Transamerica Building loomed before us. "Different groups want to redefine the American male in such a way that he becomes weakened and the defining group becomes stronger. They keep telling us that a real man is a man in touch with his 'feminine side.' But at the same time, the feminists are working on strengthening themselves, y'see. We're supposed to be planting flowers and cooking in the kitchen and they're trying to take over. See, under this reasoning, a real man is a more effeminate man." He raised a finger for emphasis. "A real man is a fag."

"I plant flowers," I said. "And cook."

"Well," he said sheepishly. "You're the exception, babe. But you know what I'm saying."

"Keep an eye on your pecker?"

"You better believe it," Donaldson winked. "And what's all this talk about the 'homosexual community'? I mean, where are they from, *Fagonia?*"

"Well, there was an island called Lesbos."

We drove a few blocks past the Transamerica Building and made a left. We then made a right and entered a multi-level car park. Donaldson drove the car up three flights and onto the roof. There were very few cars about at this hour.

We exited. A long concourse stood between the upper parking deck and the revolving doors of the entrance. We made our way towards the large concrete and steel structure with massive rectangular, tinted windows that was Michael Astor's IV palace.

We entered the building. From the outside, it looked as if the building didn't have a light on. I was surprised to see that the entire interior was well lit. I also found a chill in the air and wondered if the building was purposely kept this cool. The lobby was about three stories tall. And, despite our attempts at stealth, the clicking of our heels on the highly polished black marble floors announced our presence. I detected the subtle scent of floor wax as we reached the front desk. A clean-cut young Asian man with a buzz-cut, wearing a white pressed shirt, black tie, slacks and jacket, stood smartly behind the desk. His clip-on nametag indicated his name: Mr. Kwan. "May I help you gentlemen?"

"Is Mr. Astor in?" Donaldson asked.

"Do you have an appointment?" Mr. Kwan asked without skipping a beat.

Donaldson showed his badge. "SFPD. We'd like to ask him a few questions." He said this in an even-toned, professional manner. All the joviality he had displayed in the car was gone.

If the young man was taken aback, he didn't show it. "Let me see," he said as he checked. "Yes, he is."

"Thank you." Donaldson started walking towards a row of elevators behind Mr. Kwan as if he had permission. I followed quietly. "What floor would that be?" Donaldson asked, looking back.

"Ah. Twenty-second, sir," Mr. Kwan replied.

"Thank you. Could you please call him and tell him that we're on our way up?" he said politely.

"I'll do that, sir."

We stepped into the elevator. I could see Kwan speaking into the phone. The silver reflective doors slid shut and we could see our reflections in the doors.

"That was pretty smooth," I said. "Most people would have asked to see him."

"That would've given him the option of saying no," Donaldson said. "The more choices you give people, the more likely they are to choose one you don't like. Your best bet is to pretend you're following a well-established procedure. That kid was young. He wasn't a lawyer. Why give him an option to delay us? Besides, like you said, if the person who buried that woman is still around, he's had almost half a century to prepare his alibi."

"I like the way you asked him to call ahead."

Donaldson smiled.

"As if he wasn't going to do exactly that."

We got off the elevator and walked toward two large frosted glass doors. The inscription read, "Astor Associates." There a man stood ready to greet us. He was about five-nine and in his late 70s, with steel-gray thinning hair. His eyes were blue and bright. I noticed that he wore a Brooks Brother's suit. The material was fine, light-gray wool and had an athletic cut in the "American style." The jacket had three buttons and a natural or soft shoulder. The lapel "rolled" onto the center button, which was fastened. The shirt was wrinkle-free, pale-gray with a low collar. The tie was solid-woven light-blue silk. The pants were devoid of pleats but had short cuffs that prevented them from resting on his Cordovan Perforated Cap-toe Balmoral shoes. I like fashion, too.

"Good evening, gentlemen," he said. "The police certainly work late hours."

"Tell me about it." Donaldson smiled. "Overworked and underpaid. Oh, by the way, I'm Inspector Donaldson. This is Connor," he said, omitting that I was not a cop. "Are you Mr. Astor?"

"Oh, no. I'm Mr. Clarke, one of his attorneys. Is this something I can help you with?"

"Well," Donaldson began, "it involves a murder and we'd just as soon speak to him directly."

Mr. Clarke raised an eyebrow and folded his arms across his chest. "Murder? Is Mr. Astor a suspect?"

"No, no, no," Donaldson said as if it were a silly question. "There was a body found in one of his former properties."

"Former properties?"

"And we'd just like to ask a few questions," he continued. "But if he doesn't want talk to us- - "

"Oh no, Inspector," Mr. Clarke said, raising a hand. "We're always willing to assist the authorities."

"We appreciate that."

"Gentlemen, if you'll follow me," Mr. Clarke said.

He led us through the frosted glass doors and then through a set of massive mahogany doors into a large, spacious office. Jasmine greeted us. The room had Romanesque qualities. Tall white columns stood proudly in the four-corners of the room, as if they were really needed. White marble, intricately carved, ran the length and breath of the chamber's walls. Opulent furniture, each piece of which looked as if it weighed a ton, was arranged about a glass and marble coffee table in a circular fashion. The floor, too, was marble, white. A large marble desk sat at the far end. The configuration reminded me of a Roman oval office, only bigger.

In the center of the room stood a dignified man. Tall, at nearly 6'3 and trim, Michael Astor was a poster-boy for senior virility. His hair was steely, neatly cut and full. He had a "California tan." His eyes were green and alert. He was clean-shaven. He wore a double-breasted navy silk suit with an Italian cut. The shoulder was high and padded in what is called the "wedge shoulder" in the US. The jacket, which clung tightly about his meager frame, was without flaps and sans vents in the back. A navy pocket-square folded in the "loose points" configuration could be seen in the left breast pocket. The pants pockets were set low in the waist and diagonally cut. The high-collar shirt, like the suit, was also silk, and a lighter shade of blue. The silk tie, the same shade of navy as the suit, was held in place with a solid gold tiepin. His shoes were black Gucci loafers.

I eyed this example of modern male vanity. He barely looked sixty-five, and my expert eye decided that he had had extensive plastic surgery.

"Good evening, gentlemen," he said in a smooth baritone voice. His white teeth beamed thanks to his tan. "I'm Michael Astor. Is there something I can help you with?"

"This is Inspector Donaldson, sir, from the San Francisco Police Department," Mr. Clarke said.

"Nice to meet you, Inspector. The PBA is one of my favorite groups to sponsor," he dropped, his smile constant.

"And this is...I didn't catch your name," Mr. Clarke said, looking at me.

"Dr. Connor." I said.

Mr. Clarke noted this.

I didn't like either man so far.

The three of us shook hands. Donaldson and myself both noticed the strength and confidence in Astor's grip.

"They're investigating a murder, sir. At one of your *former* properties," Mr. Clarke explained.

"Former? Hmm. I didn't hear about this on the news."

"It was early this morning," Donaldson pointed out.

Please sit down," Astor said and all did. "Can I get you anything gentlemen - tea or coffee?"

We politely declined, though I half-expected Flavius or Julius Caesar to bring us wines on a tray and vestal virgins to feed us all grapes.

Donaldson began, "I won't waste any of your time, sir. You owned an apartment building on Sproule Street in Nob Hill back in the early fifties, didn't you, sir?"

"Yes, I did," he replied without hesitation. "Nob Gardens was one of three that my father left me when he passed on. What's this about a murder?"

Donaldson said, "Of course. A body was found in the wall of a basement apartment closet by some renovators."

"So you're talking about a murder that occurred some forty-something years ago?" a voice said from behind.

I turned to see a man, a big man, detach himself from a shadow at the far end of the room. He was young, perhaps as young as thirty. He was six-three if he was an inch and his broad-shouldered, two-hundred and twenty-pound frame was squeezed neatly into a black suit, also an American cut, with a cashmere mock-turtleneck shirt. This bulky frame was sculpted from power-lifting. His demeanor being one of blank seriousness, he seemed to look through people. I sensed an aura of contained violence and tried to imagine what it would be like to fight such a man. It wasn't a pleasant image. He was sharp, I decided: sharp and dangerous.

"Gentlemen, this is Mr. Carver, my other attorney," Michael Astor announced.

I watched him as he crossed the room, his heels failing to make a sound on the marble floor. He took a position near Mr. Astor like a Doberman. I was impressed with Mr. Carver's stealth. I also couldn't help but notice his expressionless eyes. He appeared to me as if something were missing, or lacking.

"Where were we? Oh yes, the body in one of my old buildings; that's terrible," said Astor. "But I sold that business about - " he inhaled through his teeth. " – some forty years ago."

Donaldson nodded. "Yes sir. Our preliminary investigation indicates that the woman's body was there since the early fifties. That would have been the time you owned it."

Mr. Astor nodded. "That's correct. I was given that building in 1948. A woman, you say. That's disgraceful."

"You could have called before you came in, Inspector." Mr. Clarke injected.

Donaldson shrugged harmlessly. "Well, we were in the area and I thought we'd just take a chance. I didn't want to go by your home. I figured that if you weren't in, I'd call up in the morning."

"No problem at all, sergeant." Michael Astor said. "What can I tell you about the building?"

"Did you have any trouble during that time? Any difficulties with tenants?"

"Can't say that I did. Then again, you see, I didn't have much to do with the day-to-day running of the building. I owned it but I can tell you that if there was any trouble requiring legal action, I would have been informed by one of my attorneys."

"Do you recall anything unusual, sir?" Donaldson asked respectively.

"From the 1950s?"

"Well, early fifties," Donaldson corrected.

Michael Astor IV thought a moment. "That narrows it down a bit. No," he said simply and closed his eyes momentarily.

I noticed that his eyelids weren't tan and thought it made him look sillier.

"It was a quiet building," Michael Astor continued. "I can't recall anything out of the ordinary."

"No lawsuits?"

"No," Mr. Clarke said.

"No," Michael Astor concurred, though when he said it, there was no edge to his voice.

"Any incidents of violence?"

He thought a moment. "No."

"Anybody ever disappear?" I injected.

"Absolutely not," Mr. Clarke said, his ire raised. "Do you know who the woman was?"

"No," I replied.

"No identification of any kind?" Mr. Carver asked.

"I'm afraid not," I admitted.

"The fifties," Astor began. "Not quite the idealistic time people tend to remember it as. Of course, there were no neighborhood-watch programs back then. I've been funding several for a number of years now," he injected.

"Fair enough," Donaldson said neutrally. "Would you be able to furnish us with rent records for apartment 44?"

"We should have those all on file somewhere, Mr. Clarke," Michael Astor said.

"Yes, sir. However, our files are quite extensive. If you could narrow the time-frame, Inspector, we should have no problem in getting them for you."

Donaldson nodded. "Fair enough. I'll get back to you on that."

"I'm curious," Mr. Carver began. The legal wheels of his mind could almost be heard turning. "How did you determine that this woman was in the building since the early fifties?"

Sharp, I confirmed. "I was able to base that on the style of her clothes?"

"I don't follow."

"They were new at the time of her death. The style was in vogue around the early fifties. We'll know more, though, when we do the autopsy and find out exactly when the clothes were manufactured."

"It never occurred to you that the woman could have been there from a later time and was wearing out-dated clothing?" Mr. Carver pushed.

I was impressed at the way these two worked. Mr. Clarke the senior hatchet man, asked specifics, while Mr. Carver probed for faults in our evidence. I tried to imagine what the two would be like in a courtroom and my mind was immediately filled with the image of two wrestlers, tag-teaming against a common foe. It was even less pleasant than the one of fighting Carver one-on-one. "Like I said, the autopsy will tell us more."

"But you can't say for sure how long the body has been there," Mr. Clarke picked up as if they were already in court or a steel cage.

"True."

"Easy, Tom," Astor said with a hand raised. His Tourneau watch caught the room's light nicely. "These men are just doing their job. Any records that you should require, you shall have, gentlemen."

"Absolutely," Mr. Clarke concurred.

"Certainly," Mr. Carver agreed without seeming to mean it.

"I must say that I'm worried about the negative publicity this could raise," Michael Astor began. "I do a lot of charity work for the city, and the smut-mongers would have a field day with something like this. I'm not worried, of course, for myself. It's just that the people who donate money to causes do so because they have empathy with the cause. And if my name were to be mentioned in connection with a murder in a building I haven't owned in decades..."

"Yes, sir. I understand," Donaldson soothed. "That's one of the reasons we decided to approach you the way we did. Truth is that if I cleared it with my Captain, he'd call the mayor and God only knows how many other people. That would only increase the chances of it making its way to the press."

"That's very considerate of you, Inspector," Astor said.

"I'm curious," I began. "If the building was running well when you owned it, why did you sell it?"

"There were rumors about the zoning laws changing and I decided that I didn't want to get stuck with a lemon after all the profit it had showed."

"Ah." I didn't like Michael Astor IV very much and suspected that most of the rumors about his duplicity were true. Now that I had time to study him up close, I came to the conclusion that there was something very fake about him. It took me a moment to realize that he was wearing a very expensive toupee. I wondered whether Astor's desk was really marble or plastic laminate.

I glanced about the room, noting the large bookshelf full of classics and wondered if they were real or fake as well. And if they were real, had Mr. Astor read any of them? I wanted to get up and open one and see if it was real, but didn't want to push my luck.

"Dr. Connor, are you with the ME's office?" Mr. Clarke asked.

"No. I teach over at the university," I answered.

"What then is your interest in this case?" Mr. Carver searched.

"The city has hired Dr. Connor as a consultant," Donaldson defended.

Mr. Clarke continued as if on the trail of something improper he could use later. "Why isn't the ME's office handling this directly?"

"They're a man short right now. Dr. Connor is qualified," Donaldson said, before adding, "The mayor has already signed off on this."

"Ah, the mayor," Mr. Clarke said. "Then I'm sure everything will be fine."

Mr. Carver nodded, satisfied.

They had something.

Astor straightened. "I have heard of you, Dr. Connor. Didn't you testify some years ago in the Gleason murder?"

I felt conspicuous. "Yes, sir, I did."

"Excellent work. I saw *that* on television and must say that you handled yourself well."

"Thank you."

The Gleason case was almost eleven years earlier. I had still been working for the city. A very wealthy, connected and very married old man, Alex Gleason, had died in bed after what appeared to be a particularly aggressive evening of sex with a woman half his age. Gleason, who had a bad heart to begin with and was, supposed to avoid exertion, died, supposedly of heart failure. Given the nature of his demise and his connections, efforts were made to hush-up the more embarrassing aspects of the case and simply close it. Even his wife wanted to wrap it up quickly. I, however, in my thorough manner, checked the liver and found Tubarine, a neuromuscular blocking agent. A good thing I checked too, as Tubarine remains in the liver only a short time after death. Gleason's mistress subsequently admitted that he told her he had changed his will and left her a sizable portion of his estate, so she gave him the Tubarine. Shortly after his death, she learned that he had lied. She went to jail, broke.

"Are you working this case from the University's facilities?" Astor asked.

"As a matter of fact, I am." I knew where this was going.

Astor smiled. "What a coincidence. I donated the grant that built the facility."

I smiled back. "Really? I had no idea."

"Well, anything else your investigation can tell us about the woman?" Mr. Clarke asked.

"She was about 5'7 and weighed around one hundred and twenty pounds," I said without missing a beat. "We figure she was in her mid-twenties and had jet black hair, parted in the middle with large brown eyes and full lips." I described her, speaking to everyone. All the while, though, my gaze never left Astor, who listened politely, his face flaccid and his eyes squinting in concentration as if building up her image in his mind. I thought I noticed a flicker of something in the cool green eyes for a moment but it was gone. "She was shot once in the left eye with a low caliber weapon. Probably a .22"

"My, that is sad," Astor, said, turning away. "Is that all?"

"Oh, I almost forgot. I have a photo here," I said, digging into my folder dramatically. I let that hang in the air, while I continued to shuffle about for something I knew was on top. Finally, I removed one. Mr. Carver and Clarke's hands both shot out to intercept the document. Clarke was a bit faster.

You're quick.

"I'd like to see that," Mr. Clarke said.

"Oh, it's all right, Robert," Astor said, taking the photo.

I handed it to Astor who took it and held it up. Mr. Carver leaned in over his boss's shoulder to have a look. Astor's green eyes flickered again and faded somewhat.

"Mr. Astor. Mr. Astor?" I asked.

"Hmmm, yes?" he said as if lost or groggy.

"Do you recognize her, sir?" I asked, knowing well that I was pushing my luck. I could feel Carver's stare on me.

There was a slight pause before he answered. "No," he said finally and handed the photo back toward me, but I failed to take it.

"You're sure? You hardly looked at it."

"Are you questioning my client's word, Doctor?" Mr. Clarke asked.

"Not at all," I said innocently.

"He just said he didn't know, Doctor." Mr. Carver's ire rose again before noting in protest, "This isn't a real photograph. It's a computer-generated image of some kind."

Very good. I accepted the photo, noting the slight tremmor in Astor's previous steely hands. "Well, it's not a real photo, you're right. It was generated by - - "

"If it's not a real photo, how can you expect my client to make a positive identification?" Mr. Clarke asked, interrupting.

I began, "Well, you see- - "

"Mr. Astor," Donaldson interrupted, "we appreciate the time you've been able to spare."

Astor held his hands out obligingly. The energy between Mr. Clarke and myself seemed to dissipate. "Not a problem, Inspector."

"And on a personal note, my wife loves that bash you throw every year in the park," Donaldson added.

At the sound of one of his charities, Michael Astor IV perked up. "Oh. Is she with a group?"

"She does a bit of volunteer work in the hospital. Nothing major."

"Nonsense. Time is precious and volunteered time, no mater how little, is precious and appreciated. As we get older," he began, "we come to realize how valuable a commodity time really is. Gentlemen, can you imagine how much this nation could accomplish if everyone donated an hour a week to some cause?" He shook his head with wonder. "Why, we could move mountains."

"True," I agreed. "But the environmentalists would raise hell!"

Astor laughed, his mood buoyant again. "They would indeed! I must say," he continued, "that I don't envy your task, gentlemen. How do you plan to find out this woman's identity?"

Donaldson cut in, "Connor here is going to have fliers printed to pass out around the city. He'll be on some television program as well. One of those unsolved murder shows where the audience can call in. We're also launching a web page on the Internet."

"The Internet?" Astor said with some surprise. "That should be quite helpful."

"I think it will be," I said.

"He's very photogenic," Donaldson added jokingly.

"Indeed he is, Inspector. Dr. Connor," Astor paused a moment. "I'll be watching you - on television, that is."

I nodded but said nothing. *And I'll be watching you, you motherfuckers.*

Michael Astor IV, with Mr. Clarke and Mr. Carver on either side protectively, walked us to the elevator where I made it a point to turn back and shake hands with each man. The gesture was met with various degrees of firmness and, interpretation.

"Inspector, if either one of you should have any questions, please feel free to stop by and ask anything, anytime," Michael Astor said.

Mr. Clarke stepped forward and offered each of us a business card.

Donaldson said, "I appreciate that, sir. I'll be in contact with Mr. Clarke about the records when I have more information."

"We look forward to assisting you, Inspector." Mr. Clarke said.

The elevator arrived and the doors opened. Donaldson entered first.

The elevator doors shut. We both exhaled as though we had been holding our breath for a long time.

"What do you think?" I asked.

"We're going to hear about this?"

"About what? We were on the right side of everything."

"Legally, yes," Donaldson agreed. "But egotistically?"

"I know," I said. "Did you notice he took every chance to mention the projects he has donated to?"

"I was more worried about the name the lawyer, Clarke, dropped."

I thought for a moment. "Which one was that?"

"The Mayor."

I considered this. "Well, there's no easy way to ask somebody these things."

"I know," Donaldson admitted. "I liked the way you showed the photo."

"Just trying to provoke a reaction."

"I didn't see too much."

"You didn't shake hands with him at the elevator."

"Ahhh," Donaldson said, realizing. "You're getting crafty. What were they like?"

"Sweaty."

"I know you're still kind of new to all this, but you know it doesn't prove anything."

"True," I lamented. "But it's a start."

I returned to my office later that evening and picked out the computer-generated image I felt would be the most effective. These were to be copied and would be distributed all about the city. I saw the story mentioned on the 10 o'clock news when I got home. The web page was developed and set up, as was a hotline. After the story was aired, there was a heavy and steady flow of calls and hits on the web-site, respectively. Donaldson and his men would have plenty of leads to follow.

9

SFCU: 11:09 AM

The autopsy didn't happen the following day, but two days later when Dr. Geist was able to attend. Though his buoyant temperament hadn't changed, I was shocked at his appearance. Always a tall man and heavy, Dr. Geist had ballooned to what I figured must have been nearly three hundred pounds. He walked with a cane and carried a briefcase in the other hand. I figured it must be the heart medication.

In all, I assembled a fairly impressive group. Dr.'s Maher, Trundy and Liu attended, as did two grad-students of Forensic science. One was Katherine Wilson; the other was Roger Stevenson. They answered "Absolutely" and "For the love of Buddha, of course," when asked to assist. It took me a moment to remember that Roger Stevenson never used Christian curses. That isn't to say he didn't curse; au contraire, he just never used curses that had anything to do with Christianity. As Stevenson had pointed out to me about a year earlier, most curses were directed at Christian deities'. It wasn't something I had ever considered. Stevenson didn't think this was right and so he came up with a variety of expressions guaranteed to offend every other religious school of thought except Christianity. His obscenities, as such, were the cause of many a raised eyebrow, a few explanations and more than a few arguments.

Stevenson and Wilson were in their second year of graduate school and were chosen by me, not only due to their good standing as students, but also because I felt that they would be able to keep their mouths shut about anything they might see or learn. It hadn't been difficult to enlist their help. After word had circulated throughout the student body, and the story aired on the local news, they put two and two together. Everybody wanted to help me solve the mystery. Donaldson also attended the proceedings.

I wanted nobody else to attend as I didn't know what we might find and didn't want anything to leak out. But the dean of Forensics overruled me. Given the nature of the find, those who weren't invited wanted to attend. The autopsy was held in room #4, which was used for teaching purposes. I had reserved the room once I had confirmation as to when the team would be available. I also cancelled my Friday classes.

Autopsy room #4 had a Gallery, in which people could sit and view the procedure below. The Gallery, which would be full, had video monitors hooked up. All in all, it promised to be quite a show. Although I didn't like the spectacle aspect of it, I understood it. I also took solace in the certainty that my people would do the tests and that they wouldn't talk to the press. There would be little that anybody in the Gallery could glean from merely viewing the autopsy.

Likewise, my desire to do a limited autopsy was overruled, this by Dr. Geist, as he not only wanted to obtain tissue samples from all the major organs, but wanted to have a look around inside.

The day's proceedings would, at my insistence on security, occur in three stages. The first would be the taking of photographs, X-rays and CAT scans. These would occur in private, before the autopsy and away from prying eyes. The second stage would be the autopsy itself, before the audience. The third stage would be the testing of the tissue samples obtained at the autopsy. Like the first stage, these too would be performed in private and at a later date with the doctors or staff, whatever the case might be, reporting directly to me. Each person would be responsible for his/her samples and would be instructed not to discuss their findings. I wanted to make sure that none of the findings would be leaked to the press. In the event that they were, I wanted to have somebody to blame. After everything was finished, there would be a debriefing in which we would discuss what we had learned.

With the team assembled, I laid out the plan of action. All in agreement, we donned our scrubs, booties, rubber gloves and goggles that were the standard gear in such procedures and entered the autopsy room. Roger Stevenson and I brought the body out of its berth, a freezer that kept it at a constant 21' Fahrenheit. This we set onto the autopsy table. We started by taking photos of the body; Katherine Wilson performed this task. Next came the X-rays. This was done at the direction of Dr. Trundy and took the better part of an hour as she wanted be thorough. Full-body and close-up X-rays were obtained of the entire body, with particular care paid to the head. Dr. Maher took the lead when it came time to take dental X-rays, with Dr. Trundy assisting him. Next came the CAT scans. Dr. Trundy again operated the GE machine, while Roger Stevenson and I loaded the body onto the tray.

When this was completed, the team assembled in a meeting room, where we awaited the development of the X-rays and the CAT scans. Once ready, Dr. Trundy laid out the results on a light board for all to see. She moved from one X-ray to another, making comments and pointing out what she saw as the others nodded their heads; Donaldson took notes. Being friendly with Dr. Trundy for several years, but never having made a move on her, as she had been married, I couldn't help but notice how good she was looking as of late. Divorced now for two years, the forty-something year old scientist was looking finer and firmer than she had in years. In her boredom at the museum, she must have found some time to get in a bit of exercise.

"Skull vault is intact," she said, tracing a finger across an X-ray. "Except for the area of the occipital region, which is the entrance point of the bullet." She moved to another X-ray, one that showed the bullet a bit clearer. "Bullet is still present and looks intact. No fractures or fissures about the occipital region. The bullet went right in through the eye," she stated. She looked at another. "Her left ulna had been broken," she said pointing. "Just below the elbow, here."

Donaldson took a note and asked, "Was it broken at the time of death?"

"No. See the callus here?" She pointed to a white spot on the X-ray. "When a bone breaks, a callus forms and can be seen in an X-ray within two weeks. The callus is actually new bone. This bone had been broken and repaired long before she died."

Next, she viewed the CAT scans; hundreds of cross-sectional X-ray images that were spaced at millimeter wide intervals. "I'd put her age at between twenty-five and thirty," Dr. Trundy said, pointing to a CAT scan.

"Sutures closed but still visible," Geist said, as he peered over her shoulder.

"Right," she agreed. "See?"

Dr. Trundy didn't have to explain her findings, as all present, except for Donaldson, knew what she meant. At birth, a child's skull is not one solid seamless bone but is, instead, a composite of bones that distend as the child grows. The plates come together by adulthood. In this case, the sutures of the skull's plates were closed but visible, indicative of a person between the ages of twenty-five and thirty.

Dr. Maureen Trundy continued: "Heart, lungs – kidneys, and everything else have shrunk to almost nothing; severe desiccation. Brain is intact, but about the size of an orange." She looked about, moving from image to image and then stopped. "Well, well," she said and smiled. "What have we here?"

Dr. Geist stepped forward uneasily, leaned on his cane and drew a deep breath. "Hmmm," he said simply.

"You see it?" Dr. Trundy asked.

"Oh, yes!" he nodded. His jowls shook.

"What?" I asked, speaking for the rest.

Dr. Maureen Trundy turned to the group and said, "This woman was pregnant."

"Oh my," said Dr. Maher.

"Interesting," added Dr. Liu.

"Shit!" Donaldson said and scribbled the detail into his frayed notebook. "Talk about motive."

"Allah-be darned," said Stevenson.

I explained Stevenson's situation and was met with several raised eyebrows.

Next, Dr. Lucien Maher took a look at the X-rays of the teeth and made some comments, none of which were as dramatic as Dr. Trundy's find. "All secondary teeth are present," he noted. "Except for the wisdom teeth. Nothing mysterious there. No current cavities present," he concluded, although, he pointed out, there had been "extensive work;" i.e., caps, bridges and fillings, done on her.

I warned all not to speak of anything they'd seen. The team then filed back into the autopsy room. The audience was allowed into the Gallery, the cameras positioned over and about the body and switched on, as were the monitors in the Gallery and the tape recorder.

Dr. Geist set his briefcase on a counter and stood at one side of the table. His girth was such that the others had to bunch up around the other side of the body and at the foot of the table. I stood at the head. Dr. Geist positioned the microphone a foot or so in front of himself. He set his cane aside and leaned against the table for support. The first thing he did was announce the body as being female. A seemingly unnecessary thing to do given that the naked mummy was quite clearly female, despite its shrunken state. Nevertheless, procedure was procedure and the body was announced to be a female. Next he weighed the body. "Twenty-seven pounds," he noted and then added, "The Iceman they found in the Tyrolean Alps was thirty-three."

"How's the book coming?" I asked.

"Pretty good," Geist said, and then looked up over his spectacles. "I must thank you again, Dr. Connor, for inviting me to attend. I was thinking that this would make an interesting chapter in my book, once you clear it." He paused a moment and then said, "From Iceman to the Closet Lady. How's that title grab you?"

"It's an attention getter," I admitted.

There were a few polite laughs from the gallery.

Geist performed an external examination of the body. In a normal autopsy this is done to determine if there are any bruises or punctures that could have been part of the cause of death. In this case, with the skin blackened and wrinkled, he concentrated on finding any additional bullet holes. There weren't any. Dr. Geist did, however, find several fibers in the mummy's hair. "Looks like carpet fibers," he noted as he passed them to me. I placed them in a small plastic bag and glanced over at Donaldson as if to say, you were right; she was wrapped in a carpet.

Geist took scrapings from her well-preserved and perfectly manicured nails. Stevenson put these in tiny jars and labeled each one. Strands of hair from both the head and pubic region were taken and set aside in bags.

Next came the finger printing. Fingerprints are the ridges, loops and whorls that are used to identify someone. These are formed from the dermis; that is, the underlying skin as opposed to the epidermis or top skin.

Dr. Geist looked at the fingers through a powerful magnifying glass that he had brought with him. "Epidermis has separated from the dermis on two fingers of the left hand and has lifted completely on the other three," he said, looking closely, using the table for support as he leaned in. "And separated on all of the right." He stood up and drew a breath. "Epidermis has severely deteriorated. None of the papillary ridge systems of either hand remain intact."

This was less of a problem than it might have seemed to the untutored as the lack of epidermis didn't mean that fingerprints could not be obtained; it is from the dermis, the underlying skin, that the fingerprints are formed. And it is from the dermis that prints can be developed, despite the condition or presence of the epidermis.

To do this, a mold would have to be cast about the fingers. Dr. Geist, had set molds years before when he worked on some finds in Egypt. He performed this task with me supporting him. First, he and I carefully removed the damaged separated epidermis from each finger. Next a mold of Polysulphide-rubber was cast for each finger and thumb. Dr. Geist then applied several coats of acrylic paint to the mold while I sped the drying process with a hand-held electric hair dryer. The molds were then set aside. It was hoped that from these molds a few good prints could be developed and run in an effort to discover the woman's identity.

Dr. Lucian Maher took a look at the teeth, and confirmed what he had noted earlier in the X-rays: that all teeth except for wisdom teeth were present and that she had had alot of dental work. He further noted that the gums had shrunk and confirmed the age as being under thirty. The wear-and-tear of her teeth was consistent with Dr. Trundy's estimate of the age of the deceased.

With the external exam completed and recorded, it was time to begin the internal examination. In a standard autopsy, a "Y" incision would be made starting at each side of the chest; the two lines would then meet and run down to the pubic area. This "Y" would then be peeled back on both sides and the internal organs inspected, weighed and sampled so that various tests could be performed.

In this case, the "Y" incision would not be performed, and the internal organs would not be inspected nor weighed as they had been severely desiccated and wouldn't yield anything substantial. Instead, Dr. Geist performed an Endoscopic examination and took samples of the organs. The Endoscope is a thin, tubular device that allows doctors to view the inside of a body without making large incisions to do so. It is inserted into the body via a burr hole of approximately 1cm diameter. This burr hole is made with a brace and bit. The Endoscope can be inserted into the body and through the use of lenses, mirrors and its own light source, allows the doctor to see about inside the corpse. Advancement on this device was the Fiberscope. The Fiberscope is constructed of flexible fibers as opposed to a rigid tube. It can be bent once inserted into the body and be inserted up to a depth of 2.5 meters with a diameter as small as 2.4 mm. The operator has controls that allow him or her to manipulate the Fiberscope, allowing the end to be pointed in the direction of choice. Additional devices allow the operator to suck away blood that blocked his view and even allowed him to take tissue samples for biopsy through the use of forceps built into the device.

Dr. Geist walked, with the aid of his cane, to the counter where his briefcase sat. There he took out an Endoscope and Fiberscope made of titanium. He had them constructed years earlier when he was doing his research on the Iceman, as he was afraid that stainless steel equipment might leave trace elements that could jeopardize the integrity of various tests. He also removed a brace and bit constructed of the same material.

I took the brace and bit and the Fiberscope, and set it on a tray while Dr. Geist carried the Endoscope. I used the brace and bit and drilled four 1cm-burr holes at different points in the chest. These would allow Dr. Geist various entrance points from which to view and biopsy the different organs.

Dr. Geist set down the Endoscope and picked up the Fiberscope. This he inserted into the body and then ran a cable from the monitor controls to the Fiberscope. An image from inside the mummy was visible on the monitors.

I noted that there were a few "Hmmm's" from the Gallery but no "Ohhs," or "Ahs," and for that, I was thankful. The view inside the body was more complementary than anything else; a gesture to give everyone present something to talk about, as Geist merely wanted to collect tissue samples and didn't need to broadcast the procedure. Tissue samples of all the organs were collected in this manner, with Dr. Geist having merely to remove the Fiberscope and reinsert it into another burr hole if he were unable to maneuver it to the desired organ. I wasn't worried about anyone discovering the fetus as it was too desiccated to be recognizable up close.

Roger Stevenson and I set aside each sample Geist collected in "save jars," which were labeled according to the organ. The tissues would be cut further. Some of the tissues would be re-hydrated with a solution of alcohol, sodium carbonate and formaldehyde. This would be done so that they could be cut into slices thin enough for microscopic examination. Some would be re-hydrated in a solution of water and glycerin, with alcohol added for re-colorization so that their structures would be better visible under a microscope. These would be sent to histology, where Dr. Liu would study them, performing various tests for the presence of drugs, toxins or disease. Dr. Geist also took skin samples. In addition, several samples of the fetus were taken, though Dr. Geist, ever the professional and aware of the audience above, didn't say anything about fetal tissue. Instead, he merely referred to it as the "additional samples." Neither Donaldson nor I said anything by way of warning to the others as they had already given their word not to discuss any aspect of the procedure. Both of us, however, noted the importance of this finding, as it was a possible motive for the dead woman's murder, and reasoned that the others did, too. Roger Stevenson labeled these with a nod from me.

When this stage of the autopsy was complete, we turned our attention towards the head. Dr. Geist inserted an Endoscope into the head via a burr hole through one of the parietal bones. Roger Stevenson made this one, as I wanted to give him some "drill time." I noted that Dr. Trundy was correct in her assessment of the brain being the size of an orange. The organ could be clearly seen, still attached to a bundle of nerves that ran into the neck. I had even remarked, when transporting the body in the other day that the rattling sound that could be heard coming from the body was, in fact, the brain. Dr. Geist moved the Endoscope about to get a view of the bullet but couldn't. It was no matter, as he'd be removing the brain soon enough.

Dr. Geist also passed the Endoscope in through the eye socket, as he wanted to get a better view of the path the bullet took. This was easily done as the eyes had long since emptied. He turned the Endoscope about, giving all a view of the inside of the skull.

Next came the removal of the brain. In a standard autopsy, an incision is made, ear-to-ear, over the scalp. The front of the face is then pulled down like a mask, exposing the skull, which is then cut via an electric saw and the brain removed. In this case, since the tissues had been desiccated, there was no need to reflect the scalp. Instead, Dr. Geist simply cut the head and removed the skullcap, with the skin still attached. The brain was cut free of its nerves and removed, then set in a dish of alcohol, sodium carbonate and formaldehyde. This was done to soften the tissue, as we wanted to retrieve the bullet, instead of digging through the hardened organ and destroying the tissue unnecessarily, possibly scratching the bullet and ruining ballistic tests. Just to be on the safe side, I took a peek inside the skull cavity to make sure the bullet wasn't rolling around. It wasn't.

With that, the show was over. Dr. Geist thanked everyone for attending and was given a standing ovation for his efforts.

Donaldson exhaled with a roll of his eyes. I read this as, *Scientists.*

The body was put on a cadaver lift and moved back into the refrigerator. The team retired to the conference room to discuss our findings and our next steps.

12:30 PM

It was a given that the Histology lab would, at Dr. Liu's discretion, run tests on all the tissue samples. She was interested in discovering whether the deceased had suffered from any diseases or been taking any drugs. For drugs, the tissues would be analyzed via Chromatography after being soaked in a "tenderizer" enzyme like Papain or Subtilisin and extracted by organic solvents. It was doubtful that these tests would yield anything, as it would be difficult to interpret the concentrations of any drugs found in mummified tissue. Poisons, such as heavy metals, Dr. Liu pointed out, would be easier as they would be examined by atomic absorption spectrometry, a process with which mummification does not interfere. She would also attempt to determine blood-type, no easy task, as there was no blood to test. Instead, she would examine samples of bone and muscle. These tissues would, of course, first have to be pulverized in order to produce cell-free material.

"Of course," Donaldson agreed with a smile.

Dr. Liu was most hopeful about the sample taken from the colon: a sample that weighed about twenty-seven milligrams. In an effort to minimize its destruction through chemical alteration, she planned to section it into four pieces. Saline would be added to one sample to bloat it. This piece would be reserved for the electron microscope and its 5000 fold powers of magnification. If lucky, she might be able to determine what the woman had last eaten.

Dr. Geist, who did studies and was known as an expert in molecular archeology, the study of mummy DNA, would try to type and get a DNA pattern from the deceased as well as her unborn child. A task that Dr. Geist admitted would be difficult, as the DNA would probably have broken down. The chains would most likely have begun to decay by this point, thanks to chemical changes and time, he explained. Expert that he was, if DNA could be retrieved, I knew, he'd find it.

The nails would be checked to see if the deceased had managed to get a piece of her murderer underneath them. If so, these samples too would be tested. The hair would be tested as well for whatever traces of drugs they might contain. The Polysulphide rubber mold would be used to make prints, which would be run through a computer to see if she had ever been arrested for a violent crime.

Not all of the tests would be ready at the same time. The tissue samples, blood, nails and hair would take a week or even more to be completed. Each doctor had agreed previously to perform all tests on University grounds and to submit all results to me upon their completion. The brain, once softened, easily gave up the bullet, before being placed in a save jar. The bullet was a .22. Donaldson had determined this, due to the near perfect nature of the "slug" as he called it, before taking possession of it. He would run this through ballistics personally and see if they had any weapons on file that it would match. A monstrous task considering how much time had passed, but one he would farm-out to his underlings to "Give them something to do." The real benefit would be that he had a piece of solid evidence that could be matched to the murder weapon, in the unlikely event that it should turn up.

Katherine Wilson, who'd spent hours contacting manufactures, was able to find out when the clothes of the deceased were made; but she was unable to identify the nylons. Since it was a fact that nylons weren't manufactured during World War Two, as nylon was needed for parachutes, it was a fair guess that they were made sometime after the war. A French company, "La Fleur," had made the skirt, blouse and coat. Ms. Wilson was also able to learn that these garments had come onto the American market in March of 1952 and were available until December, '54, though they had been available in France since 1950. The shoes were an American make, manufactured in 1951. The bra and panties, also French, were in the French and American stores in 1949. They were on the market until mid-1955. So, it was reasoned, she died no sooner than 1951 and no later than mid-1955. A time-frame which put the building "Nob Gardens" firmly in the possession of Michael Astor IV; a fact that pleased me more than I cared to admit as it still left him as a good suspect. Ms. Wilson also pointed out that she had picked up dozens of fibers, probably carpet fibers, from the clothing. I reasoned that these would more than likely match those found in the mummy's hair. It was, to me, a further vindication of Donaldson's theory. Either way, a microscopic examination would determine whether or not they were.

I thanked everyone for their assistance and reminded them that all information garnered was secret and if leaked could hurt their standing in the scientific community or GPA, whatever the case might be.

10

The TV segment was filmed in the morgue the following Monday. I didn't wear the trench coat or arch my eyebrow, though Donaldson, whose appearance I convinced the producers I needed, did. Wear the trench coat, that is. He was interviewed as the investigating officer.

By all accounts, I had come off well. Donaldson said to look out because I was about to get my fifteen minutes of fame, and that I should not to pass up any sexual encounters it might generate as it was only a temporary thing and would soon pass. When asked how the hell he would know, Donaldson was at a loss for words.

The segment was aired nationally. A few minutes later, the web page crashed. The police station was hit with a deluge of calls, all of which appeared to be cranks. The hotline had to take in additional volunteers to handle the volume. People called in from all over the country claiming to know who the "closet lady" was as she now known. Most claimed that she was a lost relative of theirs. Others said that she had been abducted or was a missing hitchhiker. One insisted that she was a victim of the Manson family, while another said she was Princess Anastasia. All in all, the whole thing was a sad affair with some comedic touches. A certain New York late-night talk-show host joked that this was probably the first time that a woman had ever been "brought out of a closet" in San Francisco. Donaldson, who was supposed to coordinate the cataloguing of leads, complained that he was ending up being in charge of sifting through the wackos.

I, for my part, returned to my daily job of college professor. I couldn't help but notice that what Donaldson had said about fame was true. People I didn't know waved to me. Students gave me a nod of approval as if I needed it; so did colleagues, as if I wanted it. A few of both wrote proposals on how I should pursue my case and dropped them off at my office. These I put to good use as kindling in my home fireplace. Colleagues also dropped by my office to see how the "big case" was going. Being a man who likes my privacy, I found the whole thing a bit strange - and uncomfortable.

I also couldn't help but notice the attention I was getting from the female faculty and students. There was one student in particular, Rebecca Wood, twenty-one, and a full-bodied blonde, whose clinging clothes left no doubt in the minds of the male students that everything was real. She was in my ethics class, of all things. I had noticed her as it was a small class, but I particularly noticed her paying an unusual amount of time eyeing me. I hoped that the "fifteen minutes of fame" theory would last only fifteen minutes. Time would tell.

After that, the investigation hit a lull. It was expected. We'd hoped that the show would cause a witness to the murder to appear or that an acquaintance of the victim would come forward. So far, none did. Until someone did or a lead from the hotline panned out or one of the tests yielded something, we agreed that there was no need to meet, as we had nothing to discuss. I didn't bother to check up on the others, as they were professionals. It was a respect that I even extended to my dieners as they carried out their relatively simple tasks of microscopic inspection to confirm what the others had already discovered. Several tests, performed by Dr. Liu, were completed with limited success. Due to the interference of putrefaction products, she was unable to determine whether the deceased had taken any drugs or medication but was able to report that the deceased had ingested no poisons, at least of the heavy metal variety. Also, the deceased had suffered from no diseases, she told me. Dr. Liu was further able to point out that the deceased had eaten peas. This had been deduced from the colon sample. In addition, she was also able to ascertain that the woman in question had blood-type O negative.

Katherine Wilson dropped by one afternoon to announce that the fibers in the mummy's hair and clothes were carpet fibers, from the same source, and that they were of a carpet typically found in homes. Other than that, there was nothing unique to report.

These facts, I discussed, not with Dr. Liu, as she was married and, therefore, not my type (she, I simply thanked), but with Dr. Trundy who was currently single, had been working out and now was my type. We discussed these facts one evening over dinner in a comfortable Italian restaurant that I had frequented for years and over breakfast the following morning in her more comfortable bed. A place that I had never frequented before, but made a mental point to visit again as soon as possible.

The body remained in the morgue. Slowly, other test results filtered in. The fingernail scrapings came back with no results. Donaldson rang me briefly to let me know that whoever she was, she had never been arrested as the fingerprints drawn from the molds had come up clean. On the positive side, the bullet was in perfect condition and the police would have no trouble matching it. I still had to wait for the DNA and hair tests to come back.

SFCU: 2:15 P.M.

I was sitting in my office, behind a large desk that was visibly free of the clutter that many other professors often had. I didn't feel the need to appear overworked or busy as I was pensioned by the city, and despite the fact that I wasn't tenured, didn't fear losing my job. A laptop sat on my desk and was running, though I wasn't using it. On the wall behind me were my various diplomas, degrees and awards. A small bowl of potpourri ensured that the room maintained its' French vanilla aroma.

I shifted my weight in my blue global-deluxe steno chair and it moved slightly and silently on its casters. I had finished teaching two classes that morning on autopsy procedure and was taking a break. My next and final class wasn't for nearly an hour. I was thinking about nothing in particular when there was a knock on my door.

I swiveled to see a woman standing before me. She appeared to be in her mid-sixties, with graying hair. She was a full and exotic woman with meditareaneen features, and she was dressed in a pantssuit that whispered dignity and style. Her large brown eyes held a cool sensuality that had a familiarity to them. In her arms was a box.

"Dr. Connor?" She asked.

"Yes?"

"You're the man who was on television. You're the one investigating the woman who was found in the closet," she stated, rather than asking.

"Yes, I am. Not to be dismissive," I said, "but the television show said all information should be brought to the police - "

"I know. They also said that you work at the University."

"So they did," I admitted with a smile.

She continued, "Besides, I'd prefer not to deal with the police. Not after the way they last treated us." She straightened, looking more dignified than before. I felt a renewed familiarity about her. "I believe that I may have some information for you."

"Oh?"

"Yes. You see, I'm her - - - "

"Sister," I completed.

11

I cancelled my afternoon class and had the department secretary bring in a cup of tea for Mrs. D'Angelo. I ordered all counseling appointments with students to be cancelled, and all calls, except from Donaldson, to be held. Mrs. D'Angelo sat opposite me. In fifteen minutes I knew more about the woman in the closet than all the tests in the world could have provided.

"My sister's name was Maria, she began. Maria Cialini. I am her younger sister - the baby," she said and smiled. "Theresa."

"Where are you from?"

"Our family is from Brooklyn, New York," she said gently.

I cut in, "I'm not doubting your story and I appreciate your sincerity, but what makes you sure that this woman is your sister? I mean, we've had thousands of calls."

She smiled. "Doctor, *I know*. I saw the program the other night and the computer photos you were able to create. It was like looking at a ghost. Except Maria never smiled. Not like that, anyway. Here," she said, reaching into her purse, "see for yourself."

She handed me a small black and white photo and I accepted it gently. It took but a glance to see that she was correct. The picture was of a woman in her early twenties at the beach. She was dressed in a one-piece swimsuit or "bathing suit" as they were known back then, and was posing for the camera, hands on hips. Black hair, parted in the middle, large eyes: exotic. Who was I kidding? She was downright sexy. It was she; of that there was no doubt! I looked closer at the photo. She wore a necklace; some kind of a pendant hung from the chain. I put the photo down. "You have no idea what this means to our investigation."

"And you have no idea what this means to our family," she replied.

"Tell me everything you can, ma'am." I said and then added, "More tea?" I wanted her to feel completely at ease.

"No, thank you. Maria left for San Francisco in October of 1946 when she was nineteen. She'd have left Brooklyn at fifteen if she could. Anything to get away."

"From what?" I asked quietly, so grateful for this stroke of luck and desperate to extract as much information from her as possible, but aware of the risks involved in pushing.

"Everything, everyone," she explained. "Our home wasn't so much broken as it was shattered. Our father died in the war in '41, leaving my mother to raise five children. My mother worked nights. Long hours to take care of us. Maria took care of us during the day. My uncle…"

She paused, as what I imagined was an ancient anger, long suppressed, welled up within her.

"Maria developed quickly. She looked eighteen at thirteen." She paused again.

I knew only too well what she was going to say, but kept my silence. I had seen this throughout my career.

"My uncle was supposed to help the family. Help my mother after my father's death – but he abused Maria. Sexually abused her. Maria complained to the nuns at our school and they informed our mother - Mom almost killed her when she found out. She couldn't believe that her brother would do such things. I think she just didn't want to believe it."

Theresa D'Angelo looked at an area of the wall, just above my right shoulder. "When he, my uncle, found out that Maria had told, he - he broke her left arm." Her lower lip trembled.

Sonofabitch. I deflected my gaze to the wall in an effort to make it easier for Theresa to continue. Neither of us made eye contact.

"People didn't talk about those things back then, not inside the family. And you certainly didn't tell the nuns. My mother was an old-fashioned Catholic from Italy. She didn't approve of the way Maria displayed her physical maturity. If something happened to you, we were taught that it was your own fault. Anyway, Maria was never the same after that. She didn't trust anyone. Authority, men; they were all corrupt to her. All dirty. And so was she, or so she believed - - -" She paused and looked into her cup a moment before looking at me again. "May I have another cup of tea, Dr. Connor?"

I had the department secretary bring in a fresh pot.

"My uncle died a year and a half later, but the damage was done. Maria was - - - ruined. She started staying out late. Men who thought she was older pursued her for their own ends. They wanted to take care of her and she didn't mind. Local boys wouldn't do. To hear her tell it, though, it was she who was using them. She'd get them to fight eachother over her. She'd make dates with three at the same time, at the same place, and leave them to sort it all out. My mother was mortified, and when some of the local wives came to our apartment, demanding that Maria find her own husband, my mother threw her out." Theresa stopped to take a breath. She looked as if a storm had been lifted from within.

"What happened to her then, Mrs. D'Angelo?" I inquired softly.

"She lived with some fellow, got him to leave his wife and kids. A few months later she took off with his money and that was the last we ever saw of her."

"When was that?"

She thought for a moment. "May or June of 1946."

"You had no contact with her after that?"

"I said it was the last we *saw* of her, not *heard* from her. She wrote, fairly regularly. She wrote little things like: where she was living and that she was working. She sent money to my mother, but Mama sent it back. So she started sending money and letters to me. I would use the dollars she sent me to buy candy and comics for my brothers and sisters," she confided, smiling in remembrance.

"Can you give me an idea as to when she might have disappeared?"

"Somewhere between August, 1953, and January of '54," she said matter of factly.

"How can you be so sure?" I was curious.

"My birthday is at the end of January. She never missed it. She always sent me a card with a few dollars in it."

"What about Christmas, or New Years?"

She tilted her head to one side and sighed. "One year she would, the next she wouldn't. She never missed a birthday, though."

"How do you know it wasn't before August?"

She smiled. "Maria wrote to me a few weeks after the Fourth of July," and then added, "She sent me that photo."

That was it then, I thought. She was murdered between August of '53 and January, 1954. A five-month spread.

"No chance that you could be mistaken?" I asked.

"None."

"All right. Can you tell me about her life here in San Francisco? Who she knew? Where she lived?"

Mrs. D'Angelo put the box on my desk. "I don't recall off-hand where she lived. Throughout the years, however, I kept almost every correspondence she sent me. I'm sure it's in the letters. I don't read them anymore. My priest said I have to move on. Every note, letter and card. It's all in here. In regards to your other question, she worked for a company called 'The Pyramid Group.'"

I didn't recognize the name. "Didn't your mother ever contact the police?"

"Yes, she did - with great reluctance. I knew that something was wrong when she didn't write, but it took until May of 1954 before my mother would do anything. Y'know, once a whore always a whore! God's punishment and all. We contacted the New York police and they contacted the San Francisco police. As I understood it, they found her apartment and learned that she had paid her rent until the end of November, 1953' and then she left."

"Just left?"

"Yes. The landlord said she had turned in her key and taken off – just taken off. The police said she wasn't a missing person because she had chosen to disappear. They didn't search any further."

Ok, I thought, *though strange.* "I'll need to know the address of that building."

"It's all there in the letters."

I had the incredible urge to call Donaldson, but I didn't want to ruin what was happening before me.

"Dr. Connor, please don't think ill of my sister. She was changing. She had changed."

"What do you mean?"

Mrs. D'Angelo explained, "She had met a man. I mean a good man. It's in the letters."

"Do you know who he was?" My excitement got the better of me.

"No, she never mentioned him by name. Just that he was a good man - that he taught her - the way it could be between a man and a woman and that she was in love with him. She was *in love* Dr. Connor." Tears welled up in her eyes as she said it.

I nodded.

"Tell me about her death. I know the television program said she was murdered, but I was in such shock that I'm afraid I must have missed the details."

I searched for the right way to tell her, before deciding on the unpolished truth. "Your sister - - - "

"Maria," she said. "Please call her Maria. Nobody else has in a long time."

I nodded and spoke clinically the way I had been taught. The way I had spoken to numerous victims' families whose deaths I had investigated over the years. "Maria was shot once through the left eye with a .22 caliber bullet."

"It was a man," she stated.

I shrugged. I, too, had assumed that the murderer was a man, but in light of all I had just heard, I couldn't be sure it hadn't been an angry wife. I told her this as gently as I could.

She smiled. "Oh, doctor, lots of women would've probably wished Maria dead, but a woman wouldn't do it that way. Women don't shoot, not like that. Whoever killed her was angry but calm, and methodical. It was personal. It was a man."

I nodded. It wasn't something I was going to push.

"Can you tell me anything else?" she asked. "Perhaps something they didn't mention on TV?"

"Ah, yes. Actually I can, although this may hurt you very much. Maria was pregnant when she was killed."

"I said tell me something I don't know, Doctor. That was no secret, at least between us. She told me she was pregnant in her last letter. Told me I'd be an aunt when she brought me out."

"Brought you out?"

"Oh, yes. She planned to bring me out here for a visit. She had big plans for us, her and her beau, and their baby. She sounded so happy."

"When did she plan for you to come here?"

"Seven months later," she replied.

I thought for a moment.

"That's right, Doctor," she said as if reading my mind. "My sister was five weeks pregnant when she last wrote to me."

I said nothing. Five weeks from the fourth of July, put her getting pregnant in the beginning of June. That would have made her some five months pregnant when she moved out of that apartment in November.

She dug into her purse and pulled out a card. "Here's a number you may reach me at day or night, if you should have any questions, Dr. Connor."

I took the card. "May I keep these?" I asked, indicating the box of material and photo.

"Absolutely. I want you to find this man, Dr. Connor. I want you to find him," she repeated and paused a moment before continuing. By the way she looked at me, I knew what she would say, "And kill him. Kill the man that took away her life and her baby's, just when she had found meaning in it."

I exhaled. "Easy now, ma'am. You know that - - - "

"I know your reputation, Dr. Connor," she said. "I did a bit of checking on you. I'll pay you fifty thousand dollars, cash."

I was glad I hadn't called Donaldson over. I didn't know what to say. Damn rumors.

"I understand the legal ramifications of accepting such an offer so I'll make it easy. Say nothing. When you find this person and he is dead, my lawyer will send you the money. Have you a suspect yet?"

"No, ma'am." I lied. I didn't want her going off half-cocked after Michael Astor, though the image was somewhat amusing. "Ma'am, I - - - "

"When will I be able to have her remains, Doctor?" she asked, changing the subject as she stood to leave.

I thought a few moments, grateful for the change. "Several weeks, I'm afraid," I said professionally, as if I hadn't just been offered fifty-G's to kill somebody. "We're still waiting for test results."

She shrugged indifferently. "What's a few weeks more?"

12

3:31 PM

I walked Mrs. D'Angelo respectfully to the parking lot and saw her into her maroon Honda rental. As soon as she had left my sight, I ran like a madman back to my office. I called Donaldson and gave him the *Cliff's Notes* version of what had transpired, leaving out the part about being offered the contract. "We've got a gold mine here," I explained, looking at the box she'd left me. "Employment, where she lived and God only knows what else."

Donaldson sounded happy. "This is the break we needed."

"Who owned 'The Pyramid Group?'" I wanted to know that more than anything else. "Find out where she worked and you can get records and interview her employers and co-workers." My mind was racing. "Also," I told Donaldson, "call Astor's lawyer, Clarke. Tell him to check the records on that apartment between Aug, '53 and Jan, '54."

Donaldson said he'd make a few calls and get back to me, though it might be a while.

I sat back in my chair, happy with the treasure trove that Theresa D'Angelo had provided me in information and the one she had left me in the form of the box of letters sitting on my desk. Her sister had left Brooklyn in 1946 and was dead by 1954, no more than eight years later. And she was over one month pregnant around the fourth of July. I wondered what signifigance there was if any, between her pregnancy and her murder.

3:50 PM

I spent the next twenty minutes riffling through the box of letters. They were in bundles and rubber-banded together. I undid a few of the packets and was sad to see that the letters weren't in any order by date. They were going to take a long time to go through. I took notice of the addressees. The entire first bundle was all from North Beach. That made sense to me as it was an Italian-American area and would be a likely place for a young woman transplanting herself from Brooklyn to move to. I wrote down the address, re-banded the bundle and flipped through another bunch. These too were from the same address in North Beach and were all dated between 1946 and 1947. I moved to another bunch and found an address in Pacific Heights on Green Street. I flipped through another stack and found more letters, all of which were dated between 1947 and 1953.

I picked up the phone on the first ring. It was Donaldson.

"You're not going to believe this, babe," Donaldson said.

"Well, tell me before I pick myself up off the floor," I retorted.

"'The Pyramid Group' was part of 'Golden Gate Realty.' And as you know, Golden Gate Realty was owned by Michael Astor."

"Motherfuck. The 4th? I asked rhetorically."

"Yeah, the 4th," Donaldson laughed.

"Not the 3rd?"

"No."

"Shit!"

"Right again," Donaldson concurred.

I was incredulous. "She worked for him, Cal. She worked for him and he lied right to our faces."

"Easy now, babe," Donaldson corrected. "You're half right."

"What?"

"If what you're saying is true, and I'm sure it is, then she did work for him but proving that he lied to us won't be as easy to prove. Remember, we didn't have a name for him to deny."

"We had the photo."

"Ah, he could plausibly deny having known her. Trust me. I've been doing this for years. You'd be surprised what people can pull on you. The only thing that's certain is what you can prove."

"All right. When do we go talk to him?"

"That's another thing. Seems that Mr. Carver called the mayor's office, as I knew he would. I'm sure you're aware that Mr. Astor is a big supporter of both our mayor and his party?"

"Yeah, yeah," I sighed.

"Actually, he's a supporter of whoever's in office regardless of party affiliation," Donaldson informed. "Well the mayor wasn't too crazy about the

71

questioning or the time we did it at, although nobody could fault our right to question Astor."

"How'd they take my presence?"

"Not bad, actually. I told them of your success with the photo enhancement and said something about you not being able to allow it out of your sight due to the difficulty in creating another."

Not bad. "That worked, you think?"

"Who knows? Point is, this investigation is mine. But if we do something stupid, I can't guarantee it'll stay this way."

"So, when do we go back and question him?"

"We can go whenever we want. But the mayor wants me to extend the courtesy of calling before we show up."

"Call him then."

"Right," Donaldson agreed.

"One other thing," I said, holding the piece of paper out before me. I gave Donaldson the addresses. "The North Beach one she lived in from '46 to about February of '47. The Pacific Heights one between April, '47 until 1953. It looks like she moved between February and April."

"I'll run a check on them and see what we can find out," Donaldson said. "Anything else?"

"Yeah, let's meet. "Investigations make me hungry."

"Me, too, though I'm always hungry," Donaldson quipped. "Your bar, forty minutes."

I hung up the phone and sat back to think for a moment. Theresa D'Angelo was right. Shooting her sister, Maria, in the eye was an act of an angry person, probably the act of a man. In my experience, when a person is murdered in this fashion – up-close and direct, with no other injuries - it is usually the work of a cold, calculated and precise mind: a very angry mind.

13

ALL-Night SAX: 6:20 PM

Donaldson made the call and an appointment was set up for 7:15 PM. With over two hours to kill, we met to discuss what had transpired.

A local group of amateur musicians was performing on the dais for the evening crowd. It was a trio consisting of a saxophonist, a drummer and pianist. They went for a retro look, sunglasses and black suits with skinny ties. They played as if for themselves: facing one another instead of facing the crowd. It created a sense of privacy between them and made the audience feel as if they were watching something special. The gimmick worked, I decided, as the music was good.

Donaldson and I had arrived a little after four and ordered some food. I had brown rice with mixed vegetables and a glass of water. The rice was fluffy and the vegetables crunchy. Donaldson ordered a pizza-burger and a Coke. We talked at length and in detail, pausing only to swallow. I explained to him who Maria Cialini was, where she'd come from, her family life and so forth, off the notes I had scribbled after Mrs. D'Angelo left. Donaldson listened patiently, asking almost the same questions I had asked Mrs. D'Angelo. I answered all his questions while he took notes of his own.

I explained the box that I had brought along and all it contained.

"We'll have to divide this up between us and each read as much as we can," Donaldson said. I agreed.

"Jeez," Donaldson exclaimed, when I had finished. "I wish you'd called me. I'd have loved to ask her a few questions."

My jaw ached from talking. I took a sip of water before responding. "Her coming in wasn't easy," I explained. "I was worried about her getting angry and leaving with the box. You should have seen her."

Donaldson nodded. "You did the right thing. Besides, if I come up with any questions, I can have you call her."

I nodded. "OK, so what do you think?"

"By rights, we should review all this information before proceeding. There could be a lead or even the proof that could close this case, right on this table. But I agree with you. We've got enough to go back and talk to Astor."

"Great."

Donaldson continued, "But let me tell you. Nothing is set here. We could find something in these letters that could change whatever we may think now, so we're going to go slow, be nice and see what we can see."

I nodded, before adding, "She worked for him and she was buried in one of his apartments."

"It looks bad."

I had a thought. "What did you find out about where she last lived?"

"I made a few calls after you hung up." He took his frayed notebook from his pocket and read, "The place she lived in North Beach was torn down back in the early '80s, no idea where the super is or if he's alive. Personally, I doubt it, as he would be like ninety today. But the second address you gave me is still in existence. We traced down who the super was back in the early fifties. He died in '74; wife died in '81, but they had a daughter. We think she still lives in the city. I've got a guy looking into it."

"That's good."

Donaldson looked at his watch. "It's about time for our meeting. Let's go.

7:08 PM

The drive to the financial district took longer than it had the other night. Part of this was due to the evening traffic that we encountered. Part of it was the sense of urgency that the news that Maria Cialini had not only worked for Michael Astor IV, but that she was buried in his property, had created. This knowledge had fueled the suspicion that Astor had lied and created a sense of immediacy in questioning the discrepancy in his story and his apparent memory loss. Though Donaldson showed more restraint than I did, both of us were chomping at the bit.

We reached Astor's building and went in. Mr. Kwan, as stiff and formal as he had been the first time, confirmed our appointment and we were allowed up without delay.

For me, everything about the building had lost its luster since my initial visit. That's not to say that the building had actually lost its luster. Quite the contrary, it was as sparkling and polished as ever. It was just that I was less impressed with it the second time around. I wondered whether the same would be true for Michael Astor IV. It was.

"Gentlemen," he said from the center of his office as a secretary ushered us in, "it's good to see you again." His fixed smile seemed brighter in the twilight that streamed through his office than it had the other day. His tan too seemed to glow more. He wore a Brioni tuxedo of midnight blue, which actually appeared to be blacker than the standard black. Indeed, everything- the marble floors, walls and furniture - all shone with a luster that seemed greater than it had the other day. Still, I wasn't impressed. Mr. Clarke stood off to the side, studying some documents. He raised his eyes and peered at us over his half-glasses before putting them down. Behind him, as if standing watch, was Mr. Carver. Both were wearing Italian suits.

The introductions were brief. Donaldson and I declined the offer to sit and have some tea, explaining that we'd already eaten and didn't plan to take much of his time, this time.

"By the way, Dr. Connor," Astor began. "I saw you on television the other night. You and the good Inspector."

"Thank you," I said politely, trying not to let my boredom show.

"I was right. You are very photogenic. Have you ever considered being a spokesman? I chair several groups that would be perfect for you."

"No," I declined. "I'm gainfully employed as is."

"Ah. No chance of you running for office?" he asked in a way that was both innocent and suggestive. "I'm always looking for worthy new proteges."

"That's not what really brought us over, sir," Donaldson politely interrupted.

Michael Astor IV smiled. "Of course. Sometimes I get carried away. What can I do for you, Inspector?"

"You owned a company called 'The Pyramid Group?'" Donaldson asked.

Astor nodded. "Yes, yes I did. That was part of and then absorbed into Golden Gate Realty in - - - " He raised a hand, as if the answer could be plucked from the air.

"Nineteen eighty-three, sir," Mr. Clarke assisted.

"Yes, that's right. Why?"

"I'd like to have the rental records for apartment # 44 from August of 1953 through January of '54."

"Absolutely. Mr. Clarke will have those for you as soon as possible. You've narrowed down your search, yes?" He smiled.

"Yes. We have evidence that leads us to believe that the murdered woman was killed sometime between August, 1953, and January '54 and was then buried in your building. We'd like to keep our search limited for now to that tenant or tenants who rented that unit within those months and see where it leads us."

"Excellent," Michael Astor said, impressed. "Your television show helped, didn't it?"

"It did," Donaldson agreed.

"Hmmm. The power of the media," he said. "Anything else?"

"Well, yes, actually there is." Donaldson said.

Mr. Clarke noticed the change in Donaldson's approach and folded his arms in preparation.

I noted this and it suddenly occurred to me that Michael Astor didn't get upset about the direction of the questions; his lawyers did. It further occurred to me that Michael Astor IV might well have been the first man to successfully utilize the notion of paying someone to worry for him.

Donaldson said, "We'd like for you to get us the work records for Maria Cialini."

Astor's smile remained solid. Even his eyes kept from dimming. I chalked it up to practice. His voice, however, didn't. "W - - - Who?"

I noted the crack in the armor. *I guess you can pay people to worry for you, but nobody can keep you cool but yourself.*

"Maria Cialini, sir," said Donaldson. "Our investigation has determined that the murdered woman was one Maria Cialini, age twenty-six. 'The Pyramid Group' employed her." He paused. "The murdered woman, found in one of your apartments was Maria Cialini, one of your employees," he summarized before adding respectively, "Sir."

"I have a real photo of her," I said, producing it and handing it to Astor before Mr. Carver could raise a hand to intercept or a voice to object.

Astor viewed the small black and white photo a moment before handing it back. Mr. Clarke motioned to see it so I gave it to him.

"Do you recognize the woman in the photo, sir?" Donaldson asked.

After several awkward moments, he tried to speak.

"Excuse me?" Donaldson said. Astor's voice was too low.

Astor gained focus. "Yes."

"You told us yesterday that you didn't recognize her," I chanced.

Donaldson shook his head, before either lawyer could speak, and I deferred. He didn't want to push it with two lawyers in the room.

"Would you gentlemen like a drink?" Astor asked.

We declined.

"Then I'll have your's."

Michael Astor IV, billionaire heir, real estate mogul and philanthropist, had aged twenty years in two seconds. He went to the bar and fixed himself a drink.

Mr. Clarke, who seemed to grow in size, went to his side. Mr. Carver looked at me with eyes that could have, in my opinion, bored through steel. I took the opportunity to glance at the books on the bookshelf. I was right. The books were real but apparently, never opened; the bindings were smooth and creaseless. The bookshelf, itself, was laminated chipboard, not real marble. This place was as fake as its owner.

I turned to see Mr. Clarke whispering to Astor who shrugged him off. With stooped shoulders, Astor turned to face us.

"Gentlemen," Mr. Clarke began, "Mr. Astor has chosen to speak with you against my counsel. He is doing this because he is innocent of any wrongdoing in the death of this woman and he wants to help your investigation in any way possible."

"We appreciate that," Donaldson said.

"I'd like to add that Mr. Astor could all too easily deny knowing this woman, despite the fact that she worked for him as many, many people have worked for him over the course of half a century. Not to mention all the legal muscle he could bring to retard your investigation. This he will not do, as he is an honorable man.   And it should be under these circumstances that you consider his willingness to cooperate and your line of questioning."

"Absolutely," Donaldson concurred.

Mr. Clarke patted Astor on the back. Astor took a sip of his drink. "What would you like to know about her?"

"First of all, I'd like for you to confirm that she worked for you."

"You have that, Inspector." Michael Astor said, his smile gone.

"All right, could you start by telling me everything you remember about her?"

Astor raised a hand. "I'd like to address Dr. Connor's question first. I said I didn't recognize her the other day because I didn't. That photo you showed me didn't really look like her, you see." He paused. "Didn't do her justice."

I nodded. "I understand." *Bullshit! Donaldson was right.*

"I didn't know her personally," he began. "But I made it a point to know all my employees. I remember her. She worked for me I think sometime in early 1947. I remember because we'd had difficulty in hiring good people who would stay. We'd had a lot of attrition in her department at that time. Much of the work was tedious and the few women who we hired usually left soon after - most wanted more high profile jobs about the office. I suppose, so they could meet men and find husbands. They didn't like doing jobs that had them by themselves most of the day."

"What did she do for the company?" Donaldson asked.

I noted how he used the words, "for the company" as opposed to "for you," because he didn't want Astor to lawyer up.

"She worked for the Accounting Department. Her exact tasks I couldn't tell you as my employees' tasks often overlapped with each other."

"Do you remember when she left?"

"I think it was spring of '50, though it could have been later."

I was surprised. I expected that she had worked for him until the time of her death. "I'm curious. What kind of worker was she?"

"She was good," Astor began. "Actually, she was a bit better than good. She was very competent. Independent."

"How can you remember with such certainty?" Donaldson asked.

"Like I said, we had very few women who would stay in bookkeeping. She stayed there the duration of her employment. She was given a raise for her competency."

Donaldson made a note of that. "I see. Why did she leave?"

Astor searched his memory. "I don't recall. Honestly."

"We believe you," Donaldson assuaged, though I'm sure he didn't. "Do you remember if she left or was forced out? Did she leave for personal reasons?"

Michael Astor thought a moment. "I really don't remember the circumstances. I can tell you she left of her own accord; she wasn't fired or forced to leave for any impropriety. It could have been personal. Mr. Clarke will have all the records available for you, though, and you can go through them yourself."

"Thank you. Did she ever ask for any references?" Donaldson continued.

"No, nothing. I don't think so. As far as we knew, she just left. I guess we assumed she didn't need references because like most women then, she'd gotten married. Again, records will tell more."

I asked, "Did she have any enemies?"

Astor shrugged. "Somebody who'd want to kill her? I don't believe so. God, I hope not."

"How about friends?"

"I'm sure she had them. Mr. Clarke will provide you with a list of co-workers who worked in her department. You'll have to ask them, assuming they're still alive, and that you can find them. That's the best I can do, I'm afraid."

"Believe me, sir, it's much appreciated," Donaldson said.

I grew impatient. "Sir," I began, "I have to ask this. Do you have any idea as to how or why Miss Cialini came to be buried in your building?"

"I don't." He shook his head. "With God as my witness, I have no idea." He sounded completely honest to me. Michael Astor IV finished his drink and set it down on the bar.

Mr. Clarke stepped in. He spoke with the clinical detachment that denotes a good lawyer. "Fact is, Dr. Connor, anybody could have deposited the body in that apartment. After I provide Inspector Donaldson with the records, I'm sure you'll have new leads with which to continue your search."

"I'm sure, too." Donaldson agreed.

"Inspector," Mr. Clarke said. "Mr. Astor isn't a suspect in this - - - incident, is he?"

Donaldson shook his head. "Absolutely not. I should have made that clear up front. He is not a suspect. We're merely here to gather information about a former employee." He didn't say, "who was found murdered in one of his properties." He didn't have to. "That's all."

I lacked such tact. "I just remembered something about the woman."

"What's that, Dr. Connor?" Astor inquired.

"She was pregnant."

Mr. Clarke tilted his head and Mr. Carver exhaled subtly.

"More is the pity," Astor said without skipping a beat.

Expecting to see him crack, I was disappointed. "The photo didn't show it."

"Of course not," Astor said.

"Did you know she was pregnant?" I asked.

"No," Michael Astor answered.

"Excuse me, Dr. Connor," Mr. Carver began. "How far along was this pregnancy when she expired?"

'Expired,' I thought. *That's sterile.* "Almost twenty weeks."

"Well, you see, you've answered your own question," he said. "She left in early 1950. How would Mr. Astor know about a pregnancy that took place some three years after her employment ended?"

Sharp. Spoken like a lawyer. "You're right," I said. "Let me rephrase that. Do you know if she was dating anyone during her employment?"

Astor shook his head. "No. The private lives of my employees, I never made my business. We were ahead of our time in that regard. Privacy issues in the work place. I started that." He smiled without force.

"Is there anything else, Inspector?" Mr. Clarke asked. "We have a fundraiser to get to this evening."

There wasn't.

"Inspector Donaldson, Doctor Connor," Astor began, "I've been running my companies for over fifty years. In that time I've hired many people and fired a few. I've been Godfather to more than a few employees' children and have been invited to many weddings, christenings, confirmations, bar mitzvahs and, I'm afraid, a number of funerals. Never has a murder encroached upon my companies or me. The nature of the work I do now is high- profile. If I become entangled in a murder investigation, it could - no it *would* - have devastating effects on the charities I support. This investigation, with all due respect, is bigger than the murder, bigger than I. It could effect orphans, the elderly, and vital research into half a dozen deadly diseases. So please, I implore you to proceed cautiously."

"I personally promise you that we will," Donaldson offered.

"Gentlemen," Mr. Clarke began, "please consider this when evaluating all you have learned this evening and will learn when I get you those records. If Mr. Astor had anything to do with that woman's homicide, why on earth would he have sold the building where she was buried when he could have simply kept it in his possession and ensured that nobody ever would have found her?"

I hadn't considered that. It was a good point.

"Point well taken," Donaldson said.

"I would like to inject that this woman was deposited in Mr. Astor's property for reasons of possible revenge, or if you prefer, a frame-up."

"Noted," Donaldson said.

Another good point.

Mr. Carver picked up. "I'd also like to learn more about the timing of the 'renovations' on the building that led to this discovery. Frankly, I find it suspicious."

You boys are batting a thousand. I had to admit that I hadn't thought of that, either. Fact was I didn't like Astor and so far I was concentrating on him. But as I began to think about it, Clarke and Carver had a point, actually several. "One thing, though. If what you say is true and the killer put Miss Cialini's body in Mr. Astor's building, for the reasons of embarrassment or framing, why didn't this person make the frame-up complete by calling the police and tipping them off?" *Try that one on for size.*

Mr. Clarke paused a moment, but only a moment. "Perhaps the murderer of this woman died before he got the chance or was imprisoned and died there, or just moved off."

"Good point," I conceded. *Show-offs.*

The meeting was over. Astor and his number one and two lawyers had to go to a fundraiser for the city's Leukemia Society, where Astor was due to donate approximately one million dollars. It was a black-tie affair and he didn't want to be late.

Donaldson and I shook hands with the opposition, as I saw them. Mr. Clarke ensured Donaldson that he would have all the records in his hand, by courier, in the morning. He also gave us business cards, with phone numbers at which he or Mr. Carver could be reached twenty-four hours a day for any assistance we might need. Donaldson thanked him for his cooperation.

We were nearly at the elevator when Mr. Astor called to us. He approached. He had a piece of paper in each hand.

"Inspector, you said your wife is involved with volunteer work at the hospital?"

"Yes, she is."

"Well, I don't know if either of you heard, but we've moved up the annual Astor Festival by nearly a month. It seems that there was a scheduling conflict. At any rate, the festival will be on the 30th." He handed each of us a flyer.

We thanked him again and stepped into the elevator.

"Hope you'll be able to make it," he said, his smile back in place and brighter than ever.

I didn't know whether or not I'd just been threatened.

14

8:30 PM

Donaldson dropped me back at the "All-Night Sax." There, I took half the letters and miscellaneous papers that constituted a testament to the life of one Maria Cialini. Donaldson took the other half. "I'm going to go and see if my guy found out anything about that landlord's daughter. Then I'm going to start reading these," Donaldson said before heading off.

I returned home to my spacious two-story slate-roofed brownstone in Twin Peaks. Twin Peaks was originally called "Los Pechos de la Choca," by the Spanish, and meant "breasts of the Indian Maiden." This was not the reason I chose to live there. The fact that it was the second highest peak in the city and gave its occupants a view of almost all the city, particularly the Bay, was. The view was even more spectacular at night with a good bottle of wine and a warm houseguest to share it with. My home was also near the University. I was unsure of which "breast" I lived on, though Donaldson would often ask, "How is life on the left tit?" How he had determined it was the left one, Donaldson would never say.

Twin Peaks was not developed until the 1920s due to its steep ascent. Currently it was home to mostly affluent people. Due to its height, it tended to get a bit windy and foggy. This suited me fine as it offered me a bit of variety in San Francisco's otherwise equitable weather. I enjoyed the steep hills as it allowed me to get in some good workouts, without the hassle of going to the gym, and to do so outdoors. There were also several stair-walks that could take one over the steep hills.

I drove down and parked in the driveway and exited, making my way up the stone path that cut through the neatly trimmed lawn. My home sat in a depression and was off the road far enough so that sounds seldom reached, providing me with a sense of serenity I experienced nowhere else. I traversed the steps leading to the large oaken front door, and went inside.

I had bought the house nearly five years before after years of renting apartments and owning a few condos, thanks largely to the money I made from writing. One of my books, "An Introduction to Forensic Pathology," was currently used as a college textbook. For years, I actually did own a home: a two-family, but I didn't live in it myself. I rented out both floors, paying off the mortgage with one unit and investing the other, while I lived elsewhere off my paycheck from the ME's office. The book earnings were put into safe, long-term investments. After fifteen years, I had the house completely paid for and had saved an impressive amount to allow me to buy the brownstone and do it up the way I wanted it: the right way.

I stepped into the black-streaked marbled vestibule and closed the door, disabling the burglar alarm before locking up for the night. I walked into the highly polished oak-floored living room and deposited the box Mrs. D'Angelo had given me on the area rug next to the coffee table in front of the leather sofa.

I checked the messages on the answering machine only to find it full. I pushed the forward button as soon as I realized the irrelevance of the message. The bulk of the messages were rambling: people wanting to help me in my investigation, others offering me solutions and still others wanting to hire me.

Push, push, and push.

A few were from colleagues that would speak to me later.

Push.

A few were from students who wanted to get into my classes, despite the fact that the semester was two thirds over.

Push.

How the bulk of them got my number was unknown to me.

I went up to my bedroom. Like the rest of my home, it was lightly but elegantly furnished. An elliptical rider stood off to the side. I worked out on it a few times a week. It was better than running because there was no impact on my joints and helped to keep me trim and fit.

I had seen too many homes cluttered with a cacophony of a lifetime's accumulated junk, chronicling their owner's lack of taste and I had vowed never to have this happen to me. I never understood how people had to define their space by putting something in every empty area they found. I had taken the opposite opinion when planning my dream house. Living space here was defined not by clutter and "stuff" but by a lack of it. Most of the layout was my own ideas, but I couldn't take credit for it all. I sacrificed lots of rooms for fewer, more spacious rooms. My bedroom was a perfect example. Previously, there had been four bedrooms on the second floor. I had taken two rooms and knocked down the wall between them to create the master bedroom. I kept the third as a guestroom and got rid of the fourth altogether. My bedroom, like the rest of the house, was arranged in accordance with the principles of Feng Shui. Some time ago, I had dated a woman, Elaine, who was licensed or something in the practice. Those who practiced it considered Feng Shui, pronounced "Fung Shway," something of a philosophy. As she had explained it, this Chinese philosophy recognizes that our environment has a direct effect on our emotions and health and seeks to create a harmonious milieu to live in. The word "Feng Shui" means "wind and water." Feng Shui is meant to create a feeling of interconnectedness between a person and all things. It attempts to show us how to arrange our environment to improve our health. Elaine told me that there were Feng Shui consultants, who received over one hundred dollars per square foot to advise people on how best to incorporate its principals into their lives. She wanted to do the same for me, or to me. I said all right, provided she didn't want me to make any major renovations. She started by telling me to picture the image of the perfect living environment in my head. When I told her that I thought I already had that, she "tsk'ed" me and said she'd do it herself.

In my den she recommended making the parquet floors into an octagon, and I did. She advised me to put my favorite chair into a corner. I did this as well. She wanted flowers about the house. I suggested cactus as they were low-maintenance, but she got me some leafy plants instead. She had a number of changes to make in the bedroom and I gave her free reign because I believed it would make the sex better, which it did, for her. In fact, it appeared that the whole project seemed to get her off. It was as if she thought she was going to change me, poor thing. I moved the bed to a position that offered the best view of the door. The main entrance was to be kept open and clear, as this was the "mouth of chi." (Her phrase, not mine.) She had me get rid of some of the light bulbs in favor of full spectrum lights. She bought candles and wind chimes and set up different types in the various rooms. She wanted me to repaint two thirds of the house but I said no way as I had just shelled out a bundle to have the place painted. She argued that various colors increased balance, but I wouldn't budge. I was balanced enough; her, I was beginning to have doubts about. In the end, I let her pick out some paintings and photos to hang on the walls and some area rugs to offer variety.

She installed one of those plug-in fountains. In Feng Shui, less is more. Windows had to be kept spotless, she told me, as windows were the eyes of chi, the energy of life. I thought it just good housekeeping. She had me hang a mirror over the kitchen stove as my back was to the door when I cooked. She said it would create more balance while I cooked. I suggested one over the bed; "You know, for balance," I said, but she ignored me. In all honesty, the changes she suggested did make me feel a bit relieved, though I wasn't entirely sure that wasn't because all her messing with my place had stopped. In the end, we broke up after an argument, the subject of which was that she was crowding me. This was rather ironic, I felt, considering that she was an expert in Feng Shui and spatial relationships. I missed that firm ass and realized with a bit of sadness that I'd never have the pleasure of chasing it around the house naked again. However, I did console myself with the rationale that by breaking up with her, I was removing clutter from my life and finding balance. And wasn't that what Feng Shui was all about?

I hung up my jacket and glanced about. Large, thick billowing curtains hung from the windows. A skylight above gave the option of sleeping under the stars and waking under the clouds whenever mood desired and weather allowed. A large Jacuzzi was off to the side, where I spent many a long evening unwinding after a stressful day. There was a small guestroom down the hall. I seldom had reason to use it as I seldom had who guests that spent the night. The few who did usually opted to stay with me. Male friends could rough it on the couch downstairs or go the hell home.

I undressed, laying out my clothes neatly on the satin-sheeted futon and donned my full-body, royal-blue terry-cloth bathrobe and slippers before throwing a matching full-body towel over my shoulder and heading into the my personal bathroom.

There were three bathrooms in the house, one downstairs, and two on the second floor. Like the rest of the house, they were all remodeled, but none of them like mine. Plants hung in the corners. The shower took up almost half the over-sized room. A large swing-out transparent door with a frosted-floral design served as the gateway to the chamber. A large water nozzle hung from above the center of the chamber. The shower was large. When I stood under its forceful faucet, I could reach out in any direction and not touch the walls or glass. It gave me a sense of freedom that I found lacking in others. I didn't like the crowded feeling I had in most standard showers and hated when the wet plastic curtain rubbed up against me. My shower was serene. It was deliberate.

I left the robe and towel across a hook and the slippers near the door and stepped in. A few minutes later, I was standing underneath the hot torrents. I stood there, head bowed, eyes closed for several moments, allowing the heat to open my pores before increasing it in increments.

After a time, aware of the fog that had enveloped me, I opened my eyes. I lathered myself with an all-natural liquid body-wash as I had long ago given up on the harsher artificial solid soap bars. I washed my hair with an herbal shampoo and rinsed off. I took a rubber body scrub and worked it about my lean and rangy frame. I had always been health conscious and a fitness buff. Ever since I turned forty, I had begun to get more into such things as herbs, and natural living. I wasn't fanatical, though, still enjoying the occasional beer and steak. I had simply decided to tweak certain aspects of my life to increase the quality of it. It also made me feel less guilty about cigars; the one thing I would not compromise.

Clean and sufficiently relaxed, I stepped out and dried myself. I rubbed the towel briskly against my skin, reddening it. I'd read somewhere that it was good for the circulation. I caught a glimpse of myself in the mirror and although not a vain man, nevertheless liked what I saw. When dressed, most people would have thought me skinny, but I was actually lean. My sparse frame was skeletal slim with veins close to the surface. My musculature was compact and lacked excessive body-fat, the benefits of a naturally high metabolism, giving me an emaciated appearance. I ran a face cloth about my face and head, leaving my hair damp. I put the towel on the radiator, put on my bathrobe and slippers and left.

9:10 PM

Dressed in pajamas, robe and slippers I went to the kitchen. I made myself a late meal of brown rice, mixed vegetables and some spelt bread at the kitchen-island that stood in the center of the room. As I had opted for the single life, I had long ago decided that it was worth my effort to learn how to cook. I had taken several night-classes over the years and had built myself up quite an impressive repertoire of cuisines as the stereotype of the bachelor who lived off cold pizza and milk that was more gel than liquid, was to me, overdone. I was a private man who seemed naturally suited to single life. I was well adjusted to it, which is to say that I had no pets, excessive drinking habits, vices, except the occaisional cigar, or the hostilities and regrets that marked many of my colleagues who were in similar circumstances. I liked being single and saw no need to justify my singleness to those around me. I liked the freedom. I liked the solitude. Nor was I one of those who sought to lose myself in work in order to occupy my time.

I had a glass of water with the meal instead of my usual glass of wine, as I planned to spend the rest of the evening in my study going over the letters, where I would have a drink. I limited myself to one glass of wine a day with dinner or a drink after. I'd read a few years ago that a glass of wine was good for the heart. Whatever I had, I only had one. It was one of my rules, like dating under-grad students. So far, I'd broken neither.

I took and finished dinner in the dining room and sat at the center of a large oak table. I seldom sat at the head, as it made me feel silly. The table was devoid of any tablecloth; I didn't want to hide the beauty of the finish though I set the plate and glass on a place mat, so I wouldn't ruin the finish. Mellow jazz played from the radio. I seldom watched TV.

Afterwards, I washed the plate and glass and set them out to air-dry. I rarely towel dried dishes, preferring to simply let them dry out in time and be put away later. Breakfast-ware was put away in the evening; evening-ware in the morning. It was a convenient system.

I took my box of correspondence I had gotten from Mrs. D'Angelo and went into the study to learn more about Maria Cialini.

I poured a cognac from the bar into a snifter, all the better to enjoy the aroma, and walked with it held between my middle and forefinger so it rested, cradled in my palm. This ensured that my body heat would bring out the aroma.

If the house was an extension of my body - a place of refuge and comfort from the world around me - the study was an extension of my soul, as it was a refuge from me. Originally, it had been a round-shaped living room. Not one to laze about watching television and stuffing myself with potato chips; I decided that it would better serve me as a study/library.

I'd had the floor/ceiling to the fourth bedroom above torn down, making the study into one large, two-story room. Extensive rosewood bookshelves lined the walls from the floor almost to the ceiling. There was a wheeled ladder that allowed me access to the various volumes of literature, both professional and private I had accumulated over the years. Stained glass adorned the windows, casting the room in a kaleidoscope of color on bright days. I had even commissioned a local artist to paint a fresco of a blue sky with white clouds on the domed ceiling. The room opened inward from the twin oaken, leather, cushioned-back doors. In the center of the room was a sunken rounded tan leather sofa that was flush with the floor around it. In the center of the sofa was a coffee table.

There I set the cognac and letters.

About the room were a few leather chairs and desks where one could study. Off to the left was a real, not laminated, mahogany desk and black leather chair. An apple computer sat atop it with an ergonomic keyboard that allowed me hours of writing without the risk of carpal tunnel syndrome. There was also a fully stocked bar. A fireplace sat behind the sofa.

I drew back two large cream drapes to reveal an equally large bay window that gave me a view of the city's lights. There had been a light fog earlier but that had lifted and the vista was vivid. From a small closet, I retrieved and donned a blue-velvet smoking jacket.

I set up a fire and then descended the steps to return to the sofa, where I removed a Montecristo #2 cigar from a humidor. I believe in doing things completely or not at all. I don't believe in filtered cigarettes, non-alcoholic beer or sex with condoms. If you're going to smoke, smoke. If you're going to drink, drink. If you're going to fuck, fuck.

Clipping the end with a cutter and lighting it, I took a long drag and exhaled before taking a sip of the cognac cradled in my palm. Its' sharp, sweet taste always reminded me of melting raisins.

Setting the Montecristo and the cognac aside, I opened the box and shuffled through the dozens of letters. To my dismay, not every letter came with an envelope, though every envelope came with a letter; some had several. To my further chagrin, a cursory glance through the letters showed that few of them were dated. I shook my head as I now confirmed that I wouldn't be able to simply arrange the letters by date. I was going to have to flip through every last one of them. I found that at the bottom of the box, was a book on birth control.

I had another sip of the cognac, took a long drag on the cigar and exhaled. It would be a long night.

10:23 PM

I moved from one letter to the next as quickly as I could, wanting to get through the batch in as little time as possible. I figured it would take me a few nights to get through them as it was. I was tired and getting more so with each letter. It had been a long day and I wanted to get through as many as possible. Every so often, I would turn my attention to the Montecristo or the cognac before returning to a letter.

I got a ledger and a pen from the desk so I could take notes on anything that struck me relevant: a name, place or date. The first one was dated June, '51. I read in a jump-skip fashion, reading a sentence only where it held the promise of providing me with some tidbit of information. I read quickly:

Dear Theresa,
Got a few minutes now to write to you.... The weather here is fine.... How are things with you? .... I hope to have you out sometime in the future...How are the others doing? ...How is Mom? ...I don't suppose she ever mentions me. Oh well, if you can't say anything good, I suppose one shouldn't say anything at all.... Love Maria XXX

I set the letter aside and picked up another. It was dated May, 1947. I continued to read in the same jump-skip manner, my mind tiring:

Dear Theresa,
Hope this letter finds you well - I went to the beach the other day with my beau and had a great time - San Francisco has summer all year round. At least by Brooklyn standards –

Love Maria XXX

I set the letter aside. *Who was her "beau?"* There was nothing of any value stated, no names. I flipped through a few more and found more of the same girl-talk: the weather, boys. Few dates, fewer places and no names, though. I yawned and stretched my arms skyward. Reading for work was often a tiring event, no matter how necessary, and late night reading, more so. My eyes were heavy and ached and I gave in to the inevitable, figuring that it was better to meet sleep, rather than be overcome by it. I closed my eyes to take a small nap, hoping that I would wake up in half and hour or so, the way I used to study for finals in medical school.

My mind drifted about from one random thought to another before descending through clouds of consciousness, aware constantly of my surroundings. Soon, I was aware that I was losing awareness until finally, I was no longer aware of anything. I was nowhere.

Thoughts entered this place in bits and pieces, as if filtered. Disjointed pictures of realities that weren't real, occurrences that never happened, dreams that weren't dreams, appeared in my mind's eye; a sunny day, a fence, nothing. A fence, someone in the distance and then nothing. Sound joined the montage - laughter and voices. Someone was standing over me. The dead woman, Maria Cialini stood above me. She was different than the computer generated images made her out to be. She appeared, as she looked in the picture that Mrs. D'Angelo gave me earlier, only she was in color, alive and stunningly beautiful. Wind blew through her burnished black hair. She smiled, her mouth curved opposite from the way it appeared in the computer-generated image.

"What do you want?"

Maria Cialini spoke, though no sound passed through her full sensual lips.

"What? I can't read lips."

She said something else and reached down at me. I tried to pull back and woke up, nearly falling off the couch. "Oh, shit," I said, wiping cold sweat from my brow with the sleeve of my bathrobe. *What the hell?* My heart was racing like I'd just come back from a good run. I wasn't a superstitious man and didn't believe in such things as premonition, clairvoyance or communication with people in the next world. I didn't believe in a next world. I hardly believed in the one I was in. I checked the time, 10:47. Time to get back to reading. I was sure that the adrenaline I now felt coursing through me would suffice to keep me awake for some time.

11:20 PM

My snifter was empty and the Montecristo was but cold ashes, though its fading bouquet still hung in the air. I had gone through over a dozen letters.

Reading each one quickly was an increasingly difficult task as I was becoming more tired with each line. In addition, Maria Cialini's small script caused me to take longer to get through each letter than the previous one. Furthermore, Mrs. D'Angelo had also put in a few of her own letters, some never mailed and a few returned. Many started with *"Dear Sis"* and were difficult to discern from the letters from Maria. After a time, my eyes ached and I would have to stop, tilt my head back and massage them before continuing. I glanced over the notes I had jotted into my ledger and found them lacking. I had managed to scribble a few details of Maria's life. One day she made a trip to the beach. She spent a day in Golden Gate Park. She walked the length of the Golden Gate Bridge in the spring of 1951. Her neighbor's dog barked all night long. The information provided me with a myriad of glimpses into the mind and life of Maria Cialini, such that it humanized the twisted, black pruned body that currently resided in the University's morgue, in such a way that I actually considered taking up Mrs. D'Angelo's offer. Provided I should find her sister's killer. Like the pieces of information the autopsy provided, however, they were so far useless.

As a gesture to the ironies of life, I picked a letter from the bottom of the stack and glanced over it, as I felt that with the way things were going, the answers to this mystery were probably at the bottom of the stack. It was dated February, 1947. I read:

> *Dear Sis,*
>
> *Hope you are well...getting older is no joke...make sure you always know of a good OB/GYN you can go to...Dr. Hale gave me a pelvic exam.... Why do the men who do this for a living always seem to be so socially awkward?*

My eyes jolted open and I read it again, out loud. "Dr. Hale gave me a pelvic exam."

Dr. Hale, I thought. *Who was Dr. Hale?* Pelvic exam, I read again. He was probably an OB/GYN. I set the letter down and wrote the phrase into the ledger and set the letter aside.

"Dr. Hale, Dr. Hale, Dr. Hale," I said aloud, trying to jar my memory. Though the name was familiar, I could come up with nothing. I knew a Dr. Sally Hale when I was in med school, but she'd be too young to have been Maria's doctor back in 1947.

There was a Dr. Eric Hale. I remembered him from my first year as a doctor when we both worked in the same hospital. He was still alive and was nearing eighty now. He would have been old enough, but he was a thoracic surgeon.

Seizing upon an idea, I decided to search the Internet. I got up and went to my computer. There, under various search engines, I tried the words "Dr. Hale." What I got was a multitude of names and products and other miscellaneous nonsense that made me ponder the wisdom of the Internet and lament the passing of the industrialized age. I tried the words Dr. Hale + OB/GYN and got even more of nothing.

I decided to forgo technology and picked up the original Internet: the Yellow Pages. I found several Dr. Hales in the bay area. I returned to the letter and re-read it again, my mind more focused. This time, word for word and slowly. Then I went back to the Yellow Pages, where one name got my attention.

"My, my. The plot thickens!"

I called Donaldson. I knew it was late but needed to talk to him. A few rings and Donaldson picked up.

"Cal?" I asked.

"Yeah, Connor. What's up?" he asked groggily.

"You busy tomorrow afternoon?"

"What do you call a woman who's lost 90 percent of her intelligence?"

"What?"

"Divorced."

"Are you busy tomorrow?" I reiterated.

"Just work, why?"

"We have an appointment with a gynecologist."

15

I managed to get a few hours of much needed sleep before heading off to a 10:00 AM class. I taught one class that morning before finishing at 10:55. I didn't have any regular classes on Saturday, but I had switched with another professor the day before. I had another to teach, but that wasn't until the afternoon. The third, I would teach on Monday. Despite my not being fully rested, I nevertheless noticed Ms. Rebecca Wood again paying an unusual amount of attention to me. I decided that my fifteen minutes must have been pushing into overtime. After class, I locked up my office and headed off to meet with Donaldson in the parking lot of one Dr. Martin Hale, OB/GYN.

11:27 AM

The Mission District is a working class area between Potrero Hill and Eureka Valley and is home to most of the city's Hispanic population. There are restaurants that cater to Chinese, Cuban and Salvadoran tastes. Previous immigrant waves included Jews and Irish. It is a rundown area where homeless can-collectors make their way through busy sidewalks and past mariachi bands. Murals reflected the local empathy with Central American revolutionary groups. The smells of marijuana, the thud of woofers and the occasional sound of gunfire puncture the air. Depending on how close one is to either; it can be hard to disseminate which one you heard. Mission Delores is the city's oldest structure, established in 1776. Many of the city's original settlers were buried there. In Delores Park, groups of Gays, tattoo and body-pierced slackers all convene. By day, the park is a place where games are played and dogs are walked. At night, the dealers come out. Day or night, however, it provides a great view of the city in general and of the bay, in particular. The cheap rents attract artistic types. Locals are more likely to celebrate Cinco de Mayo and Carnival, than Memorial Day or the 4th of July.

The drive took about twenty minutes. The two-story, Queen Ann style, redbrick home stood out in the dilapidated neighborhood. It was by far the best kept home on the street. The wall that ran along its front was free of graffiti as if a gesture of respect for the home's resident and what he did. I pulled into the half-filled lot and drove until I saw Donaldson's car. He sat behind the wheel reading a newspaper.

I pulled alongside Donaldson, turned off the engine and exited.

Donaldson looked up and smiled. He folded the paper and set it aside. "What's up, babe?" he asked, stepping out.

"Not much. Find anything new?"

"Yeah, but more on that later. You sure about this guy?"

I nodded. "Take a look at this," I said, handing him the letter. "At first I thought the name was familiar. I wasn't certain until I called you."

Donaldson took the frayed yellow piece of paper and looked it over. He shook his head and handed it back. "You didn't get through all the letters, did you?"

"No. You?"

Donaldson laughed. "No. I've been swamped with everything else on this case. I'll get started on them tonight."

"Fine." I indicated toward the house before us. "Shall we?"

"All right. But, ah, let's proceed with caution."

I nodded. I didn't have to ask why. Dr. Martin Hale, OB/GYN was well known about San Francisco. A successful physician, he ran a series of clinics that offered free medical services and counseling, as well as housing, to pregnant teens and single mothers. Most of the clinics were two-family homes, whose second floors served as shelters for poor unwed mothers. Volunteers and former patients did most of the help in his clinics. Though his wealth wasn't a fraction of Michael Astor's, he was well-connected and well-respected.

The public record of the man was equally well known. Dr. Hale was a "Born-Again" Christian and one of the outspoken leading members of the city's Pro-life movement. Married for over fifty years, he had a loving wife; six or seven children and something like thirteen grandchildren. He helped organize and made appearances at Pro-life rallies about the city. He was respected by the Pro-choice movement for his tact and unwillingness to engage in shrill emotional debates and name-calling. These traits were characteristic of the fringe element of the movement and so often perceived as mainstream by the media. He was a man on a mission.

The house was originally a two-family home that had been turned into a practice. It suited the family image of the man and the movement of which he was so much a part.

We entered the house and stood in the foyer. The powder and baby oil smell of infants greeted us. The inside of the house had been completely renovated. Before us were two receptionists behind a long counter. One was a matronly frosted-blonde of about seventy. The other was barely twenty.

I looked about the room. Women, mostly young and their children, mostly infants, sat about in chairs or played on the floor respectively. Two televisions hung from the ceiling and played cartoons. Toys were strewn about the room. I felt oddly out of place, as I followed Donaldson's approach to the receptionists.

The young receptionist smiled. "May I help you, gentlemen?"

Donaldson discreetly leaned in over the counter. "We'd like to speak to Dr. Hale."

"He's busy with a patient. May I ask what this is about?"

Donaldson turned his palm over, showing her his badge. This got the attention of the older receptionist, the frosted blonde. "It's police business, ma'am. We just want to ask him a few questions."

The frosted-blonde stood up. "Why don't you follow me and I'll get him for you."

We followed her to Dr. Hale's office, where she left us. A minute later, she returned. "Dr. Hale will be with you in about ten minutes."

"Thank you," Donaldson said.

We took the time to glance about the room. It was a typical doctor's office. Diplomas and degrees hung behind a neat desk. Pictures of his wife, children, and grandchildren adorned the wall, along with pictures of marches on Washington. Pictures of other children and their mothers adorned a separate wall. I noticed that many of the pictures had cards next to them. I opened a card and read:

> *"Dr. Hale,*
> *Thank you for your guidance. We made the right choice.*
> *Lauren and Lauren."*

It was an impressive testament to his endeavors.

"That's the wall of hope," a somewhat nasally voice said from behind.

We turned to see a thin, short and slightly paunchy man in his mid-seventies. He was bald on top with hair only on the sides. He grew the side-hair extra long and combed it over in an attempt to hide the obvious. It looked ridiculous. He wore glasses and had a stethoscope about his neck. His lab coat was white and well-starched. "It inspires me to continue these successes," he said, indicating the wall. "I'm Dr. Hale. Sorry for the delay, but we're kept pretty busy here," he explained.

"Not a problem," Donaldson said. "We appreciate your time, Doctor."

We made our introductions.

He asked, "What can I do to help the police?"

"Do you recall a patient by the name of Maria Cialini?" Donaldson asked.

I watched, interested to see the reaction, if any.

"I'm sorry, I didn't hear that," he said. "Could you repeat that name?"

I felt that the question was clear enough. Nevertheless, Donaldson posed it again, slower.

"I can't say that I do. When was she a patient?" he asked, his face stoic.

As a man who had been trained to keep my emotional hand close, I immediately felt that my fellow practitioner's reaction was too calculated, as if rehearsed.

"We're not too sure," Donaldson admitted. He turned to me.

"October, 1946, or later," I said.

Dr. Hale laughed. "Gentlemen. My old head has trouble remembering last month. Let me see," he said, sitting back on his desk. "Can't say that I do."

I added, "You did a pelvic examination on her."

"That doesn't exactly narrow it down, Dr. Connor. I've done thousands of pelvic exams over the years. Many women back then used phony names - - - " He stopped suddenly. "Besides, why are you interested in a patient of mine from over half a century ago?"

"She was murdered," Donaldson said simply.

"I'm sorry to hear that, but what has that got to do with her being my patient in 1946?

He seemed genuinely confused, so I explained. "She was murdered sometime around late 1953 or early '54. Her remains were recently found in an apartment building."

"I see," Dr. Hale said, taking it in. "That would change things. How did she die?"

"A .22 caliber bullet to the head," Donaldson replied.

Dr. Hale shook his head. "Tragic."

"She was pregnant," I injected, handing him the photo.

"Twice the loss," he said simply as he accepted the photo. "This is she?"

"Yes."

He looked the photo over. "My God. I remember her!" He said this with a surprise that was less than genuine.

"What can you tell us about her?" Donaldson asked.

Dr. Hale ran a hand across his silly-looking hair. "It's been so long.... but it's coming back to me. She was a troubled woman."

"What makes you say that?" Donaldson inquired.

"She was a young, single, pregnant woman in post-war puritan America. That made her troubled, Inspector."

"She was pregnant when she was your patient," I confirmed.

"Why, yes," Dr. Hale continued. "It's not like today, gentlemen. Today we don't think twice about a young pregnant woman, but then," he shook his head. "It was a different country then."

"You don't sound enamored with the past," I noted.

"Why would I be?" Dr. Hale asked.

I shrugged. "Abortion was illegal back then."

"Doesn't mean there was no problem. Things were, in many ways, worse when there was no abortion."

Worse? This took me back a bit, as it was the last thing I expected to hear from a leader in the Pro-life movement.

"Don't get me wrong, gentleman. I am avowedly against abortion. But what most of my allies in the movement don't understand is that no law will get rid of abortion until we remove the reason many young woman seek abortion."

"And what is that?" I was interested in hearing this as I had long ago written off most of the Pro-life movement as pie-in-the-sky hypocrites. I was pleasantly surprised to meet a moderate.

"Lack of options," Dr. Hale said as if it were obvious. "Now I realize that there are women who truly don't want to continue a pregnancy and will seek abortion. But I truly believe that most women chose abortion as a quick solution to a very complex problem." He took a breath and I knew he was about to launch into a speech, a common failing amongst all true believers. "I remember well the days before abortion was legalized. You know what you had then?

Illegal abortions? I thought.

"Illegal abortions," he said calmly. "Opportunists and incompetent physicians plying their potions and lack of skills and ethics at the expense of the poor and misfortunate, while wealthy women had things 'taken care of' by their family physicians."

"What's the solution, as you see it?" Donaldson asked.

"I believe that the solution to abortion is to provide options to young women so that they will chose to continue their pregnancies. That's part of what we do here," he said. "Support groups for single mothers who have nobody to confide in. We offer a place to stay for those who can't go home. Job training for the unskilled." He got off his desk. "Too many pro-life people love to march and sing about God and that's fine. But many of them, I'm afraid, would cross the street if they so much as saw a single mother."

"You sound pretty moderate," I observed.

"It's a complex problem, my friend. Too many people think a constitutional amendment will make everything all better but it won't. It didn't before." He folded his arms across his narrow chest. "If people want to end abortion, we will have to change the environment that single mothers find themselves in. And to do that," he said, "we'll have to change ourselves."

"Hmmm," I hadn't really thought about it.

"Dr. Hale," Donaldson said, "this case we're working on has been fairly well-publicized. You didn't hear about it? The closet lady?"

"No."

"We were on TV," I added.

Dr. Hale smiled. "Gentlemen, my work allows me little free-time. Besides, I don't watch TV. I find it filled with the very values that encourage young people to seek self-gratification as opposed to self-fulfillment." He paused before continuing. "I'm sure you don't want to hear my opinions on the Pro-life issue. You want to know about a patient of mine, Maria Cialini."

"That's correct," Donaldson said before adding, "The best thing for us is to check your records."

Dr. Hale squinted as if pinched. "Showing you my patients' records would be a violation of doctor - patient confidentiality."

Donaldson shrugged. "Sir, we could get a warrant and be back by the end of the day."

"If we did that," I interjected, "we'd have to make phone calls to the Judge and put in an appearance in court. Problem with that is that people can overhear what we want and what we want it for."

Donaldson saw where I was pushing and decided to take control of it before I pushed it too far. "Dr. Hale, I believe in conducting as fair and discreet an investigation as possible. But I *will* conduct it. Now if you want, we'll get the warrant, but I can't guarantee that it will stay quiet. That's not a threat; it's just to let you know that the press or anyone can get hold of this information once we start going through formal channels."

"I'll get the records, gentlemen."

16

It took nearly twenty minutes for Dr. Hale and the older receptionist to find the medical records. They weren't with the "active patients," so they had to go upstairs and search the file cabinets of "former patients." Donaldson and I sat about in the office, waiting impatiently.

Dr. Hale returned with the file. "Got it," he announced. "I was worried that she might have used a different name. If she had done that, we might never have found it." He took a position behind his desk and flipped through it. "You were right, Dr. Connor. I performed a pelvic exam on Miss Cialini in February, 1947."

"What else have you got?" Donaldson asked.

"Blood tests. The usual." Dr. Hale flipped through his paperwork. "I saw her several times starting in December, 1946." He stopped. "Hmmm. Now I remember," he said.

"What?" I asked.

"Here we are," he said as he folded over a page. "Miss Cialini had a miscarriage in October, 1947. On the fifteenth."

1947? Donaldson and I looked at one another.

"1947?" I asked.

"Yes," Dr. Hale said. "Why?"

That was six years before she disappeared.

I didn't want to give anything away, but this caught me unexpectedly. Maria Cialini was pregnant and miscarried some six or so years before she was murdered. When Dr. Hale said that she had been pregnant when he saw her, I assumed he meant the pregnancy that had occurred around the time of her death, but no. I now realized that there had been two pregnancies. This only increased the motive, I figured, as she had been pregnant when she worked for Michael Astor IV. Astor said she had stopped working for him a few years before she died, which lessened the likelihood of his involvement, but now I knew that she was pregnant while in his employment. I didn't know what to make of it, but it in my mind, it added up to motive.

I asked, "How far along was she when she miscarried?"

Dr. Hale consulted his notes. "Ten to twelve weeks," he read. "Almost three months."

Damnit! Astor will say that he hadn't noticed her pregnancy. It was plausibly deniable. "Is there anything in there about the father?" I asked, though I knew there wouldn't be.

Dr. Hale shook his head. "No. I made it a point in my practice that when a woman left personal information blank, to respect their privacy."

"When was the last time you saw her?" Donaldson asked.

Dr. Hale consulted his notes again. "October, 1951."

"And you didn't see her after that?" Donaldson asked professionally.

He shook his head. "No."

"She just stopped coming?"

"Yes."

I was frustrated. Astor had said she stopped working for him a few years before her death. Dr. Hale now said similar. It put both men clear of the time when she had disappeared. "You didn't find that odd?"

Dr. Hale paused a moment. "Like I said, Dr. Connor, it was a different time." He said this, clearly annoyed by my tone. "Many single women came and went. Frankly, many single, pregnant women simply never came back. I have an entire drawer of my filing cabinet devoted to such missing patients." He handed the report to me. "See for yourself."

I flipped through the papers. "How many months was she pregnant when she died?" I asked.

Dr. Hale was put off by the implications. "I just told you I hadn't seen her since 1951. I wouldn't have known that she was pregnant in late '53 or early '54, Dr. Connor."

I continued. "Did you ever give her a book on birth control?"

Dr. Hale thought for a moment. "No, I don't believe so."

I pushed further. "You sure?"

"Easy, Declan," Donaldson said.

Dr. Hale was about to say something when he seemed to get thrown. "Declan Connor? You're Declan Connor?" he asked.

"Yes, why?"

Dr. Hale's jaw twitched. "You're Declan Connor's son," he said again.

"That's right," I replied.

Dr. Hale's brown eyes tightened and he looked away a moment. He took a breath.

"Is there a problem, sir?" Donaldson asked.

"No. No," he said and then smiled weakly. "I knew your father," he explained simply.

"I'm sorry," I said. "I don't recall him mentioning you."

Dr. Hale shook his head. "We were never social. But we had mutual friends and we spoke on occasion."

I nodded.

"He worked at, ah, San Francisco General." Dr. Hale smiled a bit stronger.

"Actually, it was Mt. Zion," I corrected.

Dr. Hale nodded. "Oh, yes. Forgive me. I remember now." He laughed nervously. "My old head."

There was a pause for a moment or two.

"I'd like a copy of those records if I could," Donaldson said to fill the void.

Dr. Hale nodded. "I'll make you a copy. I wouldn't want you or Dr. Connor accidentally leaking my name to the press. This cause of mine is too controversial as is without my practice and myself becoming involved in a murder investigation. Lord knows, there are too many distractions as is."

I said nothing.

Dr. Hale walked to the copier and put the reports into the machine. He put them in one at a time as opposed to feeding them in through the sorter, as he didn't want to tear them, I suppose. His back was to us. Or maybe he didn't want to look at us. He wiped his forehead with his sleeve and seemed to bow his head slightly. When he was finished, he set the originals back into the file. He realigned them as they were and even used the original staple, folding the two ends back down. I figured that he was either very precise or he was playing for time.

"You're sure you never gave Miss Cialini a book on birth control?" I asked.

"Of course I'm sure!" he said immediately. "I don't believe in birth control. Ask my six kids," he smiled and handed the copies to Donaldson. "You do know, gentlemen, that I could easily have said that she must have changed her name. If I had done that, you wouldn't be able to get the file, even with your search warrant. Please consider that as you investigate."

"True," I admitted. "But the publicity would be greater if the files were missing. Don't you think?"

"Maybe," Dr. Hale conceded.

"Oh, I guarantee it," Donaldson said.

With our business complete, the two of us stood and went to the door. Dr. Hale held it open.

"I'm curious, Doctor," I asked as I passed. "What made you born again?"

"I saw the truth," he said without hesitation.

Outside, when we had made it back to our cars, Donaldson turned to me and asked, "What do you think?"

I replied, "There's an additional pregnancy here."

"You mean a miscarriage," Donaldson corrected.

"So he said."

Donaldson considered this. "What was that about a birth control book?"

"Maria Cialini sent her sister a book on birth control. It was in the box she gave me."

"It doesn't mean that Hale gave it to her. Or that she read it. After all, there were two pregnancies," Donaldson said.

"True," I said and then asked, "What now?"

"Well, I got an address on that super's daughter."

"The super who ran the building in Pacific Heights where Maria Cialini lived?" I asked, though I was clearly distracted.

"Yeah. The daughter got married and is now named Groden. She and her husband live over on Russian Hill."

I nodded, my mind still in Dr. Hale's office. "That's good."

"Yeah. My guy got in touch with her this morning. She said I could come over this afternoon. Just phone before I drop in. Want to come along?"

"Absolutely."

"You have any classes?"

"Yes, I have an afternoon class from two to three."

"That's O.K. I don't plan to go over there much before four. I also got a package hand-delivered from Mr. Clarke this morning. It contained Maria Cialini's employment records and work reports."

"Oh, Anything new?"

"Too early to tell. They confirm that Maria Cialini worked there when Astor said she did. He also gave me the rent records for the apartment that she was buried in."

"Hmmm."

"Yeah. There was nobody renting it in October of '53. But the first week of November, '53, one Tony Frazier rented the place. He kept the apartment until February of 1954. The next person to rent the apartment was Loretta Goldstein. She stayed there for four years. She died of natural causes back in '83. So, I ran a check on Tony Frazier. Y'know, criminal record, social security number."

"And?"

"And nothing. The social security number was a fake. No forwarding address. I can find nothing on him."

"False name?" I said.

"I figure."

I perked up a bit. "So we got the alias of the guy who killed her?"

101

"Or the guy who *buried* her," Donaldson corrected.

I considered this. "He was there just long enough to bury her and remodel."

"Yes," Donaldson admitted.

I don't suppose anybody there saw him?"

Donaldson laughed.

"All right, all right. How about the super?"

"Dead in '64. No next of kin."

"Anything else?"

"The rest concerns her work, progress and raises," Donaldson said.

"How about friends?"

"None that I could find. There were several co-workers, but they're either all dead or were women. And that's the problem."

"Why?"

"Because none of them currently work for Astor. They left years ago. Most got married and the records don't show what their married names were. Of the four that didn't get married, three are dead. Don't know where the others are. So it's going to be slow."

"And the rest?"

"Living out of state." He shook his head. "Like I said, it's going to be slow."

"How's the hotline working?"

"Friggin joke. I have three guys working on it. Sifting through the BS. We're making more progress here on our own. What I'm going to do is drop by later and collect what they've got."

"You know, these records mean very little," I said, indicating the file in my friend's hand.

"How so?"

"I mean there could be more and he's got them hidden. Or he could have two sets of records. Just because he was willing to dig into his files and show us these tidbits doesn't mean that he's shown us everything, or anything."

"Why do think he would do that?"

"To dis-inform us."

Donaldson was impressed. "Why not just lie and say that he didn't know her?"

I shrugged. "Maybe he knew we'd find out he was her doctor. I mean we walked in off the street so he probably realized that we must have something. Maybe he did see the story on TV and was prepared. So instead of lying up front and alerting us to the fact that he lied, he digs up some incomplete records and diverts us from the truth."

"And what would that be?"

"Your guess is as good as mine," I said simply. "Maybe he had those records set up in case anybody ever came around asking. He says she was pregnant in 1947 and miscarried. Maybe she did."

Donaldson was unconvinced. "For him to have falsified those records all those years ago, that'd have to be the greatest example of foresight ever."

"Yes," I agreed. "But you remember what I said earlier?"

Donaldson nodded. "The killer has had almost half a century to prepare an alibi."

I opened the door to my car and then stopped. "Oh, yeah, one other thing."

"What's that?"

"He seemed pretty shaken up."

Donaldson shrugged. "So, he knew your old man and then he realized that you were his son. Time catches old people off guard."

I shook my head. "My father worked in St. Mary's, not Mt. Zion."

"Old people. They make mistakes."

"He didn't know my father." I said. "This guy is lying about something."

David Feeney

17

SFCU: 3:11 PM

I returned to teach a two o'clock class. Due to its considerable size, the class was taught in a lecture hall, and was required for all under-grads, which helped to account for the large attendance. Faces, some curious, some empty, and some arrogant, stared down at me. Some took notes; others flipped through their books too quickly to be reading. Once again I found myself the center of unwanted attention. To my surprise and discomfort, Ms. Wood was in the class. She sat in the center of the hall. She smiled at me when I saw her. _Watch it, buddy._ I felt a slight flush come over me but figured I was too far away for anyone to notice. At least that's what I hoped.

When class was over and everybody was filing out, Ms. Wood commented on my television appearance. I shrugged it off with simple thanks and said something to the effect that the directors must have used a special lens or special effects and she shouldn't be watching TV on a school night and that she should be in bed. This last comment I immediately realized was a mistake. She laughed at my discomfort, realizing my faux pas and said she got to bed early and often enough. Fifteen minutes had never seemed so long.

I returned to my office and shut the door. I felt as if I were being pursued. It was worse than high school. I spent some time, actually a lot - nearly forty-minutes putting away my things and straightening up, in part, as Donaldson and I weren't due at Sarah Grodin's until about five. But also, because I wanted to be sure that Ms. Wood wouldn't be in the hall when I left. When I felt that the coast was clear, I headed over to see Donaldson.

104

4:10 PM

I arrived at the stationhouse and went inside. I found Donaldson on the second floor conferring on the phone. He saw me approach and raised a hand to wait a second. "Can I call you back in an hour or so?" he asked. "Fine, bye." He put the phone down.

"A lead?" I asked.

"I hope not," Donaldson replied.

"I don't understand."

Donaldson put on his trench coat and picked up his fedora. "I'll know more later."

4:57 PM

Russian Hill lay north of Nob hill and east of Pacific Heights. The first settlers to the area had been Russian hunters and trappers who sailed south from Fort Ross so they could trade with the Ohlone Indians and the Spanish. Black crosses with Russian inscriptions marked the graves of those settlers buried in the local cemetery. As in the case of Nob hill, the cable car had allowed people to build their country houses and cottages higher. The hill had been something of a sanctuary for writers like Mark Twain and Jack London. Even Jack Kerouac was known to come up out of North Beach to do a bit of work. The streets were mostly quiet, and with plenty of stairways carved out of the landscape, one could avail of plenty of exercise.

We took Donaldson's car and found Sarah Grodin's home right off Valpariso Street. Sarah Grodin's father had been the superintendant at the last known address for Maria Cialini. Sarah had done well for herself, I thought, as I looked the house over. It was a classical two-story Georgian home: slanted roof, and a fireplace at both ends with red brick that contrasted nicely with the white quoins at the four-corners. A white columned entrance and crown molding greeted visitors. The lawn was well kept, though not professionally, I reasoned, and had a variety of shrubs and trees arranged about the modest grounds.

Donaldson drove into the two-car driveway. We exited and made our way up the white steps. Donaldson rang the bell. The door opened and Sarah Grodin met us. Petite and dumpy with her gray hair in a bun, she was the quintessential grandmother. She invited us in immediately.

The house was as impressive inside, as it had been out. The rooms on the first floor were spacious and well lit. Plants hung in otherwise empty spaces and contained an abundance of colors that kept monotony from creeping in. There was little clutter anywhere, prompting me to wonder whether Mrs. Grodin practiced Feng Shui. She led us into a large living room that took up nearly one quarter of the first floor. Like the rest of the house it smelled fresh and floral. She offered us some fresh chocolate chip cookies that she had just baked and milk. Donaldson readily accepted, as he never turned down a snack. "Have a seat, and make yourselves at home," she said as she went to get the cookies.

I noticed the pictures of Sarah's kids, two boys and a girl. I glanced about at the other photos. They were what one would expect: baby pictures, school pictures, birthday pictures and the like. There were pictures of the kids as teenagers that looked as if they had been taken in the mid-seventies. Unless, of course, things had changed and boys and girls still wore clothes like that. There were pictures of grandchildren as well.

Donaldson sat in a large upholstered chair and I sat on the matching couch. The furniture was covered in plastic and made embarrassing noises as we sat. Mrs. Grodin returned tray in hand, with a glass of milk for each of us, and set it on the coffee table. She sat opposite us.

With everybody seated and comfortable, Sarah Grodin began. "Where should I start, Inspector?" she asked, wiping her hands onto her apron.

"We'd appreciate if you could start by telling us everything you remember about Maria Cialini."

She shook her head, stiffening her mouth grimly. "I haven't heard or mentioned that name in quite some time. I saw the news on TV but didn't think anything of it. When you called me," she drew a breath; "I got quite a start."

"I'm sorry about that," Donaldson consoled.

She raised a hand. "Quite all right. I've been going over it all in my mind. Where do I start? Maria Cialini, my gosh." She thought for a moment before continuing. "She was very pretty. I remember that because I was, oh about thirteen or so when she moved into our building and I was just starting to experiment with makeup. Maria used to give me tips. Y'know don't wear so much, how to avoid clumping the eye shadow. I must have been a sight." She smiled. "Me and my friends used to look up to her. I would wait for her to come home in the evening. My window was facing her apartment in the back and I would hear her when she came in. She had so many boyfriends." Sarah shook her head.

I dunked a cookie and took a bite. Betty Crocker had nothing on Mrs. Grodin.

"She used to bring men around?" Donaldson re-stated.

Sarah nodded. "Oh, yes. All good looking boys."

"Do you recall any of them in particular?" Donaldson continued.

She folded her hands and then wrung them on her apron, her anxiety evident. "No. At the time I remember thinking that it must be great to have so many boyfriends, but later I thought that she must have been lonely. Then one day, she didn't come around."

"That would have been around August, 1953 - or later?" Donaldson ventured.

"Oh, my. I almost forgot!" she said. "I'll be back in a moment."

Mrs. Grodin got up and left. She returned a few minutes later, a small light-blue book in her hand. "November 13th, 1953," she announced. "That's the day she disappeared."

"How can you be so sure, ma'am?" Donaldson asked.

"She was supposed to teach me how to use lipstick." Sarah indicated the book. "It's in my diary here." She opened it and read. "Dear diary, Maria didn't show me how to use lipstick today. She didn't come home at all."

Neither Donaldson nor I said anything.

"The rent card was turned in on the 25th of November." Sarah Grodin looked up, her face very serious. "A few weeks went by and I didn't see her," she said, remembering. "I would wait by the window half the night but she didn't come around. I told my father and mother." She lapsed into silence.

I asked, "They didn't report it?"

She shook her head. "My father said not to worry about it as she had spent days away in the past. He said that she was probably with someone's husband. About a week later, I was at my window. It was late and I heard movement outside so I took a look. There was a man going into her apartment."

This gained both of our attention. We shifted a bit in our seats, making the embarrassing sound simultaneously.

Sarah Grodin continued, "He appeared to have the keys. He was in there about an hour or so. He left carrying two suitcases."

Donaldson shook his head in realization. "What night was that?"

She flipped through her diary. "The 18th of November." She looked up and thought for a moment. "He made two more trips, maybe three and that was it. He was taking things out with each trip. He locked up the apartment and I never saw him or Maria again. On the 25th, my mother found the key and a note in our mailbox saying that she had left."

"Why did you do this?" Donaldson asked. "Take all these notes?"

"She was my friend," Sarah said simply, and then added, "It struck me as strange."

"Why didn't anybody call the police?" Donaldson pressed. "Didn't they notice this guy going in and out?"

"Her apartment was in the back of the building," She explained. "It was a basement apartment. There was only two apartments back there. You reached it by going around the building from the outside, not inside, so there wasn't any reason for anyone to be there, much less notice."

"I see," Donaldson said, and then asked, "I know this a silly question, but I have to ask; do you have the note?"

She shook her head. "No, I remember it, though. It was typed."

Typed? That's odd, I thought.

Donaldson obviously thought so, too. "Do you know what became of the note?"

She shook her head. "No."

Donaldson continued, "Her family reported her missing a few months later. According to the police report, she had *turned in* her key and left before the month was up. They didn't mention anything about the key being dropped into the mailbox."

Sarah shrugged. "My father was old-fashioned, even by the standards of the day. He didn't like the idea of single women having men in their apartments."

Donaldson smiled.

"More milk, Dr. Connor?" she asked.

"Oh no, I'm fine thanks."

She began again. "I remember the police coming around, asking questions about her. Did we see anything suspicious? Did she hand the key in herself? My father told them that she turned the key in one morning and left. I'd told him what I'd seen, but he sent me to go to my room. My mother was worried, but my father - - -." She bit her trembling lower lip. "He didn't like her. He said, 'People get what they deserve.'" Tears welled in her eyes and she wiped a hand across them. "She was so independent. She wasn't like other women. She was different, strong. I often wondered if my father disliked her because she had so many men or because she was independent, so strong. I think a lot of men resent women like that. Do you know what I mean?"

"I have a good idea," Donaldson admitted.

"I knew something bad had happened to her. But my parents, they said to just forget about it. Forget about *her*." She began to cry. "I stopped thinking about her," she said and then sniffled.

"Don't worry about it. You were just a kid," Donaldson said in an effort to calm her. "You have no idea how much you've helped us."

Sarah Grodin smiled and then remembered. "Wait one moment," she said and flipped through her diary. "A man came by asking about her." She said. "No, make that two men - - at two different times."

Two men came by? Who the hell were they?

"That was on...." She kept flipping. "The 26th."

"Of November?" Donaldson asked.

"No, no. January, 1954," she replied. "That was the first one. The other came on the 3rd of February."

"The man you saw empty the apartment." I said. "Was he the same as any of the others that visited?"

"I don't know."

"Did you get a look at him? Was he fat, bald, tall?"

She shook her head. "I don't know. I wasn't home when the man came by in January or the one in February. I heard my mother mention it to my father afterwards," she explained. "The man who emptied her apartment, I only saw him from behind. He wore a hat, y'know, a little cap, so I don't know if he was bald or not. I would duck down when he came out because I was afraid to be caught spying so I never saw his face. He wore a flowing trench coat. He looked heavy; I mean big. But I was so young, all men looked big. I'm sorry," she said unhappily.

"It's all right dear," Donaldson soothed.

Damn. It could be the same man, three times, or three seperate men. Each led to multiple scenarios; too many to ponder here. *Could there have been three men?*

"Oh, my god!" she suddenly exclaimed.

"What?" I asked.

"The man, who emptied the apartment," she began. "He, he, he's the one? He killed her?" She looked at each of us in turn.

"We don't know," Donaldson said.

"My god!" she repeated, her face frightened and lost. Several moments later, she regained focus. "Would you like some more cookies?"

Business concluded shortly after. We had our fill of information and cookies. Donaldson thanked her for her time and we said our goodbyes.

"Inspector," Sarah Grodin said. "Please let me know when you solve this case. I won't be able to stop thinking about her. Not this time."

"I will," Donaldson promised.

6:00 PM

We walked back to the car in silence. Sarah Grodin had given Donaldson the diary and he promised to return it once he read it and further promised, with a wink, not to read about her various crushes on the neighborhood boys. We waved to Mrs. Grodin, who stood in the door. Neither of us said a word until we had driven around the block, as we didn't want to say anything she might hear.

"Ho-ly shit!" Donaldson muttered.

I said, "He cleaned the place out."

"Yeah," Donaldson said simply.

"He cleaned the place out and turned the key in and nobody gave a damn."

"Sarah did," Donaldson corrected.

"Now we know why the police never declared her a missing person. They figured that she just left." Little things were starting to fall into place.

Donaldson nodded. "Yes. Then the killer got rid of all her stuff. Made sure there'd be no proof of her being missing. Erased her."

"And what to make of the guys who came around asking for her? Is it the same guy, three times, or three separate guys?"

"I don't know," Donaldson said. "It could be that two other men were looking for her, independantly of the man that cleaned out her place, or they may have been working together. However many it was, it strengthens the argument that one of our two killed her."

"I'm worried," I said.

"About?"

"The diary. How sure can we be she entered the information on the right days? I mean she was just a child."

Donaldson laughed. "She was a fourteen year-old *girl*. My eldest kept a diary when she was about that age. Let me tell you, young girls are meticulous about those things. It's like the minutes of a Congressional hearing. Don't worry, Declan, that diary's accurate."

We drove on a bit in silence. Then Donaldson picked up. "Oh yeah, another thing. I got a look at the police report that Mrs. D'Angelo spoke about."

"Did it tell you anything?"

"Nah. The investigating officers are both dead," he informed, and then added, "of old age. So we won't be asking them anything about what their thoughts were. The report was pretty basic. It said she was reported missing by her family. There was a bit about her handing in the key and leaving. That was all."

"Yeah, but that wasn't all."

Donaldson shook his head. "I'm more disappointed than angry. We can play Monday morning quarterback and say that the police should have done more, but the friggin super said she turned in the key, so as far as they were concerned, that was it."

I exhaled. "Then he took her over to Nob Gardens, wrapped in a carpet, and put her in the wall. I'd sure like to know how he transported her."

We were both quiet, lost in our own thoughts.

After a while, Donaldson shook his head, as if remembering. He dialed his cell-phone, while I held the wheel. He spoke briefly on the phone before saying, "You're sure? No. No names. All right, keep it to yourself. Thanks."

"What was that about?"

"I didn't want my guy mentioning names over the cellular, in case somebody in the press out there is monitoring with a scanner. They do that you know."

"Is it about that lead?"

Donaldson nodded. "I'd just as soon not get into it, buddy. I'm hoping that it turns out to be nothing. If that's the case, I don't want anybody knowing about this lead."

I had known Donaldson long enough to realize that he had seldom given a damn about where a lead might take him or whom it might implicate. But this was different and I would respect his whishes. "Sure."

"We know where she worked up until over a year before she died." Donaldson changed the subject. "I'd like to know where, if anywhere, she was working at the time of her death."

"Good one," I noted. "I hadn't thought about that."

6:15 PM

The sun was just starting to set as we reached the parking lot of the police station.

I said, "Just let me off here."

Donaldson pulled over and stopped. "I'm going to run down that lead and get back to you on it, probably tonight. Where you going to be?"

"I'll be at the school for a while, maybe an hour. Then I'm going to head home."

"All right, babe," Donaldson said. "I'll call you."

I nodded, shut the door and gave the roof two raps. Donaldson drove off.

18

6:20 PM

I had returned to the University, as I wanted to check to see if there were any messages for me. I also wanted to see if any of the tests from the labs had returned. All that was left now were the DNA and hair analysis, not that I expected either to show anything unusual. It was just that I was a man of procedure and liked to keep my paperwork in order and properly filed.

Night classes were in session and a few students walked about the campus. I entered the medical building and went to my office. There, I checked the inbox that hung off my door and found the new batch of flyers that I had asked to be printed. These were different from the originals as they showed Maria Cialini in both profiles as well as a front shot. Now that I knew who she was, though, I questioned their validity and considered having the flyers reprinted again, this time with her name and last known address. By distributing flyers about the city with her name, they could possibly jar faded memories and lead to new witnesses who knew her. Whether or not we would put these flyers out would no doubt be a matter of debate, as we already knew who she was, and also, because the police were still receiving a multitude of dead-ends. I was unsure whether this latest tactic would do more help or harm; I'd have to talk to Donaldson about it. For now, though, I left them in my inbox. I also briefly thought about whether I should contact the station that had shot the special and tell them we had the dead woman's identity so they could run a follow-up. However, since I wasn't in any hurry to be on TV again, I put that idea on the back burner.

Downstairs, I looked around the student lounge. There I saw Bud Parkins, half-asleep on a couch. He was an undergraduate who had watched the desk that afternoon. Bud worked the afternoon shift, answering the phones and taking messages. He would take the log with him at night and drop it back at the facility in the morning. I didn't mind as Bud lived on campus. He was a good kid, who could be trusted to keep his mouth shut about the mummy. The morgue was open only half a day on weekends and was now officially closed. I'd gone down there to find out if there had been any calls for me.

"Good evening, Dr. Connor. How you doing?" Bud Parkins asked groggily as I approached.

"Not bad. Any phone calls for me?"

He straightened up. "Let me see." He dug through his knapsack, searching for the ledger he used to record messages for the staff. "I think there was something for you." He flipped through the ledger. "It was a busy day," he explained.

I waited patiently as Bud continued to flip.

"Yeah, there was one," he said, handing it to me.

I took the note but handed it back. "I can't read these hieroglyphics."

"Sorry," he said sheepishly as he looked it over.

I watched him as he read over his own notes silently a moment before asking, "Can *you* read it?"

He smiled. "Ah, yes. It was a call; I remember taking it."

"Man or woman?"

"A woman," he said before correcting. "No, I think it was a man. Burt E, or Burt. Maybe Berty."

"Burt E," I repeated. "A woman named Burt?"

"It was either a man or a woman."

"I figured that. What did Burt E have to say?"

"He said, 'I knew her.'"

I folded my arms across my chest. *I knew her?* There was little need for interpretation as to what that could mean. With my luck, however, it was probably a crank.

Parkins kept reading. "And for you to meet him tomorrow at Golden Gate Park at 11:00 AM, south bridge at Stow Lake."

"That's it? How am I supposed to - - -?"

"'I'll find you,' he said. That was the last bit."

"That's all?"

"Yes."

"You're sure that's it?" I prodded.

"Yes. Sorry, but it was busy. I was answering two phones because Mrs. Littleton wasn't in and I was trying to - - -"

"All right, don't worry. 11:00 AM at Golden Gate Park, south entrance to Stow Lake."

"Yes," Parkins replied. "Frankly, Doctor, I think it was a kook."

"What makes you say that?" I asked.

"He sounded drunk, you know, slurred speech."

I considered this. "Good job, Bud. Get some sleep."

"Have a good one, Doctor." He lay back on the couch.

I took the elevator down to the morgue, using my keys as the facility had been closed since six. *I knew her.* I went over the statement again in my mind. I assumed it meant that someone had known Maria Cialini, but I didn't want to hope too much. *Why didn't the caller just call the police?* I wondered. *Why call me?* Price of fame, I figured.

The elevator "Binged," announcing my arrival and I stepped off. The smell of disinfectant was strong. Today was a cleaning day. My heels echoed as I made my way down the long hall into a pastel-colored conference room that was used by the staff for the review of lab tests. I was neither superstitious nor apprehensive about going down into the morgue at night. I shivered slightly, though I figured that was due to the change in temperature. I rubbed my arms.

I took a look around, half hoping to find Dr. Geist or one of the dieners doing some work. Some Assistants and graduate students were assigned keys so that they could come in after hours and catch up on their work. I had given Dr. Geist a set of keys as he still had some work to do, but there was nobody around. It was a Saturday; even doctors looked forward to the weekend so I turned the light off.

I exited the conference room and was about to go back towards the elevator when I noticed a light on further down the hall. I thought it odd that I hadn't noticed it when I first came in but admitted to myself that I hadn't really been paying attention.

I walked down the darkened hall unconcerned, as I figured that one of the students had forgotten to turn it off when he or she had left. I was a stickler for little things like turning out lights as they added up to budget dollars that could be better spent elsewhere.

I came to the door, from which the light bled through and took a look in. Autopsy room #2 was a room in which bodies could be stored and autopsies performed. Originally an autopsy room, there had been a mix-up with the builders who subsequently installed a row of wall-mounted refrigeration units. Once the mistake had been realized, it was decided that it would be too expensive to remove the autopsy table so it was agreed to simply keep it as it was. Beyond it was a changing room used by doctors and students. It was from the changing room that the light actually was emanating now - a cold light that cut through the otherwise unlit room.

I entered the semi-darkened room and walked toward the light. Behind me the door swung shut. I knew the layout of the room well enough to know where I was. To my right was a ceramic counter with a stainless-steel, wall-mounted sink station. On my left was a row of wall-mounted refrigerators where bodies could

114

be kept. Just off the room's center was an autopsy table. Next to it was a portable dissection table with a bucket. I pushed in the door to the changing room and took a look inside. Nobody was there so I switched the light off, turned and took a step.

Something smashed into me, lifting me off the ground and throwing me against the wall. I stood shakily and it took me a moment to realize that I hadn't slipped. I realized that I wasn't alone in the room. My night vision was ruined as I had just come from a lighted room and couldn't see six inches. But I could hear someone moving.

Something pressed against my forehead, something cold and metallic. Instinctively, I turned my head and seized at the source of the metal object. An explosion echoed in the small room, then another. I squinted from the flash of light that accompanied the blasts and could feel the discharge push my hair about. My eyes burned.

Sonofabitch! I realized. *He's got a gun!* I struck forward with my fingers and they found something soft. I had handled enough of them over the years to know that I had found an eye.

My attacker grunted and I heard something hit the ground. I realized it was the gun and would have gone for it had I been able to see.

A fist struck me in the face. I raised my hands to defend myself only to be hit in the stomach. The blow was powerful and I doubled over, once again winded and unable to so much as cough.

Hands clamped about my throat. Strong, big-gloved hands that lifted me and drove me head-first into the freezers. My head screamed numb-madness as I fought to get my bearings. I was hurt, blinded. A tremendous disadvantaged against my attacker. Hands tightened about my throat again. I had been a doctor long enough to realize that it took as little as nine seconds or thereabouts to render a man unconscious and I would have to do something quickly before it was too late.

Even with that thought, I felt dizzy, as if there were bubbles in my head. I flayed at the leather-bound hands, surprised at the size of them, painfully aware that I was weakening. I kicked feebly but to no avail.

My attacker leaned in close, his smokey breath hot on my face. "Shouldn't go looking in closets, Dr. Connor!" he hissed. "Some doors were meant to stay closed!"

He might have said something else, but I couldn't tell. I was beginning to see spots. The bubbles in my head were rapidly multiplying. I was losing consciousness.

I reached out to my side, my hand searching weakly as if it knew something my mind had forgotten. It found a metal latch, cool to the touch, and pulled on it. I heard a sound of compressed air and memory told me that I had found the handle to one of the wall-mounted refrigerators. I swung the door out and away.

The door's sudden stop and the accompanying "crunch" told me that I had a chance.

My attacker grunted and loosened his grip somewhat as I swung the door again and again into his face.

"Bastard! Little fuck!" he screamed.

The powerful hands released me and I dropped to the ground, gasping. The impact with the hard, cool floor revived me a bit. Too weak to stand and in no shape to fight, I pulled myself along the floor and away from my aggressor, whom I could hear behind me stumbling about and cursing.

I got to my knees weakly and stood, rubbing circulation back into my neck. The bubbles in my head drifted upwards. My vision had adjusted and I could see the semi-darkened room a bit better. My attacker was a large man, over six-feet tall. He wore a ski mask. I realized that I was alongside the autopsy table so I used it to steady myself as I stood. I exhaled, keeping one hand on the table. I wasn't sure if I had the coordination to make a run for it, and was afraid that movement would attract my attacker.

As it was, my attacker knew my location. I saw him now close the distance between us with a growl. I managed to get my hands up in time to block a punch to my face. Instead, I took it on my left wrist that immediately went numb.

Angry, I threw a few jabs at my attacker's face and landed at least one.

A sudden push caught me off-guard and knocked me backwards, over the table. Trays full of autopsy implements spilled to the floor where they clattered like kitchen cutlery. Their noise cut through my foggy mind and helped me to focus. I grabbed a tray and flung it at my attacker's head, hitting him dead-on.

I stood shakily to see the man come around the table. I ran, as best I could, around the table in the other direction. I bumped into the dissecting table and it rolled a bit. My attacker took a swing at me but was unable to connect with the table separating us. He ran around the table again. I followed suit and we were back where we had started. The comedic aspect of this violent incident wasn't lost upon me.

The two of us paused a moment to catch our breath and evaluate the situation.

"You're dead," he said and jumped over the table, trying to seize me by the arm, but missed, and crashed to the floor.

I grabbed the small hose that ran alongside the autopsy table and sprayed the floor between us. My attacker stood and I sprayed him in the face and kicked him in the shin.

He slipped on the tile, pitching forward. I slipped, too, but managed to grab onto the end of the table. I didn't go down.

I swung the table on its axis and smashed my attacker on the head with the far end. I staggered back a few steps as he tried to get to his feet.

I couldn't help but say it. "It seems that the table has turned."

I bumped into the dissection table and seized the bucket. I flung it at my attacker. It caught him in the face. Through the ski-mask I could see one of his eyes. The rage it held chilled me to the bone.

"What the fuck do you want?" I asked in a raspy voice.

My attacker said nothing but stood up and I could see that his ski-mask was now soaked in blood. He closed the distance between us. A glint of light in the dim enclosure caught my attention. I looked closely and realized what it was. I moved quickly and dove, sliding across the floor as my attacker rushed me.

I picked up a twelve-inch bread-knife, a standard tool of my trade.

He was onto me.

I rose and swung.

The surgical steel instrument, designed to slice through dead tissue, caught my attacker's raised hand and cut deep. I knew I had severed nerves. He pulled back, grabbing his hand and turned away shrieking.

I made a dash for the door, ran straight into the dissecting table and fell into the hall outside. I moved groggily, my body wracked with pain. I tried to run but wasn't able to manage much more than a shuffle. Behind me the door to the autopsy room flung open.

I took a look behind me and saw the tall man closing the distance, silhouetted in the dim hall lights. Determined to escape, I turned, and propelled by adrenaline, moved faster. I found a fire alarm button and pressed it clumsily.

The alarm shattered the night, echoing in the hall and in my head.

Still clutching the knife, I staggered down the hall and toward the elevator that had brought me down. I could hear the grunts of my wounded attacker as he staggered, after me.

I rounded the corner and reached the elevator. I pushed the button again and again, aware of the fact that there was no way out at this end of the hall except for the elevator, and I regretted that I hadn't taken the stairs at the other end. I cursed myself now for not having thought of it. I pushed the button again as the sound of my attacker grew louder and resolved that should the elevator not make it in time, I would make my final stand in the hall. I exhaled slowly through my mouth to calm myself, the way I used to when the pressures of a resident surgery were upon me. I looked at my hands. They were steady. I was ready.

The elevator arrived and its door "Binged," a pleasant welcome, entirely out of synch with the moment. I stepped in and hit the button. My attacker rounded the corner; his fisted hand pouring blood through the glove, dripping like a leaking faucet onto the floor. He reached out to intercept the doors before they closed, but he was too late.

I sank back against the wall and exhaled as my attacker pounded against the elevator doors. I tried to lower the bread-knife, but couldn't.

"You're dead! You're dead! You're dead!" the muffled voice screamed from the other side.

19

7:08 PM

I stood alongside the ambulance while the paramedic pressed my ribs checking for cracks or breaks. All about me there was a flurry of activity. The normally empty concourse was crowed and busy. Campus security kept the gawking students back. Some police officers were telling the Fire Department that their services wouldn't be needed, while others searched the area for any sign of the attacker. There was none. Except for the blood.

I grunted.

A paramedic looked me over. "Sorry, Doctor. Nothing seems to be broken, but you should get to the hospital and have some X-rays done."

I shook my head. "Forget it," I said hoarsely. "Nothing's broken."

"I can't prescribe any pain killers. The hospital could though," the paramedic continued.

"That's all right. I want to stay sharp," I replied without bravado.

"Here," the paramedic said, handing me an ice-pack."

I took the pack and applied it over my right eyebrow where a punch had landed. The area was swollen and tender. They had wiped my face with a damp cloth earlier to wash away the sooty residue of gunfire. That was after the police had obtained a sample.

"What was her name?" Donaldson asked.

I looked over and smiled weakly. "What's going on?"

"You tell me. I just got called at home."

I shrugged. "Went into the morgue and I almost got killed."

"Killed?" Donaldson said as he took a closer at the damage. My throat was red, raw and welted. I had bruises about my face, some tiny cuts and scratches. There were powder burns as well. It had been close.

Donaldson said, "I thought people got killed first and then went to the morgue. The last time I saw a throat as red as yours, was a young woman who was strangled to death by her boyfriend."

"I remember her."

"Oh, yeah. Get a look at him?" Donaldson asked.

"Yeah. Big, six-foot maybe more."

Donaldson took this down. "Face?"

I shook my head and winced. "Ski-mask. I told this to the other guy," I said, indicating a plain-clothes cop who was off to the side talking with a few students.

"Mitchelson," Donaldson said. "He's a good guy. I'll talk to him later. You going to the hospital?"

"Naw. I'm going to head off home and get some sleep."

"Yeah, you don't need a doctor; you are one. Besides, you're insured."

I smiled briefly. I was insured. As a P.I., I was required to be insured to the tune of 1 million dollars: one-half for bodily injury and one-half for property destruction. The bodily injury, I felt I probably earned. "Don't look so smug, you're not the beneficiary."

"Damn!" Donaldson said and snapped his fingers. "You got a ride? Because I want to take a walk about down there and see what happened."

"You know something, I'll stay. I want to have a look around too."

"Which one do you think it was?" Donaldson asked discreetly as we stepped off the elevator. There was a uniformed police officer standing at the elevator entrance. CSU people walked back and forth. The hall was fully lit and, with the exception of all the police and the large blood trail, looked the same as it did during the day. Still, a feeling of residual violence hung in the air like an airborne pathogen.

I pressed the icepack against my eye. "I've no idea," I said cautiously after we passed a young uniformed cop. "It could have been Astor; he seems about the right height, or Carver. He was the right size. This guy was strong. What do you think?"

"I honestly don't know what to think right now," Donaldson replied as we passed by a CSU person who was busy taking a sample of blood. More drops had been circled with chalk. The drops became less numerous and thinner as we walked back towards the autopsy room. "Jesus, you really stuck him. We'll have no problem getting DNA and blood type."

We entered the autopsy room where the attack had taken place. The lights were on; the room was a mess. Equipment lay asunder where the fight had taken place. Blood mixed with water ran down the drain in the center of the room, and everywhere CSU was there with bags, brushes and tweezers, dusting and sampling everything they could. A CSU man approached.

"Detective," he held up a plastic bag, "we found these in the corner."

I squinted to see what they were, but Donaldson had seen enough crushed bullets not to bother.

"Send them to the lab. Ballistics might be able to determine something,"

"I doubt it," the CSU person said. "They're too deformed."

Donaldson turned back to me. "Look, this is getting weird. There's no chance that this could have been random?"

I turned and looked at him with my good eye.

"All right, all right, I see your point. What's your diagnosis?"

I considered this for a moment. "Somebody's terrified."

Donaldson winced. "You think?"

I nodded. "It was an attack of opportunity. Whoever did this was desperate. One thing's for certain, - you won't have to bother with the hotline anymore." And I won't be going back on TV.

"Why?"

"We're getting close. The television show didn't indicate any specifics, not even the name of the victim. It must be Astor or Carver. If the killer was somebody other than those two, it wouldn't make sense to move on me. The killer must be one of the men we visited. I'm not usually here at this hour. So I must have been followed. Whichever one of those two fuckers is guilty, and one of them is, just did us a favor. He's narrowed down our search to two. We should drop in on both of them this evening and see if either of them is bleeding like a stuck pig."

"This attack could have been a professional job," Donaldson speculated. "He could have hired someone."

I considered it.

"Actually, I have to go see someone else. Don't take this the wrong way, but thankfully after what happened to you, it'll be little more than a formality."

"What do you mean?" I asked not understanding.

Donaldson motioned for me, in a way which I knew meant he had something to say that he didn't want anybody else hearing. We stepped to the side, where we were relatively sure of privacy. He spoke softly. "Remember the lead I told you about?"

"Right."

"That's where I'm heading," Donaldson said.

"I'd like to tag along."

"You should go home and get some rest."

I shook my head. "No. I wouldn't be able to sleep even if I did. Let me go. I promise not to say anything. Like you said, this is just a formality."

Donaldson considered this a moment, then nodded. "All right, let's go."

I turned the icepack over to keep the cold on my eye. "Where's this mystery suspect live?"

"He's not a suspect."

"Oh yeah, sorry."

Donaldson spoke. "We know where she lived from mid-1947 to November of '53. But we also know that she lived in North Beach earlier."

"Right. The address was on some of the letters Mrs. D'Angelo left me," I said. "October, '46"

"So, you know what I did?"

I shrugged.

"I had one of my guys look up Maria Cialini's name in the court records. I was curious to see if she had ever been involved in any legal action. This morning I learned that a Maria Cialini was involved in a lawsuit against her landlord in North Beach back in March, '47. It seems that he tried to have her lease canceled, as he didn't like her boyfriends coming around. He wanted to throw her out and *keep* the balance of her lease."

"Asshole."

"It gets better - or worse," Donaldson said grimly.

"Hang on. I'm getting confused about all these apartments. How many have we found now?"

"Just three. The two that she lived in and the one she was buried in," Donaldson clarified.

I was even more confused now. "What relevance does her first apartment have for us?"

"None." He waved a hand. "Listen. This is the thing that I had to have checked out. The apartment isn't important. What *is* important is the name of the lawyer who handled her case."

I felt a growing sense of unease. "Who was it?"

Donaldson paused before answering. "Jonathan Emerson."

"Jonathan Emerson," I repeated so it would jog my memory. "I should know this name?"

Donaldson nodded. "Play with it a bit."

It suddenly dawned upon me. "Jack Emerson. The Federal Judge?"

"Yes."

"I suppose we'll have to proceed with caution," I said with a light laugh.

"You better believe it," Donaldson said.

"I've got a few questions to ask Jack."

"Tell it to the Judge," Donaldson replied.

"I think I will."

20

8:16 PM

Pacific Heights is a neighborhood where caterers deliver their wares to courtly mansions, and limousines linger outside consulate offices and private schools educate the progeny of the privileged. One can still find homes constructed before World War I. There are also condos. It is an area where old money and new coexist quite well.

Federal Judge Jonathan Emerson's home sat atop a long winding driveway on its own private hill. Tall pine trees, neatly trimmed, stood protectively about the cut-stone Tudor mansion and formed a natural barrier, denoting the extent of his property. Two stone chimneystacks stood like brackets at either end of the house. The exterior walls were half-timbered. Tall diamond-paned windows were on the first and second floors, while arched windows could be found on the gabled attic. A fountain sat prominently in front of the house, spurting water endlessly. The front door too was gabled. There was a gatehouse off to the side. Cast from the same stone as its neighbor on the hill. This one had mostly bay windows and a large oriel window at the far end. There was a single stone chimneystack in the center of its roof. Both dwellings had elegantly carved terracotta about them.

As we approached the front gates, a man with a flashlight waved for us to stop. Donaldson rolled down his window, showed him his badge and was waved on with a nod. Donaldson eased slowly up the shrub-lined driveway, as he and I noted not only the number of cars parked about the property, but more significantly, some of their exiting owners. Their owners read like a "who's who" of San Francisco's social community.

"Isn't that that lawyer guy?" I asked.

Donaldson nodded. "Lewis," he said. "Of Lewis and Lewis."

"It's like a lawyers' convention."

"And Judges," Donaldson added.

"Looks like he's having a party."

"It's patronage," Donaldson corrected.

"What do you mean?"

Donaldson smiled. "Don't you read the society pages? Everyone knows that he'll be appointed to the Supreme Court this year. They're paying their respects."

Donaldson drove the car around the illuminated fountain, past the valet who was standing out front. He eased into a spot and turned off the engine.

"I can't believe this," I said. "First a billionaire philanthropist. Then a well-respected pro-life activist. And now we're questioning 'Jack' Emerson, Federal Judge and all but nominated Supreme Court Justice?" I shook my head. Despite the presence of all the other cars, I felt wrong about us parking on these grounds, by that house. I felt like I'd stepped back in time. It was as if we were violating something. "I guess we'll have to take it easy."

"Very."

We made our way to the front door, where a grey-haired butler, complete with tux, and smile, waited.

"Good evening, gentlemen, may I help you?"

"No, thank you." Donaldson said. "I'll find my own way." He showed the badge discretely before adding, "It's a professional matter." He never stopped moving and neither did I.

I figured the butler was considering following us but didn't as there were other people entering. The house had an elegant simplicity about it. Pewter candelabras led us down a gray, cut-stone floored hallway, while our heels echoed our arrival.

"Before you ask," Donaldson said, "let me explain. I didn't want to give the butler the option of ushering us into some side-room and seeing the Judge at his leisure. I want to see the man in his environment before I approach. But," he said emphatically, "we still handle him gently."

"Because he's a Judge."

"Partly," Donaldson admitted. "But also because he has a stellar reputation. I stood before him on a few occasions and I've always found him professional and committed."

I shrugged, not entirely interested.

Donaldson explained that few citizens who knew anything about the Civil Rights Movement hadn't heard of Judge Emerson. He had been prominent in some of the bigger Civil Rights cases that had come out of the fifties. He could be seen in some of the old photos with Martin Luther King. He was one of the few whites associated with the movement before it became fashionable. As time went on, he took on other Civil Rights issues and became very prominent in the burgeoning women's movements and later the gay rights movements. His stance was simple: equal rights for all. All movements were, in his opinion, concerned with human rights.

We entered a large reception room. Here, too, the walls were of stone as were the columns. Despite the walls, the room was warm and personable. The furniture was mahogany. People sat about or chatted in small groups. The windows had long, billowy tied-back curtains complete with swag and valance. An oak chimney-piece, intricately carved, in what appeared to be the Emerson family crest, stood watch over the fireplace. A large oriel window offered the guests a choice view of the English garden in the backyard. Donaldson and I were pleasantly surprised to find that the affair was not formal. Men wore suits while the women wore the feminine equivalent. With the exception of the caterers, there wasn't a tuxedo or evening gown to be seen. Still, we felt out of place.

"If we're not good, I suppose he'll call the mayor?" I commented.

"He could just shout across the room. He's right there," Donaldson said indicating with his jaw.

I said nothing but instinctively turned and walked after Donaldson in another direction.

People clotted together in little cliques. Every now and then, one would hemorrhage off, drift away and congeal with another group. I eyed the scene looking for Judge Emerson before realizing that I didn't know what he looked like.

"See her?" Donaldson asked, indicating a thin, statuesque woman of about seventy, elegantly dressed and talking to a small group of people in a corner.

"You mean Audrey Hepburn?" I asked.

"Yeah," Donaldson said and nodded in agreement. "That's his wife of, I don't know, fifty years. She does a lot of work with the disabled. Her name is Geraldine I think."

"You sound like a fan."

Donaldson was a bit miffed. "My wife reads the social pages. She tells me this stuff."

"Aw."

He elbowed me gently, looking toward one of a multitude of dignified men standing about the room. This one, however, had his back to us and was holding court to several people. They arranged themselves about him in a horseshoe fashion and hung onto his every word.

I followed Donaldson as he walked about the group, gradually coming around to face its attraction: Judge Jonathan Emerson. Popularly known, as "Jack," he was tall at nearly 6'4," and very broad-shouldered. He was a distinguished looking man dressed in an impeccable Saville Row dark gray, double-breasted suit of English design. The shoulders were soft and lightly padded. The armholes, which I could see as he raised his hands, were cut high. The two side vents were cut high as well. The trousers had two pleats and the pockets were located at the seam. He wore a light blue, high-collar broadcloth shirt and a dark blue tie. The choice of broadcloth over Oxford this time of year was significant as broadcloth is of a tighter weave and thus smoother and more refined. A blue pocket square, folded in the loose-stuffed style, could be seen in his jacket pocket. His shoes were black, plain-toe Oxfords. His full head of steel-gray hair was cut neatly. He could have been Cary Grant's double with looks that probably made many middle-aged men hopeful that they too, could look as good when they got to be his age, and elderly men jealous that they didn't. And I had a feeling, that women of all ages wondered what it might have been like to have known him, way back when. He had an aristocratic bearing and a magnetism that could be best described as Kennedyesque.

If one were forced to pick an outstanding feature from all of his outstanding features I would have picked his eyes. Wide and intelligent, they were the palest of blues, but hinted at such knowledge and sensitivity that they made me, and, I imagine others who found themselves in their gaze feel special, as if they were the center of the universe.

We waited patiently before him, unconcerned that anybody from the group would notice two sudden stragglers, as it was my opinion that these people wouldn't have noticed a bomb going off.

A hand touched each of us on the shoulder. "May I help you, Inspector?"

We turned to face an older man. Average height, and thinly built in a striped three-piece black-flannel suit of English design.

I wondered whether he was comfortable in a flannel suit, as something tropical at this time of the year would have been more complementary to the body. I couldn't help but notice that the lines were continuous, not pinstripes, which were actually finely dotted lines and not really stripes at all. The jacket was double-breasted with six buttons. The gray Oxford cloth shirt had a broad collar and button cuffs. The vest had four pockets and held his gray tie firmly in place. He had the visage of mongoose with sharp piercing green eyes that saw through everyone and into every situation. His bald, bullet-shaped head shone under the lights and he wore a hearing aid. He was not naturally bald, though; his head was shaved. I noticed that he was overly formal, bearing all the mannerisms of a repressed individual. I figured that he was a man imprisoned by occupation, class and fashion.

"I'm Mr. Issacson." He offered his hand, which Donaldson shook.

We both knew well who Samuel Issacson was. Sam, to his clients, he was one of the best criminal defense attorneys in the state of California. Issacson, a big believer in the rights of man and the all-too-prone-to-abuse legal system of the day, had opted to defend the innocent from the system itself. This included several death-row inmates whose innocence he had proven. He was currently on a board of attorneys pushing for the utilization of DNA evidence to get wrongly convicted death row inmates one last chance. He had defended a wide variety of people in his career and built a reputation for being the legal gun-for-hire for the guilty-rich. Still, I found it hard to dismiss him as just another shyster who defended guilty clients who had money; Issacson had defended greater numbers of people, who were by all accounts, probably innocent. This included cops and doctors.

"Dr. Connor," I said, shaking his hand and noting the strong grip.

With the fluidity of a Maitre'd, he turned us away from the crowd standing around the Judge and guided us to a quiet corner of the room.

Anyone watching us from a distance would have thought we were old friends. I knew what was going on, but understood it to be one of the social skills of a class of people who prided themselves on tactfulness.

"I'm a friend of the Judge's. Can I help you with anything?"

"We need to speak to him," Donaldson began. "It's a matter concerning a case and his name came up. We just want to straighten a few things out." He said this as if it was of no real concern but he had to do it.

Mr. Issacson offered a gentle challenge. "If that's the case, I'm surprised you didn't call his office and set up an appointment instead of dropping in on him unannounced - at a party."

Donaldson, who had learned a few maneuvers in social Judo himself, replied, "We didn't know about this get-together. If we had, we wouldn't have stopped in."

"Would you like to sit down, Doctor?" Issacson asked, as he took a better look at my bruised and somewhat puffy face.

"Ah, no. I'm fine," I said. "Thank you."

"I see."

"Like I said," Donaldson began, "we got some information on a case and we're just going through the motions."

Issacson nodded.

"But it involves a murder. That's the reason we came over tonight," Donaldson finished.

Take that, I thought.

"I see," he said, absorbing the impact of this, before redirecting us toward a side room.

"We'd just as soon not go through official channels. You know how these things can get out."

Hi-ah!

As Donaldson said this, I noticed he avoided the word "leak" due to the implied threat usually associated with the word in these situations. I noticed he also made sure that the words he did use were uttered with respect, not so much because he was frightened of Issacson or any other lawyer for that case, but because he had a tremendous amount of respect for Judge Emerson.

"Indeed," Issacson nodded. "Why don't you follow me."

He moved with the nimbleness of a retired acrobat, making his way through the crowd, and led us into an elegantly furnished chamber off the reception room. There he invited us to have a seat while he got Judge Emerson.

Donaldson took a cursory look around the room, while I took in the details of the highly polished, ornately inscribed wood paneling that adorned the walls. A long oak table and chairs stood in the center. Sounds from the party outside bled through the thick stone walls. A few minutes later, the door opened and two waiters walked in. One carried a tray of assorted hors d' oeuvres. A second, with a tray of assorted drinks and bottled water, followed.

"Thanks," I said as they exited. I took some hors d' oeuvres from the table as well as a napkin and grabbed a bottled water. "One of the perks of the job? First cookies and now appetizers," I said, before adding, "Why don't you grab something?"

Donaldson patted himself on his expansive belly. "Almost thirty years of appetizers and I built a shed for my tool. You keep doing P.I. work long enough and you'll look the same. Then we'll see how many college chickies want to spend detention with their favorite professor."

I would have said something but my mouth was full so I smiled instead. And then ate another.

The door opened and Samuel Issacson entered, followed by Judge Jonathan "Jack" Emerson. The effect of his presence and in particular the eyes were only magnified now that we had a private audience with him.

"This is Inspector Donaldson, SFPD and this is Dr. Connor, sir," Issacson said, leading the older man in.

"A pleasure," Judge Emerson said, then shook each of our hands in a two-handed grip, neither of which was cut. Not that I expected they would be, even though he *was* the right size. I was overcome with the feeling that we were the recipients of the attentions of a great man. I felt special and couldn't help but return his honest smile.

"Nice to see you again, sir." Donaldson dropped.

Judge Emerson raised an eyebrow. "We've met?"

"In the course of work. You signed a few search warrants for me, oh eight or nine years ago."

"Yes, yes of course," he replied.

"They are investigating a murder, sir. And your name came up," Issacson injected.

"Oh? In what capacity?"

"Do you recall a woman by the name of Maria Cialini? Donaldson reiterated yet again. "She was a client of yours back in March of 1947."

Emerson considered this. He seemed to be on the verge of nodding. "A bit more information, Inspector. It's been a long time since the forties."

"You represented her in a suit she brought against her landlord." Donaldson prodded. "A man by the name of - - - "

"Felini," Judge Emerson completed. "Oh, yes. I remember that case."

Mr. Issacson seemed surprised. "That's astonishing. I can't remember 1997 that well."

Judge Emerson continued, "I remember taking the case, but I don't remember trying it."

"It was settled out of court," Donaldson explained.

"Hmmm," he said. "Memory fades with time."

Donaldson removed from his jacket and handed him, photocopies of the case he had obtained.

Judge Emerson took the documents, put on his glasses and began reading when a burst of laughter from outside the room pierced the environment.

Judge Emerson looked annoyed. "Why don't we go to my study? It's quieter there," he said.

Outside, somebody laughed again.

Emerson led us out a back door and down a long hall, at the end of which he stopped and looked to his left, then right.

"Right, sir," Issacson prompted.

"Oh, yes, of course," he continued and turned to Donaldson. "House is so big I'm thinking of putting up those maps, the kind you see in the museums that say 'you are here' around the house. That way I can find my way to the kitchen late at night."

Donaldson smiled.

He led us into his private study, held the door open and ushered us in. Standing in the doorway, he turned and said to Issacson, "It's all right, Sam. I'll take it from here."

"I don't mind," Issacson said.

"Hold down the fort," Emerson said as he closed the leather-padded door on Issacson before he could object. He turned to face us.

"You sure you don't want your lawyer with you, sir?" Donaldson asked.

"Sam? He's not my lawyer. He's a friend. Bit of a protective one. I've known him since we were at Harvard. He helped me when I was starting out. Besides, I am a lawyer and a Judge. Let's sit down, shall we?"

We arranged ourselves about the center of the spacious room, Donaldson and I on one set of Italian leather chairs, Emerson on the other. Next to each chair was a small end table with a translucent puffy lamp atop it. Between us was a glass coffee table. On the walls all around us sat a lifetime of books and documents dedicated to every aspect of his occupation. Between them were photos of him with Civil Rights leaders, like Martin Luther King and Jesse

Jackson, women's rights organizations and leaders like Patricia Ireland, The National Organization of Women, and Gloria Steinem. Emerson read the photocopies over casually, making comments like "Ah-ha," or the occasional "Hmmm." A few times his sharp eyes seemed to glance far away as if he were staring at something separated from him by space, or time and he was trying to see it clearly. But those all-knowing, wise eyes never once dimmed. Finally, he looked away, reached under his glasses with his thumb and forefinger and rubbed his eyes. He put down the photocopies.

"Yes. This refreshes my memory, Inspector," he said slowly. "Good thing you brought it over as many of my older records are in storage."

"Really?"

"Yes. I'm in the process of having all my records stored on CD and entered into a database."

"That's a good idea," Donaldson said.

"We have to keep up with this new technology." He paused a moment. "You seem to have everything pertaining to the case. What else can I tell you?"

Donaldson took a moment to explain about the murder of Maria Cialini, her burial in the wall and that we were searching for anyone who had known her.

"That's terrible!" he said. "I heard about it on television the other night. I must admit a weakness for some of those mystery shows. I thought you looked familiar, Dr. Connor."

"I was on too, sir. Briefly," Donaldson injected.

"Oh? I must've stepped out for a moment." He looked toward me again. "If you don't mind my asking, what happened to you, Dr. Connor?"

"I ran into a critic," I joked. "But you should see the other guy."

Judge Emerson laughed lightly. "Good for you." Then he returned to business. "The television program didn't say anything about her name. Least I don't recall that having been the case."

"Her identity was only recently obtained. We haven't released it to the public yet."

"You work quickly, Inspector."

"We've been putting in a lot of overtime," Donaldson admitted.

Emerson nodded. "I see. And she'd been buried there all those years?"

"That's correct."

"Nobody ever declared her missing or," he paused, "or looked for her?"

Donaldson shook his head. "It would appear that whoever murdered her went to great lengths to make it appear that she had moved away."

"My gosh." Judge Emerson stopped again and appeared to drift a moment before returning. "I handled a case for her involving her landlord. He wanted her out because she had brought men in late at night. He wanted to cancel her lease and keep the balance of her rent. I argued to his lawyer that under letter law, she hadn't violated any aspect of her lease. She'd paid her rent in a timely fashion and hadn't altered the environment of the domicile in question. His argument that she had altered the 'moral' environment of the building was weak at best. The fact that he wanted to keep her balance weakened it further. I pointed out that we'd probably win and then we'd counter-sue him for defamation of character. In those days, that was 'trail blazing' for women's issues. Can you imagine? In the end, his lawyers were able to help him see the futility of his case. He was a greedy man who attempted to take advantage of a young single woman in full use of her legal rights. It was a ridiculous case. I guess you could say it was one of the earliest examples of a frivolous case."

"You have a good memory for details, sir," I said.

"You never forget your first cases," he said. "I imagine it's the same in medicine."

"It is," I agreed.

"What can you tell me about Mrs. Cialini, sir?" Donaldson asked. "As a person."

He thought a moment. "Not much, I'm afraid. I remember that she was very determined not to be pushed around by her landlord. She had a toughness, you know? A strength. She wanted to win. I told her that if we went to trial, the other side would make an issue of her male friends. That they'd try to push the 'moral' issue and that it could be embarrassing. But she wasn't afraid. She was in the right and that was that. I found that very impressive. Not only for the time, but also for her age. One got the feeling that they were dealing with someone much older, even though I had a few years on her. She was also smart, not book-smart like a student," he explained. "But intelligent from experience. Again, very impressive. I often wondered what had become of her. Why would anyone have wanted to kill her?"

"She was pregnant," I slipped in.

"Hmmm. You didn't mention that, Inspector,"

"I didn't think it was relevant," Donaldson said, and threw me a look. "Since we're on the subject, sir, we also know that she had a miscarriage. What was her health like when you knew her?"

Emerson considered this a moment. "You're asking me politely - and I appreciate that - if she was pregnant when I was her lawyer."

Donaldson said nothing.

"Fair enough. I met her a few times at the library. I didn't have an office yet. I was just starting out. She seemed healthy, though not pregnant."

I asked, "You never met her socially then? Did you know any of her friends?"

Judge Emerson shook his head. "I'm afraid not. I kept strange hours and went to few parties or socials then. Not like today." He handed the photocopies back to Donaldson. "I don't know what else to tell you."

Donaldson stood, as did Emerson and myself. We'd heard enough. "I thank you for your time sir." Donaldson said.

"No problem Inspector. Any time. Let me walk you out."

Judge Emerson opened the door to his study. His wife, Geraldine, was standing there.

She was even more radiant and elegant up close, I decided.

"I was just about to knock." She smiled. "The guests are asking where you are."

"We're just coming out now, dear." Judge Emerson said with a smile.

We introduced ourselves briefly, then made our way back up the hall toward the party. Sam Issacson approached. "The fort is held down. Everything all right?"

Emerson patted him on the shoulder. "Yes, yes. Just straightening a few things. If I remember anything else, Inspector, I'll call your office."

"I'd appreciate that, sir." Donaldson replied.

"Why don't you and uh…." he hesitated.

"Dr. Connor," Issacson injected.

Emerson smiled. "Yes, Dr. Connor. Why don't the two of you stay and make yourselves comfortable?"

"That's very kind of you, but I have to get back to the station," Donaldson declined.

"And I have to get back home," I added.

We had walked a few steps when I asked, "Sir, how did you come to be Maria's attorney?"

Emerson cocked his head as if the motion would knock loose a lodged memory. "I honestly don't know. I might have been referred.

It was darker and a bit cooler when we exited. We were almost at the car when we heard footsteps approaching from behind. We turned. It was Issacson. "Inspector, Doctor, I just wanted to thank you."

Donaldson didn't understand. "For what?"

"For your discretion." He raised a hand and caught his breath. "As you know, Judge Emerson is close to being nominated to the Supreme Court. This will mean a Congressional hearing. The conservatives, ever desperate to prevent a liberal from being nominated, will be on the lookout for any scandal to prevent his nomination. Just the mention of a murder investigation could be all they need to harm the Judge. That's why I jumped on you about not calling earlier." He adjusted his hearing aid.

"We understand. And I don't blame you. We're just going over the names of any people who might have known her. It's just background," Donaldson assured.

"I see," Issacson added.

"We don't have much to go on," I confided.

"Nevertheless, your professionalism and discretion is appreciated."

"Think nothing of it," I said. "You should see some of the people we've been talking to."

We watched as Issacson made his way back across the gravel and into the mansion.

"Glad that's over with," Donaldson began.

"Why's that?"

"You saw him. He had nothing to do with her death."

I said, "Got to check every lead."

Donaldson shrugged. "Like we agreed earlier, whoever went after you did so because we're getting close. I wasn't even able to confirm this lead until a few hours ago. Let's go."

We reached the car.

"Strange guy," I said.

"Issacson?"

"No, the Judge."

"What makes you say that?"

I tilted my head, the way I often did when offering a diagnosis. "He was wearing two different color socks."

"I hadn't noticed."

"It wasn't a big deal. Not like one was black and the other yellow. One was navy and the other black."

"Maybe he's color blind," Donaldson offered.

I shrugged. "I just thought it odd."

"I'm going to radio in and have a car by your place every hour. I don't want this guy, whoever he was, to take a second shot. I suggest you take a few precautions. Know what I mean?" Donaldson asked after we had driven a while.

I nodded.

"I'm also going to drop you off at home. Give me your keys and I'll have your car in your driveway when you get up."

In no mood to argue and grateful for the gesture, I took my keys from my jacket, and removed the car keys from the set. I handed them to Donaldson. "I could drive," I said unconvincingly.

"Forget that," he said, then asked, "You're not going to work tomorrow, are you?"

I laughed hoarsely. "No."

"Good for you," Donaldson said.

"I'm going to go to the park."

21

9:20 PM

I closed the front door to my house and reset the alarm. I made my way through the noiseless darkened home without turning on any lights and headed straight up to my bedroom. Some of my single colleagues had told me that they often left lights on or music or both, so as to make their homes or apartments seem "alive" when they came home in the evening. Others, the more desperate I figured, kept little pets like a fish or parakeet. Something low-maintenance that would depend on them, but was easily disposable without much by way of conscience making them feel guilty, should the little critter die. Such were the little tricks to make the mind forget momentarily that the body was alone and probably would be forever. I never engaged in such silliness as I felt that compared to where I worked, any place was full of life. It was one of the fringe benefits of being surrounded by death all day long. Besides, I didn't like animals and considered the rest a waste of electricity. (I was a stickler for such things)

After putting my clothes away and changing into my pajamas, I went into the corner of the room and knelt at the foot of the dresser. I opened the bottom drawer and from beneath some light sweaters, I removed a small cedar box. I stood and walked to the nightstand with the box where the light was better. There, I opened it.

It had been a gift from Donaldson. Something I'd received when my PI license had become official. It was something I never expected to use until one day when asking some routine questions, the otherwise congenial lady of the house came at me with a knife. I never learned why she did it. She hadn't been a suspect. I guess she was having a bad decade and just flipped. I had fought her off, but not until she performed a few surgical moves of her own, cutting me up nicely and ensuring that *I'd* have to see a doctor. In truth, if I had to do it again, I reflected from my recovery room that weekend, I'd have shot the bitch.

I removed the .357 nickel-plated magnum revolver from its foam berth. It was a simple weapon that I was licensed to carry, should I feel the need, and on whose operation I had passed a course. It even came with a shoulder holster.

I opened the weapon and light glinted off the barrel as I inspected it. I took one of the speed-loaders from the foam and emptied its contents into the cylinder.

"It only holds six bullets," I commented to Donaldson when I'd first seen it. Like many people, I was used to movies where all firearms came with thirty-round banana clips. I'd forgotten that that they still made *wheel guns* as Donaldson called them. I seldom carried it as it made me feel silly, and except for the times when Donaldson dragged me down to the range to do some shooting, and that one time in self-defense, I never fired it. I wasn't a very good shot, either.

"You only need to hit them with one," Donaldson had replied.

I closed the barrel with a distinct "Click." *Precautions indeed.*

22

Golden Gate Park: 10:47 AM

Nestled between the Great Highway, Stanyan, Fulton Street and Lincoln Avenue, Golden Gate Park was something of a garden spot for city dwellers and suburbanites alike. Some 1,000 acres in size, it offered such attractions and distractions as: an Arboretum, Botanical Gardens, the Japanese Tea Garden, Museums, Tennis courts, baseball diamonds, a golf course and two man made waterfalls at the base of a man made mountain.

I walked through the throng of revelers slowly. It felt good to be outside in the fresh air. The swelling on my face had gone down and my sunglasses covered most of my bruised eye. The only indications of the previous night's events were the few cuts on my face and the red marks on my neck that peaked out from beneath my beige mock turtleneck.

Michael Astor's Festival was one of the city's highpoint events and was always ensured a good turnout. One couldn't have picked a better day, I thought. Everywhere I looked, I saw different events for different people. Each event or attraction was representative of some charity or organization. Most of the events were geared towards handicapped children as they made up the bulk of Astor's interest.

Astor employees, identified by their blue shirts and nametags, were in charge of the various events. There were pony rides and three legged-races for youngsters. Clowns handed out balloons and performed simple magic tricks for toddlers. A wiffel-ball game for older kids was starting in the distance. For the seniors, there were dances going on beneath tents as various bands playing the music of their youth belted out old favorites. There were separate tents for jazz, big band, swing and ballroom.

I took all this in and was impressed, though in the back of my mind I kept asking myself; *Why would a man do this? Gratitude? Guilt?* I glanced at my watch. I still had a few minutes so I made my way toward the bridge.

I didn't regret not telling Donaldson what I was doing here, as I was sure that he would have insisted on having a few plainclothes officers shadowing my every move. This wasn't something I wanted, as I wasn't sure that it would pan out and I didn't want to waste Donaldson's time, especially since it was the weekend. Besides, I had all the protection I needed suspended from my right shoulder. Not that I thought I'd need it in the park, but after last night, I wasn't taking any chances. *Who was this Burt E that Bud had mentioned?* Was he friend, foe or fake? Was he here to help me, hurt me? Was he here at all?

Despite the reassurance that kept pulling beneath my right shoulder, I couldn't shake the feeling that I was being watched. Every so often I would turn around and take a look back into the crowd only to see no one and feel stupid. I told myself that I wasn't paranoid, as somebody had tried to get me. It helped a bit.

Up ahead, I could see Michael Astor on a raised stage. Well-dressed in a dark-blue suit, he was saying something, but with the reverberation from the PA system and the applause, it was difficult to hear anything, so I drifted closer.

"It's great to have so many people here this morning," Astor said, looking about smiling, as people politely applauded. "I always prefer to have our get-together in the spring as it is always a time for hope and possibilities."

More applause.

I caught Astor's gaze. He looked at me a second too long and glanced away.

"I, uh," Astor paused, his smile dropping momentarily. "I hope that everyone will get around to taking part in all the events." He paused again, his smile strained. "And don't leave any food."

The audience laughed collectively and applauded some more. I noticed one of his lawyers, Mr. Clarke, seated off to the side. I looked about but couldn't find Mr. Carver. *Where is Mr. Carver?* I wondered. *Did I carve Mr. Carver?*

I walked off, not because I didn't want to cause Astor further discomfort, but rather because I didn't want to be late for my appointment. I was unsure whether Astor's discomfort was due to my physical appearance or the fact that I was able to appear at the day's events at all. The only good thing I could see about Astor was that his hands and face were free of damage. I would liked to have seen Mr. Carver's hands.

I turned and bumped into a man.

"Excuse me," he said.

I had to look up to see who it was. I was a bit surprised to see that it was Judge Emerson. He wore a beige cotton gabardine suit, a straw hat and a light oxford shirt, beige suede shoes and a thin tan tie. He looked every bit the colonial gentleman out for a casual stroll in the park. "Good morning, Judge," I managed to say. His wife Geraldine was alongside him. She was dressed equally casually in a summer dress. "Ma'am," I acknowledged.

She smiled and nodded in recognition. "Good to see you again, Doctor."

"Good morning," the Judge said and he paused. "Dr. Connor, I'm surprised to see you here."

"Really?" I didn't know what to make of that.

"Are you all right, Doctor?" Emerson asked. "You look like you've been in a brawl."

"I got mugged," I said simply.

"Really. Where?"

"In the morgue."

"Oh yes. You mentioned that at the party. I believe you've met my wife?

I turned my attention to Geraldine Emerson. "A pleasure, ma'am."

"Thank you, Dr. Connor."

The Judge asked. "Are you here with anyone, Doctor?

Inspector Donaldson perhaps?"

"No, I came alone. But I'm here to meet someone." *I couldn't help but drop it.*

"Very good," Emerson said before turning to his wife. "Ger, Dr. Connor is working on that murder. You know the one that was on that show the other night."

"The closet lady!"

"Yes," I replied.

"How's the investigation coming along?" she inquired.

"My investigation is definitely getting somewhere," I hinted.

"Taking a day off from your investigation?" Emerson asked.

"No. Actually I'm here to investigate a piece of it."

Judge Emerson considered this. "I see. Well best of luck with it."

I replied, "Thank you. And might I add that the hors d'oeuvres Friday evening were terrific."

"Thank you," Judge Emerson said.

"Friday night? That party was last night, Doctor; Saturday," Geraldine Emerson corrected.

"Oh, that's right. I must have gotten bumped on the head a bit harder than I thought," I said politely.

Geraldine Emerson smiled civilly, though her eyes held something else.

Judge Emerson said, "Well, we must be going, Doctor. I want to get over to the swing tent. I've been promising my wife I'd take her out dancing for some time now."

137

I nodded. "A pleasure to have met you again, ma'am," I said as they continued in the other direction.

I turned and walked a few meters. It was nearly time to meet this mystery person at the southern bridge of Stow Lake. I covered the distance in a few minutes. As I approached, I had to slow my stride as a group of seniors were walking before me at their own pace. Some rolled along in wheelchairs, while others walked with canes.

Stow Lake lay at the base of Strawberry hill, a 428-foot tall man-made mountain. I walked over, stood at the stone bridge and looked into the 15 million-gallon reservoir a moment. I could see a few fish swimming below. I turned my attention away from the lake and eyed the crowd. It was then that I saw Dr. Hale staring at me. Some twenty yards away, he wore green corduroys, black shoes, a white shirt and a blue windbreaker. Like myself, he was wearing sunglasses and had his hands in his pockets. I stopped and decided to play the same game, so I just stared at him across the crowd.

After a while I got bored, so I waved to Dr. Hale, but got no response. I considered giving him the middle finger to provoke a reaction, but decided against it.

"Did you see my son?" an elderly man asked as he passed by.

"Ah, no." I said, momentarily caught off-guard. I took my eyes off Dr. Hale to view the man. He was small and at least eighty. By the way he looked at me, I could tell that the poor fellow was medicated.

"He never visits," the old man continued. "Why don't he visit?"

I felt uncomfortable and walked a few feet. I reacquired Dr. Hale, who had also moved but who nevertheless kept his gaze on me.

"Bobby?" an old woman asked as she grabbed at my hand.

"What?" I asked a bit put-off by the distraction.

A second old woman arrived, and stood next to the first. She put a hand on my shoulder. Though sympathetic, I was made uncomfortable by their attention.

The first old woman held her grip and touched a bruise on my face. "Who hit my baby?" she asked in a sad voice.

Her touch stung my face and I pulled back. I felt stifled. I had never liked being in crowds and liked even less being the center of attention in one. A sudden wave of claustrophobia washed over me.

"Ladies, ladies!" a commanding voice called. "We have to go now."

I looked to see a woman, of no more than forty, approach. She wore the blue shirt and nametag that identified her as one of the festival's organizers. She took the first old woman's hand and began to lead her away. "Sorry about that, mister. It's hard to keep track of them all."

"It's all right," I replied, embarrassed more than anything else.

She smiled. "Sometimes they're like kids."

The second old lady reached for me. I smiled and nodded politely at her.

"Come on now, Gertrude," the younger woman said, taking her by the hand. "That's right. Say bye, bye, Gerty."

I turned and looked about for Dr. Hale as the crowd thinned. He was nowhere to be seen.

2:00 PM

I sat on a chair at a tent near the bridge and looked about. Much of the crowd had bled away and was enjoying the free food that was set-up on large tables underneath some of the tents. I wasn't hungry. I glanced at my watch and decided that I had wasted enough time. *Must have been a crank*. Disappointed and angry, I left.

23

8:15 PM

I sat in my study with my feet up on the coffee table. I had ordered out from a Chinese restaurant, as I didn't feel like cooking that evening. I was feeling very anxious. The case had yielded some quick results at first. We knew who the victim was, where she had worked and lived, and who her doctor; lawyer and former employer were. Then it seemed to stop. And it could have very well stopped there if someone hadn't beaten the hell out of me.

I thought about the three men the case had introduced to me, and how each one rated as a suspect in the murder of Maria Cialini.

Each one was as good as the next, I decided. Michael Astor had been a wealthy man even back in 1953. He had denied knowing Cialini when first approached and only admitted to knowing her when we had proof that she worked for him. She had worked for his company and was buried in a building owned by him. *Had some inter-office tryst led to murder?* However, his lawyer, Mr. Clarke, had a good point: If Astor had been involved in her death, why would he give up control of her burial place by selling it? He could have easily afforded to hold onto it forever.

Dr. Hale was an OB/GYN in 1953 and a respected family man. An affair with a younger woman could certainly have ruined one and maybe both. I couldn't help but wonder what had caused him to become a born-again Christian. Was all his work with young pregnant women a sop to a guilty conscience? Maybe he and Maria had been romantically involved, though Hale hardly seemed her type.

And what of Judge Emerson, champion of women's rights? He had been her attorney. Was there some relationship that had gone awry? He too had been a married man. Back then, an indiscretion with a client would have ruined his marriage, not to mention cost him a lot of credibility with the movements he was trying to further.

The more I thought about it, the more I realized that the attack on me was the best proof that one of them was guilty. It made no sense that another person would have attacked me when the identity of the woman was still not publicly known. I doubted the Judge's involvement, though; as the attack on me was precipitated before we had questioned him. Just the same, I'd keep Judge Emerson in mind. Unlike Donaldson, I had no special reverence for Judge Emerson. And what about his wife, Gerdaldine? She was sharp I diagnosed. I hadn't forgotten nor had I bought her excuse for being outside her husband's study the night before. *She was listening in.*

The more I thought about it, I began to realize that all three men had more to lose now than they did in 1953. Just the mention of a murder investigation involving them could ruin all they had worked for.

So who had the most to lose? Michael Astor IV, philanthropist and friend to the city? Dr. Hale, pro-life activist and distributor of much needed medical help? Or Judge Emerson, progressive thinker and probably a Supreme Court justice in the making?

Each man had everything to lose. It dawned upon me then that the reason for killing Maria Cialini might have been very simple, not having anything to do with what they were into at the time of her death. Just because Astor was a wealthy young man at the time didn't mean that he had any more reason to kill her than a sharp new attorney or an up-and-coming doctor.

What to make of her actual death then? From what I had been able to gather, Maria Cialini tended to instill many emotions in the people around her, most of them extreme: anger and jealousy from women; lust and anger from men. A bullet to the head hardly seemed to be a crime of passion. It was too deliberate, too planned. She must have pissed somebody off. She must have been holding something over one or more of them and he had decided to act. *Or was it an angry wife?*

What about Astor having been framed? Could either Emerson or Dr. Hale have known about the building belonging to Astor? I considered it for a moment. Emerson could have found out whom she worked for from her. And I knew only to well what a person would tell their doctor. Who, if any of them had gotten her pregnant the first time? And what about the second? Was it the same man, or two different ones? Had she been blackmailing one of them, or more than one? Were there connections?

Who the hell attacked me in the morgue? It didn't seem to have been Astor or Emerson. They were the right size, but I had cut that guy; that much was certain.

141

Hale wasn't big enough, despite his hands being hidden at the park. Or had it been Mr. Carver, Astor's personal attack dog? Or was it a professional job then, like Donaldson suggested? All three had the money and, I suspected, the connections to hire a bruiser.

I decided to stop thinking about the case as my questions only led to more questions. It was conceivable that we would never find out who killed her. Our evidence thus far only showed that they had known the victim. We had no evidence to show motive or opportunity. We could request that each take a blood test to see if it matched with the unborn fetus, assuming we could determine its blood type. I tried to imagine the court battle that would ensue over that one. This case was a fucking minefield, I decided. If we accused any one, the media blitz would be enormous. If we accused the wrong one, the defamation suit would be staggering. Imagine going up against a billionaire, the pro-life movement or a Judge. Nor was this a list of suspects that one could simply threaten or frighten. These men were connected. Each was powerful in his own way and hounding them would bring repercussions that neither the mayor's office nor the police were willing to risk.

I turned my attention to the box of letters set out before me. I read; Hey kiddo…the park was beautiful…. Gerty prefers to dance! I stopped and noted the last part again, "Gerty prefers to dance!" *Who was Gerty?* I skimmed the rest of the letter but her last name wasn't mentioned. The letter wasn't dated. I read another two letters but found nothing of any value.

I set them aside and reflected for a moment. *Gerty, Gerty, Gerty,* I thought before saying aloud, "Burt E. Burty?" Bud Parkins had said at first that it was a woman who had called me at the university before changing his mind. I had been at the park but nobody had approached me. Except for the two old ladies. The young woman had called one of them Gertrude.

"Say bye, bye, Gerty."

"Ah, hell." I had been so distracted by Dr. Hale that it hadn't occurred to me that any of the seniors might have been the one who had called me. Oh no, had Hale seen her? Did he know her? What about Astor or Emerson - had they seen her? And if so, was there any danger in that?

I got up from the couch and went to my desk. I found the flyer that Astor had given Donaldson and myself the other day. I looked it over but it didn't mention which senior citizens' groups were being represented. Reluctantly, I got the number for Astor's attorney, Mr. Clarke, off the card he'd given me and dialed. Aside from the potential risk, I didn't like calling him, but if Mr. Clarke knew who she was and if she was a threat to Michael Astor IV, then I knew I was already too late. If Clarke didn't know, or if she was no threat to Astor, then it could do no harm. Either way, I had to find out the name of that old folks' home.

"Paul Clarke," the voice answered.

"Yeah. How you doing? This is Dr. Connor."

"Oh," he seemed surprised to hear from me. "What can I do for you, Doctor?"

"I need the names of the seniors groups that were at the festival today."

"There were several, Doctor. There were veteran groups, grandparents against drunk driving. Any idea which one?" he sounded suspicious.

I thought for a moment. "This group was from a retirement home. They had people escorting them around."

"That would be 'Sunset Homes.' Why?"

"I'm planning for my future," I said and hung up.

24

8:27 PM

It took me only three minutes to find out where "Sunset Homes" was located and another two to put in a call to Donaldson. "Meet me at 'Sunset Homes,'" I told him and hung up. I got into my car and left immediately. I knew that I should have told Donaldson more, but I had lost too much time as it was by not having talked to Gerty. It wasn't until I was halfway there that I realized I should have brought a cell-phone, called "Sunset Homes" and told them to check on Gerty, but I had been too busy checking my .357.

"Sunset Homes" was located in an area called the "Inner Sunset." The area is built on sand dunes on the western side of the city, immediately south of Golden Gate Park. With the exception of where I was headed, the layout of the streets was very symmetrical. Both Caucasians and Asians populated the neighborhoods. Most of the homes were stucco.

The drive was short, though twelve minutes never seemed so long. There was a gate at the entrance where a large man in a rent-a-cop uniform sat on a chair with no back, viewing a small color television to pass the time. He told me that visiting hours were over. I showed him my credentials, which amounted to my medical and PI's license and "ordered" him to inform the night staff that I was on my way up, before speeding off. I drove along the lengthy winding driveway a bit too fast, but kept on going, nonetheless. I knew that it would be at least another five minutes before Donaldson arrived, as he lived further away than I. There was a parking lot in front of the building for those residents still mobile or independent enough to drive. Or those who still had somewhere to go.

I got out and looked around. Long, green peaceful hills sloped down to the road I had just come up. The main entrance was ahead. All was quiet. I knew I should wait by the car but couldn't just sit back and wait for Donaldson to arrive and say, "Ok, let's go in." The building was cream stucco with a beige, slanted Spanish tiled roof. It looked like a resort from the distance. Each unit on the ground floor had an air conditioner sticking out. The top windows all had small balconies.

I bounded in the front entrance. The automatic doors parted as I approached and I saw the front desk. Behind it was a short man in his early thirties watching TV. I wondered if he were watching the same show as the guy at the front gate. It was obvious that the call hadn't gone through yet. It was probably the first "situation" the guard had had to deal with. I crossed the thin beige carpet quickly and silently.

"Excuse me," I said startling the attendant. "Do you have a woman here by the name of Gertrude?"

"Visiting hours are over at seven," the young man replied flatly.

"I need to know if you have a woman by the name of Gertrude here!"

"How the hell would I know?"

"Look it up."

"Who the hell are you anyway?"

"I'm a private investigator," I said unconvincingly, feeling stupid.

"Fuck you, Dick Tracy. I'm calling the police."

"They're already on their way. Look, I have reason to believe that a woman's life might be in danger."

"All right," the young man said. He raised a hand as if to appease me. "I'll look it up."

"Thanks."

It wasn't until I caught a glimpse of myself in the mirror behind the desk that I realized the sudden change in attitude by the young man had more to do with the fact that the .357 had shifted and was now exposed, than any understanding on his part.

"Gertrude is her last name?" he asked.

"No, her first."

"We only list last name and first initial. I'd have to look them up individually."

"Which women are listed with a first initial of G?" I asked.

The young man scrolled down the screen. "O'Connor, Gail," he read. "Vidal, Georgette; Myers, Gertrude."

"Gertrude Myers!" I pounced. "Good. What number?"

"Ah, 310."

"How do I get there?"

Exasperated, the young man said, "Follow me."

145

David Feeney

He led me down a gently lit hall, wide enough for wheelchairs, marked "Ladies Wing." The décor, I noticed, was serene. Green leafy plants hung in corners or rested on pedestals. Photographs and posters showing the elderly enjoying their lives appeared at regular intervals. Messages telling them to "Go for it," "It's never too late," and "You only live once," encouraged them to try everything from swimming to line dancing and golf. It was overly clean, boardering on sterile.

We made several turns, half of them wrong, and had to double back. "I'm not supposed to leave the desk," he complained.

I said nothing.

We arrived at room 310.

"Here it is," the young man said needlessly as I knocked on the door.

"Mrs. Myers?" I called. "Gerty, are you all right?"

"Not so loud; you'll wake the rest of them. They'll never go back to sleep."

"Have you got a key?"

"I left them at the desk," the young man said weakly.

"Great!" I kicked at the door latch.

"Careful, fella, you'll break it," the man protested.

"That's what I'm trying to do,"

"Gerty, open up please!" the young man said.

All along the hall, doors began to open. Heads popped out to see what was going on.

"Now you've done it!" the young man said.

I kicked the door open, .357 out.

"Oh shit! Get back in your rooms," the young man said before adding, "Gun!"

There were screams as I ignored him and entered the room. I reached in and flicked on a lamp that sat on a small table. A light came on and exposed about half the room. I stepped in and took a look about. The bed was empty and looked as if it hadn't been slept in. I looked around and saw why.

In the corner of the room, seated in a large chair was the frail form of the old woman from the park. The television was on in front of her. She wore a white nightgown. Her white hair fell to her shoulders. She appeared to be asleep. She was so peaceful. I'd been in the death business long enough to realize that she was asleep, permanently.

I put a hand to her neck to check her pulse. She was warm but there was none. Gertrude Myers was dead, but not long dead. On the floor, by her hand was a bottle of pills. Several were spilled onto the floor.

"What the hell is going on here?" I wondered aloud.

A sudden motion caused me to look up. Someone wearing a ski mask and trench coat stared in at me from outside the sliding door a moment, then ran off.

146

"Got you!" I tore at the curtains, found and unlocked a sliding door, pulled at it and stepped outside.

It was cooler now than it was before. Darker, too. I held the weapon ready and looked about. I took a few steps, bumped into some chairs and fell down. It took me a few seconds to realize I was standing on a patio. I was able to make out the shape of white patio furniture. Cursing, I got up and listened.

I heard footsteps moving away and gave chase. I rounded the corner and saw, some thirty feet away, the shape of a man in a trench coat as he ran down the couple of steps that separated the patio from the golf green. He opened a gate and ran across the golf course that stretched up the back of the retirement home. I ran down the steps to the fence and fumbled with the gate before entering the field. I intended to catch this guy once and for all.

I ran in a controlled, deliberate fashion, having been told long ago by Donaldson that it was easier to chase than be chased. The "chasee" had to watch where he was going, always fearful that one bad step could cause him to fall and end everything. The chaser, on the other hand, had only to pace the chasee and hope that he fell.

I rapidly closed the distance, gun in hand. *Was this the man from the morgue?* My quarry didn't appear to be very tall. *Was it somebody else?* I smiled inwardly. Old man, whoever the hell you are, this is going to be fun! I could hear the man ahead panting. He was running for the back fence but I knew he wouldn't make it. Donaldson was right; just pace him. The only thing that could ruin this would be if he were armed.

The trench coated man stopped running. He turned, drew a weapon, and let off two shots in my direction.

I ducked and hit the ground awkwardly as the bullets raced past me, one a bit too close.

The man fired another three shots. He then turned, covered the distance to the back fence and disappeared into the brush.

I raised the .357 and capped off two rounds. The report was like dual thunderclaps that echoed across the green. Adrenaline made my hand shake and the shots went wide. I picked myself up, reached the back fence and climbed it.

I jumped and rolled down the soft lawn on the other side. A few meters ahead was a street running through a residential area. I got up and ran onto the street.

A car bore down on me, with its high beams on. I hurried back onto the side of the road as it blew by me and up a hill. Angry, I jumped back into the center of the street. I could see the head of the vehicle's single occupant. I emptied the remaining three rounds at the retreating vehicle. The rear windscreen blew out as the car climbed, accelerating. The vehicle swerved before straightening itself as it cleared the hill.

David Feeney

I stood alone on the road; my weapon smoked as people in the neighborhood ran out of their homes to see what had happened. I felt so many different emotions: angry that I hadn't been able to speak to Gerty; happy that I got to send a message to the trench coat man; disappointed I hadn't put the bullets through his head instead of the car. I was also sad that she was dead.

The sound of the car dissipated, leaving me alone with the shadows.

"Late nineties Volvo," I read. "2M7-4 something."

25

8:48 PM

Sunset Homes swarmed with police, CSU and more than a few EMS teams. It was a sight that I was becoming used to. All the residents, except for the ones most heavily medicated were up, probably for the rest of the night. Most were giving their accounts to the numerous police, about what had been for many, the most exciting night in a long time. Some talked at length about the young man with a gun in the hall. Was he a suspect? What did he do? Did he kill Gerty? Some argued over whether they had heard eight shots, half that, twice that, or none at all. Others said it was motorcycles driving by. Some wanted to call their kids, to get them out of this "crazy house," while others, mostly World War II combat veterans, told them all to shut up. All the while the desk clerk tried to convince them, sans success, that there was nothing going on and that they should all just go to bed. I gave a statement as well. To make matters worse, some little guy named Redd ("My friends call my Red rooster," he informed me) kept approaching me, once he discovered I was a doctor, as he wanted to get his Viagra prescription refilled. "My regular doctor won't give me any for another week," he complained.

"With good reason, I'm sure," I told him.

"Yeah," Redd smiled. "But I need it tonight. I gotta make the rounds." He winked.

Not wanting to be the cause, even indirectly, of the deaths of any more elderly women, I declined. "Go back to your own coop there, rooster."

"Ah," Rooster complained. "It's all right for you. You're still on the prowl. I got to make do here." He smiled again. "I've never been so popular."

149

8:50 PM

Donaldson and I viewed Gerty's room as Carla Ryan, of the ME's office, finished zipping her up. Late thirties, single and pretty, I'd never made a move on Carla. The timing was never right. The room was light in furnishings, yet comfortable. She had her own little desk with a keystroke typewriter on it. A small adjustable light was positioned over the desk.

I asked Carla, "What does it look like?"

"No sign of a struggle," she said. "I'd say either she died of natural causes or she took too many pills."

"Natural causes?" I was incredulous. "He was right outside the window. He shot at me!"

"I don't doubt it," she said. "I'm just telling you what I got. Who knows, maybe you interrupted a murder. Autopsy will determine."

I shook my head. "How long has she been dead?"

Carla Ryan said, "We've got early non-fixed lividity and she's still warm. Under three hours. I'd say closer to two. No rigor yet."

"Two hours?" I exhaled. Non-fixed lividity occurrs within three hours after death. Simply put, the skin will blanch or whiten when pressed. Rigor mortis is the stiffening of the body due to the depletion of the muscle's energy source, Adenosine Triphosphate, or ATP. Rigor starts to show after four hours. By this point, the body will be noticeably cooler. Rigor is a poor indication of time of death due to different amounts of ATP in people's bodies, but lividity is an accurate estimate of how long a person has been dead. "What about the door?" I asked Donaldson.

Donaldson had the look of a man who had been called to work after he'd begun to unwind for the evening. He wore no tie and his shirt was half-tucked. "It might have been jimmied. No scratches. If so, it was by a pro with tools."

"Anything missing?"

Donaldson shrugged. "There doesn't seem to be anything touched in the room. Furniture hasn't been moved. Everything lines up with the indentations in the carpet. Clothing is in place as far as we can tell. Desk hasn't been disturbed. Could it have been a burglar that you surprised?"

"I doubt it. Matter of fact, I'm pretty sure the weapon he fired was a .22. Want to bet that ballistics matches them to the bullet pulled from Maria's head?"

"It'll be difficult to match," Donaldson said. "The three slugs that CSU found out back impacted against the wall. They're completely deformed. The rest they're still looking for. And if it is," Donaldson continued. "Why would the killer use the same weapon after all this time?"

8:53 PM

Later, after the commotion had died down, I told Donaldson about the message at the university, my day in the park, Gertrude Myers and how I had found her. Carla Ryan was still in and out so we spoke in hushed tones. She noticed this and said, "Secret messages in the boys' club? I'll leave you guys alone." Then she exited the room.

I sat on a chair. Donaldson stood opposite me. The room looked different with all the lights on. It was less mysterious and smaller.

"What about the car?" I asked.

"That's probably the only good thing we've got. They're running the plates now. That'll take a while, as the number you gave us was incomplete. Car's probably stolen," Donaldson figured.

"Maybe. Then again, whoever came here tonight must have done so because Gerty Myers posed a threat to him and he saw her in the park with me."

Donaldson nodded. "If that's true, our visitor tonight didn't have much time to plan. This was spur of the moment. Maybe he didn't have time to improvise and just took a chance."

"Exactly," I agreed.

"Dr. Hale, Judge Emerson and Astor were all at the park?" Donaldson reiterated.

"Yeah."

"You know, you're supposed to tell me what you're up to."

"I was worried it might be a crank," I offered in defense. "Besides, I knew after what happened to me in the morgue, you'd want to have me wired and covered."

"And I would have," Donaldson confirmed.

I objected. "And maybe she wouldn't have approached me."

Donaldson nodded. "Maybe. If this was a murder made to look like an accident, then it was very well done."

"Somebody's covering his tracks. Just like when he cleared out Maria's apartment. He's getting rid of people who have information on her. Check out Gertrude Myers. I'll bet she worked for our buddy, Mr. Astor."

"I will. She's probably one of the women who got married and changed her name."

I took a breath. "We're getting close. Somebody's frightened."

"No kidding! If he gets any more frightened, you'll be dead. It's just pure luck that he hasn't killed you yet, anyway!"

Carla Ryan returned and collected up an evidence bag containing Gertrude Meyer's bottle of pills.

"Hang on a second there," I said. "What kind of medicine was she taking?"

Ryan turned the bag over and looked at the small prescription bottle. "Ticlid."

"What's that for?" Donaldson asked.

"Treatment of stroke," I replied.

Ticlid, a.k.a. Ticlopidine Hydrochloride, was a platelet aggregation inhibitor. A stroke is quite simply a brain attack and is often referred to such. Similar to a heart attack except in the case of stroke, blood and oxygen is cut off to part of the brain. Depending upon which part of the brain is affected, vision, speech or movement can be impaired. Because the brain doesn't register pain, often a person is unaware that they are having a stroke.

I shook my head in realization. Gertrude Myers had had a stroke some time ago. That explained her strange behavior at the park. She had grabbed me, but was unable to speak clearly. That's why Bud Parkins had had trouble understanding who had called as her speech was slurred from a stroke.

"You know, Connor," Carla said, "some of these old people take the wrong amount and...."

"Yeah, yeah," I said. I knew it all too well. A bit too much and she would be disorientated, like she was at the park. Way too much and she could die. Especially when taken in combination with other medication. It happened more times than retirement homes cared to admit and would explain a lot of what had happened today. Of course, nothing would explain the armed trench coated man. "May I see it?"

"Sure," she said as she handed me the bag containing the bottle.

I glanced at it a moment. "You know who could fake a good murder as an accident?" I tossed the bag to Donaldson.

Donaldson read the name off the prescription. "Dr. Hale."

26

8:58 PM

The director of Sunset Homes, Michael Sullivan, who was to be called in, in the event of an emergency, arrived. The evening's occurrences, in the opinions of all concerned, qualified as one. He arrived, looking harried. His hair was disheveled and he wore no socks; just old, sloppy looking shoes. The three of us sat in his small office.

"Mrs. Myers had been living here for about fourteen months," he began, reading through his records. "She had a stroke and her family opted to send her here so that she would be given supervision whenever she needed it."

"Is it common practice to allow patients here to take their own medication?" I asked.

"First of all, Dr. Connor, Mrs. Myers wasn't a patient. We consider all our people here as tenants," Mr. Sullivan explained. "And yes. Many of our tenants do take their own medication. It allows them a measure of independence. We encourage that. We also check up on them to make sure that they do take it. If we suspect that one isn't, then we take the appropriate actions."

I nodded. "What was her maiden name?"

Mr. Sullivan consulted his records. "Goldman."

Donaldson noted this in his notebook. "What can you tell us about her? Did she have visitors?" he asked.

He searched through his records. "No," he said, looking up. "Her husband died five years ago and she'd been living on her own. She has a son who lives in New Jersey but she liked the coast. After her stroke, the son's interest in her lessened."

"It usually does," I said. "What can you tell us, if anything, about her doctor?"

"Dr. Hale?" He brightened. "He does a lot of work with seniors here. He's been doing it for years. It helps to keep down costs. We're quite grateful."

"What exactly does he do?" Donaldson asked.

Mr. Sullivan said, "Dr. Hale has been volunteering his time and services for years. He helps to provide healthcare for some of the residents with limited means. He performs physicals, get's low-cost medicine for some. He comforts others. Nobody makes house calls anymore. They're lucky to have him."

9:10 PM

As we walked down the hall, Donaldson turned to me. "What do you think of that?"

"That's some coincidence, him being her doctor," I said, keeping an eye out for old Rooster.

"True. What about the medicine?"

I considered this. "It's on the up and up. I'd still like to ask him where he was this evening."

"Yeah," Donaldson said. "Let's do that."

27

9:34 PM

"Dr. Connor and Inspector Donaldson! Are you two out of your minds?" Dr. Hale asked, standing in the door of his mission district office/home. He wore pale blue pajamas, a royal-blue terrycloth bathrobe, slippers and a look of disgust that could not be described.

I got a glimpse of his hands, and much to my disappointment, they were uncut.

"First you ask me about a patient from fifty years ago and now you're actually accusing me of murdering a patient I barely know?"

"No, Doctor, we're not." Donaldson soothed. "We - - - "

"The hell you're not!" Hale screamed, loosing his cool, his voice shrill.

"Are you saying that you didn't know Ms. Myers?" I asked, sticking it further.

"Of coarse I knew her!" Dr. Hale exclaimed, red faced. "She was my patient!"

"We just want to know where you were this evening," Donaldson continued as if he hadn't been interrupted.

Dr. Hale was exasperated. "I was at a dinner with some friends. I just got in," he said calmly after several moments.

"Name of friends," I said without emotion.

Dr. Hale, recognizing that he had lost his cool, matched my detachment. "Clare and Michael Holmes."

155

"Doctor," Donaldson said, attempting to alleviate the tension between us, "a patient of yours was found dead an hour ago and a man was seen running from her room."

Hale paused. "My god. I didn't know that!"

Donaldson took a breath. This was a clear mistake as it allowed me, obviously angry about having been shot at and nearly run over, to ask the question, "How'd you get back so soon?"

"You bastard!" Hale said with venom. "I ought to sue you."

"How long have you been her doctor?" Donaldson interrupted.

"I've been working with Sunset Homes for about fifteen years now. How long had she been there?"

"About one year," Donaldson replied.

"Excuse me for not having a better memory, Inspector. I see some one hundred or more patients there twice a month. I can't remember everyone perfectly. No doctor can. Not when you deal with *living* patients."

I said nothing.

Donaldson continued, "Were you prescribing any medication for her?"

Dr. Hale took a breath and thought a moment. "I was treating her for stroke with Ticlid. She had one a while back. Not serious, in the sense of life-threatening, though all strokes are serious. Her's was bad enough. It impaired her speech. I prescribed Ticlid for her to prevent the likelihood of another."

"Did you know anything about her personally?"

Hale shook his head. "Her speech center was impaired. We didn't talk much as I saw so many people. But she was able to speak; though some days were better than others."

"All right." Donaldson said. "That's about all we need, Doctor. I apologize for dropping in on you like this, but - - - "

"But you thought you'd see if I was still in my running shoes," Dr. Hale replied.

Donaldson said nothing.

"Good night, Inspector."

"Good night."

Dr. Hale began to shut the door then stopped. "Dr. Connor, what branch of medicine did you specialize in?" he asked rhetorically.

"You know, it's pathology."

"The dead. It figures," he said with contempt. "You should have studied medicine and not death. It would make you less suspicious." He closed the door.

I turned and exhaled. "Prick."

"Don't look at *me*," Donaldson said, searching the mirror as he changed lanes. "You fucked up back there with your questions."

I looked out the window. "We should go and visit the Holmes family tonight and talk to them," I said simply. "Make sure that Hale was with them."

Donaldson waved me off.

"Why not?"

"You're fishing. Besides, I can check that out in the morning. You don't honestly think that he killed her, do you?"

"I don't know what to think."

"First of all, we need to wait for the autopsy. Then we'll see."

"When's that?"

"Tomorrow morning. That pathologist is back from his vacation."

I nodded. "Miller. I want to be there."

"We'll see."

"What's the problem?"

"The problem is how I'm going to explain to my boss how the hell you came to be running around an old folks' home with a gun, trading shots, when you're supposed to be advising me."

"I already made a statement."

"Not good enough."

"Tell them the truth. I got a lead and called you. I was worried for the safety of a potential witness and I acted."

"You sure did!" Donaldson said. "Fact is pal, this stunt might not be so easy to talk around."

I changed the subject. "He was Gertrude's doctor. Maria's too. Quite a coincidence."

Donaldson, though sympathetic, was unconvinced. "I agree. It is quite a coincidence, but think for a moment. Do you think he'd kill a patient, when it could only attract more attention to him?"

"Yes, if she had something to say that would prove him guilty."

"I don't think he did it. Besides from what you told me, there's no way that guy ran that fast or climbed a fence."

"I didn't get that good a look at him." I defended.

"Even so. He's not the one. Go home, buddy. Get some rest. Get laid," Donaldson perscribed. "You'll have to make out a formal statement in the morning."

"At any rate, we've got two strikes on Astor and now two strikes on Dr. Hale."

"What about Emerson?" Donaldson asked.

"Just one so far. But that could change."

28

10:40 PM

I sat in my study and stared at the ceiling. A glass of wine sat atop a doily on the coffee table. I didn't want to think about the case anymore. I took a sip. The .357 lay next to the bottle. The last few days had left me anxious, angry and brimming with untapped energy.

The doorbell rang. I stood, grabbed the gun and made my way through the house, keeping against the wall as I moved. I reached the front door quietly and opened it, weapon ready. It was Rebecca Wood. She carried a small package under her arm.

I exhaled and lowered the weapon.

She told me that she had found some flyers in my inbox at the university. I'd forgotten to bring them home, due to the attack. She said she had heard about the attack the day before and asked if I was all right. I said I was.

I chalked her up then and there to being an adrenaline junky. She was excited by violence. Not towards anyone in general, but in the life of the men she was with. She had dated jocks and guys who rode motorcycles. She would probably eventually marry a cop. She found dangerous men and men in danger a real turn on.

She mentioned how she had seen me on TV and I smiled politely. She asked me if she could come in and I said "s-u-r-e."

I took the flyers from her and brought them into the kitchen. I offered her something to drink and she opted for a beer. I knew where this going, and that I shouldn't, but I blamed it on my being worn out, tired and beaten up. She commented on the bruise on my eyebrow, before she touched it and asked if it hurt.

"Only when I look," I said.

She laughed.

The conversation went from the kitchen to the study and wound itself about such subjects as the case, what it was like to work with the police and a hundred other things that had little to do with the business at hand. She commented on the design of the study and I gave her the abridged version of how it came to be.

Eventually, her concentric comments narrowed themselves down. Which was good, as I had been debating whether I should assist this seduction or just hijack it. She said that she had noticed my looking at her in class. I told her that I couldn't help it as she stared at me a lot. The circle grew tighter when she mentioned teacher-student relationships and asked my opinion on such. I felt stupid for answering the question but said that what two consenting adults did was their own business. She agreed, saying that it was a stupid rule and then laughed, saying something about "Don't ask, don't tell," before adding that she had heard that about me. She mentioned a friend; Sarah McCarthy who had graduated a few years earlier and I said I remembered her well. *Now I'm the topic of graduate 'hen sessions,'* I thought. The conversation hit a lull and I decided that she had taken it as far as she could. Between the accumulated tensions, anxieties and frustrations of the last few days, I felt that I had earned it. "Ms. Wood," I asked, "would you like to go to bed with me?" Sex was best, I believed, when it wasn't too personal. "Ms Wood" smiled and said yes.

The first round, as I referred to it, was destined to be brief. It was exhilaratingly so and encompassed the best qualities of sex: free, and free of meaning. It was sex for the sake of sex. She had almost all her clothes off before I had discarded my shirt. This was no trick as all she wore was a summer-dress, no bra with panties and shoes. She had only to undo the straps that arced over her tan tennis-toned shoulders to allow the dress to fall, before she stepped out of it. She bit her lower lip when she saw the bruises about my ribs and I felt vindicated in my earlier appraisals of her.

I had to steady her as she slid out of her panties and stumbled, nearly falling over with a giggle. Her body was full and well curved. Her hair fell freely just below her shoulders. Her full natural breasts swayed as she tugged at my pants, and the display excited me. Though nude, she carried herself with a giddy confidence that I admired in a woman. I found her bountiful and more appealing than the thin and bony image of feminine beauty that was currently being sold to women and inspired all manner of ridiculous diets with disastrous results.

She eased me out of my briefs and onto the Italian leather sofa. She climbed atop me gently and put her hands on my shoulders to control her descent. I held her full hips. She "Hmmed" with her eyes closed as I came to full rigidity within her. She rocked her hips back and forth until she found a good fit. Her moist heat was intoxicating.

There are few things in life as invigorating as sex and I had long ago decided that there was no sex better than that with a twenty-two year old woman. Few things in life could measure up to firm natural breasts that had yet to suffer the traumas of gravity. I believed that it took an older man to appreciate what a young woman had to offer, as they often didn't know what they had themselves.

My training as a surgeon left my hands as deft as an appraiser's eye. I ran those hands across her youthful body, expertly surveying the vistas of her physique. They were not found wanting.

She held the back of my head in her hands and pulled gently on the hairs of my neck while I teased out one of her nipples until it was nice and taut. As she pressed in against me, I caught her scent. I admired the golden tan she'd obviously worked hard to achieve, and the way it ended clearly demarcated at her soft white breasts. She took the unfinished glass of wine and had a sip. She poured the rest of its contents across her breasts and I lapped it up quickly (I was worried about it running onto the carpet or sofa).

Her excitement nearly surpassed my own as she ground into me with vigor. What she lacked in skill she made up for in enthusiasm.

She jumped off me a moment later. "Hang on," she urged as she took my penis into her mouth. The sudden warmth of her mouth sent a shiver through me.

I placed a hand on her head. I had read somewhere that "the blowjob" was considered offensive by women over thirty-five and obligatory by women under thirty-five. I had found that to be largely true. Society's self-appointed moral cops blamed this on the most recent political scandal. Pleasantly, it was one of the few benefits of the collapsing American culture and was, in my opinion, Bill's ultimate legacy!

She sucked the head for a time with short sudden movements, but only the head. She flicked her tongue across the glans. She took me full in her mouth again and tongued me from base to head, working me slowly. The change in technique kept me from becoming fully erect. She drew me out slowly, deliciously.

I stood.

"Don't bother," she told me, but I ignored her advice.

She ran her hands gently inside my thighs. She held my erection in her hand and lightly stroked it while she tongued my balls. She varied the stroke, its tempo and pressure, as I stiffened in her grip.

I felt my legs flutter and sat down on the couch.

"Told you not to stand," she said and looked down and took me again.

I felt myself rising and lay back. My dick hurt, actually ached. I felt as if I were losing a battle and was retreating against an enemy who couldn't be stopped.

She opened my legs with her hands so she could get in closer, tighter.

"Just finish," I gasped from between clenched teeth.

"Hmmm," she hummed. At first I thought that it was in acknowledgement, but no, it was part of the act. And it sent a wave of pleasure through me. She "hummed," and increased the tempo. Her head rose and fell steadily and deliberately. She moved quicker, her "humm," steady and sure. I put my hands back, closed my eyes and stretched out as I felt myself drifting.

"Come for me, baby," she urged. Moments later I felt myself spill. I erupted and she continued sucking harder, spurred on by my convulsions and siphoning away whatever was left in me.

I exhaled, feeling the past week's tensions and frustrations lift.

She wiped me off with the edge of her dress and then sat on my lap.

The second round was more restrained. Her initial energy was spent and I was thankful as mine was still to be tapped. Like a marathon, it was the journey that counted, unlike the sprint, which concerned itself with getting from A to B.

I led her to the bedroom and gave her a playful, but firm smack on the ass as she jumped onto my futon. She sat on the futon, slid away from me coyly and crossed one leg over the other. I knelt at the foot of the futon and held her by the ankles, halting her retreat.

Taking advantage of recovery time, I pulled her toward me and opened her legs slowly. She offered no resistance but lay back instead. I kissed her knee and then gently set it over my shoulder. I did the same with the other and moved slowly along her inner thigh. As I drew in closer, I got a better view of where I was heading and couldn't help but admire her attention to detail. Neat and trimmed into a tight triangle, it reminded me of a well-manicured lawn. I found this far more attractive than the "Mohawk" look that many young women today considered fashionable. Or the "shaved" look and whatever issues that attempted to resolve.

She drew in a breath when she realized where I was going.

"It's your turn," I told her.

I tongued her gently, searching between the folds until I found what I wanted and manipulated it, as she moaned encouragement. She placed her hands on the back of my head and held me in place while she heaved against me, not that I had any intention of leaving. It took me almost as long to bring her to the brink, using finger and tongue to draw her out, as it did me, as she was already partway there. She shuddered. Her hips raised off the satin sheets against her will. She gasped before settling down.

Rested, ready and aroused by her encouragement, I kept her legs over my shoulders and entered her. My hands found hers and pulled myself in closer, compressing her frame and allowing for deeper penetration and better control. Now satiated, she had less energy but still managed the occasional wiggle. I tried a few different tempos until I found one that suited me. I maintained the pace using it to siphon off the remainder of my own pent-up energy. Whereas the first round, she had sprinted, this one was like a leisurely jog, so I sat back on my haunches and enjoyed the view.

After a time, I withdrew and told her to turn around. As she did, the sight of her full ass beckoned me.

She looked back with a flip of her hair. "Woof, woof," she joked.

"Quiet," I said. "There may be a test later."

I entered her easily from behind and with hands on her hips found my momentum again. Soon, I felt a growing tension about the head of my penis. I ignored the initial urge to quicken my stroke, as I knew my body. Prior experience had taught me that it was better to stride on to victory, for if I tried to sprint these last few yards, there'd be no winner.

So I strode on, depleting my body and looking up at the ceiling until my body was nearly through. She assisted me nicely in the final moments with a few sudden and well-timed counter-gyrations. I grunted once through clenched teeth, as my knees got weak. My quads cramped and I felt myself throb inside her: strong at first and then weaker as I slumped down on top of her.

We lay awhile, basking in the warmth of one-another's bodies and reveled in the heady floating sensation that is the hallmark of conciliatory copulation. Neither of us spoke for quite some time. She traced a finger about my chest as I cradled one of her buttocks in my palm as if weighing it and kissed her fully on the mouth.

"Connor," she began after a while.

"Dr. Connor," I corrected. Had to keep some distance.

"Dr. Connor," she smiled, "what's the difference between fucking and making love?"

I considered this a few moments before commenting. "I think that 'fucking' is sex you do *to* the other person for your own benefit and 'making love' is something you do *with* another person for their benefit," I said before adding, "Or a common benefit."

"So we fucked first and then made love afterwards," she surmised.

"Yeah. I think so," I said before correcting, "Actually, you fucked me the first time and then I made love to you and then I fucked you." I thought about it for a moment. "That seems about right."

She shifted her weight until her face was over mine. "So I should make love to you."

"Right now that wouldn't be making love," I said simply.

"What would it be?"

"Attempted murder!"

Rebecca laughed at my humor. "Not now. Later."

"We'll cross that bridge if we get to it." I was a man who knew my limitations. I had seldom in my life made love more than twice in one evening and on those few occasions when I had been inspired to do so, hadn't found the third really worth the effort. I wondered if Ms. McCarthy had told her my well-stated position on the subject: that if you did something right the first time, you didn't have to do it again.

"Come on. You can do it later," she encouraged.

"I don't know," I said. "But thanks for the vote of confidence."

"Why not?"

"Cause I've fallen," I mimicked with a laugh, "and I can't get up!"

Rebecca Wood laughed as well. "You're a doctor. Don't you have Viagra laying about?"

"You mean like in a mint bowl?"

"Yeah."

"No, I don't." I never felt the need for it. "Besides, I'm not that old, dear."

She shrugged. "I was going out with a football player once about a year ago. He used to use it. He was only twenty-two."

I rolled my eyes. "Dear" (I often called them dear), "if I use Viagra, you'll be using crutches."

After a time she said, "Con, I mean Dr. Connor," She corrected in mock seriousness.

"Yeah," I said, my eyes closed.

"I'm going to use your bathroom."

"Yeah," I said and then added as she got up, "Don't go poking in my cabinets." I never understood why women did that.

"How about your drawers?" she joked.

"Too late."

9:25 AM

I awoke before the alarm sounded. I felt drained and invigorated at the same time. It was about time for me to get up, so with regard for the sleeping form beside me, I eased off the futon and walked quietly to my private bathroom.

I shut the door gently and stepped into the shower. I adjusted the temperature and flow until I found a level and intensity that was to my liking. After a time, steam rose about me, fogging the room as water pounded the taut muscles between my shoulder blades. I felt a breeze on my back and smiled. I had a visitor.

She wrapped her arms about my waist. And as she pressed her body firmly against mine, she found me ready. "One for the road?" she teased.

"Hi, there,"

163

"I thought you said two was your limit," she said as she gently cupped my balls with one hand while the other gently stroked my over-worked erection.

"It's morning," I explained before adding, "Looking for anything in particular?"

"I found it. I thought I'd help you with those hard to reach places."

We took turns and took our time lathering one another. Our hands, well soaped, sought out every aspect of the other's body. There, we half-soaped, and half-massaged each other until settling upon a rhythm that we both enjoyed. After a time she turned away from me, maneuvering her ass against my erection where she ground against it. She took my soap-slicked hands and put them between her legs. "Double-click my mouse," she told me.

I almost laughed at the phrase but didn't want to ruin the moment. My trained surgical hands worked precisely and with firm gentleness manipulated the folds of her pussy. I worked her into a fury before easing off somewhat when I felt her shudder. Without breaking momentum, I used one hand to cup her breasts, first one, and then the other as she leaned back against me.

"On the bed," she said suddenly.

I understood her dilemma as I remembered well the early days of my own sexual encounters. In the moments before orgasm, I often couldn't make up my mind which position to do; often I wanted to do all at once, so intense and immediate was the feeling. We rinsed off under the torrents. I kept one hand on the action, keeping her in a holding pattern.

We went back to my bedroom. The cool air revived me, hardening me to the job, literally at hand. There, we sat on the futon and stretched out, she in my lap. My left hand still stirring her while the right hand found a breast.

She followed suit taking my erection and stroking it, a bit rough at first as she was excited, but I didn't mind. We quickly found our rhythm, though she was well ahead of me.

The whole thing reminded me of a game of "chicken" where the object was to get the opponent to blink first.

"Ah-ah-ah." Rebecca blinked and blinked and blinked....

"I won," I said jokingly.

She said nothing but smiled and exhaled. She let go of me and curled up in my arms. I held her for a while and brushed her hair out of her face with my hand. She exhaled. "Woo. That was fun."

"Welcome back." I said.

She looked up at me. "What's for breakfast?"

29

10:40 AM

"More pancakes?" I asked over my shoulder.

"No, I've got plenty," she said as she twirled a piece of pancake in the maple syrup before consuming it.

I felt rested and ready to face the day. I had gotten dressed in a pair of Dockers and a polo shirt. Her stuff was still in the study so I gave her my bathrobe to wear while we had breakfast. I checked the pans on the stove. I always cooked my breakfasts in the reverse order of their cooling rates. For example, I had long ago noticed that pancakes cool quicker than omelets or hash browns. So when I made breakfast for myself, I made the hash browns and the omelets first and then the pancakes. That way, by the time the pancakes were ready, the hash browns and the omelets would still be warm.

I shuffled up the remainder of the food onto my plate and walked over to the island. There I sat opposite Rebecca. I tilted my plate and let a few hash browns slide onto hers.

"I'm fine," she said.

"Finish it up," I ordered.

It was her third helping. All considered, she had great appetites, I decided: four pancakes and a good-sized omelet. Not to mention the sex. I started in on my ham-cheese-and-tomato omelet and was surprised at my own appetite. I alternated eating, taking a piece from the omelet, then the pancakes and then over to the hash browns.

Conversation between us was nil, as there really wasn't anything left to be expressed. I appreciated the fact that she didn't see fit to fill this time with a lot

165

of clutter, polite empty-talk, devoid of meaning and meant to fill the quiet. I was happier still that she didn't want to talk about *it*, her favorite part and so on. I considered it a failing of the young that they always saw fit to discuss these things; to find some hidden meaning or relevance in the act. Instead, she busied herself with the morning newspaper. I thought about my accumulated tensions and anger of the past few days, and how effectively they had all been dissipated. The attack in the morgue had left me brimming with adrenaline. I reflected and hoped I'd shown her a good time. I had never been one to neglect a woman. I thought of my friends and associates, the way many of them lamented the death of regular sex, never mind oral, and decided that they probably took their wives for granted.

I indicated the orange juice and she nodded, so I filled her glass. After empying the rest of the juice into my own, I took another mouthful of the omelet.

"Do you want a section of the paper?" she asked.

I nodded.

"Sports, politics?" she prodded.

"Comics," I replied. It was to me a higher quality of fiction then the rest of the paper, which I seldom read. I had it delivered every day, however, as it made good kindling in my fireplace. I also had it delivered, as it was cheaper.

There was a knock at the front door.

"Want me to get it?" she smiled.

"No," I said firmly.

I crossed the distance to the foyer and opened the door.

"Morning, babe," Donaldson said.

"Yes it is." I would have tried to stop Donaldson from entering so I could "shoo" Rebecca out the back but Donaldson walked right by me. Besides, I had never "shooed" a woman out of my home yet. I realized that I wouldn't live this down, so I simply followed my friend through the house. In truth, I was feeling too damned good to care.

"How's life on the left tit?" Donaldson asked and then noticed Rebecca, who, not understanding the joke, arched an eyebrow and looked at me. I waved her off.

Rebecca stood, put her plate into the sink and said, "Morning."

"Yes it is." Donaldson said. "Something smells good," he continued, trying to fast-forward the moment.

Rebecca walked to the study and shut the door. She stayed in there a few minutes. All the while Donaldson and I bantered on about such subjects as the weather, how clear the view of the Golden Gate was, and why was it called "Golden Gate" as it wasn't gold but red. Then she emerged, said her good-byes and left.

I was happy that she didn't kiss me goodbye and happier still that she hadn't said anything about seeing me in class.

The front door shut.

"The legend lives!" Donaldson declared without missing a beat.

I was worried that she could have heard. "You told me to get laid," I said quietly.

"Yes, I did." Donaldson agreed. "I used to think it was bullshit, y'know, about you being a lady's man. A viscous rumor created to discredit your wholesome Catholic upbringing." He put a hand on my shoulder. "You did go to Catholic school didn't you, Connor?"

"Yep."

"Were you an alter-boy?"

I nodded.

"Ah-sure now, Father," Donaldson said in his best Irish accent, which wasn't very good, "I don't know what happened. One day he's serving the church and the next day he's cavorting with women. It must have been the kneeling." He laughed. "I was starting to get worried about you, Declan. You know, the other rumor: single guy, doctor, teaches college, living in San Francisco. And this place is so well put together, neat and stylish even. People see all this and they ask, 'Why no wife; why no women?' and then someone says 'Well y'know, I heard that he's - - - '"

"I got the picture."

Donaldson took a breath, "But now I can tell them. Tell them all. Our little Connor likes pussy." He laughed.

"Oh yes," I agreed. "Pussy is our friend."

"Speak for yourself," said Donaldson. "Tell me something. How old was she?"

I shrugged. "I didn't card her."

"Come on, buddy?"

"Old enough to drive," I said simply.

"Twenty-one? Two?"

"Thereabouts," I said as I gathered up her plate and cutlery and set them in the sink.

"Hmm-hmm. There's nothing like having sex with a twenty-two year old."

"How would you know?" I fired back.

"I must have read it in a book," Donaldson concluded.

I ran the water on the dishes. "Remind me to get you the Playboy channel for your birthday."

"I gotta ask," he paused for effect. "Did she blow you?"

I took a dishrag and started cleaning a glass. "A gentlemen never talks."

"Oh, come on," Donaldson implored. "I'd tell you."

I laughed. "What's to tell?"

"Hey, hey - - - "

"Did you want something to eat?" I asked, changing the subject.

"Y'know, scientists have discovered a food that diminishes a woman's sex drive."

"What's that?"

"Wedding cake."

"Here," I set a plate on the island.

"Thanks," Donaldson said, sitting down.

I dried the dishes as Donaldson sat at the island and ate.

"I've got a few questions about what happened last night," I began.

"Such as?" Donaldson asked.

"Such as, did Hale's alibi about being with the Holmes family check out?"

Donaldson nodded. "Yes. He was there; the wife too. I spoke to them this morning. Next?"

I wasn't surprised. "What about the car?"

"It was stolen from a suburban shopping mall about an hour before your run-in with the mystery man."

"No prints?" I asked.

"Of course not."

I said nothing.

Donaldson took a swig of orange juice. "Guess who the owner was?" he asked, seriously.

I noticed the change, stopped drying and turned. My bruised face hardened. "Who?"

"Geraldine Emerson," he said calmly.

"The Judge's wife? You're kidding me!"

"No. She was at Macy's in the mall and when she came out, the car was gone. I talked to mall security and the officer who took her statement. The car was swiped about an hour before your run-in."

"You're sure it was her car?" I couldn't believe what I was hearing.

Donaldson nodded. "A 1998 Volvo. License plate number was 2N9-410. You gave us 2M7-4."

"I wasn't wearing my reading glasses."

"No big deal. It was found this morning over in the Tenderloin district."

I said rhetorically, "So she has an alibi."

"Tight as a mink glove," Donaldson replied and took another bite of pancake.

"You spoke to her?"

Donaldson nodded, his mouth too full to respond.

"Why didn't you call me?"

Donaldson swallowed. "Cause my boss told me you're not supposed to be involved in the investigation. You're just an advisor. Your little stunt last night raised a few eyebrows. The fact that you were contacted by the victim and that you probably interrupted a crime in progress are the only reasons the city hasn't pulled the plug on your involvement."

I was silent.

"The real problem was your buddy, Dr. Hale. He complained that we were harassing him, actually just you," Donaldson corrected. "I was called onto the carpet about that. I told my boss that I brought you along due to the medication in question and that I needed your expertise on how to approach Hale. It appeased them a bit, but they're still leery. So, if you're going to tag along in the future, you'll have to leave the questioning to me."

"What about the Judge?" I asked.

"He was having dinner with a few old legal buddies, all Judges, all respectable. The mayor was there, too."

I was exasperated and shook my head. "This is bizarre."

"I've been thinking about it all morning," Donaldson began. "Personally, I think the use of the Judge's wife's car was a ruse."

"How so?" I was interested, as there was such a mountain of conflicting evidence that it was becoming increasingly difficult to sift through it all.

"We visited Astor a few days back. Then we learned of Dr. Hale and spoke to him, right?"

I had finished drying and took a seat opposite Donaldson. "Right," I concurred.

"When did we visit Judge Emerson?"

"After I was attacked in the morgue."

"Exactly," Donaldson agreed. "But the same night," he added.

"But he saw the special on TV," I said.

"Sure, but he's a smart man. Do you really think that if he was involved in this, he'd attack you when he couldn't even be sure that the identity of the victim hadn't been established?"

"That would really be tipping his hand," I admitted.

"Not to mention the risk," Donaldson added.

"Maybe he was moving fast. Anticipating the inevitable," I suggested.

Donaldson shook his head. "And if it was him, why then use a car that could be traced back to him so easily? He would have had a couple of days to plan it out. Why be so stupid?"

"He or she wasn't expecting me to show up at the old folks' home?"

"She?" Donaldson shook his head. "You don't really believe that it was the Judge's wife last night, do you?"

In truth, I didn't. It was just that in the past few minutes, my mind had replayed the chase across the green again and again. There was something about the way the assailant ran that I'd noticed but hadn't really considered until Donaldson told me about the owner of the car being Geraldine Emerson. The trench coat person had descended the stairs daintily, and had run with hands extended. He had run the way little girls do, as if afraid to fall. It had struck me as feminine, though I hadn't thought of it until now. I reiterated this to Donaldson.

Donaldson rejected this theory completely. "I think that whoever killed Maria Cialini panicked after we visited, and after failing to kill you, decided to point the finger at the Judge in some way so as to take the spotlight off himself. And that leaves you with - - - "

"Mr. Astor or Dr. Hale," I said. "Only Hale had an alibi last night and I'm sure if we checked into it, Astor would have one, too."

"Right, but think about this. Astor had two days to mull over what we said. And on the second visit, we told him who she was, that she worked for him, etc. If he's the one, that would certainly have felt like we were getting close. And don't forget that lawyer. Carver could have jumped you, and Clarke could have been at the old folks' home. You said in your statement, he was of average height."

I nodded. "We haven't seen Carver in a while. I'd like to get a look at his hands."

"Plenty of time for that. What about Dr. Hale? We approached him that very morning with her name and everything. It would have been quite a shock to him that we made that much progress in just a few days," he said before adding, "If he's the one." Donaldson pushed his plate aside, finished. "Guess who else I spoke to this morning?"

"You've been busy. Who?"

"Harold Davidson."

I shrugged. "Who's that?"

Gertrude Myers' son in New Jersey."

"I don't follow."

"Gertrude Goldman married a fellow named Davidson a while back. They divorced and she married Myers a few years after. Both husbands are deceased," he explained.

I exhaled skyward. "What did the son have to say?"

Donaldson shifted in his chair. "Not much. He confirmed the basics, where she lived and all that."

"What about who she worked for?"

"That too. She worked for the Pyramid Group around the same time Maria Cialini worked there. I consulted that list Mr. Clarke gave me to get the specifics," Donaldson said. "She was there all right. Same department. Same timeframe. She left the company about a year after Maria disappeared."

I nodded.

Donaldson looked at his watch. "Let's catch that autopsy.

170

30

We didn't go directly to the morgue. On the way over, Donaldson remembered that he'd had to have me confirm that the car they had in the impound yard was, in fact, the one that attempted to run me down at the Sunset Homes. The impound yard was on the way to the morgue and we had plenty of time. I viewed the vehicle and said that, due to the bullet holes, it probably was, as I didn't get much of a look since I had been too busy diving for cover. "Not to worry," Donaldson told me, as the ballistics would confirm. We also made a quick stop at the Police Lab, where I relinquished my .357, which I now carried everywhere. Donaldson had them put a rush on the test, so I could have it back ASAP. The rush was done in light of the two attempts on my life; one deliberate, the other incidental. The technician, known for his competency and tact, promised that I could pick up my revolver in a couple of hours. With this accomplished, we went to the morgue.

City Morgue: 1:04 PM

The city morgue was different from the University's in several respects. First, it was a few decades older and its architecture reflected such. Secondly, it lacked the atmosphere of the university's morgue. Not that any morgue has much of an inviting environment, but here the emphasis was on sterility as opposed to style. The primary colors and components were white tile and stainless steel with bright fluorescent lighting as opposed to pastels and diffused lights. One thing consistent between the two morgues was the smell of disinfectant.

We introduced ourselves at the desk and were soon greeted by a young man named George Rham who led us to the changing room. We met Dr.'s Miller and Matthews who were already "suited-up." The introductions were brief. All knew eachother or had heard of one another. I knew Miller and Matthews as I had worked with both of them in the years before my leaving the ME's office. Donaldson knew Miller from having met and consulted with him on several cases and he knew Matthews by reputation.

It took Donaldson and myself only a few minutes to don the gowns, booties, facemasks, gloves, et al. Next we were led into the autopsy room where they would be performing the procedure. Dr. Miller, fresh from his week in the mountains, would lead. Dr. Matthews would be his assistant and George Rham would be the diener. Donaldson and I would watch.

George Rham exited to retrieve the body of Gertrude Myers. While he was gone, Miller and Matthews laid out the equipment they would be using. Saws, various scalpels and bread-knives were set on a tray, as was an oscillating saw to cut through the skullcap.

Though I hadn't performed a procedure in this room in some time, I felt right at home and quite comfortable with the fact that I would merely be watching.

George Rham returned and wheeled in the still clothed corpse of Gertrude Myers. Donaldson and I stepped back as Dr. Matthews and Mr. Rham lifted her body from the gurney onto the autopsy table.

Dr. Miller spent a few minutes taking photos of the body from various angles. He worked quickly and quietly. The only sound heard was the "POP" of the flash.

Next the body was unclothed and the white nightdress and underclothes set aside. I noticed that the doctors had a difficult time removing her clothing as she was still in a state of rigor mortis. A state that wouldn't be resolved until thirty hours after her death, although rigor mortis would be fading now and her neck and jaw would already be slack. I also noticed that her skin was greenish-red in color, an indication that the she'd been dead between eighteen and twenty-four hours. I knew that if I touched her body, her skin would have been clammy.

Dr. Miller took another set of photos, tracing his previous angles in reverse until he wound up back where he started.

With this done, Dr. Matthews weighed and measured the body while Dr. Miller prepped the X-ray machine. X-rays were taken and sent to the lab for developing. These would later, along with the rest of the materials from the autopsy, be placed in a file called the autopsy protocol.

Dr. Miller adjusted the microphone that hung from the ceiling. "This is case number 70-1066, Gertrude Myers. The body is that of a well-nourished woman of seventy-nine. She has green eyes and white hair. She is sixty-three inches long and weighs one hundred twelve pounds." He read this from a piece of paper that Dr. Matthews had handed him. Dr. Miller went on to note, the condition of her teeth, her scars, as well as moles and the general condition of the body. He noted that rigor mortis was still present, though it had lessened about the neck and jaw. Her hands and fingernails were checked for fibers, blood or skin, but none was found. Hair samples were taken from the head and pubis and set aside. The genitalia were also inspected for signs of injury. Vaginal and anal swabs were taken as well. With the external examination completed, it was time to begin the internal examination. A thoracic-abdominal incision, a.k.a. a "Y" incision, was made from shoulder to shoulder across the chest, crossing the breasts where it met at the lower part of the sternum. There it continued down to the pubis.

The cartilage connecting the ribs was cut and the heart exposed. Dr. Miller opened the pericardial sac and took a sample of blood. This he handed to Dr. Matthews who set it aside. It was from this sample that Gerty's blood type would be confirmed as they already had it from the records from Sunset Homes.

Next the heart, lungs, trachea and esophagus were removed "en bloc" (all at once). Each organ was weighed by Dr. Matthews and noted by Miller who also examined each organ before sectioning them. The sections were set aside in "save jars" and would be utilized later in microscopic examination.

Next, the abdomen was examined for damage, and the fluids contained therein were aspirated and set aside for further analysis. The organs of the abdomen were removed, weighed, examined and sectioned. The stomach contents were emptied and a sample was taken. Samples of urine were obtained from the bladder. These organs, too, were all removed en bloc.

Nothing out of the ordinary was found and, in truth, I wasn't surprised. It was in the head that I expected to find the cause of death, although it was also possible that the stomach contents or blood would yield the presence of Ticlid or other drugs.

They turned their attention to the head. Dr. Miller first checked the eyes for petechiae, tiny red specks; actually hemorrhages that would denote strangulation, suffocation, hanging or choking. These he checked along the mucous membranes inside the eyelids, but found none. Dr. Miller took a scalpel and made an intermastoid incision from ear to ear across the scalp. He peeled the scalp forward, exposing the skull. The skull was cut away making the brain visible.

"Here we are," Dr. Miller announced.

"What's that?" I asked.

"Hemorrhagic stroke," he explained. "Subarachnoid hemorrhage, to be precise."

I moved to get a better view. There are two types of strokes, ischemic and hemorrhagic. Ischemic is caused by a blood clot in one of the arteries of the brain. Hemorrhagic stroke is best described as a "blowout" of a blood vessel in the brain. A subarachnoid stroke is a type of hemorrhagic stroke where an aneurysm bursts in one of the large arteries or near the membrane surrounding the brain. In the case of subarachnoid hemorrhage, blood spills into the area about the brain that is surrounded by protective fluid. This blood-contaminated fluid ultimately encompasses the brain. Hemorrhagic stroke occurrs in about twenty percent of all strokes, yet accounts for about half of all deaths. Subarachnoid hemorrhages are easily spotted at autopsy as the aneurysm itself often is, too.

"Have a look," Dr. Miller said. "See that?"

I didn't have to strain my eyes to see the hemorrhage. She had died of a stroke, no doubt about it.

With the autopsy completed, all that remained was to return the organs to the body and sew the "Y" incision back up. Tests and studies would be performed on the blood, urine, hair, stomach contents, et al, but wouldn't be back for a few days at best. For Donaldson and myself, the process was over. We had our cause of death and didn't need to see anything further.

"Let me know if tox comes back with anything," I said before we left.

31

3:12 PM

The drive back to the lab was quiet. I was having difficulty putting the results of the autopsy into perspective as I reviewed them again. I wouldn't have believed them at all, if I hadn't been there and seen it for myself. Gertrude Goldman-Davidson-Myers, despite the fact that a man or woman with a gun was attempting to or had broken into her apartment, had died from a stroke some two hours previous to the attempted break-in. I turned it over again. It had all seemed so clear when I entered her apartment. She was in her chair, dead. An intruder was outside having just picked the lock. It had been obvious to me that the intruder's presence and her death must be connected. *But she had been dead for two hours!* Likewise, I knew that the shock of seeing a man wouldn't have been enough to cause a stroke, not a subarachnoid hemorrhage. Had she died of a heart attack, there might have been a chance that the intruder could have caused it.

We picked up my .357 from the lab. The technician had completed the ballistic test and was satisfied that the bullets in Geraldine Emerson's car had, in fact, come from my weapon, thus confirming it was the car that had nearly run me down the night before. Donaldson thanked the technician and told him he owed him one. The drive back to my house was equally quiet as both of us, I, in particular, tried to assemble all the pieces into a coherent picture.

3:31 PM

"I wish we'd waited until this morning rather than heading over to Dr. Hale's last night," Donaldson said, sitting at my kitchen island. "We could have avoided a nasty run-in and getting my bosses upset about your involvement."

"No evidence of foul play, no bruising, no trauma of any kind," I reiterated. "Not even so much as a hair out of place. The ME emptied her stomach and there was no trace of pills. And the lab will prove the obvious." I shook my head. "A stroke. What are the odds?"

"Considering it was her second," Donaldson reminded, "I'd say pretty good."

"That's not what I meant," I said. "I meant, what were the odds of it happening last night, that way?"

"Maybe she felt the stroke coming on and was going to take her medication when it got her." Donaldson said.

"No. She wouldn't have realized that she was having a stroke. The brain doesn't feel pain," I informed before returning. "I saw a guy, somebody on the patio. What did your guys come up with about the sliding door?" I couldn't let it go.

"It may have been jimmied," Donaldson said. "If it was, it was professional. Probably used a laminated lock pick. So we can't tell if he was breaking in or had already broken in."

"It was open when I was there. Coffee?" I asked.

Donaldson nodded. "I believe you," he said defensively. "Look, you and I have been over this. Some of the guys at the station have a theory."

"What is it?"

"That you bumped into a burglar before he got a chance to break in."

"I doubt it."

"Or that your burglar jimmied the lock and stopped when he heard you kicking at the door."

I considered it. With the coffee ready, I poured Donaldson a cup. "Sugar?"

"Two. No cream."

I added the sugar and gave him the coffee.

"Thanks," Donaldson said. "Either way, you have to consider that the burglar had nothing to do with this case or her death. I mean, if he did, he'd have had to hang around for a couple of hours. That makes no sense. Believe me, buddy. Over twenty years on this job, you'd be surprised how one thing can turn out to be something entirely different. Or nothing at all."

"What are the odds of somebody breaking into an apartment two hours after the occupant died of a stroke?"

Donaldson shrugged. "Strange coincidences, I'll give you that."

"Yes."

Donaldson said, "As unbelievable as you may find it, I've got another one for you. What are the odds of an elderly woman dying of a stroke two hours before a burglar tries to break in and minutes before you come crashing in?"

"As of right now, they look pretty good."

"They sure do."

"One thing, though. Would a burglar break into a room with the light from a television set on inside?"

Donaldson shrugged. "All kinds of thieves out there. Getting ballsier all the time. Besides, this one had a gun, remember?"

I nodded. "It's hard to forget. Speaking of the gun, what has ballistics been able to put together?"

"Not much. They found six slugs altogether. All of them .22s and all of them deformed. They hit off the side of the retirement home. Getting a match will be impossible."

I said nothing. I flipped through the flyers that Rebecca Wood had brought over.

"What have you got there?" Donaldson asked.

"The new flyers." I held one up.

Donaldson motioned and I handed him a few.

"We don't need these anymore," he noted.

I viewed the image of Maria Cialini for a moment before answering. "I'm not sure. I may have some use for these yet."

32

3:48 PM

Donaldson left soon after, as he had to get back and "Earn a paycheck." I had to teach an afternoon class, to repay a colleague, and headed off a few minutes later. I didn't head directly to the school. Instead, I went over to a Staples super store. There, after several moments of contemplation, I wrote on, and then faxed one copy of the flyer with Maria Cialini's computer-generated image. After that I headed over to a cyber café where I scanned the flyer and E-mailed it. After searching the web a few minutes and confirming the address, I scanned the flyer again and E-mailed it. After that I went to school.

4:55 PM

The class went off without incident. Students filed in; I spoke wisdom. A few questions were raised, answered, homework was assigned and students filed out. It was just another day in academia.

I walked back to my office, where I checked my inbox. Finding nothing, I entered and settled down, thinking about the work that lay before me.

There was a knock at the door and I looked up to see Rebecca Wood. Her white shorts accentuated her tan legs and the cutoff shirt gave emphasis to her flat stomach and full bust. She looked good. As much as I liked seeing her, I was a little uncomfortable about the fact that she had dropped by my office. I figured that this visit had little if anything to do with school and hoped I hadn't made a mistake that I'd regret.

"Hello, *Doctor*."

"Good afternoon," *Thank god she's using titles.* "What's on your mind?"

"Well," she said entering the office in a way that made me uneasy, but I didn't show it. "I was wondering if you had decided on which students you were selecting for the exchange?"

The exchange? It took me a moment to realize that she was referring to the exchange program the university ran with its sister school in the UK. Every year several students of above average merit were selected to study overseas for a semester. It was a prestigious honor, and the selection, in which I had some say, had been determined months before. "Well, yes I have," I answered. Fact was that I got to pick two, sometimes three students.

"I was wondering," she began, "if I'm one of them."

I felt the beginnings of something; exactly what, I didn't know, though I was sure it was only a matter of time before I'd learn, so I played along. "Actually no," I said neutrally. "I've already picked two students."

"But you could pick three, right?" she pushed.

"I could, but - - - "

"Why not pick me?" she asked with a shrug.

My discomfort was peaking as the beginnings of whatever I felt were taking shape. The hairs on my neck stood up. Rebecca Wood was a good student, no doubt. However, the simple fact was that she wasn't of the caliber required to succeed in such a program and to send any student into a program, for which they weren't suited wasn't fair to either them or the program. I'd never really considered her as I felt that she'd be in over her head. I tried to convey this to her. "Your work, Ms. Wood, while good doesn't - -"

"Are you aware of the school's policy concerning professors engaging in sexual relationships with students?" she interrupted, the warmth in her eyes, gone.

There was a moment of silence in which my discomfort finally took shape in the form of a noose. One, which I now realized was fitting snugly about my neck, and into which I had literally stuck my own head.

She continued, sounding more like a law student than a medical one. "Section four of the school's handbook says that- - - "

"I'm aware of the policy," I interrupted. I didn't want to play anymore.

"- - - any such relationships are strictly prohibited and can result in the immediate loss of tenure by the offending faculty member," she concluded.

I said nothing. I felt trapped, didn't know what to do and I was furious.

"All I want is to study in Europe for a semester," she said simply.

"I could deny it happened," I countered.

"Yes, but unlike Monica, I didn't take my dress to the cleaner."

She's got you, I realized. *DNA evidence.* "If I were to recommend you - - - "

"I want to go," she corrected. "I don't want be recommended."

"If I get you in, then what happens?"

She shrugged in that sexy way that right now held no special appeal for me. "Then nothing. I go and that's that. I'm sorry. I tried to earn it, but the competition was tough."

I knew that I was trapped, but it was against my nature to simply roll over. "I'll have to think it over."

"I don't have time for you to think it over. The list is due soon," she pointed out.

I nodded. It was due the seventeenth of this month if I remembered correctly. I hadn't thought about it in some time as I had already made my picks.

"I'm sorry, Doctor. I think you're really cool, but - - -" she shrugged again and then left.

"You idiot!" I said to myself. I felt old and stupid. I opened the bottom drawer of my desk, took out a bottle of Bailey's Irish Cream and set it on the desk. I also took out a flask that looked like a beeper. Donaldson had given it to me as a joke. It was a novelty item that could be set to beep the owner to have a quick swig. I filled the beeper/flask and put the bottle back in the desk.

A moment later, Rebecca stuck her head in the door. "Oh yeah," she said. "I won." Then she was gone.

I took a swig of Bailey's, and then clipped the beeper/flask to my belt.

33

27th St. & Douglas St.: 8:00 PM

I sat in my Mercedes. To my left was Douglas Park, nestled in between Noe Valley and Diamond Heights. It had rained a little earlier and an oily smell wafted up from the streets. I'd been there nearly an hour, as I didn't want anyone to get the drop on me. I had selected this place and street as it gave me ample view of the park and anyone approaching it, be it by car or by foot. I thought back to the actions that had led me there and wondered if I had done the right thing.

As a doctor, I'd been taught that sometimes one has to fight disease offensively. That is to say, not merely to wait for disease to come to you, but to go out, meet it and defeat it on its own ground. This is often done in the form of vaccinations and other methods of preventive medicine. It was with that attitude that I had taken some flyers and sent them via E-mail and Fax to each of my three suspects; Judge Emerson, Dr. Hale, and, of course, Michael Astor IV. On each flyer was a simple message…

I know what you did to her.

None of the flyers were signed. No threats were made. None were needed. The implications of those seven words, I reasoned, would mean nothing to the innocent, but quite a lot to the guilty. Beneath the message was a time and place. Each place was different and the times were separated by one hour. This gave me plenty of time to go from one place to the next, should no one show up. I had done this because I was tired of being a target, as stationary targets tend to eventually get hit even by the most inept shooter. It was only a matter of time. I was tired of living at the whim of unknown assailants. I didn't like having to look over my shoulder everywhere I went. I didn't like carrying a gun all the time, as it really didn't make me feel safe, though that's exactly what I was doing. I didn't like that everybody always had an alibi and that they all were in a position to put pressure on the investigation, my investigation. I was angry and felt stupid over what I'd gotten myself into with Rebecca Wood. I hadn't told Donaldson what I was up to; he wouldn't have approved. But I had never let a sickness rest. That's not the way you defeat it. You harried it, you shook it up, you wore it down and you hunted it untill it was of no harm to anyone. Whoever had killed Maria Cialini was indeed sick and I wasn't about to let him or them rest.

I glanced at my watch; it was a few minutes past eight. The Judge was late, I noted, if indeed, Judge Emerson was guilty. The Fax had been sent to his home office, as he didn't have E-mail. This was better than if he had an office elsewhere, as I hadn't ruled out his wife. I thought about the Judge and wondered whether he was the one, going over what I knew about him for the umpteenth time. Jack Emerson was aristocratic in bearing and from a good background. He had known Maria Cialini from when he had defended her in a lawsuit she had brought against a landlord who didn't like her lifestyle. All he had then was his family's name, his burgeoning career and, of course, his wife. *Was there more?* Had he gotten Maria pregnant only to have her miscarry? Was he the cause of the second pregnancy? Such an event today would scarcely raise an eyebrow, particularly after the shenanigans the country had been recently put through by its elected officials. But back then, in 1948? Such an occurrence would have destroyed an up-and-coming lawyer's hope of ever attaining a Judgeship. The fact may or may not have hurt his credibility with the Civil Rights and women's movement, but may have been enough for him to kill over to protect his career.

And what of his charming wife Geraldine Emerson or his friend Mr. Issacson? Had they any part in this? The Judge could have been the man in the morgue; he was the right size. For that matter, he could have been the man whom Sarah Grodin saw going in and out of the apartment so many years before. The wife could have been at Sunset Homes. Except, of course, I reminded myself that I was attacked in the morgue before Donaldson and I had approached Judge Emerson. Would a man, or a husband and wife team, take such a chance and tip their hand, risking getting caught at a time when he or they couldn't have known that we knew of any affiliation with Ms. Cialini? Could the person at Sunset Homes who had run so femininly, been the Judge's wife, despite what Donaldson had found? Maybe Emerson, the wife, and Issacson were in it together, each one doing his/her part to help the group. *Whoever it was couldn't have known that I had been on my way over to Sunset Home; nobody knew.* That being the case, stealing the car to point the finger at the Judge had been a pathetic, half-baked attempt to implicate him.

I checked my watch again. It was nearly twenty-five past the hour and nobody was in sight. For whatever reason, Judge Emerson wasn't going to show.

It was time to get to the next meeting point. *Who knows*, I thought to myself, *maybe he is innocent. Maybe they all are.*

May flower & Carver: 9:07

It had taken me only fifteen minutes or so to make my way over to Bernal Heights and to the park of the same name that now lay before me. This spot, like the other, offered a good view of anyone approaching. I had done a drive by this street in case Dr. Hale decided to show up early and wait for me. The street was deserted, so I parked and waited. As it was, the good doctor was already seven minutes late.

Dr. Hale, a leading figure in the city's pro-life movement, gynecologist extraordinarre, founder of numerous free clinics for pregnant teens, finder of homes for unwanted children and caretaker of the aged. I ticked off the titles and accolades. He had been Maria Cialini's gynecologist from the time she'd come out from New York, but had stopped seeing her some two years before her death. Of my three suspects, Dr. Hale would best know the specifics of her miscarriage and possibly of the pregnancy itself.

Had Hale been the father? I wondered. A pro-life doctor impregnating a patient back then probably wouldn't have been well received by the movement, particulary, if she had had an abortion. He would be even less well received in today's radicalized atmosphere. Perhaps she was making demands on him, demands to leave his wife, demands for money. Everyone had his breaking point.

And why did he become "born again?" What had he said? *"I saw the truth,"* or something to that effect. I wasn't a religious man, but I knew that many people who professed to be "born again" often went through some great tribulation before their "rebirth." What was his tribulation - was it murder? Dr. Hale could have been at Sunset Homes, I reasoned, alibi aside. *He was Gerty's doctor, as well.* But what of the morgue attack? Who had that been? And what of the large man that emptied Maria Cialini's apartment, or the men who came asking for her? Could Sarah Grodin have been wrong? Could it have been a smaller man?

The fact was I didn't like Dr. Hale and part of me hoped that he was guilty and that he would make another attempt on my life, now that I was ready.

A car passed by, but never even slowed. I waited around for a few minutes to see if it would return or if anyone else would show, but no one did. I checked my watch: 9:21. I considered waiting a while longer, but decided against it. Why bother? The flyer had been specific enough. The doctor was definitely not making any housecalls tonight. I started up the Mercedes and headed for my final destination.

Duboce Ave & Walter: 10:02

I eased back into my seat. Ahead of me lay Duboce Park in the Filmore district. All was quiet. Even the sounds of the settling engine had long since died out, leaving me alone with my thoughts. I was disappointed that no one had shown up thus far. Disappointed that Dr. Hale hadn't made an appearance. In truth, I hadn't really expected the Judge to show up, *had I?* I pushed my frustration away to focus on the moment and its potential subject, Michael Astor IV.

Michael Astor IV was something of a west-coast legend. He had inherited a number of properties from his father and in the space of a few years, had parlayed those holdings into a real estate empire valued in the billions before dedicating himself to philanthropic pursuits.

She worked for him! From the time she came out to San Francisco until about two years before her disappearance, Maria Cialini had been his employee. Was she more than just another pretty face around the water cooler? Astor was known to have been something of a playboy. Married three times, he had several children and was often seen linking arms with various models and actresses at his events. The public, mostly due to his charity, winked at this bit of male vanity. His kindness, it was said, knew no bounds. My studies into the human mind told me that often such personalities demonstrated extremes of behavior, love and hate, kindness and cruelty, generosity and vindictiveness. Would an affair even back in the late '40s have hurt him? Perhaps, but he wasn't a public figure then, just an up-and-coming mogul. His name had been more powerful than he was, back then. It was possible, I reasoned, that a scandalous divorce from his first wife could have crippled his not-yet-formed empire and seriously set back its growth by several years. I had learned that Astor and his first wife divorced in 1955. Why? Maybe he'd had an affair and the wife had had enough. Perhaps Maria Cialini was holding an affair and the resulting pregnancy or even a miscarriage over his head. Could all his public kindness be reparations for some unknown private cruelty? Who could tell, maybe his philanthropy, which didn't come until years later, was the rich man's version of being "born again." Perhaps, it was his way of giving back after having taken so much.

She was found in his building, my mind reiterated, or at least a building that he owned at the time. Hiding her in one of his buildings would certainly have taken care of what to do with the body, ensuring him of an area that he could control indefinitely. The fact that he sold the building a few years later didn't necessarily mean that he'd had nothing to do with her death, as his lawyer tried to make us believe, but could have indicated a level of confidence on his part. He was confident that enough time had passed and that she hadn't been missed. It was now safe to let go of the property.

Astor was vain and kept himself in good shape. He could have been the man in the morgue. For that matter, it could have been Mr. Carver. Astor also could have also been the man seen cleaning out Maria's apartment, and Mr. Clarke could have been at Sunset Homes. When I factored in the lawyers, the possibilities only increased, and in my mind, increased the likelihood that Astor had been involved. The fact that the other two hadn't shown only reinforced the possibility that any second now, Michael Astor, or more likely one or even both of his lawyers, would appear to take care of this latest mishap. I tried to imagine Mr. Clarke and Mr. Carver showing up in their Jaguars and Corvettes or whatever they drove. I pictured them in black Armani suits and Bruno Magli shoes with knit caps, handguns and steak knives at the ready. Maybe they'd even bring a few trash bags to take care of the problem. The image was somewhat comical, but given their obvious devotion, particularly in Mr. Carver's case, and the way they worked together, I figured it wasn't entirely off the mark. On the other hand, I had called Mr. Clarke the night I went over to Sunset Homes, and by that point, Geraldine Emerson's car had already been stolen. Another thought entered my mind, a holdover from my ponderings. Could two of the suspects have been working together? What if Dr. Hale and Judge Emerson were in cahoots, to coin a phrase, or Dr. Hale and Astor, or Astor and Emerson?

I rubbed my eyes. When I considered these possibilities, the combination of scenarios was such as to make me dizzy. I'd have to draw it out with a flow-chart to make proper sense of it all. Still, my mind raced on with endless questions. How had Dr. Hale been able to afford setting up all those clinics? Was it entirely through savings, or had he a wealthy benefactor? Had he done a favor for somebody? Three men, all powerful in their own way, each with various levels of connections in the city, and each with much to lose, and I, the investigator, taking the scenic route to nowhere. Still, I had to do something. I had to shake things up.

A quick glance at my watch told me that if it was Michael Astor, then he or his emissaries were running late and were probably not going to show. *What had I done wrong?* I tried to think how each man would have interpreted the arrival of the Fax or E-mail. A legal mind like Judge Emerson's could have easily recognized the banality of such a threat and reasoned that he could afford to ignore it. He might just as easily have dismissed it as a crank. A man like Dr. Hale, I figured, would have been startled and easily pushed toward action. Michael Astor, the businessman, acting on the advice of counsel, could have ignored it or ordered his men to act for him. Maybe it was all a mistake. No. I figured, whichever man had committed this murder would have been startled into rash action. The message, seemingly omnipotent in its insinuations and directed at him alone, demanded action. I hoped it would be interpreted as something beyond the killer's control; something that threatened all his best-laid plans; a threat from the past that had returned to destroy his future. It was 10:31. Maybe none of them received it, I mused. With a final look around, I started the engine, eased the Mercedes out and headed home. It was several blocks later that I made an interesting discovery: I was being followed.

34

10:37

At first I hadn't paid much attention to the car that was behind me. It was only after I had made two additional turns that I picked up on it. Normally this wouldn't have aroused any suspicion, but I had been particularly paranoid the past few days and the single car on the otherwise empty streets caught my attention. I made a few more turns, doubling back and contradicting my previous direction. Sure enough, the other car followed suit.

I couldn't make out the type or model of the car, only that it was about three blocks behind me and was keeping pace. The knowledge that I was being followed excited me somewhat as it indicated to me that perhaps, I finally might make some progress after all and that the night's actions weren't in vain. The fact that I was being followed, more than likely by a murderer who had escaped detection by nearly half a century, and who despite his cool planning must be somewhat rattled, didn't frighten me, for as always, I had a plan.

I drove at a steady pace, keeping the Mercedes comfortably within the speed limit and headed west. I got on the Central Skyway and headed south on Route 101. Sure enough, the other car stayed with me, keeping a safe distance in the light evening traffic.

Does he know that I know? I tried to imagine what the other driver must have been thinking. *Who does he think I am? Does he care?* I squinted and tried to get a look back at the other car. As far as I could see, there was only one person in the vehicle and I had to fight the urge to slow down and get a better view, as I didn't want to lose my quarry. My training as a surgeon had taught me patience and planning, skills that would be brought to bear before this night was through.

I drifted casually over into the far left lane. The other vehicle followed suit. I did this on purpose. When I found the exit I was looking for, I put on my turn signal indicator and moved from the far left to the far right lane, crossing four lanes quickly like a person who had nearly missed his exit. But not too quick, like a person who was trying to lose a pursuer. Behind me, I could see the other car swerve suddenly; trying to keep up and slightly cut off a small pickup.

Not too experienced in tailing, are we? I noted. An amateur, I surmised. I made the exit and got off in the Mission District, pursuer in pursuit. There was no traffic in the area at this hour. I nonchalantly sped up and put several blocks between my pursuer and me. The pursuer did likewise. I made a left just as a light turned red.

This is where it would get interesting. I went a few blocks quickly and came to a stop. I waited a few moments until I could see the other car jump the light and close the distance.

"Don't worry, pal, you won't lose me. I promise," I said before making a turn and speeding off out of sight.

That ought to rattle your cage.

I waited again until my pursuer came into view and hung a left onto Mitchell Street, which curved and came to an abrupt stop. There was a blind alley that ran parallel to Mitchell Street. It didn't have a name, but was wide enough to fit my Mercedes. I had started my career with the ME's office as a driver, working the night shift. I knew every block of this city and had picked this area for any potential ambush as it stacked all the odds in my favor. I brought the car to a sudden halt, and reversed into the alley, making sure that the passenger side would be facing my pursuer. I killed the lights, kept the engine running and waited, after removing my foot from the brake. I didn't want the break-lights to tip off the other driver.

The moments dripped like a slow IV, but I was good at holding myself in check. I kept the engine running and the stick in neutral. I undid the safety strap on my holster. The .357 was loaded and I had brought along several speed loaders. I was ready.

Come to daddy, motherfucker!

As if on command, the pursuing vehicle passed by, slowly. As it did, I could see the driver's silhouette looking around, searching. *One person,* I was certain. I popped the clutch and applied the gas. I could hear the other car screech to a halt as the driver realized he had reached a dead end.

I sped out and stopped, effectively blocking my pursuer's escape and turning the dead end into a cage. The pursuer's vehicle reversed suddenly and then stopped within a few inches of the Mercedes. He was trapped. The moment had arrived. This was the tricky part.

I jumped out, drew the .357 and took up a defensive position behind my car. From there I could see the driver's side and, if necessary, empty my weapon into it. "Put your hands up!" I said in my loudest and most commanding voice.

Several tense moments passed as if the driver were contemplating his options. *Don't give them any options,* Donaldson told me, when dealing with perpetrators. *Take charge.* "Get your hands up or I'll shoo- - - "

The driver raised his hands and I could see that he held no weapon.

"Kill the engine, *now!*" I said. *That's it. Take control. Maintain the momentum of inevitability.*

The driver complied. The engine went silent and it was just my pursuer, myself and the silence of the alley.

I was aware in the sudden silence of a pounding and realized that it was my heart and I fought to maintain control of both the situation and myself. The thought, what if my pursuer had confederates? entered my mind. *What if they were entering from behind me now, closing the distance, and closing the trap.*

No. My mind whispered calmly. No. There was just one and I had him. I took a breath and regained my calm. "Keep your hands where I can see them." I came out from behind the safety of my car and closed the distance. *Keep the pressure up; don't give him time to think.* "You are trapped," I said as I reached the car, weapon raised and pointed it at - - -

"Dr. Hale," I said simply.

35

Dr. Hale, his hands raised, said nothing. He merely regarded me, through the open window, with a look that I couldn't quite surmise. Fear? Anger? Hate? "Making a housecall?"

"What do you want?" Hale asked in that manner that had irked me more times than I cared to remember.

"Why are you following me?" I asked.

"I don't know what you're talking about. I was just out for a drive when you blocked me and - - - "

"Don't even start that shit," I interrupted. "You've been tailing me since I left Duboce Park, maybe earlier."

Dr. Hale was flustered. "I did nothing of the sort - - - "

"I see you got my E-mail," I interrupted.

Dr. Hale squinted. Things were becoming clearer.

"That's right. I sent the bait and you bit-down, pal."

Dr. Hale staggered forward. "You're crazy, do you know that? When I - - - "

"You're 'born again,' right? Maybe you've got something you'd like to get off your conscience. The truth will set you free."

Dr. Hale snorted and was about to make a comment when I noticed something on the seat next to him, something shiny. Dr. Hale noticed my stare and moved his right hand.

I put the barrel of the .357 to his neck. "Do it, Doctor, and I guarantee you'll meet your maker tonight. Miss Cialini as well."

This last comment stung Dr. Hale. "You really are ignorant, you know that? What's your specialty again, autopsies?"

"You know it is." I was getting tired of this. Tired of the games.

"Dr. Death," he said with contempt before adding, "It's a disgrace that they even count your kind in the medical profession."

"What?" I was incredulous that this worm of a man was insulting my calling.

"I deal with life. I help people become families, but you. What attracted you to the field, your lack of bedside manner or the fact that there's so little chance of malpractice? Or maybe you're afraid of life?" He looked me in the eye and said quietly, "Some doors shouldn't be opened, Dr. Connor. You might not like what you find."

I had heard enough. My training as a surgeon had taken me as far as it was going to; indeed it had taken me into overtime. Fact was, the stresses of the past few days, the attack in the morgue and my nearly being shot and run down at Sunset Homes had gotten to me. Coupled with the fact that I was being blackmailed by a student, had been followed, and was now being insulted by what was at this moment my number one suspect, who was armed, was too much. I decided I was going to take my stress out on Dr. Hale. Right now.

I holstered my weapon, murderer Hale might be, he was no fighter. He never even attempted to go for the gun next to him. I seized Dr. Hale by the arm and applied pressure to the Ulnar nerve, more popularly known as the "funny bone," though there was nothing funny about what I was doing. When the nerve is struck, most people experience a spasm that numbs the lower arm. However, this spasm occurs if the nerve is struck momentarily. When the nerve is manipulated properly, the pain is excruciating, and best of all it leaves no bruises.

Donaldson had advised me not to leave bruises if I was going to assault somebody. When asked how I was to do that, my buddy had laughed and said, "You're the doctor. Can't you do something with nerves?" After some consideration, I realized the validity of Donaldson's advice and I had an idea.

"Dear God, what are you doing?" Hale screamed. "What about your oath, as a doctor? Ahh!"

I leaned in close. My ire was peaked. "I don't practice medicine anymore," I said calmly.

I pulled Dr. Hale from his seat, out through the open window and onto the ground, never letting go of his arm, the pressure on the nerve constant. "That's right, Dr. Hale, man of life. I am Dr. death." I said this in a way that gave Hale pause. Gone was the anger of a few moments before only to be replaced with an eerie calm. I was in the zone. "I've forgotten more about murder, torture, suicide and death than most people will ever know. I can make a sadist say 'enough.' I can teach a dominatrix a whole new repertoire. I'm more of an authority on death than your average cleric, and I'm going to take you on a guided tour of pain, suffering, and if necessary, your death, unless you start giving me something other than lies and attitude. Either way, I'm going to wipe that smug look off your face. What I replace it with is entirely up to you." I continued to massage the nerve gently, sending ripples of fire through Dr. Hale's already overloaded nervous system.

"Sweet Jesus, you're a monster! What do you want from me?" he pleaded. Sweat poured from his reddened bald head. I noticed that his hair, usually combed over to hide this fact, had fallen back. He looked ridiculous.

I stopped massaging the nerve, as I didn't want to burn it out, but kept pressure on it to maintain a certain level of pain. Oddly, it was similar to what I had done the night before with Rebecca Wood, only now I was keeping Hale hovering in agony. "You were following me, yes?" I said this more as a statement, not a question.

"Yes, yes I was," Hale, said weakly, the smugness gone.

"You got my E-mail," I continued.

Dr. Hale nodded, eyes clenched, tears streaming down his face.

I was unsure whether the tears were from regret or from the pain I was inflicting. In truth, I didn't care. I hadn't finished exerting myself on this man. "Let's have it!"

"Have what?" the old man gasped.

"The truth!"

Dr. Hale began to cry, providing sound to the tears. "I got the E-mail - I was shocked. Why was this happening to me? I was scared, so I drove down and followed you. I didn't know it was you."

"Why the gun?" I asked, eyeing the weapon on the seat. It was an automatic, a 9mm, wrong make, and wrong caliber.

"I was scared," he gasped. "I thought you might be her killer."

"Bullshit!" I said, beginning the massage again. "I want some truth." I paused a moment before adding, "End it, Doctor."

Something in Dr. Hale broke. "All right, all right! I thought that someone knew."

"Knew what?"

"About - - - " he whispered. "Miss Cialini - I killed - - - "

"You killed her."

"No," he said as if admonishing a small child. "I didn't kill her. I killed her baby."

"What?" I hadn't expected that.

"She didn't miscarry," he sobbed. "She had an abortion."

Abortion! "You performed it?"

"Yes."

I noticed that Dr. Hale was shaking and I realized that his nerves were shutting themselves down from overuse. Sweat poured from his face and his fist was clenched, useless. I released my grip on Dr. Hale's arm and took a step back as the older man slumped to the ground. He massaged his forearm and fist.

Both of us were exhausted.

I asked, "Who was the father?"

"I don't know."

"Was it you?"

"Depended on when you asked her," he said simply. "Sometimes she said it was; other times she said it wasn't. It depended on her mood. And she was very moody."

I said rhetorically, "So you were having an affair."

"You must be a PI," the old man said and then laughed.

I ignored this. It was a good sign when a suspect laughed. This often meant that they had given up, were finished lying and were attempting to deal with the futility of their situation with humor. "Was she threatening your practice? Your marriage?"

Dr. Hale nodded. "She did, at first. Said she wanted the procedure or she'd ruin me. I gave her that book on birth control, but she just laughed and said that it was 'too little, too late.' So I did it."

"That's why you became 'born again,'" I said simply.

Dr. Hale nodded. "I've lived with that mistake every day since. I should have let her ruin my job. One life is not worth the sacrifice."

"That was the first pregnancy. She was pregnant when she died. Who was the father?"

"I didn't know she was pregnant again. She stopped coming to my office in 1951. I told you that." He looked worn out. "I told you the truth. She came back for some checkups, but then she left. That was it."

I considered this in silence.

"I'll tell you this," Dr. Hale resumed. "As sorry as I am about what happened to her, she probably deserved it."

"Why is that?"

"You were right. She was the reason I became 'born again.' I'd never met a woman like that. Way ahead of her time. She had a helplessness that I later determined she could turn on and off like a faucet. That's what attracted me, you know, the helplessness. She was," he paused as he searched for words he didn't normally use, "open. Sexually open. She did things that up until then I had only heard of. She got into me like a drug. As soon as she was pregnant, though, she turned 180 degrees. Making threats, calling my home. I had to do something. I knew how to perform the procedure, so I did it in my office." He became angry at the memory. "She wouldn't stop harassing me until she got what she wanted."

I said nothing. In light of what was going on with Rebecca Wood, I felt a momentary solidarity with Dr. Hale. It didn't last long, though.

Dr. Hale continued, "She came back for a few checkups and then that was it. I never saw her again. I figured she must have moved on.

I weighed this.

"Whoever killed her was a man she took advantage of. I guarantee it. She probably angered the wrong fellow. You said that she was pregnant. She was probably blackmailing some new fellow and he killed her," Dr. Hale concluded.

"You say that in a very blasé fashion," I commented.

"Were you expecting me to cry, Dr. Connor? For her? You can't expect to go around using men like that and think that you can get away with it."

"You had an affair with her, and she blackmailed you into performing an abortion on her. She could have ruined you. That's quite a bit of motive, Doctor."

Dr. Hale shook his head solemnly. "Yes, but I didn't kill her."

"Convince me."

Dr. Hale looked up at me. "I'm not a killer," he said simply. "You can charge me if you want. But I didn't do it. Why would I admit to all this unless I hadn't killed her? You don't think your strong-arm tactics would get me to tell you anything I didn't want to, do you? Truth is, I'm not a killer." He reiterated.

I looked down on the old man, sitting pathetically on the ground. I searched his eyes and – believed him. Dr. Hale was many things, I realized; a killer wasn't one of them. I couldn't explain it, but I was certain Hale wasn't whom I was after. Sometimes a truth is so blatant, so obvious, that it stands of its own accord and needs no proof. I eyed the gun on the seat. "I assume the gun is licensed."

"Yes, I got it a few years ago," Dr. Hale said, rubbing his arm. "Some of my clinics are in rough areas and I carry it for protection. Addicts think they can get drugs from my clinics."

I realized that tonight's exercise had been in vain. I had succeeded only in riling an old man into following me to an alley. I had hoped to shake something loose and succeeded in shaking my belief in my own abilities to reason. I had nothing. I couldn't even charge the doctor with speeding. *Great.*

"I forgive her," Dr. Hale said softly, "for what she did to me."

I snorted. "You're being kind to yourself. Considering that you got her pregnant and then performed an abortion on her."

"That's if it *was* my child. With a woman like that, how could I really be certain?"

"Don't follow me again," I said simply. I got into my car and drove off, leaving Dr. Hale alone in the alley, sobbing.

36

SFCU: 12:15 PM

I arrived early and taught my classes that morning. Afterward, I dropped by my office. There was no particular reason for my visit. It was just part of my routine. I'd decided to tell Donaldson about the night before and my setting it up. I felt bad about what happened. Actually, I just felt bad. Not about roughing up Dr. Hale. I wasn't sure why I was doing this and decided that it must be a form of penance for the unrepentant.

When I reached my floor, the department secretary, Mrs. Genaro, told me that Dr. Sekor, Dean of Faculty, wanted to see me – immediately.

I'd little interaction with Dr. Sekor in the past, and could only wonder what he would want with me "immediately." His office was on the other side of the campus, in a building I seldom frequented. By the time I reached the building, I had some inkling as to what it could be about and hoped that I was wrong. I wasn't.

"Shut the door, Doctor," Dr. Sekor said when I arrived. "Have a seat."

I did as requested and took a seat across from Dr. Sekor. The room had a polished smell to it. There were but four or five years and forty pounds between the two of us, all of which were in Sekor's favor. I had met him on a few occasions and my general impression of the man was that he was a stickler for rules. Dr. Sekor had a way of over-talking a subject. He would often start at the furthest recesses of the actual subject and with each question; slowly approach the true subject at hand. He often spoke about a topic so as to take forever to get to the point. It reminded me of the vortex action of a toilet flushing or a black

195

hole. I felt that Dean Sekor liked the sound of his own voice. It was a common failing amongst administrative types.

"Dr. Connor, do you enjoy working for this university?" he began obliquely.

I did my best to conceal my shock, as I couldn't bring myself to tip my hand. "Absolutely."

"We let you use our facilities for your side-interests; you assign our students various tasks. All in all, I'd say what we have here is a fairly beneficial symbiosis," he meandered.

I said nothing.

Dr. Sekor rambled on, sitting back. "I can't imagine why anyone would do anything to jeopardize such an arrangement."

I nodded, pretending not to understand the implications and ignoring the sensation of a vortex swirling beneath me.

"Dr. Connor, I'll be brief."

That'll be a first.

"My office received an anonymous call earlier saying that you were engaging in a sexual relationship with one of your students. You know about the policies of this institution concerning such relationships."

Flush.

"Yes I do."

"What is it?" he asked.

"Section four of the handbook says that any such relationships are strictly prohibited and can result in the immediate loss of tenure by the offending faculty," I recited without hesitation.

Dr. Sekor nodded. I imagine he didn't know whether my ability to quote a handbook that nobody read was because I was an astute academic or because I had read it over for legal purposes and didn't know which would have been worse. "Good," he said simply. "I'm not going to ask you whether or not it is true. I'm simply letting you know that a complaint has been made."

I added, "An anonymous complaint."

"Correct. That's why I'm not going to push the issue. Had it some backing, I'd have to push…. *further.* I'm just letting you know."

"All right. Is that all?"

"Yes, for now."

The walk back to my office was slow. *Anonymous caller,* I thought. *Who dropped the dime on me?* Dr. Sekor didn't have much in the way of details. Could Rebecca Wood have made the call? Did she do it to quicken my decision? Was it another student? The last few days had been nerve-racking, and had taxed my cognitive powers to their limits; last night had only compounded that. This last bit of information from Dr. Sekor was about as much as I could take. I decided not to think at all. Instead, I would go to my office, talk to Donaldson and then go home.

When I arrived, Rebecca Wood was waiting.

"Good afternoon, Doctor," she said simply.

"You must be joking."

"Excuse me?"

I looked about the hall, and seeing no one, led her into my office. I kept the door open.

I spoke quietly because of the open door. "Did you tell any of your friends about us?" I asked this clinically, the way I would ask a patient if they'd taken a prescribed medicine. Any other way would be to add to the tawdriness of my dilemma.

"No, of course not," she said.

She seemed genuinely taken back by this. "You didn't by any chance make a call to the Dean and tell him about us?"

Ms. Wood shook her head. "He knows? God no. I didn't."

I exhaled. Her reaction seemed honest, but didn't it always?

"No, he doesn't know, not for sure. But he's suspicious."

"No, I didn't say anything. I just came by to see if you made up you mind."

"No, I haven't," I said, happy that she was still talking code. "I've been pretty busy."

"Well, you better make up your mind. You've only got a few days left."

"I'll think it over tonight."

"All right." She relaxed a bit. "I didn't call anybody. What good would that do? I'd only do that if you'd refused."

I tried to interpret this as a positive, but couldn't quite do it.

"I've got to go," she announced.

I said nothing. When she left, I sank back in my chair. Someone was setting me up. Someone was fucking with me. *Little bitch,* I thought, and for the second time, I felt a kinship and understanding with Maria Cialini's killer and a brief flickering sympathy for Dr. Hale. I wondered for a moment if the anonymous caller had anything to do with the case, but was too tired to consider it seriously. So I called Donaldson.

37

"You did what?" Donaldson asked.

I said nothing. Actually, it was the second time Donaldson had said this. Instead, I sat back in my chair. If I thought that Donaldson was going to come over to ream me out, I wouldn't have bothered. What was the point in confessing over the phone? As it was, I didn't feel better for my honesty and decided that it definitely wasn't my best policy.

"I'm sorry. You said something?" Donaldson continued.

"You wouldn't have OK'd it if I had told- - - "

Donaldson was angry. "You're damn right I wouldn't have OK'd it. What the hell were you thinking?"

I spoke calmly, the way I would to an irate patient or family member. I knew that I had crossed the line but didn't want to push Donaldson over it. "You're not the one who's been getting shot at. I had to do something. I guess I wasn't thinking," I shrugged.

"I'll say. I'm the investigator; you're the consultant. You don't go around running stings of your own. What if the killer had shown up?"

"What if he did?" I asked quietly.

"Oh great, just what we need. Bad enough that the mayor's looking for some excuse – anything to get you off after the pressure that Astor's put on him. If Dr. Hale were to go to the mayor's office - - - "

"He won't."

"How can you be so sure?"

I shook my head. "He just won't. He didn't do it."

"That's another thing. You've had a hard-on for this guy being the killer and now you think he didn't do it. Why?"

"I looked in his eyes."

Donaldson's tirade was cut short and was replaced by sarcasm. "Well, I guess that's all we need then."

I was about to reply when there was a knock at the door. Roger Stevenson looked in; a folder was in his hand. "Ah, excuse me, Doctor. You wanted to know when the tests got back."

"Thanks," I said simply, taking the envelope and returned to my seat.

"Tests on the mummy?" Donaldson asked, trying to change the subject.

I nodded as I flipped through the lab results. Nothing out of the ordinary, I decided. One was the result of the DNA test performed by Dr. Geist. I read lightly over the material, picking out the details I wanted as if looking for a specific purchase on a credit card. I reached a document dealing with an analysis of Maria Cialini's hair. "Bimeth," I said, uncertain.

"What's that?" Donaldson asked.

"Bimethorate; it's a drug."

"What's it for?"

I shrugged. "I'm not entirely sure. I've got a weird feeling, but I want to check it out first."

38

University Library: 1:30 PM

I stood on a ladder. We were on the third floor of the library, in the non-circulating section. The third floor served as a repository of what might be known as the ghosts of medicine's past. It was there that the university kept older reference books and texts generally not sought by the student body. This information had since been proven inaccurate. New methodologies had deemed the originals irrelevant. I searched along the shelf until I found the reference guide I needed. I took the book off the shelf and climbed back down the ladder.

"Found it?" Donaldson asked.

I nodded. "Yeah, it should be in here."

I sat at a small desk with the reference book in front of me, the lab results next to me. Donaldson sat at another. I flipped through the book and read intently. I turned and looked at the lab results. "Dr. Hale said that he *performed* an abortion on Maria Cialini."

Donaldson thought for a moment. "That's what *you* said."

"That's what *he* said," I confirmed. "Performed the procedure in his office were his exact words."

"Right. So?"

"Maria Cialini didn't have cancer by any chance, did she?"

Donaldson shrugged. "I don't know."

I closed the reference guide. I knew. She hadn't. I'd seen the reports on the tissue samples. "Dr. Hale didn't *perform* an abortion on Maria Cialini," I said simply. "Not a surgical procedure."

"How'd you figure that?" Donaldson asked.

I explained in uncomplicated terms how human hair grows at a rate of about half an inch per month and how drugs and medication get stored in the hair. I told Donaldson how each hair acts as a chart of not only what drugs a person has taken, but more importantly, when. It is similar to the way in which the depth of soil samples can determine the history of a region; its mineralogical makeup and so forth.

"Yeah, I've read all about that. But how accurate is it? Can you tell when she ingested it?" Donaldson asked.

I raised a hand. "Theoretically. The accuracy of the time can't be guaranteed as far back as we're going. But we're developing some new techniques here that could extend the accuracy considerably. Modern techniques can only go back accurately about ninety days from the ingestion of the drug."

"So what have you got?"

"According to the test results, she had Bimethotrate in her system."

"All right, what's Bimethotrate?"

"It's a chemotherapy drug."

I explained the history of the drug. First used in 1945 to treat leukemia and breast cancer, Bimethotrate worked by inhibiting the growth of newly developing cells. Unfortunately, this very aspect that was so effective in blocking cancer cells from growing, was also effective in halting the growth of a fetus. In the proper dosage, it was fetotoxic. "Cal, he chemically induced an abortion on her," I concluded.

"Not necessarily. She could have had an abortion with another doctor," Donaldson said.

"That's hairsplitting," I said; then added, "No pun intended."

Donaldson thought for a moment. "Are you sure there's enough of the drug in her to have induced an abortion?"

I shook my head. "No. The presence of Bimethorate deteriorates over time, so there's no way to determine how much was originally injected."

"How much of this drug would it take to induce an abortion?" Donaldson asked.

"As I remember it, abortionists would perform several injections over a period of weeks, sometimes as many as six. The drug would build up gradually, halt the developing fetus and ultimately induce abortion. It was a time consuming process and one had to be careful to watch out for various complications and side effects."

"What kind of side effects?"

I paused, allowing my memories of the drug's history in back-alley abortions to surface. "If the procedure wasn't successful before the second trimester, it had to be stopped, as prolonged usage beyond the first trimester increased the risk to the mother. It had something to do with long-term build-up of the drug. Another problem was that sometimes the doctor in question would start the treatment too late and had to stop because the second trimester was about to begin. In those cases, the child could be born, premature, undeveloped, with various health problems or even born retarded."

"Jesus!" Donaldson said with equal measures of sympathy and disgust.

I continued. "The other problem was that since all this was being carried out illegally, there were no recognized standards or dosages. Doctors had to play guessing games based upon the weight of the mother and then improvise. There were no hard and fast rules. Dosages for this drug had to be precise. Too little and the buildup wouldn't arrest the development of the fetus. Too much and the buildup could not only kill the fetus, but the mother as well."

Donaldson shook his head. "Sounds very risky."

"It was," I agreed. "They were never able to perfect the technique and it was dropped a few years later."

"So you can't prove that he was the doctor who prescribed that drug for her. Or that there was even enough in her to induce an abortion. Or when it was injected into her."

"No, I can't. But even so, he was her doctor. He lied to us. He lied to me. You know he did. He said she had a miscarriage. He then says he performed an abortion, a procedure. He knows he didn't. He never said anything about injecting her with Bimethorate. Why? Why would he lie about the way the abortion was performed?"

Donaldson was running out of angles. "Maybe another doctor performed it and he was just cleaning up someone's mess."

"Why lie? The fact that he lied is enough to warrant another interview."

"Won't he know that you can't absolutely tie him to this drug?" Donaldson asked.

I knew that Dr. Hale would be aware of forensics science in general and would have some knowledge of what hair analysis can determine, but he wouldn't know of its limitations. "No," I said without hesitation. "He specializes in life. I'm Dr. Death."

39

2:05 PM

It took us about fifteen minutes to find out where Dr. Hale was for the afternoon and almost another twenty minutes to get there. We found him at the Concorde, a large banquet hall, where he was attending a Pro-life brunch. We entered the single-story red-carpeted facility and walked around until we found the correct hall.

As fate would have it, his table was located in the center of a room of two hundred-fifty people. He was seated with a woman who appeared to be his wife - the frosted blonde receptionist in his office - and his daughter, son-in-law and granddaughter.

I spotted them before Donaldson and walked across the hall. Donaldson followed. I couldn't help but notice how worn Dr. Hale looked. He appeared harried and defeated - gaunt - as if the life had drained out of him.

Dr. Hale saw us approach and his face belayed his displeasure at seeing us, and more, fear. He stood slowly. "What do *you* want?" he said looking at me.

"We'd like to talk to you, sir." Donaldson said.

"Can't it wait until later?"

Donaldson shook his head. "I'm afraid not. We have to ask you a few questions."

"I've answered all *your* questions, Dr. Connor," he said with obvious annoyance.

"Not all," I replied.

Dr. Hale considered this for a moment, and then excused himself. His wife started to object as their daughter and son in-law looked on concerned, but Hale patted her hand. "It's all right, dear," he said, and walked with us to the back of the hall. There, we found a quiet spot.

"What's so important that you have to interrupt me when I'm with my family?" Dr. Hale asked.

"Bimethorate." I said simply.

"What?"

"You heard me, Bimethorate."

"What about it?" he asked defensively and then corrected: "Wh, what is it?"

I held up a finger. "No, no. You said 'What about it?' Don't you pretend that - - -"

Dr. Hale shrugged. "I don't know what it is," he said unconvincingly.

"OK, you want to play it stupid, fine. You performed a chemical abortion on Maria Cialini," I stated.

The word hit a nerve.

"No I didn't."

I took a step in closer and launched my bluff. "I have a lab test that shows that Maria Cialini had Bimethorate in her system at the time you said you *performed* an abortion on her."

Realizing the faux pas, Dr. Hale looked around, trapped. "Why do you keep digging, Dr. Connor?" he asked, flustered. "What's the matter with you? I confessed to having an affair with her, and with performing an abortion on her. What else do you want?"

"I want to know why you said you performed an abortion procedure on her when you injected her with Bimethorate."

"What's going on?" a voice said from behind.

We all turned to see Dr. Hale's wife, the frosted blonde, approach.

"Ma'am," Donaldson began, "we have to ask your husband a few questions. I don't think you want to concern yourself with - "

"My husband and I have no secrets, Inspector," she said. "He told me about this years ago and we've worked past it. My husband has suffered enough. He didn't kill that woman, but you can go and make a case if you wish. And you'll lose and then we'll sue you and this city."

"Ma'am, we're not trying to 'make a case' against your husband, but we are going to ask him a few more questions," Donaldson responded calmly.

This break provided Dr. Hale with the moments needed to find an angle and mount a counterattack. "Just because she had Bimethorate doesn't mean I gave it to her."

Hale's ignorance in forensics showed. I neutralized this attack easily. "You were her doctor. You ran blood tests on her. That's standard. You would have known."

Dr. Hale drew a breath. He was shaken, but struggled on. "I didn't think you'd understand," he hesitated. "I wanted to keep it simple."

I was unimpressed. "Didn't think I'd understand? I'm a doctor. Try again."

Hale's composure began to crumble. The old man was off balance.

I cut off any further defense before he got a chance to launch it. "Bimethorate was used for back-alley abortions. You know that."

The discrepancy showed on Dr. Hale's face. He was about to say something but I allowed him no quarter.

"And don't give me any crap about how it was somebody else and you had nothing to do with it."

With his retreat cut-off, Dr. Hale looked about, momentarily dazed.

I recognized his dilemma and knew that now was the time to shut him down. I spoke fast; using my words the way a prizefighter uses his fists to put away a stunned opponent. I would feel sorry for him later. For now, there would be no mercy. I laid it out for him, mixing science with bullshit. "You lied to the police; we got that. We can show that she was given Bimethorate while under your care, which means that she had an abortion. We know Bimethorate chemically induced the abortion from the hair analysis we ran. You can't say that you didn't know about it because you were her physician at the time. You ran tests; you knew. You knew because you did it."

Dr. Hale looked ahead and I could see that he was weighing what he'd heard and was still working on an angle.

I continued my onslaught. "We're going to do a blood test on her unborn child and we're going to match it to yours, and then we're going to get you for murder." I pointed a finger at Hale for emphasis.

Donaldson, recognizing my expertise in this arena, kept silent.

The mention of the word "murder" shocked Hale back into the present. "I didn't murder anybody," he shook his head. "And you can't force me to take a paternity test."

"We don't have to. I'm going to leak this shit to my friends in the press."

"No!" Dr. Hale said, his voice breaking.

"You evil bastard!" Hale's wife said.

I shook my head knowingly and bluffed. "She was having your kid and you killed it. Later, when she was having another, you killed her. I guess it was easier that way. Kill two birds with one shot!"

Dr. Hale shook his head, frustrated. "You've got it all wrong. She was my patient earlier. She stopped coming to me in October, 1951. We," he hesitated, "had an affair. She became pregnant and I performed an abortion, gave her Bimethorate." He corrected. "That's all."

Neither Donaldson nor myself said a word. Both knew enough that once a suspect begins to confess, it's best not to push them any further, but to allow them to go at their own pace. You had only to guide them gently or roughly as the situation might dictate, according to the suspect.

Dr. Hale labored. His breathing was heavy. "She said she didn't want to carry my child to term. I was able to get Bimethorate for her, but I injected it. I kept two sets of records on her. She said she wanted a child with someone better and that I didn't cut it."

Dr. Hale was falling apart. I didn't even bother to glance at Donaldson. Both of us recognized it.

Hale continued: "One set was in case anybody asked about her; the other so I could have a clear record of how I had treated her." He shook his head as memories and feelings long suppressed returned. It was like he was trying to shake them from his mind. "She was blackmailing me," he said. "She was going to tell my wife. Said she was going to cry rape! I could've lost my license, my practice, my family."

For the second time in twenty-four hours, I felt a momentary connection with Dr. Hale in light of my own situation. But as before, it was brief.

It was at this time that I noticed Dr. Hale remove the automatic he'd had the night before, from his coat pocket. "Cal - -" I said as a warning.

Donaldson saw it, too. He reached for his hip holster but we all knew he'd never get it out quickly enough.

Dr. Hale had the drop on us.

"Wait now, doc," Donaldson cautioned with a hand raised.

Dr. Hale raised the weapon and then placed the muzzle to his own temple. His previous agitation was gone. His face was resigned.

"Honey, no!" his wife urged.

Dr. Hale was oblivious. "You just had to keep digging, didn't you?" he said, looking at me.

Donaldson had his weapon out and pointed at Dr. Hale, something, which I realized with a bit of irony, did little to deter a person bent on suicide. *Maybe it would encourage him?*

I looked at Donaldson who gave a brief shake of his head. Neither of us was close enough to jump Hale. The distance was just great enough to leave us a split second too late.

"You don't have to do this," I said. "It's all over."

Dr. Hale laughed. "You think so. If you knew what I did, you'd want this gun. No Dr. *Connor*. It isn't over yet," he said with something other than contempt. "It's just beginning."

I interpreted Hale's laugh as a bad omen. It demonstrated to me that he had nothing to lose and was resolved to a course of action.

"Sweetheart, don't," his wife, pleaded. "It's all going to come out. You know that. We discussed this. We can survive this."

"I don't want to survive this," he told her before turning back to me. "Some doors should be left closed."

And then he pulled the trigger.

40

SFCU: 4:40

The next two hours were occupied with: sealing off the crime scene, keeping people away from body, and the growing puddle, waiting for the Medical Examiner to arrive and taking statements from the witnesses, including Donaldson and myself. All in all, there wasn't much to say. There were only three witnesses. In the end everyone was allowed to leave, myself included. I felt bad that Hale had killed himself. However, I did not feel bad about the act as I considered him a coward. The act left us one suspect short and no closer to finding the killer. I did not feel responsible for, "driving him to it." He'd been edgy from our first meeting. Guilt had "driven him to it." I was certain of that. He had simply taken a forty-six year, scenic route. In truth, I was happy to get out of there. Donaldson would stick around and tell the captain what had happened – again.

I returned to the University. I went to my office, as I wanted to clear my head but didn't want to go home. Also, there was something bothering me, aside from the obvious, but I couldn't put form to the feeling and wanted to be alone to think about it. I checked my inbox. There was a single package in a large manila envelope. It was addressed to me, but had no return address, so I opened it and had a look inside. I pulled out a folded letter and read it. "Not again." I went inside my office and gave Donaldson a call.

Police Station: 5:00 PM

Donaldson opened the envelope that I had just handed him and removed a small book. He wore latex gloves and held the book at its edges.

"What is it?" I asked.

"It's a ledger of some kind," he said, "There's no name on the cover but it's obvious that it belonged to Mr. Astor. I recognize some of his properties listed here. There could be prints."

"Tests will confirm," I said.

"They sure will," Donaldson said, referring to the science of handwriting identification. Simply put, handwriting identification attempts to determine whether or not someone wrote a document in question. A professional handwriting examiner determines this by studying such things as the slant of the letters, how they are joined or separated, even the use of capital letters. Handwriting examiners can even determine whether a person was using their other hand when writing because the nuances of writing with the proper hand were carried over to the other hand, as these nuances were beyond the control of the writer. Even if an individual were to trace another's handwriting that, too, can be detected as the "stops" in the writing will not be the same as that of authentic handwriting.

"What does it show?" I asked.

Donaldson flipped through the ledger gently. "It looks as if Mr. Astor was keeping two sets of records. You can see it here," he said, pointing. "The first column shows the actual amount derived and the second shows the amount declared for purposes of taxation. Over here's the difference." He paused a moment as he looked closer at an area. "And these look like bank account numbers here." He closed the book gently and placed it in a plastic bag. "Michael Astor was screwing the government out of some tax money."

"The book proves this?"

Donaldson nodded. "It lists incomes from his various properties, how much was declared and earned as well as the difference and where it ended up. It will be an easy thing to determine if the prints are his and whether these bank accounts were in his possession."

"Who do you think wrote it?"

Donaldson shrugged. "We'll run tests. You have some samples of her writing. His we'll obtain."

I nodded. "Sounds like a good reason to kill somebody."

"Particularly if she had stolen the book and was blackmailing him," Donaldson added.

"We've got enough here to go after him, don't we?"

Donaldson nodded. "Yes." Then he saw the note in my hand. "What does *that* say?"

I held up the note. "It's a letter from Gerty. Just that she couldn't go on anymore knowing what had happened and that she hoped that this would make something right." Then I added, "I don't like this," handing Donaldson the note. "Look at the signature."

"It's typed," Donaldson noticed. "Like the rest of the note."

"What kind of person types a note?" I asked.

"The kind that's on medication for a stroke. Gertrude Myers was taking that tickles stuff."

"Ticlid," I corrected.

"Right. Besides the lab will be able to determine whether this letter was typed on her typewriter or not."

I nodded. That was true. The keys on the typewriter in her room would be compared with the impressions on the note. The ink, too, on the note would be compared with the ribbon on her machine. Even the paper on which it was written could be tested to determine whether it came from any paper in her room.

Donaldson read over the note. "It's typed 'Gertrude,' not Gerty. It doesn't go into her relationship with Maria Cialini or anything." He straightened up in his chair. "Look, buddy, people who are about to kill themselves often use maiden names or nicknames or what-have-you. Others are very formal. Some perform little rituals. One time I worked a case where a guy killed himself but washed all the dishes and put them away before his wife came home. Who can explain it? Believe me, these things are simpler than you'd believe."

I considered this.

"This is the best evidence we've got. Maria Cialini worked for Michael Astor. She got hold of evidence of him withholding money from the government and he killed her and put her into one of his buildings. I say we get this thing printed, enter it as evidence and then we go and confront Mr. Astor."

"Fine."

41

Continental Dinner Hall: 6:15 PM

We entered the hall and I stopped to take it all in. Michael Astor IV sat at the center of a long table on a dais. He was dressed typically in an Italian suit, blue. Like the others, this one too was silk and single breasted with three buttons. Next to him was a female *friend* some forty years his junior. He adjusted his blue woven silk tie and looked out at the room before him.

It was a lavish room with thick, plush red velvet drapes. Waiters and waitresses walked back and forth, trays in hand, making sure that everyone's glasses were filled. Central air ensured that the guests were comfortable in their seats.

Seated about him were leaders of the various charities that he had supported over the years as well the city's elites and various dignitaries including the mayor. In the crowd, seated at round tables, were members of these organizations. A haze of chatter hung about the room.

Next to Michael Astor was Robert Thomlinson, head of the largest cancer society in the city. Thomlinson stood and tapped his microphone. The room grew quiet.

Thomlinson, well trained in the art of public speaking, delivered a deliberately calm tribute to their benefactor. The theme of his speech was concern and charity and was interrupted only by polite applause.

Donaldson and I walked along the far side of the hall. We were followed by two plainclothes police officers. Donaldson motioned for the plainclothes to stay back, while we approached the table.

Mr. Clarke saw our approach and rushed to intercept us, walking in the hurried, stiff-legged, exaggerated manner of the self-important. "You've got to be kidding," he said with a combination of anger and surprise. "You can't speak to him right now. He's about to receive an award."

"We're not here to speak to him," Donaldson said. His voice deliberately trailed off with an air of mystery.

It took but a second for Mr. Clarke to look over to the two officers and realize what was happening.

"You're joking," he said.

"Do I look like I'm joking?" Donaldson asked.

"Right now? This can't wait until later?"

I said. "It's waited some forty-seven years."

"I'm looking forward to seeing the evidence you think you have," Mr. Clarke said and then added. "One moment please."

We watched as Mr. Clarke ascended the dais and spoke with Michael Astor a few moments. Astor looked down and I thought I could make out the words "You're kidding." Both were aware of the interest they had attracted from the tables nearest them. I shrugged my shoulders as a bead of sweat ran down my back.

Michael Astor IV stepped off the dais and approached with Mr. Clarke. He looked solemn. "We can't discuss this here, Inspector?" Clarke asked without pretense.

"I'm afraid not."

"Was the police escort really necessary?" Mr. Clarke asked.

"It's standard operating procedure." Donaldson replied professionally.

Mr. Clarke asked with disbelief, "Is he under arrest?"

Donaldson informed, "If he wants to be." Then he added, "We're going to ask him some questions. Not later, not here."

"You're not going to cuff him, are you?" Clarke continued sarcastically.

"Not if he comes along quietly." Donaldson was all business.

Michael Astor smiled. "Oh now, you'll have no trouble from me, Inspector."

Donaldson indicated the direction in which Astor should walk. Astor went first, followed by Donaldson, yours truly, and Mr. Clarke.

"You've crossed the line gentlemen," Clarke said. "Say nothing, sir. We're going to sue this city."

Michael Astor IV, for his part, smiled and shook hands with guests, as he made his way through the room.

42

Police Headquarters: 6:45 PM

The second floor interrogation room was not a comfortable place. Small, it made for feelings of claustrophobia when you put in three or more people, and between the suspect, his lawyer, and the police, there usually were. The color scheme was cacophonous and sought to capitalize in the interrogated, the feelings of confusion they were experiencing. The floor was tiled an unsightly lime-green and the molding about the door and the mesh-covered single window that faced the street, were bright blue. The chair was metal and previous occupants had largely torn out the thin padding, a combination of nerves and anger. It scraped like nails on a chalkboard when it was moved. Worse than that, there was no air-conditioning. The stench of accumulated fear permeated everything. The chair was an uncomfortable place to sit and was in the center of an uncomfortable room. The room was uncomfortable, as it was meant to be.

"She worked for you. Gertrude Myers worked for you. You and Maria Cialini were falsifying your income and withholding money from the government. Maria blackmailed you and you had her killed and hidden in one of your buildings," Donaldson speculated.

We sat about the table. Donaldson and I sat on one side of the table and Astor and Mr. Clarke sat on the other side. Michael Astor shifted uncomfortably in his chair and grimaced as it shrieked.

Somewhere behind the two-way glass, I knew District Attorney Ramsey and Captain Wilson were watching. Wilson would pay particular attention to the proceedings and hope that this went somewhere, especially in light of what had happened earlier. It had been because of Hale's suicide that Michael Astor IV had been frisked soon after he'd been brought in. One dead suspect was enough for one day. I guess they didn't want to take any chances.

I regarded Astor and couldn't help but feel a bit of sympathy for him. He looked shell-shocked, like a POW in one of those old Vietnam films. He appeared older, listless. He glanced down and seemed to focus on nothing in particular. His head seemed to be at a weird angle, but I realized this was because his toupee had shifted slightly. His usually vibrant face was slick with sudation. His pocket square sat crumpled before him and was soaked two-toned with perspiration. Stains of sweat spread across the collar and front of his shirt like a bullet wound. Silk, I knew, was resistant to dry cleaning's efforts to remove perspiration. It would have to be handwashed. I had difficulty picturing Michael Astor IV washing his shirt or anything else by hand, though the thought of him handwashing his own clothes in prison was an interesting one.

The door opened and Mr. Carver, smartly dressed in a double-breasted, Brooks Brother suit entered, briefcase in hand, and scowl in place. I looked to see his hands for bandages or cuts as each came into view. Neither had so much as a chipped manicured nail. It was a bad omen.

Mr. Clarke spoke. "All you have is this ledger, which I want to see - "

"You will," Donaldson said.

"- - - and assuming that this ledger is legitimate, a big assumption at that, that's all you have. You can't prove my client killed that woman. What about opportunity?"

"Who needs it? His prints are on the ledger. The bank accounts are yours," Donaldson said. "The jury can read anything into it they want to."

"Inspector, you and I both know that fingerprints do not last for forty-seven years on leather," Mr. Clarke said, referring to the fact that the ledger was leather bound.

"That's true," Donaldson reiterated. "However, they'll last a hell of a lot longer than that on unglazed paper."

Mr. Clarke considered this.

I was sure that he had familiarized himself with forensics as it applied to forgery, handwriting and such things as latent prints, as these had often been the preferred modus operandi of several of his clients. With regard to what Donaldson had said about prints on unglazed paper, it was true. Latent prints could be raised from paper thousands of years after they had been left. Currently, there are two techniques to retrieve prints from paper: fuming and spraying. When spraying, one uses Ninhydrin, a.k.a. Triketo-hydrindine hydrate. Over 90 percent of all prints involving paper brought into court are developed with Ninhydrin. Prints generally take twenty-four hours and as long as a week to develop. Ninhydrin reacts with the amino acids contained in the perspiration in the print and can range in color from orange to purple. Heating and humidifying the print can shorten this time. This, however, was a side issue, albeit an important one, which I believed, Clarke would consider as needed. For now, I knew he would think as a lawyer and instinctively attack the lack of proof before him.

"You've got strings of information, that's all," he said at last.

Donaldson countered, "Give me enough string and the jury will tie it around his neck. The ledger goes a long way towards motive. Astor is a man of means. Opportunity he could buy. Wait until those prints and handwriting results come back."

"You're half right, Inspector," Astor said. It was the first words he'd spoken since they brought him in.

"Don't say anything," Mr. Carver urged.

"It's all right," Astor said, dabbing at his blackened fingers with the silk handkerchief, trying, with little success, to remove the fingerprint ink. He'd been fingerprinted when we brought him in, in order to compare his prints to those on the ledger. We had also obtained several samples of his handwriting. "Why delay the inevitable?"

"Sir," Clarke urged, "this ledger might not pan out. We should wait until - - -"

"Wait until it does?" Astor replied. "This could be a bluff, but with the way things have gone so far, I wouldn't bet on it. Why make it harder on myself than it's going to be? I don't know if the ledger was written on unglazed paper or not. What is unglazed paper anyhow? Besides, the simple fact is that I didn't kill the little tart." He straightened in his chair with a screech. "My prints are in the ledger. They've got me," he said slowly and then added: "On the fraud and tax evasion, but that's all. I didn't kill her."

Donaldson started. "Why should we believe you? You've lied to us up until now."

"Maria Cialini and I had an affair and I was holding out on the government, but that was her idea," Astor informed.

"Really?" Donaldson asked.

I hadn't considered this and despite the fact that it could be a complete lie, it was very interesting.

Astor continued, "Yes. She said she had this idea that we could skim a bit off each property and use it to put money towards other properties. She was quite the little bookkeeper. You'll find that she did all the entries. The book is all in her handwriting. At the time, I thought it was a pretty good idea, too, until she started demanding a cut from each of the accounts. Then she left the company and took the ledger with her. I still don't know where she hid it, much less managed to smuggle it out of my house as I always kept it in a safe in my bedroom." He smiled a moment and then the smile died. "Then she started calling me. She had the ledger and said if I didn't pay her, she'd hand it over to the IRS. So I paid her. Check those accounts and you'll see that some of them were in her name."

Mr. Clarke said nothing.

That's the reason why we couldn't find out where she worked after she left his employment; she was living off blackmail.

"And then?" Donaldson asked.

"Then nothing. She stopped calling. I don't know whether it was November or December of '53. I continued to keep paying for a few months; then I stopped."

"And she never responded?" Donaldson asked.

"That's right."

Donaldson continued, "You didn't find that strange?"

"I found it a relief. Wouldn't you? I didn't question it. She stopped calling and that was it. I thought she'd moved away and I hoped it was for good."

"Weren't you worried about the ledger?"

"Of course I was. After a while I hired a private investigator to check up on her. He asked around and told me that according to her landlord, she'd moved out that November. I spent years investigating into and searching for both her and the ledger, but nothing ever came of it, so I decided that she had either dropped out of sight - she always talked of moving to Europe - or that something had happened to her. Frankly, I'm glad to see that it was the latter."

The PI was the other guy looking for her.

"What about Gertrude Myers?" Donaldson continued.

"Who's she? You mentioned her before."

"Her name used to be Gertrude Goldman," said Donaldson. "She worked for you as well - in the same department as Maria Cialini."

Michael Astor shrugged. "If you say so. Off hand, I don't remember her."

"What has this woman got to do with this investigation?" Mr. Clarke asked.

"She was the one who sent us the ledger."

Michael Astor shrugged again. "So? I didn't know she had it."

"I'd like to question her," Carver injected.

I entered the conversation (and imagined DA Ramsey on the other side asking, 'Why is he in there?'). "She' dead. Someone broke into her apartment the other night. Maybe he was looking for the ledger."

"She was murdered?" Mr. Carver asked.

"No. She died of a stroke," said Donaldson.

Mr. Clarke took over. "Which night?"

"The thirtieth," said Donaldson. "Between six and seven."

"Mr. Astor was at a meeting in his office. Until eight. There were several other people present. I'll give you their names and numbers."

"What about him?" I asked, referring to Mr. Carver.

"I was there as well," Carver said calmly.

"So Astor could've paid someone," Donaldson said.

"Yes, but I didn't," said Astor. "Inspector, my lawyer once told you that if I had killed Ms. Cialini, I would have had to be stupid to sell the building she was buried in. Do you recall that?"

"I do."

Astor continued, "Then doesn't it seem only natural that a billionaire searching for a missing woman all these years would have found Mrs. Myers and the ledger years ago as opposed to the other night?"

"Maybe," Donaldson acknowledged. "But she lived out of state for a long time. You didn't know her married name. She only moved back a few years ago. Maybe our investigation prompted you to renew your efforts."

"Ridiculous."

Donaldson added, "She did live in a home for the elderly that you helped to support for the last year."

"If that were the case, don't you think my client could have found a woman living in a home he supported a bit sooner?" Mr. Clarke hit back.

Donaldson obviously hadn't considered this and was momentarily stopped.

Clarke continued, now that he had a toehold. "Besides, how would my client know that this woman had the ledger to begin with?"

Donaldson hadn't considered this, either.

Mr. Carver took a verbal swing. "Can you say exactly when Miss Cialini was killed?"

"We believe that she was killed November 13th," Donaldson stated.

Clarke stepped in. "One moment, gentlemen." He opened his briefcase and dug about a few moments. "After your last interview, I took the precaution of retrieving and reviewing all of Mr. Astor's travel records from August 1953 to January, '54." He withdrew a folder and opened it. "Here we are," he said. "Mr. Astor was in New York that week, looking into some new properties to purchase."

He handed the documents to Donaldson who looked them over.

"And I wasn't born yet," Mr. Carver smirked.

The tag team is working its magic.

Mr. Clarke continued, "Feel free to contact all the people there; they are all living." He paused a moment. "And never mind this nonsense about we'll just put it out there and let the jury decide, because if that's the best you've got, get ready; we'll mount a defense that'll make the O.J's 'dream team,' look like legal aid."

Donaldson was about to say something.

"Gentlemen," Mr. Clarke interrupted, "I told you earlier that you should consider the strong possibility that whoever killed Miss Cialini and put her in my client's building did so in order to frame my client. I submit to you that the release of this information is for the same end. You should check out this Myers woman's background. Fact is, you have absolutely no proof to convict this man of being involved in the murder and only your opinion that he could have hired somebody. This ledger was written by the *victim*," he said sarcastically. "And proves only that they were involved in a tax scheme; that's all." He looked at the two-way mirror on the wall. "My client will plead guilty to fraud and tax evasion and that's it. He'll cut a check for the difference and pay the fine."

I imagined on the other side of the window, Captain Wilson looking at DA Ramsey, who probably was shaking his head. He'd say something like: "The ledger only proves that he and Cialini were involved in fraud and tax evasion, at best." He'd point out, that they might have been able to get Astor indicted for murder or conspiracy. But in light of the alibi checking out, that was now doubtable. And we all knew it would check out. He'd say, "Indicting him is one thing, convicting is another." Then he'd add, "Cut him loose."

Mr. Clarke turned to Michael Astor. "This happened almost fifty years ago. Since then you've given back ten times what you took. A thousand times. People will understand."

"Will they?" Astor asked.

43

I was off the next day, Wednesday, and took Thursday off too. I decided that I needed a break, in light of all that had transpired. Donaldson said it was from all the high-quality sex I was getting from Rebecca Wood. I slept in and continued to read the letters, but discovered nothing new. Word was that DA Ramsey wasn't going to push with murder as Michael Astor had a solid alibi as to his whereabouts at the time of Maria Cainlini's disappearance, and because they had no proof that Astor had hired anyone to kill her. They weren't even going to pursue tax evasion charges. He would simply have to pay a fine. I felt that they were afraid to go up against a well-connected billionaire.

The tests on the ledger came back. All was as Astor had said: The prints were both his and hers; the writing was in her hand. Some of the bank accounts in the ledger were in Maria Cialini's name. Some were still active.

For all intents and purposes, the case had hit another snag. We knew that the only person left from our original list was Judge Emerson, but we had less reason to suspect the Judge than we did Astor. It could have been Dr. Hale, but we wouldn't be questioning him anymore.

SFCU: 12:58 PM

I returned to the college Friday and put in a full day. I saw Ms. Wood in the second class. She said nothing but merely stared at me. I also noticed that several students, all female, smiled/smirked when I looked their way during the lecture. *Great, everybody knows!* For a moment, I thought that maybe I was imagining their reactions or at least embellishing them, out of paranoia. A second glance and the giggles it brought told me that I wasn't imagining anything. An astute man, I realized exactly what was going on. Rebecca Wood was turning up the heat; reminding me that time was running out. *Message received, bitch.*

I went to my office at the end of the day and checked my mail. I found a small envelope with a bulge at one end. I removed the envelope, and read the name and return address on it, Gerty Myers, Sunset Homes. Both were handwritten.

"Not again!" I said and looked into the envelope.

Inside was a folded piece of paper. I opened it and the tiny bulge slid out. It was a heart-shaped locket on a chain. It was the one that Maria Cialini was wearing in the photo that her sister, Mrs. D'Angelo, gave me.

I read the shaky, hand-written note,

Dear Dr. Connor,

My name is Gertrude Myers. I was a friend and co-worker of Maria Cialini's at The Pyramid Group. For years now I thought that she had simply moved away but when I saw her on TV I was forced to face the unsettling reality. In a sense, I guess I always knew. I don't know who killed her, but I can tell you about the men she was seeing. I tried to meet you at the park but my medication sometimes gets the better of me.

Maria left me something that I have enclosed. I hope that it is of some help. I'm only sorry I didn't come forword sooner, but it's been a long time. Memory fades. I'd write more, but my medication makes if difficult. I'll tell you all I know when you come to visit me.

Gertrude Myers

"I'll tell you all I know when you come to visit me." I put the letter down. "Great." I opened the locket, took a look. Inside was a nice photo of Jack Emerson and Maria Cialini, cheek to cheek. I closed it. "Oh boy!"

1:40 PM

"It never rains but it pours," Donaldson said, as he looked over the note. "What do you think?"

I sat back in my chair and put my hands out, exasperated. "I don't know. Something is not right here."

Donaldson nodded. "I agree. We receive evidence that seems to implicate Michael Astor, but the information is typed and that indicates that it could be forged. Except that the lab informed me that the note mailed to you was typed on Gertrude Myers' typewriter. Now we have a handwritten note with evidence that indicates Judge Emerson. Thing is, do you think the note was really written by Gertrude Myers?"

"It's too easy to check out," I said.

"True."

I hypothesized, "If the handwritten note is authentic, then the typewritten note must be a fake, meant to divert attention towards Astor."

Donaldson nodded. "And if the handwritten note is a fake, then it was meant to push us to the Judge."

"Right," I agreed. "Thing is we can't determine that the typewritten note is a fake. We can, however, determine whether the handwritten note is."

"OK," Donaldson said.

I continued. "We must also consider the fact this letter doesn't mention the ledger. That gives credibility to the notion that Mrs. Meyers had nothing to do with the ledger being mailed to me."

"Good point," Donaldson conceded and then added, "Either way, we can agree that one of these notes is false and the purpose of it was to implicate one man over the other."

I nodded. "Right. Now, let's pretend that the handwritten note is legit for a moment."

Donaldson agreed. "OK."

"Assuming that to be the case, then somebody wanted to frame Astor. Who?"

"The guilty party," Donaldson said and then paused. "Emerson?" He shook his head, unconvinced.

"It would look that way." I said and postulated: "The locket is the same one as in the photo. They obviously had a relationship that he didn't admit to. That means that he's lied to the police."

"So did Dr. Hale and Michael Astor," Donaldson countered and then added, "But they were each hiding a crime."

"That doesn't mean that Emerson wasn't hiding something also. Everyone has a skeleton in their closet," I suggested. "The handwritten note feels right."

"All right then," Donaldson said, "All puns aside, how do you explain the typewriter?"

I thought for a moment and then raised a hand. "Bear with me," I said and then offered, "What if the typewriter was planted?"

"You may be onto something; keep going," Donaldson encouraged.

I nodded. I *felt* as if I were onto something. "What if the break-in at Gertrude Myers' room wasn't meant to steal the ledger as we thought? What if it was meant to plant the typewriter, so the note would be legitimized in retrospect?"

"What about the fact that she was dead?" Donaldson asked.

I shrugged. "Let's say the killer was going to kill Gertrude, plant the typewriter and mail the note, but when he arrived, she was already dead - a stroke of luck for him. No pun intended."

Donaldson said, "That would have to be one serious case of foresight."

"True. All we have to do is get a sample of Gertrude Myers' handwriting from her personal effects and compare them. If they match, then we have to assume that the typewritten note was false. That's just logic."

"I suppose," Donaldson admitted.

I continued, "Let's look at it this way. What did the ledger and typed note do? It made us suspect Astor. We brought him in for questioning and would have indicted him except for his alibi. Maybe it was meant to do what it did."

Donaldson stated, "The mayor is screaming murder to my captain over our questioning of Mr. Astor. I won't even go into what they're saying about Dr. Hale's suicide." Donaldson opened the locket and took a look at the photo again.

It took an hour to obtain samples of Gertrude Myers' handwriting from Sunset Homes. It took a little over three hours before a handwriting identification expert was able to say with absolute certainty that the letter mailed to me was written by Gertrude Myers. In that time, he compared several samples of her writing with that of the mailed letter.

"Now we go after the Judge?" I asked, after the expert had rendered his opinion.

"Yeah, now we go see the Judge."

David Feeney

44

Pacific Union Club: 6:15 PM

The Pacific Union Club was a dark Connecticut brownstone on Nob Hill at the corner of Mason and California. Originally, the Flood Mansion, it was built for James Clair Flood, in 1886. Flood, who'd made a fortune in mining, had been impressed with the brownstones in New York. He entrusted Augustus Laver, a London trained architect, to build a mansion that reflected that style. The Flood Mansion was for a time the only mansion on Nob Hill built of stone. The rest were built of wood. It was due to this fact that the mansion survived the fire of 1906. The style of the building was Italian, reminiscent of London's "gentlemen clubs." The mansion's bronze fence was considered by many to be the finest in Victorian metalwork. The Pacific Union Club bought the mansion after the fire, when the Flood family moved out. Architect Willis Polk remodeled the mansion, lowering the tower and adding two wings. Windows were added to the third floor, creating another story. The rooms inside were designed with eastern opulence. The Pacific Union Club was formed in 1881, via a merging of the Pacific Club and the Union Club and was perhaps the most exclusive men's club on the West Coast. I knew these tidbits, as I had sought membership in the club in the past few years, but was unable to attain such, as I lacked the necessary connections.

Donaldson and I strode into the lounge where we were greeted by the sweet combined redolence of a dozen types of cigars. The scent was powerful and impossible to separate. Judge Emerson was nowhere to be seen, but Mr. Issacson was, entertaining a few friends. A moment later, Emerson emerged from a men's room off to the side. Issacson walked up to him and straightened his collar.

222

Emerson sat down in a leather-backed chair. He wore a deep, rich, blue-velvet smoking jacket and beige corduroy pants. An H. Upmann cigar rested in one hand, a brandy in the other. The other men in the room wore similar jackets of blue, red and green. All held cigars of various descriptions and brands like H. Upmann, Montecristo #2, Romeo y Julieta, Ramon Allones and the always overpriced Dunhill Montecruz. A cedar-wood humidor sat on the highly polished oak table. I wondered what these guys talked about. I would have given nearly anything to relax here after a day's work, smoking jacket and all. I'd bought mine when I thought there was a chance of my gaining membership.

"Good evening, Judge Emerson," Donaldson said quietly as we approached. "We'd like to talk to you for a moment."

"What is this about?" Issacson asked.

"It concerns our investigation," Donaldson said vaguely.

"The Cialini murder? I thought you already arrested someone for that."

"No," Donaldson corrected. "We questioned someone, but it turned out to be a mistake."

I kept my mouth S-H-U-T!

"As is this," Issacson said. "I'll save you the embarrassment of having to apologize later. And the lawsuit if you leave now."

"That's not an option," Donaldson said.

Judge Emerson motioned gently with his hand and the three of us followed him to a small room, off to the side. "What's the question, Inspector?" Emerson asked calmly.

"You said that you did some legal work for Maria Cialini in March of '47," Donaldson began.

"That's not a question," Issacson remarked.

Donaldson didn't like being interrupted. "We can do this at the station."

"Please continue," Judge Emerson said.

Donaldson began again, "You said that you did some work for her and that was that."

"That's correct. That was in March, 1947."

Donaldson took out the locket and chain. "Sir, this locket belonged to Maria Cialini. Does it look familiar?"

Judge Emerson said nothing. He took it and looked it over.

Issacson stood next to him. He saw the inscription. "It says 'From Jack.' You can't be suggesting that - - - "

Emerson opened the locket.

Issacson saw the photo. "Ah, God," he said.

Several moments went by and I felt as if the Judge was struggling with some inner-demon. Finally, he spoke. "I had a relationship with Maria Cialini." He said with regret, "A sexual relationship - "

Issacson became agitated. "I want it on record that Judge Emerson cooperated in this investigation."

"After he was cornered," I added. *I hope he's not armed.*

"You're trying to build a case on this?" Issacson asked.

"I'm trying to get to the truth of your client's relationship with the victim," Donaldson said before saying to Emerson, "It's noted."

Judge Emerson sighed and said. "Yes, I had a relationship with Maria Cialini in 1947, shortly after I took on her case. The case was against her landlord, who was attempting to evict her, wrongfully. It came at a time when I felt that my marriage was over. My wife was living with her mother and we had no children at that time. It was wrong, but I got involved with Maria. She was so," he searched for the words, "strong; strong in every way possible. A natural-born feminist, she could have been very prominent in that movement. Especially in the early days when they were still building up the grass roots. It was a wonderful relationship. And yes, I did know about her past. Not who the men were, but that there *were* men involved. Did you know she was sexually molested by an uncle, Inspector?"

"Yes," Donaldson said.

"But she was a survivor. Using men was her only weapon, you see. Truth was that she wasn't a bad person, just abused. She had never been in a relationship with a man who respected her. All that changed. We spent many months together. During that time, she went through a change, but it was slow going. At one point, I thought that we might get married. Then my wife came back and said that she wanted to work things out and get back together. Maria and I decided to take some time off so I could decide what was best. I decided that it would be best if I got back with my wife."

"Just like that?"

"I'd taken an oath, Inspector. It meant something to me then and it still does."

I felt the sincerity in Emerson's voice, such that I didn't question it.

Donaldson continued, "You never saw her again?"

"No, that isn't true. I saw her from time to time and we remained friends," Emerson corrected. "She was interested in bettering herself and I would often recommend various books for her to read. The last time I saw her was sometime in mid-1953. Later, I realized that I hadn't heard from her in some time and I dropped by her place and asked about her, but they said that she had moved out."

The second man who came around asking for her, I realized.

"Didn't you find that odd?" Donaldson asked.

"I didn't know what to think. I thought she had simply left. I told my wife everything. She stayed with me."

Issacson was agitated. "That locket proves nothing, except that they had a relationship. Have you found out when this murder was committed?"

"November 13th, 1953." Donaldson replied.

Issacson thought for several seconds. His eyes looked up and darted back and forth as if the information he sought was written on the inside of his head. "Dear God!" he said. "Judge Emerson was at a week-long seminar in Boston." Then, turning to the Judge, he added, "You remember, Jack; Paul Waterson and that other fellow, Schumann, were there."

"Bill? Oh yes. I remember that now." Emerson smiled.

Issacson continued, "I'll be happy to furnish you with proof, Inspector. You know, if you had just asked us his whereabouts I could have told you. But you had to go play special agent. Jeepers, Inspector, what would his motive have been? They were having an affair? How about method? He doesn't even own a weapon? Opportunity?" Issacson put his hands up in disgust.

"We didn't think it prudent to accuse the Judge of any wrongdoing," Donaldson explained.

"So that's it," Issacson said. "He's guilty of having an affair. We could have settled all this a long time ago if you'd only told us the day, or at least the week, she died."

"We didn't know at that time," Donaldson said. "You could have been straight with us from the beginning and we wouldn't have kept digging. This other stuff had nothing to do with our investigation, but when people lie to me, I tend to focus on those people."

"Wait," Emerson said. "You said earlier that she was pregnant when she died."

"Yes," I said, and as I was curious, pushed: "She had been pregnant twice, once in '47 and again in 1953. She had an abortion."

"Boy or girl?" Emerson asked.

"Boy."

"I never had a son," Emerson said simply.

Something had been bothering me about the pregnancies and I didn't know what it was, so I asked, "Were you the father?"

"Of which one?" Emerson asked.

I pushed my luck further. "Either - both."

Emerson shrugged his shoulders. "I didn't know about the second pregnancy."

"And the first?"

"She wouldn't say. In truth, I suspected that she didn't know. She had a lot of secrets and I didn't think it my place to push. In all honesty, I always felt that she'd get around to telling me on her own. I'd offered her help but she turned me down. She said she could manage on her own."

"Don't worry, sir. Nobody need know about this. I trust that Inspector Donaldson is honorable enough not to seek publicity on what is essentially a private matter?"

"All I wanted was the truth," Donaldson said.

Issacson put his hand on Emerson's shoulder. "It's not the end, sir. Just go back in that room and be yourself. Nobody will ever know. You can still achieve your goal."

"I'd know. I do know." He patted Issacson's hand and straightened up. "I tried to forget about this and for years now, I have forgotten. But every now and then I would think about her and I wondered where she was and why she just left. Now I know why. Someone murdered a woman that I was in love with. I can't go on and keep silent about this."

Issacson was incredulous. "About what? You didn't know what happened to her. You didn't have anything to do with it. You had a relationship with a woman over a half-century ago. It's not relevant."

"You were always a good lawyer, Sam," Judge Emerson said. "It's a matter of character and that's always relevant. I can't have the knowledge of what happened to that poor girl on my conscience."

"How is that related to your character?" Issacson asked, disturbed.

Emerson smiled. "Because I broke an oath. I gave my word before God and my wife, and I broke my word."

"No. You can't, sir. Your goal - - - "

"Being a Supreme Court Judge was never my ultimate goal. My goal was to help people and I've done that."

Issacson was about to say something, but Emerson cut him off. "If people can accept my past and my lapse in character, then I will be nominated. But they will know exactly what type of man they're dealing with. The American people deserve that." He turned to us. "If that's all, gentlemen, I have an announcement to make." He took a few steps and turned back. He looked confused. "Dr. Connor, you said that her pregnancy ended in abortion. You were referring to the second?"

"No, the first." I corrected.

Judge Emerson considered this for a moment before saying, "She told me that she gave the child up for adoption."

Adoption? This was something new. "Was it a boy or a girl?" I asked.

"I honestly don't recall her saying." Judge Emerson turned and walked back into the room. There the gathered crowd cheered him like a conquering hero. I motioned to Donaldson. We didn't want to hear the "I have sinned speech." We felt badly enough as it was.

Issacson simply sat in a chair, too stunned to do anything.

45

The next few days found the District Attorney's office making multiple statements that neither Michael Astor IV nor Judge Emerson were suspects in the death of "the closet lady," and apologized to each. The speculation concerning Michael Astor was the greatest, and various scandal-mongers had a field day with the facts of the victim having worked for him, being found in his building and having assisted him in a tax-fraud scheme.

Dr. Hale's death, which previously had been thought of as a mere suicide and therefore not deserving of attention was currently undergoing a second look and a bit of revisionism in the press and cable news shows. Some of the gossip columns carried a story that Dr. Hale, the prominent Pro-life spokesman, had also been questioned with regard to the murdered woman and was actively trying to confirm this from the police. Leaks to the press centered on the woman's previous "miscarriage/abortion" and what, if any, the doctor's role in that might have been.

Nor was Judge Emerson spared. Various rumor-mills wove tabloid tapestries of how His Honor too had been questioned about the woman's death; information that was obviously leaked by one of his *friends* at the Pacific Union Club. The papers were awash with stories of the now "former" potential Supreme Court Judge nominee's confession that he, too, had had an affair with "the closet lady."

News outlets of all slants gave way to the numerous conspiracy theories surrounding three well-respected men and their links to Maria Cialini. Some speculated on the love-triangle aspects of the case while enemies and rivals of all three men hinted of cover up and payoffs or favors.

Cranks called in twenty-four hours a day insisting that they had seen each man, two of them, or all three, kill her at the same time. Everyone agreed that the reputations of these men were severely tarnished. Neither Michael Astor IV nor Judge Emerson could be reached for comment as they were in seclusion.

Michael Astor IV hired a PR firm for damage-control but it was too late. The circus had arrived; it was three-ringed and he was in the center. He was asked to step down from the boards of several charities. Some commentators said that it was only a matter of time, though, before he would be invited back, citing that there currently was a shortage of billionaires in the city and none who were as charitable.

Dr. Hale's wife, in response to the accusations of his alleged guilt and complicity in the murder of Maria Cialini, brought on by his suicide, made public in a press conference the reason she believed her husband had committed suicide. It was learned that Dr. Hale had, in his early days, brokered several illegal adoptions with single mothers for some prominent citizens. Furthermore, it was through these adoptions that Dr. Hale was able to fund some of his early clinics. She went on to state that Dr. Hale took his own life, because of the guilt he felt over the "adoptions," and that to her knowledge; he hadn't committed any abortions on any patients. The abortion aspect had been leaked to the press and was particularly disturbing to her. The names of the adopted would not be made public, as Dr. Hale had, before his death, taken the step of destroying the records of all the women who had sold their children.

The stories weren't only reserved for the three one-time suspects. The rest was reserved for the Police Department, the DA's office, the city, and especially Inspector Donaldson and his advisor, yours truly, as both of us faced defamation suits from Michael Astor and Dr. Hale's wife. "Shit rolls downhill," Donaldson told me. The mayor pulled the city's funding of me. I turned in my report and returned to teaching. In truth, I was glad to be finished with the affair. Besides, I had enough problems of my own. I was still sore from the can of whoop-ass that someone had opened on me. However, I was unable to put the case completely aside. Dr. Hale's wife's comments about her husband never having committed an abortion could be dismissed as a faithful wife protecting a husband's legacy, not to mention his clinics, but what to make of the admission that he was the middleman in a number of illegal adoptions? Why would Dr. Hale confess to performing abortions he hadn't performed? Why not confess to the adoptions? To my way of thinking, abortion was far more offensive to Pro-lifers than adoptions, no matter how illegal. So why lie? I decided that the best course of action would be to learn whether or not Miss Cialini's first pregnancy had resulted in childbirth. For this task, I contacted Dr. Trundy. I recalled that pregnancy often left marks on the hipbones of the mother and that these marks could be seen in some X-rays. I believed that they were called the "scars of pregnancy." Dr. Trundy informed me, much to my forgetfulness and embarrassment that when a woman is in the late stages of pregnancy, her body releases a hormone called "relaxin." This hormone loosens the ligaments of the pelvis in preparation for the impending birth. Relaxin also softens the bones so that the movement of the child's head can produce a groove (pre-auricular sulcus). The presence of this groove or sulcus does not mean that a woman gave birth, as a stillbirth could have occurred. The "scars of pregnancy" prove that a woman has been pregnant, which can be seen in X-rays as well as CAT scans.

"Scars of Parturition," on the other hand, occur along the birth canal and only occur during birth if the child's head was too large for the canal. This produces pitting, which can be viewed via X-rays or CAT scans. It doesn't mean that the child was deformed per say, although that can be the case. It simply means that the child's head was too large. The mother's birth canal could have been contracted via nutritional deficiencies. Unfortunately for me, not all births produce these scars. Indeed, they are rare. Still, it was all we had to go on. "Scars of pregnancy," she summed up, only proved that Maria Cialini had been pregnant. "Scars of Parturition," if they were present, would prove that she had given birth.

"I'll have a look at the X-rays and CAT scans," she told me. "And I'll get back to you."

I was anxious to know what she'd discover. Personally, I doubted there was anything to it. However, what if the Judge had been right and Maria had given up her first child for adoption, instead of aborting it. How would that alter the equation? If she did give up her child for adoption, what happened to that child? Did one of the three suspects have it? Was he or she living out there somewhere in obscurity? Did he or she even know that they'd been adopted?

Today it is common practice to inform adopted children of the circumstances of their origins. It hadn't always been the case. When Maria was pregnant, before such terms as "birth mother" and "biological father," were used, many people chose not to tell a child that they had been adopted. Some adopted children didn't learn until later in life. Some never learned at all. In my case, I had been aware of my adoption from an early age. My parents made it clear that I had been selected and that I was *special.* If Maria Cialini opted for adoption and we learned the identity of the child, would it be moral or ethical to inform him, or her of what had become of their birth mother? Had he or she looked for their birth mother? Would he or she care?

Donaldson was still actively interviewing and basically sifting through the kooks. The opinion by all was that the case was unsolvable.

SFCU: 1:15 PM

I had led a team of third-year medical students through an autopsy that afternoon. The procedure went well, nobody got sick and they only dropped the kidneys and the liver.

The day came to an end and I realized that this was the first truly normal day I had spent in a few weeks. It felt good and made me glad that I did this PI stuff on a part-time basis. My bruises had faded and I figured that I'd workout soon, maybe a jog in the morning. I still hadn't figured out what to do about Rebecca Wood but reasoned it wasn't a question of *if* I buckled to her demands, but when.

I removed my gown, booties, gloves, facemask and cap and disposed of them in the hazardous waste container. I washed the face shield with a liquid disinfectant and set it out to dry. I walked past the storage room that harbored the remains of Maria Cialini and wondered when the police were going to allow the family to take possession of the body or whether in their desire to get beyond this case, they had forgotten about her completely.

"Dr. Connor."

I turned to see Roger Stevenson approach. "Yes?"

"I was in autopsy room #2 and I was cleaning up and I found this." He held out a metal object in his gloved hand. "Thing is, I can't identify it."

I looked the object over. It was wafer-thin and about six inches in length; each end turned at a right angle, going in opposite directions of the other, ending at about an inch or so. I had never seen the device but had a good idea who could identity it.

2:05 PM

"It's a PLT," Donaldson said.

"What's that?"

"A professional lock tool. A lock-pick," Donaldson simplified. "Actually, it's a tension wrench used to turn the lock after you've picked it."

"Holy Shiite!" Stevenson said.

"You're sure?" I asked.

"Yeah. It's professionally made." Donaldson held the device by its edges to view it under the light. He wore a single white glove and reminded me of Michael Jackson, but I didn't point this out to him. He, however, pointed out to me scratches that ran parallel to the pick's edge.

"What does that mean?" I asked.

"It shows that this pick was 'stoned' by a professional. See, when you cut a pick out of steel, you often have scratches or wavy imprints. These have to be smoothed out or the pick could get stuck when it's inserted into the lock. You do this by oiling the pick and moving the stone along the direction the edge will travel. You have to be careful because if you 'stone' the edge too long, you can change the contour and ruin the pick before you even start." Then he added, "This one was meant to last."

"How can you tell?"

"Because he 'blued' it."

"Like a firearm?"

"Pretty much. Picks are blued to protect them from rusting. It also keeps the edges from becoming rough again. Some folks immerse their picks to blue them. Others wipe the bluing agent on or use a brush, though you have to be careful not to leave streaks. This one appears to have been immersed." He turned it over.

"Where did you find it?" Donaldson asked Stevenson.

"In autopsy room #2," Stevenson reiterated. "It was in a corner, by the changing room."

That's the room I was attacked in.

"Hmmm. It's got prints," Donaldson observed.

"Prints?" I knew well the ramifications of this discovery.

"Did you touch this?" Donaldson asked Stevenson.

"No. Dr. Connor doesn't allow us to touch any instrument without wearing gloves."

"Thanks for your help, Stevenson," I said.

Stevenson made his good-byes and then his exit. We walked down the hall as Donaldson placed the lock-pick into a plastic bag.

"That was found in the room I - - - "

"I know," Donaldson interrupted and added, "and I think you're right."

"That this thing belonged to the guy who attacked me?"

Donaldson nodded. "He must have dropped it in the fight and it got kicked into the corner."

"Jeepers." I couldn't believe this turn of luck.

"Let's get it down to the lab and see what we can see," Donaldson said.

46

Police Crime Lab: 5:08 PM

The Automated Fingerprint Identification System is a database in which the fingerprints of all convicted criminals in the state of California are stored. Also known as CAL ID, the system offers police the possibility to match as little as a single print from that of all convicted criminals and is operational in several states. Donaldson and I worked up a partial profile of the person we were looking for, white male over 65. These two facts would allow the technician to exclude thousands of people from the search at the outset.

The technician sat back in his chair. "Willie Knox, a.k.a. Willie 'The Fort' Knox."

Donaldson stood at a coffee machine in a corner of the small room. "Tell me about him."

The technician typed away. "Born 1922 – That makes him 78 - A whole list of convictions for theft, burglary and assault. - Entered the Army at age 18. - Gets out in 1944, honorable discharge. – Back to his old profession, only now he's hitting banks and pulling armed robberies. – Who says military service doesn't provide skill training? - Must have done, let's see – twenty-five, no – twenty-six years in various prisons for convictions, including eight years for murder of an associate."

"You're absolutely sure of this guy?" I said, standing behind him. "No chance of a mistake?"

"Not a chance," the technician ensured. "I got nine points of similarity. These prints are unique."

"Oh?" Donaldson commented. "How's that?"

"The thumb has arches," he informed.

"Hmmm." Donaldson considered this.

There were in all, three major divisions of fingerprint patterns: arches, whorls and loops. Sixty percent of prints are loops, thirty something percent are whorls and about five percent are arches. Different fingers often have different patterns. Thumbs most often contain whorls, not arches. Arches are most often found on middle or index fingers. Arches on a thumb are unique and indicate little chance of a mistake.

"Print it," Donaldson said. "Print it all and get me the name of his current or last parole officer."

6:00 PM

It took almost an hour to track down Martin Bryant, Willie "The Fort" Knox's last parole officer. Bryant explained to us that his introduction to Knox had occurred almost a decade before, when Willie had been found in possession of stolen goods. It was Knox's last conviction, but as far as Bryant was concerned, it didn't mean that after over sixty years of crime, he was finally reformed. Willie Knox was a career criminal, though not a very successful one. In the world of career criminals, Willie Knox, in his opinion, could best be described as a failed businessman. The only thing that had stopped his life of larceny was advancing years and the fear of dying in prison.

"What's he like?" Bryant repeated. "He's an asshole."

Donaldson said, "Our information said that he killed somebody, another career criminal type, Paul Sanford."

Bryant thought for a moment and ran a hand across his curly graying hair. "Oh yeah. Sanford was a driver on a bank job they did in '45. He tried to make off with Willie's cut so Willie found him and shot him." He paused. "Once. Right through the eye."

I noted this without comment.

"What is he like now?" Donaldson asked. "Activity wise."

Bryant thought for a moment and shrugged. "I haven't seen him in a couple of years. He's in my semi-retired file. Last time I saw him, he was – well, like he always was, six-two, two-ten. A heavy drinker – smokes. He was married there for a time. Actually, he was married a few times, between prison stints. Last one left him because he beat her within an inch of her life. She didn't press charges, though. Why do you ask?"

"I have to bring him in," Donaldson explained.

"Well, you better bring help!" Bryant told him.

"That bad?"

Bryant said, "This guy's taste for violence made him one fearsome bastard in his day. Got a whole bunch of medals for bravery and valor in the war, though. Showed them to me once. What do you suspect him of?"

"Assault, for starters. We're also looking into an old murder." Said Donaldson.

"Look," Bryant warned, "if you're going to bring this guy in for anything, you better bring in some serious backup. Last time I saw him he had a few drinks in him and we got talking about life in today's prison, and he said that there was no way he was ever going back. He was really scared, y'know. Said he'd kill any 'mother-fucker,' who tried to bring him in."

Donaldson acknowledged this with a nod.

"I've seen it in other parolees. They're real tough in their youth, but then they get a bit older and the idea of dying 'inside' really terrifies them. Most get this way when they hit their forties. I guess old Willie took a bit longer. And don't let the age fool you. I never saw it, but Willie used to tell me that he bought an AK-47 from a guy in Colorado and that he wouldn't hesitate to use it."

"Great," Donaldson said.

47

6:30 PM

The Tenderloin was the perfect place for someone of Willie "The Fort" Knox's pedigree. Crime, prostitution, drugs; drag queens and transvestites all abounded in the area's run-down hotels, many of which charged by the hour, and some, it was said, by the quarter-hour. In the preceding century, police who worked that area were given higher wages. This allowed them to afford better meat, hence the name. Despite the new developments in residential settlement, this by the influx of Asian refugees, it was still a place where one preferred to drive through rather than walk. Some business owners referred to the area as the "theater district," as there were many theaters there, but it didn't really catch on. Not even the jazz or blues bars were enough to persuade me to venture about at night. Bryant gave Donaldson Willie's address and Donaldson had it checked out. The police found the building, a rundown six-story walk up and were able to confirm discreetly through the landlord that Willie was in fact a tenant. A SWAT team was brought in quietly. The landlord, who tried to make it a point not to know his tenants, knew Willie well as Willie had threatened him often enough. Donaldson pointed out to me that Geraldine Emerson's stolen car had been dumped some six blocks away and we both admitted that it was a good omen.

"Are you sure he's inside?" Donaldson asked the landlord and adjusted his bulletproof vest for the tenth time.

"Yes. I haven't seen him leave his apartment in two or three days."

"All right then." Donaldson turned to the officer in charge of the SWAT entry team. "We'll take a quick look inside. If he's not there, we're out."

The landlord, not wanting any trouble, gave Donaldson the key and made him promise that he wouldn't tell Willie that he had given it to him. Donaldson agreed.

The SWAT team was in position in the hallway just outside Willie's apartment. All the masked members of the twelve-man group were dressed in full-body armor, Kevlar helmets, and carried H&K MP5SD3 sound-suppressed 9mm's. Some carried ballistic shields. Donaldson mentioned that he knew or knew of each member of the team. All had been outstanding police officers before their acceptance into SWAT, he told me. They were trained to be team players and they played to win. I was at the end of the hall, so as to stay out of trouble. Donaldson stood next to me.

Sergeant Marshall, the leader of the SWAT-entry team, approached us. "There's a television on in a back room."

"OK. What do you think?" Donaldson asked.

"Probably in the back. If we knock or 'crash' the door, he'll have almost five seconds before we can get to him. More than enough time. That's, of course, if he's in the back room."

"Let's use the key and sneak in on him," Donaldson suggested.

"All right. Problem is that he could have the place wired to prevent anyone from getting the drop on him. But we'll take the chance."

Donaldson looked at me. "Hang here, buddy. We'll be done in a minute."

I nodded. *Don't worry.*

Donaldson gave Sergeant Marshall the key and the two men returned to the awaiting team. Two men with ballistic shields stood outside the door on either side. Donaldson took up a position behind the entry team. I stayed back by the stairs. Technically, I wasn't supposed to be here as the city was no longer paying me as a consultant, but Donaldson allowed me to ride along since I had delivered the evidence that led them to this place.

Sergeant Marshall looked at all his men and made a series of gestures with his hand. Each man nodded, indicating that they understood the plan.

Sergeant Marshall inserted the key and turned it gently. There followed a distinct "click."

Next to him knelt a man holding a fiber optic monitor used for looking under doors. He gave the "thumbs-up."

Sergeant Marshall turned the handle slowly.

On the other side of the door came the sound of shattering glass.

"We've been made," Sergeant Marshall said. "Go! Go! Go!"

He pushed the door in and the two officers with ballistic shields took the lead. They carried their shields with one arm while 9mm Berettas protruded from a slot in the front. This, I imagined, offered them the ability to fire while advancing and being fired upon. The team rushed through after them, no doubt anxious to get a jump on their tipped-off quarry and disappeared from sight.

From my vantagepoint, I imagined them moving through the apartment, weapons ready. Each man, shouldering, kicking in a door or otherwise entering a room, swept his weapon about, checking for targets before announcing, "Clear."

It was over in a few moments. The "all clear" was announced. Donaldson motioned for me and we both entered the dirty dwelling. We passed SWAT men standing in various doorways. They were relaxed but ready. We reached the backroom, where four SWAT's had convened.

"Clear," one of them announced as we stepped inside.

"Ripe," said another.

Even before I got inside, I caught a smell that I had come across too often in my previous profession. I didn't have to ask what it was. A combination of feces, urine and only I knew what else.

The room was dingy at best. A television was on in the corner. A ratty-assed, beer-stained couch was against the opposite wall. Bits of fluff and stuffing hung out in the parts where it had been worn away. Wallpaper was peeling and the ceiling had water-stains due to leaks from the unit upstairs. Willie "The Fort" Knox sat in a recliner, blistered and swollen from expanding gases, leaking fluids from his every orifice. Bugs traveled freely in and out of his mouth, eyes and nose. A single bullet-hole entrance could be seen in the left eye. I looked for an exit wound, but there was none. A trickle of dried blood ran out his eye and down his face. A small caliber revolver was clutched in his right hand.

Donaldson removed the revolver from Willie's puffy, blistered hand, and gently placed it into a plastic bag. "22," he announced.

I noticed Willie's right hand. It was heavily bandaged. "Yeah."

"Dr. Connor," Donaldson announced. "Allow me to introduce you to Willie Knox."

"We've met."

The Medical Examiner arrived and took the body. Someone turned the television off. A cursory search of Willie's apartment turned up items that chronicled his miserable existence: a few pictures of him in his Army uniform. A set of lock-pick tools, bound in a leather case and incomplete by one tension wrench, sat on the television. An AK-47 was found under the couch. A key was found on his key ring that subsequently led to a locker at the local Y, which contained a few items that would later be identified by Maria Cialini's sister as having belonged to Maria: things like a hairbrush, a few family photos and her jewelry.

"He rigged a beer bottle over the door knob. That's what crashed when I turned the handle," Sergeant Marshall pointed out.

"A makeshift alarm," Donaldson surmised.

I nodded.

"How long do you think he's been dead?" Donaldson asked.

I diagnosed, "Couple days, judging by the bugs and the bloating. An entomologist will be able to tell you for sure."

"The Mayor should be happy," Donaldson announced.

"Why's that?"

"It has an ending that people can live with," Donaldson explained. And then added. "Congratulations, buddy, looks like we found our killer."

"It does *look* that way, doesn't it?" I mused.

"You don't think this was a murder, do you?"

I shrugged. "It's all very neat."

"It is," Donaldson acknowledged. "There's no evidence of a break in. But let's say that Tommy was murdered. How on earth did his killer get out? The windows are all locked, from the inside and so was the door. If Tommy Knox was murdered, how did his killer rig the bottle over the door, and manage to get out while leaving this place all locked up, from the inside?"

I hadn't thought about that. "Be a neat trick wouldn't it?"

48

All-Night Sax: 12:17 PM

The local band played to the afternoon crowd. I drummed the fingers of one hand on the end of the table. The other was wrapped about a club soda. I seldom drink beer and never in the afternoon. Donaldson had a coke.

Donaldson said, "We try to find out who put a skeleton in one closet and end up uncovering a whole bunch nobody knew ever existed."

I nodded. "Do you believe what Hale's wife said about him killing himself?"

"Grief?" he asked. "Maybe. He was always a bit edgy. I mean, here's this guy who's helped so many young women. Only problem was that it was all built on shady adoptions."

"That's the thing that's been bothering me. Why did he lie about giving her an abortion, when he was actually involved in an illegal adoption?"

"To protect the lie," Donaldson explained. "I mean look at it this way; he wins all these awards and accolades for being so moral, when it was really a case of the end justifying the means. I'm not saying he didn't do good things. I'm just saying that in order to do good, he had to do some shady stuff. After a time, he was probably able to put the shady stuff in the back of his mind, like it didn't happen. Can you imagine the shock he must have felt, when we showed up asking questions?"

I was unconvinced. "He'd lie about an illegal abortion to cover up illegal adoptions? I mean, isn't the abortion the greater of two evils if you're in the Pro-life movement?"

Donaldson nodded. "Yeah, but he figured that if he admitted the abortion, then you wouldn't look any further. If he admitted to the adoptions, that would

239

invite more investigation. It could have hurt his clinics, more than a single abortion over half a century ago."

That made sense.

"Also," Donaldson continued, "an investigation into the illegal adoptions could have threatened to disrupt some of those families he helped create."

"Even his cowardice was noble."

Donaldson agreed. "That's how it's being interpreted. His way, he's gone, he takes the secrets with him, the families remain anonymous and his clinics are free of his baggage."

"Judge Emerson said that Maria Cialini didn't have an abortion. That she gave her child up for adoption."

"Right, I heard."

"What do you make of that?" I was putting together some ideas of my own, but I wanted to see what my friend had to say.

Donaldson deduced, "Well, someone is either lying or is mistaken, O.K?"

I agreed. "O.K."

"Dr. Hale would be the one who'd know for sure, so I'd say that the Judge is mistaken."

"Not lying?"

Donaldson shook his head. "Naah. I doubt it. Maybe he was lied to. It wouldn't be the first time Miss Cialini bullshitted some guy she was involved with."

"That's true," I conceded.

"Why? What do you think?" Donaldson asked.

"What if Dr. Hale was lying? What if he didn't give Maria Cialini an abortion, chemical or otherwise, and instead she gave the child up for adoption, via his extra-legal service. That would certainly be something she'd have over him."

Donaldson agreed. "True. In that case he'd be lying because he wanted to protect the identity of the adopted child or the adopted family."

"Right. And that's entirely possible. I mean if he was willing to kill himself to protect the identities of the children, he'd certainly lie about it. If he did, I guess what I'm wondering is, what happened to her child? And who was the father?"

Donaldson took a drink. "Well, that's the sixty-four thousand dollar question, pal. The answer to which Dr. Hale took with him to the grave."

"One of those guys knew." I was certain.

Donaldson shrugged. "Maybe. She could have been shafting some other guy, too. God only knows how many guys she pissed off. Maybe Tommy Knox was the father."

I hadn't thought of that. "I doubt it. He wasn't her type. You know. But if the kid was adopted," I pondered, "who got him? Or her?"

Donaldson shrugged.

I could tell he wasn't really interested in this case anymore. As far as he was concerned, the matter was a done deal. I couldn't blame him. "Maybe one of our suspects took the child."

Donaldson said, "Michael Astor had four kids in all. Judge Emerson had four and Dr. Hale had six. I'm not too sure of the dates those kids were born, but I'll bet there were a few around the time of Maria Cialini's pregnancies."

I began, "Astor's second son, Paul, was born in late '49. Hale's - - - "

"You've been doing some extra work," Donaldson noticed.

I continued, "DNA tests of each could determine - - - "

"DNA?" Donaldson said. "You'd never get it."

I started to say something but Donaldson held up a hand. "Doesn't matter; y'know why?"

"Why?"

"Because it's over. Besides, you're assuming she had the child. For all we know, she had the abortion."

I sighed. "Why do you think Knox attacked me? I mean, we had no evidence to link him to anything."

"Because he didn't want to go back to jail for murder," Donaldson replied. "Our expert was able to match his signature to the rent card of Maria Cialini's apartment. We were able to find it from the rental company's records. Knox was afraid that we were closing in on him." He took a sip and continued, "And don't even start with any nonsense that maybe he wasn't the killer. The bullets pulled from his head and Maria Cialini's both matched, and the murder weapon to both was found in his hand."

"It's weird."

"People do weird things when they get older. Think about it. A woman he killed and dumped almost half a century ago is found and suddenly her face is everywhere. He wasn't too bright."

"If that's the case, then he must have sent the ledger and the fake letter from Gerty," I reasoned.

Donaldson nodded. "Looks like you were right on that one. He broke in and planted the typewriter so the ledger would be legitimized later."

"Then how did he know Gerty?"

Donaldson shrugged. "Maybe he knew of her through Maria."

"He's probably also the man who cleared out Maria's apartment after she died," I theorized. "That would explain how he got the ledger."

Donaldson agreed. "Exactly."

"Tell me this. She was involved with a doctor, a successful real estate man and an up-and-coming lawyer. What the hell was she doing with an armed robber?"

"Some women like dangerous men. Some are turned on by violence, y'know?"

I couldn't help but think of Rebecca Wood. "I suppose."

"I don't know," he said. "Maybe she was in on some scheme with him and held out."

I considered this.

"My lawyer and PBA rep tell me that these lawsuits will be dumped. One, they have nothing as we were doing our job and two, they don't want any more negative publicity."

I was quiet a moment and then said, "Out of all three, Judge Emerson was the only one who showed remorse, yet his rep is as screwed up as the other's."

"Y'know, they all could have avoided the embarrassment if they'd been straight with us upfront instead of trying to hide everything," Donaldson said and then added, "Everybody's got a skeleton in their closet."

I was quiet. I was troubled.

"What?" Donaldson asked.

"There's something else that bothers me about Willie Knox," I said cautiously.

"What's that?" Donaldson asked.

"We've assumed that he was the guy who sent me the ledger and therefore must have been the guy who broke into Gerty's."

"Right."

"Yeah, but the guy I chased seemed a bit smaller. Thinner he was - - - "

"Running away from you at night in the dark and you never got any closer than thirty feet from him," Donaldson reminded.

"True," I admitted. "But I can't help but think that there were two men."

"No way. Willie Knox was a burglar. He did a lot of breaking and entering in his life. Who knows, maybe he had a partner we haven't caught onto. It's a possibility. He ran with a lot of guys in his life. I got a look at his rap sheet; it's two inches thick. Personally, I doubt it, though," he then said with certainty. "He broke into Gerty's and he broke into the morgue."

I took a sip of the club soda. "What if the lock-pick was planted?" I dropped.

"What? Connor, come on now. I - - - "

I raised a hand for patience. "Just hear me out. What bothers me about this case is that I see a pattern that's happened twice." I took a moment to run it through my mind. "First, we get the ledger mailed to us and then Gerty is dead. Now I accept her death as from natural causes, but we both agree that the break-in was to plant the typewriter, right?"

"Right," Donaldson agreed.

"Now if we take this to be the case, then we have to assume that the burglar was going to kill Gerty. After all, the letter only works if she's dead. Otherwise, we'd interview her and find out that she didn't write it. Second, the lock-pick was found in the autopsy room and we go to find Willie Knox dead. My problem with this is that room was cleaned twice since the attack. Why didn't anybody find the lock-pick before then?" I asked. "The pattern in both examples is that we have evidence that is delivered to us or we trip over and then the persons who are the presumed source of that evidence are found dead." I shook my head. "It's very neat. I feel as if a third party is manipulating us, pushing us toward one suspect and then another. The ledger pointed us at Astor; the lock-pick, toward Knox. That's the pattern."

"His fingerprints were on the lock-pick," Donaldson reminded.

"That's another thing. Cal. How many professional burglars leave fingerprints on their equipment? He was wearing gloves in the morgue. Could a guy be that stupid?"

"Yes!" Donaldson said resoundingly. "One third of all property crimes have usable prints left at the sight. Connor, sometimes an accident is an accident and a burglar bungles. In my experience, the guy who looks like he did it and has the murder weapon and has done this before *is* guilty! Maybe your students aren't cleaning up as you instruct. You're making this too complicated. Maybe it's because of your training as a pathologist; always looking for some hidden meaning in everything."

"Creature of habit? What does the brass say?"

"Case closed. Ask anybody. It's a done deal."

I finished the club soda and rubbed my eyes with one hand. "I'm going home."

"Probably going to meet that student, huh?" Donaldson asked.

"Shit, that reminds me!" I looked at my watch. I'd call Rebecca Wood when I got home and tell her I'd grant her demand. "I can't help but think, maybe Knox *did* have an accomplice."

"And maybe you are mistaken," Donaldson said.

I tilted my head. I didn't believe it.

"I just found out something else. Remember the Pacific Union Club, where we found the Judge?"

I nodded.

"Well, Michael Astor was a member of that club, too. Has been for like thirty years or so."

"Point being?"

"Point being," Donaldson explained, "we have no idea, given the scope of our investigation, if either two, or all three of those guys knew each other. For all we know, all three of them could have been involved in her murder." He shrugged. "It's just something I thought about the other day."

"'If you only knew the things I did,' he said. What do you think he meant by that?"

"What do *you* think he meant?" Donaldson counter-asked.

243

I shrugged. "I think there are two possible meanings. He could have meant if you knew what I *knew* or he could've meant if you knew what I *did*.

"What's the difference?"

"If we knew what he knew or what he did." I played with it again. "Then he said you'd want this gun. Did he mean 'you' in general or 'you' in particular?"

Donaldson shrugged.

"And what was that bit about, this isn't over; it's just beginning?"

"You're reading too much into it. He was losing it. Don't pursue it or you'll lose it, too." Donaldson advised.

"I gotta go," I said. "What about you?"

Donaldson took another sip of his coke. "Nah, I still got some time left. I think I'll stick around a bit and listen to the band."

I stood and took out a few bills.

Donaldson said, "Don't bother, I'll get it buddy."

"All right. Thanks."

"Thank you, Connor," Donaldson said. "It was a tough case, but you did well." He smiled. "Who solves a forty-seven year old murder anyway?"

I nodded and walked toward the exit.

"You got a ride?" Donaldson asked.

"Nah," I said with a wave of my hand. "I'll take a cab."

Epilogue

David Feeney

1:03 PM

I stood on the corner of Jersey and 18th Street. The last few days had been confusing. But in truth, I was glad to have it all behind me. The case was closed and that was it.

It was getting warmer and the wind blew through my tightly cropped hair like a whisper, telling me that summer was close. I ran a hand across my hair. Behind me I could hear the lively sounds of piano and saxophone that emanated from the bar, All-Night Sax: a one-story structure with a cut-stone façade and a slate roof. Two prominent windows stood on either side of a large oaken door.

I bought a paper from the machine and looked over the headlines. A moment later some kids came running around the corner and it reminded me of when my friends and I used to sell papers in that area. Actually, that very spot if memory served.

A cab slowed and came to a stop, its rear passenger door right in front of me. I got into the cab, thinking about the future and how I would spend the evening with a long hot bath, and a brandy. I noticed as I got into the cab that the "On-Duty" light was off, but figured the driver was just coming on shift. It also occurred to me after I'd gotten in that I hadn't signaled for one, but thought nothing of it.

"Nice bar," the cabby said, after we'd driven a bit.

I paid little attention. I was looking out the window. "Yeah, it is," I said finally.

"It used to be called the 'Great Sax.'"

"Oh, when?"

The cabby looked into the mirror. "Back in the early fifties."

I said nothing. I was thinking about the street corner I had just left and had a sense of deja vu that wouldn't pass and demanded my attention. Fragments of memories filtered through my mind. And I remembered:

I was selling papers. The older boys, two of whom were my cousins, had put me up to it. We were visiting relatives who lived nearby. "Ask that lady," they told me. "Paper, ma'am?" I said to her. She asked me the cost and I told her. My young mind didn't know the cost of papers or anything else so I said something, probably too much: "Thirty cents" or something. The other boys had chased me three blocks to get it. I was too small and couldn't outrun them so I put the quarter in my pocket and surrendered the other, a nickel or dime. I told them that I had dropped the quarter. I figured that it was better to have one coin than to lose both. I bought myself some candy after they ran off. The woman - I thought - that street - those eyes. She had touched my cheek and I felt a blush....

It was her! I realized, as a flood of emotions coursed through me. I had met Maria Cialini! When was that? How old was I? Could that have been the last day of her life?

247

David Feeney

The cabby said something. He sounded annoyed, as if he had repeated himself more than once.

"What was that?" I began. "I'm sorry - " It was only then that I noticed we were on the Southern Freeway and were heading south along Route 280 instead of towards Twin Peaks. It occurred to me that I hadn't even given the cabby an address.

"I hope you're happy," the driver said in a gravelly voice. His rage-filled, bloodshot eyes, and then his face filled the mirror.

The voice was familiar. It took me a second to recognize the face only because it was so out of context. Unshaven and sweaty, he looked like he hadn't slept in days. "Issacson," I said simply.

The taxi accelerated violently.

"You ruined a good man. Not like those other two cowards."

I knew that I was in trouble. "Hey now, fella, what are you talking about there?" I said, hoping to stall.

"It's all your fault," Issacson said. "The police had this chalked up as unsolvable. How the hell did you get involved anyway?"

"It was the officer in charge's idea," I said, relieved that Issacson was still talking.

"Pity he didn't get in with you. It would have saved me the trouble of going after him later."

I tried the window lever. It spun freely. The window stayed shut. "I don't under - - - "

"You can knock off the psyche shit, Connor. You see, it's my fault."

"Your fault what?"

"It's my fault that the Judge met that whore in the first place." He pounded the steering wheel twice and looked about.

I said nothing. *Let him confess: buy some time.*

"I was working in San Francisco before Jack arrived. I had done some work for Astor in one of his earlier scrapes with the law. When she needed an attorney, he called me up and asked me to help her out." He looked at me in the mirror. "That bastard was dumping her on me. I didn't have time, so I called Jack and he took on her case." He slammed his fist on the dash. "I delivered her to my friend."

The taxi weaved in and out of the sparse traffic. Cars beeped and braked. People shouted abuse. Issacson didn't seem to notice and didn't stop.

"Nobody forced him to have an affair with her," I asserted.

"That's what you think. You should've seen that piece of ass in action. Man oh man, nobody could refuse her," Issacson said.

"Nobody forces a man to break his word," I reiterated.

"Like you and that piece of fluff that dropped by your place the other night? Yeah, I saw her. Followed her back to the school. I've been watching you. Was it

248

good, Doctor? Isn't that a violation of some agreement the college has with its students? How would you like it if she called you up and said she was going to rat you out? What would you do? What would you do to keep your little skeleton in its closet?"

"You made the call to the Dean," I realized.

"I had to try to get you off this case somehow. Problem was that the Judge really fell for her. He was considering getting a divorce until his wife called him and said she wanted to get back together. The Judge was having a crisis of conscience. That's the kind of man he is. He had to make a decision. So did I. I found out where she lived. I knew all about Astor screwing her."

"Did Astor know about them?"

"No," Issacson dismissed. "He's an idiot."

"Then Mr. Knox enters the picture," I prompted.

"Yeah. I heard about him through a colleague who was doing work for the VA. Knox was a soldier and used his benefits. I gave Knox some of my legal attention, off the record. He was looking at serious time and I got it dismissed. He owed me. All he had to do was get rid of the body and clean out her place. That plus he stole me a cab. He taught me some tricks as well, like hot-wiring cars and how to pick a lock. I picked her up the same way I picked you up, and on the same street."

My mind was filled with the image of Maria Cialini getting into the taxi. I felt the déjà vu lapping at the shores of reason, but nothing came of it. "Knox got you the ledger from her effects."

"That's right. I sifted through her crap. Kept some in storage because I knew it would make for good motive in the future, should she ever be found. The poetic notion of putting this on that prick Astor wasn't lost on me when I found it."

"So you and Willie Knox became buddies then?"

"No," Issascon said. "I gave him some advice on a few cases and then he went up for a few years and I didn't bother with him. He approached me years later; said he wanted free counsel. I was doing better then and didn't want him ruining what I'd built. He tried to blackmail me but I had his prints on some of her stuff and told him to beat it. He left me alone after that, until you appeared on that show, with her picture. Then he called me. He was frightened because he knew that the rent card was in his handwriting and he was afraid of going back in."

"So you had him try to kill me," I said calmly.

Issacson sneered. "Yeah. I said that you were the only real threat to us and told him where to find you. I was surprised that you were still alive. Willie must have lost his edge; too much drinking."

"How on earth did you manage to put the bottle over Knox's door and get out of his apartment, yet leave everything locked from the inside?"

"You like that one? Willie taught me that. I won't tell you how I did it, though. If I did, there'd be no secrets," Issacson said with a wink.

Great. "What about Gerty? Explain that."

"I saw you at the park and I recognized her. I researched all of Cialini's old friends. I was following you. I almost had a heart attack and figured she was going to talk to you. I didn't know if she had anything, so I figured it was time to use the ledger and get rid of her. When I got to her place, she was already dead. I couldn't believe it so I just planted the typewriter. Then you showed up."

"You used Mrs. Emerson's car. Why?"

Issacson smiled. "I figured that either you or that cop," he confided, "would figure that the car had been stolen to point the finger at the Judge."

"All of that would be seen as an obvious frame-up as both the Judge and his wife had alibis," I said.

"Of course. After I sent you the ledger, I figured you and that cop would do the logical and indict Astor. I didn't know that Gerty had mailed you anything. That threw me. I knew that you'd eventually figure that the typed note must be false and thus Astor was being framed, so I decided that the best thing was to put it all on Willie, plan B. He was always a back-up in my mind, but also a good gopher."

"So you had the lock-pick planted."

"Yeah."

I felt vindicated. "How the hell did you get that inside the autopsy room?"

"I'm a criminal defense attorney. I have contacts everywhere. People owe me - thieves, mobsters, politicians," he said with a smile. "Students. If I need something planted, it gets planted," he paused a moment. "So I called him up and said I had a plan. I dropped by, took care of him and left the evidence."

"What did you think of the Fax?"

"What Fax?"

"The one I sent Emerson accusing him of being the murderer."

"You would pull a stunt like that," Issacson said with disgust. "I never saw it."

That explained it. I had never considered the possibility that the right man had never seen the Fax.

"You don't have to do this," I reasoned. I tried the door locks but the mechanism was disconnected.

"Yeah, I do. I know that the police would've just let this go but not you, Connor. You'd have kept poking around on your own. You'd have found out that I was Knox's lawyer on some early cases and you'd have a connection. Dr. Connor, you might have even discovered that I worked for Astor or that I gave Miss Cialini's case to Jack. I did a bit of research on you too, Doctor. I know all about you."

The cab slowed and exited Route 280 in Bay View and headed west.

"She changed," I said.

Issacson sneered. "Right. You should have heard her when she realized what was going to happen. She started talking about how this one was real and how she was pregnant and in love with Jack."

I was oblivious as I was caught in a moment, another time, and another place. The tide of déjà vu returned. I remembered:

She stood before me, her long hair blowing slightly in the breeze. She smiled that half-smile and got down on one knee, her beautiful face, filling my vista as she leaned in close and whispered- "I'm your real mommy. I'm going to take you to be with your daddy very soon."

She kissed me lightly on the cheek. She went to the cab, turned and waved, before getting in. The cab pulled away.

The world fell out from under me. I was devastated. "She was my mother," I realized. "I was the first pregnancy."

"What was that?" Issacson asked.

I said nothing. A wave of nausea swept over me. I felt as if I were going to throw up and had to breathe deeply to prevent myself from splattering the partition between us with my lunch. Though, after the tide had subsided, I thought it wouldn't have been such a bad idea. I drew a breath and asked with a measure of spite, "If they were in love, then what business was it of yours?"

Issacson turned and stared back at me. "Because I was in love with him."

It took a moment to sink in, although in retrospect, it was obvious.

"Didn't expect that?" he asked. "You figure that I should be out cruising the Castro? Just because I don't limp-wrist my way through a conversation." He shook his head. "I was his protector. We were friends in college. Even then you could see that he had it. His ideas, his interpretation of the law, his insight. You could see that he would affect change. I helped him get set-up after he graduated. Got him a few cases concerning civil liberties and discrimination against minorities and women. Astor dumped her on me and I delivered her to Jack." He sneered. "You say that they were in love; I'm in love with him! But I knew enough to keep it to myself once I realized that it would not be reciprocated. I knew that if I were to pursue it, it could hurt his fledgling law practice and I would never do that. When you really care about someone," he said, "you do what's right for them, not yourself. You sacrifice. And if I wasn't going to do that to him, I sure as hell wasn't going to allow her to ruin him. Which is what she would have done. You know her background. She ran with anybody and everybody." He shook his head with anger. "She whored herself on every man she ever met. She sucked her way to the top. Why do you think they call it getting a-head? It would've been only a matter of time before she ran off with somebody else and left him a wreck."

Filled with anger and loss, I asked. "So you're the self appointed protector, is that it?"

"You could say that. Jack was heading for great things. I couldn't let that whore ruin it. If I hadn't stepped in, he'd have been ruined and several movements would have lost a voice. He was heading for the top from the beginning. I couldn't let anyone ruin that, not me, not her and not you."

I felt spiteful. "He'd never have made it, you know. Not to the Supreme Court."

"Why not?"

"Because he has Alzheimer's."

"Don't say that!"

"It's true and you know it. It took me a while to pick up on it but I noticed the signs: the forgetfulness of dates and recent events; the way you or his wife were always nearby to keep an eye on him. Sometimes he wears two different color socks. The way you folded down his collar at the club. Always someone to take care of him. Except when he spoke to Inspector Donaldson and myself in his office, without you. He seemed a bit lost that evening in his hall. When I saw him at the park, he had forgotten what night the party was."

"Shut up!"

"Don't get me wrong. He's still in the early stages. I'm sure he can function quite well. But he'd never stand up to the scrutiny of a Congressional hearing. Time was the one thing you couldn't manipulate," I said, and then, hoping to rattle Issacson's cage, as it was obvious that I wasn't supposed to leave this taxi alive, asked, "Does he ever forget to tuck himself in?"

"Shut up!" Issacson said with disgust at the insinuation.

I knew I had hit a nerve and agitated it further. I hoped Issacson would blow his own brains out. "Does he ever walk around with his gavel out?"

Rattle.

"Stop it!"

"Order in the court! Order in the court!" I laughed.

Rattle. Rattle.

"You're sick, sick!"

"Ever have to tuck it in for him? Bet you'd like that."

Rattle. Rattle. Rattle.

"FUCK YOU!" Issacson screamed and slammed my side of the cab into a guardrail. The metal shrieked but the vehicle continued.

I lamented the fact that people tended not to pay attention to reckless cabs. It was also ironic that the old adage of there never being a cop around when you needed one was holding up splendidly. I knew the area we were heading towards from all the bodies found over the years: Hunter's Point Naval Reservation.

Hunter's Point Naval Reservation lay just south of Hunter's Point: An area known for drugs, and violence, as well as a few family-oriented communities. There was also a well-known art community that held viewing and purchases three times a year.

Established in 1868 by the California Dry-dock Company, the Naval Reservation encompassed 638 acres and was the site of shipbuilding, maintenance, sub-modification and repair until it was closed in 1974. Congress purchased the site in 1939 and the Navy changed its name to the San Francisco Naval Shipyard. This name was changed in 1970 to the current, Hunter's Point Naval Shipyard. There was base-housing that the Navy had built to house workers during World War II. After the closure of the yard, buildings were leased to small businesses. There was a naval ground that still dismantled the odd ship. A few old sailors nevertheless fixed tugs and eked out a living there. The area was also something of a sore spot for local environmentalists due to years of improper waste disposal.

"I have other criminal clients, Connor," Issacson said slowly. "You ever hear of Tommy the torch?"

"No. Afraid not."

Issacson smiled. "Sorry. That's the name his lawyer calls him, behind his back, of course. Tom Kowolski is his real name. He burnt three buildings in a week back in the mid-seventies; killed five kids."

I nodded. I had seen the bodies.

Issacson looked at me through the mirror. "I gave him advice, too."

The taxi sped up and entered the reservation. It was like a small city. Warehouses and buildings of various sizes lined the streets. Piles of trash, bricks and sand rose up in the few empty areas.

"You know," I offered, "as a physician I must say that suicide would be completely acceptable at a time like - - - "

"Fuck you!"

A man's got to try.

We sped underneath a bridge connecting two warehouses.

"I'll teach you, Connor. No burial in a building; no preservation. I've learned from my mistakes."

He drove towards a large warehouse a few hundred yards away. All around, I could see the bay, ships, and warehouses and found it increasingly difficult to ignore the feelings of fear and isolation that swept through me. Suddenly, I remembered. Now was as good a time as any. I'd heard enough. I took the .357 from out of its holster and leveled it at the partition with two hands.

"It's bullet proof," Issacson pointed out, though his voice displayed some concern.

I fired five rounds at Issacson's head. The heavy weapon jumped in my hands and its report sounded like a string of explosions in the enclosed vehicle.

The partition was indeed bulletproof, but, nevertheless, fragmented from the concentration of gunfire. A chip of Plexiglas caught Issacson in the corner of his eye. "Ah, damnit!" he yelled as he raised a hand to fish it out.

253

I barely heard what he'd said and doubted that Issacson could either as my ears rang from the gunfire. The smoke and the smell of powder were strong, particularly as neither of us could open a window.

Issacson's eye bled profusely from under his clenched fist and down the side of his arm. He lost control of the taxi and swerved on the asphalt before driving into a pile of sand.

I saw it coming and turned my shoulder into the impact. I hit the Plexiglas but didn't break it. It was obviously people-proof as well. The impact caused me to drop the .357.

Issacson, who wasn't wearing a seatbelt, hit face-first into the steering column. He groaned but was mostly still. Smoke swirled about the vehicle.

A moment later, the engine died.

I coughed and moved a bit. My shoulder hurt. Smoke stung my eyes. I reached into my jacket and pulled out a speed-loader from my holster. I searched the floor and found the .357.

Issacson looked up slowly into the mirror, his face bloody and smashed. He saw me reloading. "Too little to late, Connor. You'll burn for this."

I opened the .357 and emptied the spent shells onto the floor.

Issacson opened his door with difficulty, then reached back in under the driver's seat. A high-pitched "beep" was heard, though barely audible. "I did everything for him. I even got him to go to that seminar so he'd be out of the city and would have a clear alibi." He half got out of the taxi. "I sacrificed." He said. "And when that wasn't enough, I sacrificed her and now, I'm going to sacrifice you."

I released the bullets into the chamber and snapped it shut. I leveled the weapon and fired three shots at the partition, hoping I could shatter the already damaged Plexiglas, but it held. *Probably made in China.*

Outside, Issacson hit the ground awkwardly and got up. He walked away from the taxi slowly, with great difficulty. He didn't look good. He didn't look back.

I decided to try my luck on the side windows as the Plexiglas partition wasn't going to give and I was low on ammo. I fired one into the rear passenger side window opposite me.

The window was bulletproof. It fragmented, but held.

I slid over and put my back to the window I had just shot, turned and fired at the opposite window. Same result.

I was getting scared, but surgical training prevented me from allowing it to affect me, or, as I had been taught by a colleague years before, "It's OK to have fear; just don't let fear have you." I looked over my shoulder and saw Issacson running away through the rear window. I had only one bullet and only Issacson knew how many seconds left. I pointed the weapon at him through the rear window and fired.

The bullet blew out a small hole, but missed Issacson. The rest of the window spider-webbed. I tried to kick at the hole, to make it bigger but couldn't get any leverage, so I had to use my elbow. I elbowed the hole, again and again, enlarging it. First pain, then numbness spread through my arm as I hit the Ulnar nerve.

The hole got larger and I started to push myself out through it. I put a hand out first and then my head. I used the other hand to force the window away from my body. Glass cut me from every angle. From a distance, I imagined it looked as if the taxi was giving birth to me.

I climbed out of the taxi and onto the trunk. Bloodied and battered, I sucked dusty air as if it were pure and healthy O2. I coughed. My feet cleared the window and I felt a "pop." It struck me odd that I didn't hear it. Then I felt the heat.

I rolled off the trunk, and hit the ground in a heap then, got up awkwardly and trotted a few meters. I looked back to see the taxi engulfed in flames, and realized that I couldn't hear it because I was still deaf from the gunfire.

I turned in the direction that Issacson had staggered, rounded the corner of a warehouse and trotted on a bit. I looked about and saw nobody. I moved to the corner of a small building. In the distance, Issacson ran towards an abandoned Naval Destroyer. I holstered my weapon, as it was empty and, thus, useless and impeded my running. I moved quick, quicker than Issacson and soon narrowed the distance between us. Issacson was barely speed-walking fifty meters ahead. I vowed that he wasn't going to hop over any fences today.

The Destroyer was a football field in length or more, and several stories tall. Its name been scraped away along with most of its serial numbers. It was in a state of limbo. It had been towed in from Hawaii a few years earlier and was to have been renovated, then restored as a museum and finally dismantled, respectively and in that order. In the end, none of these plans had played out due to military cutbacks, lack of donations and budget cuts, respectively and in that order. So the Destroyer sat in the naval yard, half- disassembled but still afloat.

Actually, I didn't know whether it was a Destroyer. I thought it was because I could tell an aircraft carrier from its landing deck and a submarine was shaped like a cigar. But this thing could have been a cruiser or a frigate for all I knew. Whatever the hell a frigate was.

Issacson moved up the rickety gangplank. I closed the distance to twenty meters when Issacson turned, weapon in hand. I hit the gangplank, which creaked and bounced a bit as a bullet ricocheted off the rotting wood next to me. The gun report was audible, but barely. Issacson disappeared into the destroyer.

I stood up and followed, shakily. My left knee hurt from the fall. I entered the structure carefully, sticking my head in a moment and pulling it out. I realized that it was so dark inside; I couldn't see three feet ahead of me. Issacson could be right inside the door and I wouldn't hear him, so I simply entered.

I stood inside the door for several seconds, collecting my thoughts and giving my eyes the valuable moments needed to adjust to the darkness. Above me, I thought I heard something crash to the floor.

Darkness fell away from my eyes like veils and I was able to discern my environment. Ahead of me was a narrow hall, some open hatches or doorways and a flight of steps that went up. The hall had been stripped clean. I went to the stairs and cautiously looked up. I heard a "bang" echo above. *Did he fall?* I climbed up the steps. Shafts of light crisscrossed me through holes, where some of the ill-initiated dismantling had begun. I squinted as I climbed.

Near the top, I caught movement out of the corner of my eye and ducked. It was a trick Donaldson had taught me. "If you think a weapon is pointed at you and you turn to look, you just wasted a second when you should have been ducking," he had told me. "So just duck."

Bullets impacted above me harmlessly and dully. It was then I realized that the "crash" and "bang" I had heard was Issacson firing his weapon. *He was waiting for me all along.* He must have thought he saw me. He must have – *He can't hear me. He's still deaf.*

I looked up to see Issacson fumbling with bullets, dropping half of them, from behind a door. I noticed that he didn't have his hearing aid in. He must have lost it in the crash. Between that and the gunfire, he was most likely, completely deaf. I had an idea. I pulled out my .357.

I dashed from the stairs to a door, two down from Issacson, weapon in hand.

Issacson fired again in a panic, and the shots hit the door harmlessly. His weapon clicked empty. He ran from door to door until he was at the end of the hall. There he struggled with a door, cursing as it opened slowly on rusted hinges. He pushed the door out and light flooded in, brilliantly blinding us both. Issacson stepped into the light.

I followed behind him; one arm raised to ward off the light, and stepped onto the deck of the Destroyer. I stopped suddenly as my eyes adjusted. Half the deck had been ripped out and large gaping holes threatened to deliver the unwary into the superstructure and certain death bellow. Only a thin walk space, one steel beam wide, offered me safe passage.

Across the chasm, Issacson, gun in hand, staggered and tripped. He got up pathetically and reached into his pocket. He took out something shiny. I squinted and made out that it was more bullets. *How many more?* I wondered. How Issacson had gotten over there without falling was a miracle.

He attempted to load the weapon but his hand shook. He raised his hand, still holding the bullets, throwing shade onto his face. He searched around for me.

Now or never. I'm in the open. "Issacson!" I screamed as loud as I could, and hoped he could hear me.

Issacson looked over and I pointed the .357 in his direction.

I pulled on the gun the way children do, pretending that it was loaded. Pretending that I was shooting.

Issacson ducked and dropped his bullets. He must have thought the weapon had fired. He couldn't hear. He jumped/half stumbled backwards, off the deck and into air. He tumbled head over feet straight down the side of the destroyer. His head impacted against the side with a "smack-gong" before he fell, still alive, into the water with a silent splash and into the path of an oncoming tug. He never heard what hit him.

I walked over and stood on the edge of the deck as the tug driver struggled in vain to bring the small ship to a stop. This tug wasn't going to stop for a hundred meters or two minutes or whatever came first. Issacson disappeared beneath the tug. The polluted water churned red. I stood there for a few minutes until Issacson's body bobbed back up in the wake of his own blood. I had to make sure; after all, Issacson was a lawyer. Satisfied that Issacson was dead, I turned and walked back through the ship.

1:27 PM

I walked across the yard, my mind reeling with all I had heard. I wasn't sure how much of it to believe, and aside from Issacson's guilt, wanted to believe none of it. *Was one of the three suspects my father?* If it were the Judge, I doubted that he'd remember given his condition. Dr. Hale wouldn't be talking and if it were Astor, I wouldn't want to know. I wondered what Donaldson would say when I called him. With regard to Miss Wood, I had a sudden insight as to how to deal with her; not only would I grant her wish; I'd see to it that she'd get put into the honors program. *That ought to put her in over her pretty head.*

Finally, I wondered, how many days it would be before Mrs. D'Angelo, *my aunt* sent me a check for 50Gs. *Did she know who I was when she approached me? Is that why she came to see me?* I realized, with some concern, as I took a handkerchief from my pocket and dabbed my forehead, that my reputation was intact, if not enhanced. *Could Maria Cialini have been my mother? Or had I imagined it?*

I stopped. It suddenly hit me as to why Dr. Hale would have committed suicide. Earlier, I'd thought it was because Maria Cialini's baby had been adopted and not aborted. But what if I had been the baby? Hale had seemed caught offguard when he realized who I was at our first meeting. He had definitely lied as to knowing my father. Pieces were falling into place and I didn't like the picture they made. *"If you knew the things I did,"* Hale had said. "The things he did. The illegal adoptions." I took the beeper/flask from my hip and had a sip of Bailey's. The sharp chocolate slid down easily and felt good.

"Some doors shouldn't be opened," I said simply.

257

My cell phone vibrated in my pocket. I dug around until I found it. *Too bad I hadn't remembered this earlier.* "Yes?"

It was Dr. Trundy. "Hey, Declan, how you doing?"

"Speak up." I still couldn't hear very well.

"How are you?" She reiterated.

"I've been better."

"You busy?"

"No."

"I went back over the X-rays and CAT scans like you asked and you were right. She had given birth previous to her death."

"Oh."

"Yeah. I should have picked up on that. The scars weren't visible on the X-rays but I found them on the CAT scans. I should have noticed them at the autopsy but I guess I was so caught up with discovering her pregnancy that I didn't focus much on anything else. Sorry about that. Sometimes we fail to notice things right in front of us."

I said nothing.

"I hope that makes things better," she said.

"Actually, that makes them worse."

Dr. Connor will return.

About the Author

Born in New Jersey, David Feeney lived in Ireland in the early 1980's. He attended Jersey City State University, where he studied film, theater and creative writing, before earning a BA in Communications.

He enlisted in the US Army Signal Corps in 1991 and was stationed in K-town, Germany. Upon receiving his honorable discharge in 1994, he attended Montclair State University, where he studied History and German, graduating with a BA in 1997.

Currently, he divides his time between the USA and Ireland. A Skeleton In The Closet is his first novel and is the first of a planned series.

Visit my website at, www.askeletoninthecloset.com

Printed in the United States
3014

9 780759 644632